BEST OF
B E S T
LESBIAN
EROTICA
2

BEST OF
BEST
LESBIAN
EROTICA
2

Edited by

Tristan Taormino

CLEIS
PRESS

Printed in the United States.
Cover photograph: Siege
Cover design: Scott Idleman
Text design: Frank Wiedemann
Cleis logo art: Juana Alicia
First Edition.
10 9 8 7 6 5 4 3 2 1

The following stories are reprinted from *Best Lesbian Erotica 2000:* "You Know What?" © 1999 by Cara Bruce; "Thermal Stress" © 1999 by María Helena Dolan; "Center of Attention" © by Dawn Dougherty; "Becoming Stone" © by Sandra Lee Golvin, "Descent of the Butch of the Realm" © 1987 by Judy Grahn reprinted from *The Queen of Swords*, first published by Beacon Press and now available at www.serpentina.com; "Always" © 1999 by Cecilia Tan first appeared in *Herotica 6* ed. by Marcy Sheiner (Down There Press, 1999). The following stories are reprinted from *Best Lesbian Erotica 2001:* "Grand Jeté" © 2000 by Toni Amato; "Monica and Me" © 2001 by Rachel Kramer Bussel was published in *Starf*cker* ed. by Shar Rednour (Alyson, 2001); "Blood and Silver" © 2000 by Patrick Califia first appeared in his book *No Mercy* (Alyson, 2000); "sex hall" © 2000 by MR Daniel; "The Rock Wall" © 2000 by Peggy Munson; "Splitting the Infinitive" © 2000 by Jean Roberta first appeared online in *Jane's Net Sex Guide;* "Business Casual" © 2000 by Lauren Sanders first appeared at Nerve.com; "Sometimes She Lets Me" © 2000 by Alison L. Smith. The following stories are reprinted from *Best Lesbian Erotica 2002:* "Symphony in Blue" © 2001 by Betty Blue; "Good Old Tyme" © 2001 by Linda A. Boulter; "Anonymous" © 2001 by Amie M. Evans first appeared in *Harrington Lesbian Fiction Quarterly* (2001); "Etched in the Flesh" © 2001 by Sacchi Green first appeared in *Zaftig* ed. by Hanne Blank (Cleis Press, 2001); "Redemption" © 2000 by Michael M. Hernandez was first published in *The Academy: Tales of the Marketplace* ed. by Laura Antoniou (Mystic Rose Books, 2000); "Farewell to Rain Woman" © 2001 by Thea Hutcheson; "The Word Nebraska" © 2001 by Tennessee Jones. The following stories are reprinted from *Best Lesbian Erotica 2003:* "LIVE: By Request" © 2002 by Samiya A. Bashir first appeared at www.kuma2.net; "Keeping Up Appearances" © 2002 by Kenya Devoreaux; "Cop-Out" © 2002 by Rosalind Christine Lloyd first appeared in *Bedroom Eyes* ed. by Leslea Newman (Alyson, 2002); "Gravity Sucks" © 2002 by Skian McGuire; "Boys" © 2002 by Ana Peril; "At Long Last" © 2002 by Madeleine Oh; "Elizabeth" © 2002 by Julie Levin Rosso; "Luck of the Irish" © 2002 by Kyle Walker. The following stories are reprinted from *Best Lesbian Erotica 2004:* "Loved It and Set It Free" © 2004 by Lisa Archer was published in *Awakening the Virgin 2* ed. by Nicole Foster (Alyson, 2003) and later appeared in *Best American Erotica 2004* ed. by Susie Bright (Touchstone, 2004); "Look, but Don't Touch" © 2002 by Sparky first appeared at www.dykediva.com; "You Can Write a Story about It" © 2003 by Jera Star; "To Fuck or Get Fucked" © 2004 by Rakelle Valencia; "Does She Look Like a Boy?" © 2003 by Tara-Michelle Ziniuk. The following stories are reprinted from *Best Lesbian Erotica 2005:* "Lessons" © 2004 by S. Bear Bergman; "The Second Hour" © 2004 by L. Shane Conner; "Roulette" © 2004 by Shannon Cummings; "Fee Fie Foe Femme" © 2004 by Elaine Miller; "Envy" © 2004 by Teresa Lamai first appeared online at www.erotica-readers.com (March 2004).

TABLE OF CONTENTS

Introduction
Tristan Taormino

I have learned that you can't wait for the muse to come to you; you have to go grab her by the hair of her head.

—ANN BANNON

Lesbian sex on the page made its mass-market debut during the golden era of lesbian pulp novels in the 1950s. Cheaply produced and widely distributed, these novels featured sapphic story lines with racy covers that promised strange sisters, forbidden love, and unconventional encounters. While many were penned by and for men, it's well documented that there were a handful of lesbian authors—though plenty of lesbian readers—of these best-selling paperbacks. Unfortunately, dykes didn't always fare so well in these stories. One reason was that their fates reflected their times, an era when queer women lived literally in the shadows, their bars routinely raided, the closet necessary for survival. In addition, many publishers insisted there be no happy endings because they did not want to be seen as condoning homosexuality. In the end, incest, abuse, alcoholism, and mental illness plagued lesbian characters, and two women rarely rode off into the sunset together.

Equally disappointing to actual queer readers must have been the oversubtlety of the sex: The juicy details promised by these novels' tempting covers was rarely delivered with much specificity or authenticity. The illustrations were often hotter than what was found between the covers—images of soft-core sex that either was toned down or focused more on implication and titillation. Explicit—or, for that matter, realistic—explorations of lesbian desire and fucking were few and far between. It's curious to note that one early novel, *Women's Barracks* (written by a lesbian), was singled out by the House Un-American Activities Committee in 1952 as pornographic, though it was no more explicit than others like it. The same year that one book got a triple X rating from the government, Patricia Highsmith's novel *The Price of Salt* was published (under her pseudonym Claire Morgan). It sold a million copies, and—even more impressive—it had a positive resolution.

Last summer, I had the honor of moderating a dialogue at the LGBT Center in New York between two of the leading figures in lesbian pulp, novelists Ann Bannon and Marijane Meaker. Both women talked about how they came to write lesbian novels, how they met, and what dyke life was like in the New York City of the 1950s and 1960s. While Meaker had been in several lesbian relationships that she drew on for her writing (including her two-year partnership with Patricia Highsmith), Bannon was a married suburban mom who'd never met—let alone loved or fucked—a lesbian when she wrote her first sapphic novel. (In interviews, she often refers to this as not having done any "field work.") She admits that the characters and stories in that first book, *Odd Girl Out*, were based solely on her imagination. After it was published, and thanks in part to mentoring by Meaker, Bannon found the underground lesbian community and did get to do some hands-on research for the rest of her novels. But with or without it, her tales of Beebo Brinker and friends, like the work of other lesbian novelists, resonated with plenty of lesbians, and the books continue to be enjoyed by new generations.

As I read through the last six books from the *Best Lesbian Erotica* series to collect my favorite stories, I was struck by how much the world of written lesbian lust has changed. And not only when it comes to healthier relationships, realistic depictions, and, yes, happy endings. While writing about lesbian desire can require just as much courage now as it did in the 1950s, the authors no longer need to plant subtle references or hint at simmering desires. Erotica writers have gone full balls (and cunts) out, with no sexual act or taboo ignored. Pleasure in lesbian erotica today is not simply a promise, it's a priority, a pussy-driven narrative, a button-pusher, a political statement. Not only has the level of explicitness dramatically shifted, but writers now enjoy complete freedom to explore themes, characters, and fantasies that challenge convention and knock propriety on its head.

Whether it's lesbian sex at work ("Business Casual" by Lauren Sanders) or a lesbian sex worker (Tara-Michelle Ziniuk's "Does She Look Like a Boy?"), the stories in this collection reflect how far literary lesbian sex has come in half a century. Nearly all the stories would probably have made Ann Bannon blush (back in her day, that is). For example, the title alone of Rakelle Valencia's "To Fuck or Get Fucked" conjures a post–sex war quandary, nods to the pleasures of penetration, and makes an unapologetic statement about dyke desire.

While butch/femme was *the* archetypal lesbian relationship in the 1950s, its changing dynamics and passionate complexities continue to inspire many of us. Witness femmes getting what they want in stories like "Center of Attention" by Dawn Dougherty, "LIVE: By Request" by Samiya A. Bashir, and

"Roulette" by Shannon Cummings, or tag along with butches on the prowl in "Becoming Stone," "Thermal Stress," and "Cop-Out." In fact, the importance of gender identity, and how it affects our bodies and our sex lives, is a major theme in this collection in stories by Alison L. Smith, Tennessee Jones, Ana Peril, S. Bear Bergman, and Jera Star.

By 2005 the lesbian erotic imagination has evolved to explore nearly every genre of fiction; happily, most of them are represented here. Consider the historical fiction of Julie Levin Russo, whose heroine courts Queen Elizabeth; a dirty fairy tale by Patrick Califia; and a futuristic sci-fi adventure from Linda A. Boulter. Some writers have even succeeded in inventing their own genres (see Skian McGuire's techno-porn and Rachel Kramer Bussel's star-fucking smut).

In addition to sexing up the form of fiction, other erotic stories in this volume illustrate just how the world of lesbian courtship, dating, and sex have expanded. "Anonymous" by Amie M. Evans, "sex hall" by MR Daniel, "Look, but Don't Touch" by Sparky, and "You Know What?" by Cara Bruce read as hot examples of dykes taking advantage of anonymous and public sex. At the heart of S/M erotica lies power, and I believe that power dynamics fuel much of the best erotic writing, whether it contains the specificity of sado-masochism (like Michael M. Hernandez's "Redemption") or not (Jean Roberta's "Splitting the Infinitive"). Power can be expressed in myriad ways: a crush on an older woman (Kenya Devoreaux's "Keeping Up Appearances"), a pair of cuffs (Elaine Miller's "Fee Fie Foe Femme"), or an elaborate scene (L. Shane Conner's story "The Second Hour").

Some of my favorite sex stories are those that explore intense relationships and timeless emotions. The writing of Kyle Walker, Sacchi Green, Peggy Munson, and Betty Blue features complex pairings fueled by yearning, secrets, and memories. The power of self-discovery and growth at different stages of life drive "Farewell to Rainwoman" by Thea Hutcheson, "Loved It and Set It Free" by Lisa Archer, and "Always" by Cecilia Tan. Darker feelings, those of heartbreak, longing, and jealousy, are at the center of "Grand Jeté," "At Long Last," and "Envy."

The stories in *Best of Best Lesbian Erotica 2* track some of the crucial changes in lesbian sex—how we do it and how we represent it. They map just how wide-ranging our desire and our imaginations can be. And they continue what Beebo Brinker and her pals started. Ann Bannon and all our writing foremothers have given us a gift: the confidence to grab that muse by the hair, drag her to a dark corner, have our way with her, then write about it later.

Tristan Taormino
December 2004
New York City

Center of Attention
Dawn Dougherty

There was something about being out with her family that made me want to fuck her.

Maybe it was how better looking she was than the rest of her family. Maybe it was the fact that I couldn't have her that made me want her so bad. All I know is that when we all sat down to dinner at the restaurant I could barely look at my menu from wanting to slip underneath the table and unzip her pants.

Her parents had just gotten back from an extended vacation when they called to invite us to dinner.

"Please don't make me look at pictures," I pleaded as we got dressed. I twirled my hair around my fingers and knotted it up on top of my head.

"You don't have to look at pictures," she said as she pulled her shirt over her head. "But you do have to keep up with the conversation."

I let out an exasperated sigh as I sprayed my curls in place and slipped my earrings on. "I'm ordering a very expensive meal."

"Yes, honey."

"And if your brother makes one comment about church I'll let him have it."

"Yes, dear."

"Are you even listening?"

She came over and gave me a kiss on top of the head. "I'll be downstairs."

The minute we got to the restaurant and she hugged her parents I was wet. By the time the waitress took our order I had my hand on her thigh. As her brother droned on about the new secretary at work I wrapped one of my black leather boots around her pant leg and started to inch it up toward her knee.

She smiled and nodded her head at her brother and gave a little smirk I knew was meant for me.

"You okay?" she asked quietly as the waitress dropped a bowl of steaming pasta in front of her.

"I could be better."

After we ate she got up to go to the bathroom, and I stared at her ass as she walked away.

"So how is your family?" her mother asked, interrupting my thoughts.

"Oh, they're fine." I managed to keep them entertained until she came back.

We kissed them good-bye after cappuccino and tiramisu and drove out of the parking lot.

"Why is it that when we go out with my parents you can't control yourself?"

I wiggled my way over to her side of the car and stroked the outline of her breast. "I don't know. It's the same way at parties. You look so good when you're talking to other people."

"It's because I ignore you, and you know it," she looked down at me. "You can't stand not being the center of attention. Admit it."

"I don't know what you're talking about," I said as I kissed the side of her neck. I was thinking about how good she smelled when she pulled the car over to a rest area.

"What are you doing?"

She stopped the car and turned off the ignition.

"Do you have to pee?" I asked. "I don't think they have a bathroom here."

"Do me a favor and get out of the car."

Two men had just raped a sixteen-year-old boy at a rest stop a few months before, so I was a little apprehensive. I got out and she met me around on my side. It was dark, and there was only one other car parked almost half a mile away.

"Honey, this isn't exactly safe."

She ignored me and grabbed both my arms and pulled them around my back and kissed me hard on the lips. She snaked her tongue inside my mouth, pulled my wrists back hard, and held on to them both with one hand. She continued to kiss me as she grabbed the hem of my skirt with her free hand and pulled it up just under my ass and squeezed.

Several cars whizzed by, and I looked up to see if anyone was pulling in.

"Pay attention, babe," she said. With a smooth motion, she let go of my skirt, grabbed the top of my underwear, and pulled it down to my knees.

"It's really too busy here," I said. She wasn't listening. I wondered how many people were about to see my ass hanging out.

She put her entire mouth over mine and gave me a hot kiss, pulling back only to bite down hard on my neck, collarbone, and shoulders. I was sure she was leaving marks. She pushed me up against the passenger door, and I yelped as the handle dug into my hip. I'd be bruised from head to toe before the night was over.

She unbuttoned the first three buttons on my sweater and unsnapped the front of my bra. Then she pulled up the hem of my skirt and tucked it into the waistband leaving my ass and pussy fully exposed. I felt like a fool with my underwear still around my ankles, but she didn't seem to notice as she stepped back and checked me out. I was glad I wore my black boots. They looked great.

She opened the back door and told me to sit on the edge of the seat. When I did, she knelt outside the car, pulled my underwear off, and spread my legs. The wetness between my legs kept my lips from parting. She took my left ankle and placed my foot on the armrest. My right leg stayed planted on the ground. My lips spread wide and the air on my cunt felt cool.

She leaned back on her heels and took a slow, even breath. As she did I saw someone's headlights flash across the car. I sat up halfway, startled and nervous.

"Shit!" I said.

She didn't move. "Wait," she whispered. "They may just drive by."

The car stopped about thirty feet behind us.

We both sat frozen waiting for something to happen. They had to be able to see us. The car stayed there for almost a minute, then slowly backed up to about fifty feet away and turned their lights off.

Through the rear window I could see it was a man and a woman. They watched us for a minute, and then they turned to each other to kiss. In a minute her head disappeared into his lap.

We both looked at each other.

"I don't mind if they don't mind," she said. "Besides, they'll never even see your face, honey." She leaned forward and pushed me back down on the seat.

4

I lay back tensely, and she had to press my knees apart until they rested in an open position. I wondered how much of my legs they could see. I wondered what the women at work would think if they knew my girlfriend fucked me at a rest stop while some guy got his dick sucked and watched.

Then with total precision the very tip of her tongue grazed just the edge of my clit. I forgot about the voyeurs as she shot her tongue out and hit me again. I moaned and pulled my thighs in toward her head. She pushed them away and kept her hands planted on the inside of my legs.

"Do you like them watching?" and her tongue was at my clit again. She flicked her tongue over my clit four or five more times then stopped and pulled my hips a little farther out the door. This time she slowed down and used her tongue in small, tight circles. My pussy was arched up off the seat to meet her. My tits lay open across my shirt and bounced to the rhythm of her tongue.

She stopped.

"Roll over."

I did, and she pulled me down so my knees and ass were outside the car. They definitely had a full shot of me now. Then she pushed my skirt up to my waist, and I heard her unzip her pants. I looked back to see her slide a fat dildo out of the crotch of her pants.

She had packed for dinner out with her parents.

I smiled.

She pushed my knees farther apart and my boots scraped across the dirt. She bent her head down, pushed my cheeks apart, and slid her tongue into my ass. Her movements were slow and juicy, and I practically dripped onto the ground I was so wet. I love to get fucked up the ass.

She dipped her tongue into me and rimmed me hard. I pushed my ass into her face and used my own hands to spread myself even wider. She groaned from deep inside her throat as she met my resistance with her entire mouth.

After a minute she slowed and then stopped. She spread my ass farther and placed the tip of the dildo outside of my asshole. She dropped it down and pushed it slightly into my cunt to get it wet, then brought it up again and slowly started to push into me.

I lay still while she worked it in. She placed both of her hands on my hips and used them for leverage. After a few minutes of slow rocking the dildo was all but an inch in. She paused then pushed the last inch in hard and held it there tight inside of me.

She brought her hands up to my shoulders and pulled them back as she started with slow short pumps. She gradually increased her speed when she felt me pushing against her. I felt the leather smack against the inside of my thighs. She was on her knees between my spread legs with her hand on my shoulders fucking me up the ass with my favorite dildo. I was in heaven.

She took one hand off my shoulder and brought it around to the base of my cunt. She moved up to my clit and started to massage me. My ass tightened around the dildo, and I gritted my teeth. She bent over and rested her head between my shoulder blades and whispered in my ear.

"Come right here, baby, with me up your ass and these two getting off on you."

She clamped her teeth down on my neck and bit and kissed me while she stroked my clit. My ass loosened, and she moved into strong pounding strokes. I grabbed the edge of the seat as I came. My body jerked hard as she pushed and continued to rub her fingers over me.

I imagined them watching me come and wondered if they'd ever seen two dykes do it before. I bit my lip and strained my arms as I held onto the upholstery.

She slowed and lay on top of me for a minute breathing, catching her breath.

"Whore," she joked. I pictured how we must have looked from fifty feet away.

"You're the whore! This was totally your idea."

She sat back and slowly eased the dildo out of me. My muscles contracted with the final pull out, and I relaxed. I pulled my skirt back down over my ass as she took the dildo off and threw it onto the floor in the back seat.

"I hope we don't get pulled over."

I'm sure the cops would love to confiscate a dildo off of two lesbians.

"Can you see them?" she asked looking back. She was wiping the dirt off of her knees.

I nodded my head. I didn't particularly want to see them. What if they were totally gross and disgusting? I wanted to imagine them as gorgeous and bisexual.

As I got into the front seat I felt the stickiness between my thighs and squeezed them together tight. My ass hurt as I adjusted myself and put my seat belt on.

"They're driving by."

I looked in the rearview mirror, and sure enough their car was inching toward ours. We both sat waiting to see what they'd do. As they passed they just smiled and nodded. The woman was fixing her hair. The man just grinned. They didn't look gorgeous or bisexual.

As she started the car, I curled up around her arm.

"We need to go out with your parents more often."

"We sure do," she said as she pulled out onto the highway and headed home.

Always
Cecilia Tan

Morgan was always the one who wanted a child. Even when I first met her, before we got involved, before we got engaged, always the talk of motherhood with her, of empowering Earth-mother stuff and of making widdle baby booties. I, on the other hand, had always said I would never have children, was sure somehow that I would never decide to bear a child, and yet I had always thought about it, secretly. So when I fell in love with Morgan, and she fell in love with me, and we had a hilltop wedding where we both wore white dresses and two out of our four parents looked on happily, I figured I was off the hook on the parenting issue.

This was, of course, before John, and way before Jillian. But I'm getting ahead of myself.

Back up to the summer of 1989. New England. Cape Cod. Morgan and I are in a hammock in the screened in porch of her aunt's summer house. The night is turning smoothly damp after a muggy day, cars hiss by on pavement still wet from the afternoon's rainshower, the slight breeze rocks us just enough to make me feel weightless as I drowse. I am on my back with one foot hanging out each side of the hammock; Morgan rests in the wide space between my legs, her spill of brown curls spread on my stomach and her knees drawn up close to her chest. The hammock is the nice, cloth kind, with a wide wooden bar at either end to keep it from squeezing us like seeds in a lemon wedge, not the white rope type that leaves you looking like a bondage experiment gone wrong. Morgan's hands travel up my thighs like they come out of a dream. It never occurs to me to stop her. Sex with Morgan is as easy and natural as saying yes to a bite of chocolate from the proffered bar of a friend. Before her fingers even reach the elastic edge of my panties I am already shifting my hips, already breathing deeper, already thinking about the way her fingers will touch and tease me, how one slim finger will slide deep into me once I am wet, how good it feels to play with her hair on my belly, how much I want her. With Morgan, I always come.

Imagine afterward, lying now side by side, holding each other and sharing each other's heat as the beach breeze turns chilly, when I decide to propose to her. I am gifted with a sudden and utter clarity—this is the right thing to do. It has been six years since I came out as bisexual, three years since I began dating women, but something like ten years of getting into relationships with men and constantly trying to disentangle myself from them. It's not that I don't like men. I like them, and love them, a-proverbial-lot. But I've never been able to explain why it is I've always felt the need to put up resistance, to define myself separately, to have my foot on the brake of our sex lives, with a man. I always do.

But here, with Morgan, the urge to resist is not even present. Maybe it has nothing to do with men versus women, I think, and maybe it has everything to do with her. She's the right one. And she says yes.

So we got married, that part you knew. Marriage for us did not mean monogamy, of course—rather we defined it as "managed faithfulness." We had our boundaries, our limits, our promises, and our outside dalliances were allowed. But when you're happily married, who has time or energy for all the flirting and courting and negotiating with someone new? Neither of us did for several years. And that's when John came into the picture.

Morgan always toasts the bread a little before she makes cinnamon toast. Always two ticks on our toaster oven's dial, then on goes the butter and sugar and cinnamon, and back in for the full six ticks. I've tried making it without the pretoasting and can't tell the difference, but she insists.

A raw spring day in Somerville, me in galoshes and a pair of my father's old painting pants with a snow shovel, cursing and trying to lift a cinderblock-sized chunk of wet packed snow off the walkway of our three-decker. On the first floor lives our landlady, one frail but observant old Irishwoman Mrs. Donnell, on the second a new tenant we haven't yet met, a single guy we hear walking around late at night and never see in the morning. Hence me trying to shovel the late-season fall, two April-Fool's feet of it, because I'm pretty sure no one else will. Morgan inside rushing to get ready for work, emerging soap-scented and loosely bundled to plant a kiss on my cheek as she steps over the last foot of unshoveled snow onto the sidewalk (cleared by a neighbor who loves to use his snowblower). She's off to catch the bus to her job downtown as facilities coordinator at the Theater Arts Foundation. I heave on the remaining block of snow with a loud grunt and perhaps it is my grunt that keeps me from hearing the noise my back must surely have made when it cracked, popped, "went out" as they say.

I am hunched over in pain, cursing louder now and not caring if Mrs. Donnell hears it, when another person is there, asking if I'm all right. His hands are on my shoulders and he slowly straightens me upright. It is the new tenant, wearing an unzipped parka and peering into my face with worry. I tell him I'll be all right; he says are you sure. I say yes but I'm clearly not sure—it goes back and forth the way those things will until it ends up somehow with me in his apartment drinking some kind of herbal tea and then lying face down on his Formica counter with my shirt on the floor while his thumbs and palms map out the terrain of my back.

In the theater world a backrub is a euphemism for sex. ("Hey, come upstairs, I'll give you a backrub." "Oh, those two, they've been rubbing each other's backs for years.") So you'd think I'd know. But no, there's no way obviously that he could have planned that I'd try to lift too much snow. No, it was an honest case of one thing led to another. Maybe a couple of resistance-free years with Morgan had dulled my old repeller-reflexes, and we...well, in specific, after they had done their magic with my spine, his hands strayed down to my ribs, and he left a line of warm kisses down my back. He had longer than average guy hair, straight and tickly like a tassel as it touched my skin. I moaned to encourage him, my body knowing what I wanted before my mind had a chance to change the plan.

Morgan always says I plan too much.

My father's oversized pants slid to the floor and kisses fell like snowflakes onto the curve of my buttocks, feather light, and then a moist tongue probed along the center where it went from hard spine to softness. We got civilized after that, and went to the bedroom and it wasn't until we were lying back having one of those postcoital really-get-to-know-you talks that Morgan came and knocked on the door. No bus, saw your galoshes on the second floor landing she explained at her seeming clairvoyance, to which I replied This is John.

John always says, "How do you do" and bows while he shakes two-handed when he's formally introduced.

Our first threesome happened right away, that night after dinner fetched on foot from the Chinese restaurant on the corner. On our living room floor, the white waxy boxes and drink cups scattered at the edges like spectators, the elegant curve of our bay windows standing witness to his hand between my legs, Morgan's mouth on his nipple, my lips on Morgan's ear, John's penis sheathed between us, my chest against his back while he buried himself in her, her tongue on my clit, his nose in my neck, my fingers in her hair, our voices saying whatever they always said, mmm, and ahh, and yes. I didn't know if this was going to be one of Morgan's experiments in excitement, or one of my few dalliances, or one of John's fantasies come true. What it was, which I didn't expect, was the beginning of something more solid, more intricate, and more satisfying than any twosome I had known.

John always buys two dozen roses on Valentine's Day, which he gives to Morgan and me one rose at a time.

When was it, maybe a year later, when Morgan became director at TAF and John, who was in computers, had a discussion with Mrs. Donnell about buying the building. Morgan always loved housewares, I've always loved renovation and design. The idea hit us at Christmas dinner, Morgan's parents' house in Illinois, her mother on one side of her, me on the other, John on my other side, and all manner of relatives near and far spread down the two long tables from the dining room into the ranch house living room, in folding chairs brought for the occasion in minivans and hatchbacks. Turkey so moist the gravy wasn't needed, and gravy so rich that we used it anyway. Wild rice and nut stuffing heaped high on John's plate, shored up by mashed potatoes, his vegetarian principles only mildly compromised by the addition of imitation bacon bits on green salad. Family chatter and laughter, Morgan's father sometimes directing men's talk at John. And somehow the discussion turning to Mrs. Donnell and her plans to sell the house, and somehow our three hands linked in my lap, under the table, and John announcing to everyone, suddenly, that the three of us would buy the house together, voicing the thought that was at that moment in all three of our heads, even though until that moment we'd never contemplated the idea.

I always clean the toilets and the sinks but I hate cleaning the shower and bathtub. John, who has a slight paranoia about foot fungi, loves to do the shower and tub. If only we could convince Morgan to do the kitchen floors.

If my life seems like a series of sudden revelations, that's because it is. The most recent one was watching Jillian walk her stiff-legged toddler's walk from one side of our living room to the other. I knew then what Morgan looked like as a child, what her exploratory spirit and her bright smile must have been like when she was knee high.

The night we made Jillian we had a plan. We didn't always sleep together, or even have three-way sex together, but we knew all three of us had to have a hand in her creation. For months we had charted Morgan's period, her temperature. We cleared a room to be a new bedroom and put a futon on the floor, lit the candles and incense (we're so old-fashioned that way) and made ready. Imagine Morgan, her long brown curls foaming over her shoulders, her back against the pillowed wall, her knees bent, framing her already seemingly round Earth-mother belly, watching us. John kneels in front of me, naked and somber-faced. I will not let him stay that way for long.

I begin it with a kiss. I kiss Morgan on the lips and then John and we pull away from her. I take his tongue deep into my mouth, my hands roaming over his head and neck, and he responds with a moan. My hard nipples brush against his—my hands on his shoulders I continue to kiss and wag my breasts from side to side, our nipples brush again and again. Then I am licking them, my teeth nipping, my hands sliding down to his hips, one hand between his legs, lifting his balls. He gasps and throws his head back. My mouth is now hovering over his penis, hardening in my hand. I reach out my tongue to tease. Instinct begins to overtake the plan, his hands are reaching for me, he pushes me back, his mouth on mine, his tongue on my nipples, his fingers seeking out my hottest wettest places and finding them. He knows my body well, he slides two fingers in while his thumb rests on my clit.

Morgan watches, her belly taut, her hands clenched in the sheets.

He is slicking his hand wet with my juices up and down his penis, and then he climbs over me, my legs lock behind his back, and he settles in. Tonight there are no barriers between us. I let go with my legs and let him pump freely. If I let him I know he will grant me my secret wish, to make me come from the fucking, from the friction and rhythm and pressure and slap and grind. I am sinking down into a deep well of pleasure, his sweat dripping onto me, as he becomes harder, hotter, faster, tighter, his jaw clenched, and I become looser, and further away. The turning point comes though with a ripple in my pelvis, and then every thrust is suddenly bringing me closer to the surface, up and up again, drawing me in tighter, closer, until my wish comes true. I break the surface screaming and crying, and calling out his name, and thinking how good it is to have learned not to resist this....

His eyes flicker with candlelight as he strokes my hair and jerks from me—the plan is not forgotten after all. His penis stands out proud and red and wet and the strain of holding back is evident in his bit lip. Morgan's nostrils flare and she slides low on her pillows. I go to her, my fingers seeking out her cunt, which is already dripping, my mouth smothering hers, our tongues slipping in and out as I confirm what we all already know. She is ready.

And I put myself behind her, my hands cupping her breasts, my legs on either side of her, as John lies down between her legs. My fingers sneak down to spread her wider, to circle her clit and pinch her where she likes it, while he thrusts slickly, my teeth in her neck, her hair in our faces, the three of us humping like one animal, all of us ready.

Morgan always comes twice.

There's nothing like a grandchild to bring parents around. So Jillian has six grandparents and none of them mind enough to complain about it. We always have them here for Christmas now, we've got the most bedrooms and the most chairs. Jillian will always be my daughter. John always shovels the snow. And Morgan always says we could make Jillian a sibling— that it could be my turn if I want. I don't know. I just know that I love them always.

Becoming Stone
Sandra Lee Golvin

Summer is becoming. Gone to Africa says A. Now you on the blue couch becoming my fist. My arm becoming the cradle. Your hair becoming the yellow dream.

I did dream you another summer. I was trying to decide about my life. I was believing in the *I* of decision making. I was believing in the *I* of dreaming. Now that *I* does not know so much and would say you dreamed me or perhaps the dream dreamed us both. An old lady's corpse was being kissed. In the kissing she became you, the fairy tale princess. Someday my prince(ss) will becoming. I will becoming her. Or him. We had not yet met, my *I* and yours. Not then. Not that summer.

You were wearing chocolate panties. Even now, with my fist inside, the wet silk wraps my wrist at the place where it wants cutting open. You let me be the one who knows. I so wanted that. I have a chocolate dick, the one A never liked because it looked too real. You don't mind though. You're such a girl. Until you, being the girl was *my* job.

When you first approached I had no way to understand. You, all Midwest blond, the wife and mother, legs long as prairie sky. Can you hear the longing for what I thought could never be mine? Me, the frog, my lipstick androgyny a cover for what only you saw living in stone.

You would chip away my protection bit by bit until I knelt naked before you in an attitude of wanting. I did not make your job easy any more than the stone yields to the chisel with the first blow. No, persistence was required, and more than that, desire. Inexorably you made me, a me who I did not know was there. Is the figure the creation of the artist or is it hidden there in rock, only waiting to be revealed? Am I now what you imagined, or was I always so?

It's not only the change in clothes, the end of dresses and wide-brimmed hats. My hips have narrowed, my jaw grown more square, suddenly I know how to let my gaze linger on the pretty girl as if I might presume to know her. And my friends, those few who remain, do not recognize me. All of this I want to say you wrought. Lady of alchemy, Aphrodite of dreams.

Another one last night, another not able to reach you. You were in a Presbyterian hospital by the sea. You had given birth to our daughter. Things are breaking all around me. Things made of glass like the nautilus you brought me from Paris after you already knew you were done with me. (That week with your mother rendered me an impossibility.) Still months later I dream of you and my hand awakens hot, curled in on itself, bereft of you.

Jealous of my own fist. It knows something I never will. Your wet heat imprinted in traces at the grooves that mark the knuckles. My palm forever empty of the sweet, flat place at the base of your spine. My thighs that held the curve of your ass, lonely. I never held a woman that way before. Don't you see?

I was your mother, your boylover, and you my midwife, my child.

There was A, for many years my man. I'd been faithful to her. You had your husband and two sons, your woman lovers on the side (you'd brought them out). For nine months I refused to be one of them. You always got what you wanted, on your terms. This time you wanted a real dyke. I needed terms of my own.

Then A went to Africa.

When the sculptor works with stone, a long time passes where nothing shows. There is a circling and a tapping, and it is all an act of faith. Then comes a moment, seemingly out of nowhere, in which what has been only surface and raw edges suddenly becomes the thing that was always there. The soul in the stone unfolds.

I don't want to tell this story. Once it is written it is over. I can't bear that. When the phone rings I still imagine it might be you. When it is silent I wonder why you do not call. How ridiculous I am.

The moment.

You didn't come to class, and we exchanged angry messages. I remember I called you chickenshit. You gave it right back. Your temper opened up the place in me where violence fuels my sex. It felt good, the lust and the killing rage. Made it possible for me to say I humble myself and demand your presence at the same time. You liked that and came to find me at the beach. As I told you to do. In the parking lot I didn't say hello, just pulled your head down to mine and gave you the kiss you'd been wanting. What I wanted was to fuck you there in public. I didn't. I made you demonstrate your desire though, all the way back to my house, and a man on a bicycle rode by calling "Lovers, yoo-hoo, lovers" like an enchanted bird.

I made you wait on the blue couch while I searched for the poem. The one by Judy Grahn where Ereshkegal Butch Queen of the Underworld dares Inanna Queen of Beauty to face her secret want. This is you, I said, Queen of Beauty. And you were, too, so lovely in the shock of what you had provoked in me. I grabbed your hair, that blond mane, tight and read to you. Do you remember the words?

> *Strange to everyone but me that*
> *you would leave the great green rangy*
> *heaven of the american dream,*
> *your husband and your beloved children,*
> *the convenient machines,*
> *the lucky lawn and the possible*
> *picture window—to come down here below.*
> *You left your ladyhood, your queenship, risking*
> *everything, even a custody suit,*
> *even your sanity, even your life. It is*
> *this that tells me you have a warrior*
> *living inside you. It is for this*
> *I could adore you.*

My fist is remembering the rough of your hair.

You cried as I forced your face down into my lap. Being a dyke isn't fun and games, baby. It's serious business. It's warrior business. Like the poem says. I think you complained then, that I was being hard on you. You should thank me for that, I shook you, thank me for caring enough not to play your little secret on the side. For caring enough to try to bring you down here, to my world. To where you want to be. You cried some more. And then you thanked me. You did.

You were the most beautiful to me then, all your perfect passing prettiness stripped away by real grief.

Was that when you bared your belly, so that I could witness the site of your devastation? Not only the scars of childbirth, but the ravages of bulimia, the muscles destroyed by years of laxatives and vomit. I thought of napalm, dead places too poisoned for anything to live, and I believed I understood something about the price of your fortune.

You were a connoisseur, bred for private jets and crystal. I was proud you'd picked me. Cocky. At one point—not that first night, but soon—I put Mick Jagger on and danced for you to "Gimme Shelter." *We all need someone we can cream on,* he sang. Baby, you squirmed with so much delight I thought I was king of the world. You had the power to put me there. And to take me down. You were the Queen of Beauty, after all.

I wouldn't let you touch me. I don't know how I knew to do that.

Not much happened that first night. You remembered your boys whom you'd dumped at a neighbor's for a minute, not knowing I had other plans. I didn't like it, you leaving in the middle of a scene. You begged for a return engagement the next night, and I said I'd think about it. In the morning you called, and I told you what to wear. A dress with a full skirt. No underwear. A more interesting bra. You confessed you'd thrown out all your sexy bras and bought plain ones because you thought that's what lesbians like. Since you were trying to please me I forgave you. But I was clear. I wanted you in lace.

So cool and yet out of my mind. What was happening to me? My hands, my hands, my hands do all the remembering.

I put on my man's suit. You swooned at the door. Trousers, you whispered, eyeing me in a way no girl ever had before. I said we're going out in public. Your assignment is to let everyone know you are with me. That you're mine. We went to the Pleasure Chest. We looked at dildos and porn. I said I need to know what you like. You fumbled, dropped your keys, acted silly. Then I took you to an upscale industry panel on gay parenting. The kind of thing I hate. But I endured it because I wanted you to see there were people like you with children and money. I wanted you to be able to imagine a life with me.

I think that was the night I danced for you. Yes, I'm sure of it now. You got on your knees in front of me, undid my slacks. It was a mistake to let you touch me. I knew it right away but didn't know how to stop. You went home to your husband, and I raged all night, feverish to find my way back to that place of power I'd let slip away under the stroke of your fingers.

At 6:00 A.M. I telephoned, woke you. I knew he'd be gone already. Come to me now, I demanded. I'm not through with you. Of course you couldn't comply, couldn't leave your boys. What can I do for you, you asked. I said I need you to touch yourself. As if you were me. Now. And you did. Are you touching yourself? Yes, yes I am. Are you thinking of me? Yes, yes I am. Does it feel good. Oh yes. Do you want me to fuck you? Yes. Say it. Yes. Please fuck me. Now say this: I'm a dyke. I'm a dyke. I've always been a dyke. I've always been a dyke. I love women. I love women. I want to be fucked by women. I want to be fucked by women. I want to be fucked by you. I want to be fucked by you.

That afternoon you told me you'd decided. No more lies. You wouldn't come to me again until you told him. It was not what I expected. I didn't believe you. That you would risk everything. *Even a custody suit, even your sanity, even your life.* To come to me. To come to yourself. But you had already made the plan to speak with him that night. I was in awe.

Walking the long stretch of beach miles beyond home I thought only of you and your courage. How I could hold you while you did this warrior thing you could only do alone. For three days and three nights I hadn't taken in food or been able to sleep. Running on some other source, my body feeding on a part of itself I no longer needed. The detritus of my own passing. A fire burned. What becoming was happening to me? Then I remembered the poem, the invocation between us. How for three days and three nights Inanna hung on the peg of the underworld stripped to nothing. And when they stole into Hell to find the Queen of Beauty, they found Ereshkegal writhing on the ground beside her, out of her mind. Giving birth to Inanna.

> *Yes, I am the Butch of the Realm, the Lady*
> *of the great Below. It is hard for me*
> *to let you go.*
> *When next you say "you bitch"— "wild cherry"—*
> *and "it just happens"—*
> *you will think of me*
> *as she who bore you to your new and lawful*
> *place of rising,*
> *took the time and effort*
> *just to get you there*
> *so you could moan Inanna*
> *you could cry*
> *and everyone you ever were*
> *could die.*

You told him you were a lover of women. He said that's okay, just tell me the truth. I slept then.

We had one more night before A returned from Africa.

You were waiting for me when I got home. I had on trousers. You wore a red dress. Tight so I could know you had nothing underneath. You had made me dinner. Up against the kitchen counter, I wrapped my hands strong around your rib cage. You said, You make me feel so female. You said, You're my man. I think I died then. In that moment. Everything I'd ever pretended to be. Gone. With you in my hands.

I must have taken you on my lap then, on the blue couch, the sweet of you all over me, and I think I called you Baby, Baby. You must have moaned or I did and then my hand went looking for you. I remember my hand and the weight of you and my face in your hair. Jesus how you opened to me. Let me reach up into the wound, curl inside and fill your empty places. Did I do it? Did I ease the rawness for a moment? Is it sacrilege to try to speak of this? To describe the unnameable? Something eased in me, a coming home, a landing. Into a hot pink hyperactive stillness.

Who is screaming? My hand has not forgiven me for leaving. If I'd believed I could not return I would never have left. But I thought it was only the beginning, and that night I wanted you to have it all. So I strapped on the chocolate dick, lay you down on the carpet among the pillows, and knelt over your belly.

I traced the folds and pocks of that tender place with my fingers, a sureness in my hands that meant something about arriving into a knowing that was mine and more than mine—a birthright, an ancient lineage. I guess I was praying for a healing when I saw them. Judy Grahn and Pat Parker and other butch elders there in the room. I didn't say anything at the time because I didn't know if I was going crazy. You had taken me so far from all I'd been, I could easily have been out of my mind. They gathered around us to watch. And then I knew they were there to welcome me into a secret circle. Into the same sacred holy office they'd held for me two decades before in Berkeley, when I was trying to find a way into my life and their poetry was all I had to go by. I've never had a vision before, actually seen people not in the flesh. Even now talking about it I know it sounds like fiction. But those poet butches were there with us, and they were telling me what I needed to know. That I had descended to the underworld and now had to learn to live there. That it was not at all clear between you and me who had taken whom down. That this was not only your initiation, baby, but mine. That they would watch over me on the long rock road ahead.

That was the moment, really. You know the rest. How I

left A to wait for you, how school ended, how you said you needed to not see me while you went through the process of divorce. I didn't tell you how stupid I felt that last time you came by. Me in my new trousers I'd bought with you in mind. You asked me about them, as if you knew I was trying to look sexy for you. As if you knew how I needed you to find my way home. I knew better than to let you kiss me on your way out the door, but I couldn't stop myself. If only I'd really done it, gotten on my knees and pleaded, in the attitude of the beggar you'd revealed in me. Chipped away, bit by bit, with your wild beauty.

Stone is a living thing. Only more slow moving than most. There are processes. Once in a great while eruptions come, fire, ice. It is in these moments that the stone comes to know itself as stone. Its limitations. Its capacity. Its longing.

You Know What?
Cara Bruce

I work in a place "nice girls" don't usually visit. Starting about four in the afternoon I enter a black-covered doorway underneath a flashing marquee that reads: "LIVE GIRLS—ALL NUDE." I am a performer, a dancer, an exhibitionist. And I like it.

Sometimes I strip on stage, but mostly I work the booths. The booths in my joint have a tiny bit of glass at the bottom. They are open so I can see everything the john is doing, and he can see me. If a girl wants to make some extra money she can let the guys touch; there is also a security button if they get out of control.

I like it this way. I like to watch the men jerking off. I like to look right in their eyes as I shake my tits and move my shaved pussy up and down in front of their faces. Some girls hate to know what the customers are doing, but not me. I'm causing it; therefore I own the reaction. I want to know what I own. This is why I make the most money.

I don't usually let anyone touch, I just like the watching. Just the two of us, making each other hot as hell in a space as big as my bathroom closet.

One day I was working the booths, it was pretty slow. A couple of guys came in, one just sat there, staring at me. I don't like it when they just look. I want participation. Makes me feel as if I'm doing a better job. One guy jerked off, came in about two strokes. Made me feel as if I was doing *too* good a job. Then this woman comes in. Now sometimes we get lesbians or prostitutes with dates, and once in a while there are girls who come in with their boyfriends. Usually these women won't even look at me, they look at the floor, their feet, their boyfriend, or they try to make out to distract themselves from the show. It's like they're embarrassed for themselves and for me. I always try and dance harder to force their attention. The couples never stay long.

So anyway, this woman comes in. She is hot. I look at her, dressed in her chic black business suit, little skirt, blouse, and matching jacket. And the first thing I think is that she might be a cop, but she sits down and puts some quarters in. The lights come on, and I can hear a faint beat of music from whoever is dancing outside, so I start to grind my hips and toss my hair.

The woman stares right at me, as if she's daring me to show her what I've got. So I do. I look right back in her eyes and start fucking an imaginary body, real slow and sensual like. And she keeps looking. She drops more quarters in, and she spreads her legs.

She's not wearing anything underneath, and I wonder if she went to work like this. Her legs are spread wide, and she's shaved bare as well, giving her big and thick lips plenty of air. Now I'm thinking maybe she's in the business, and I start sort of showing off for her.

I bring my cunt down right in front of her face, and you know what she does? She breathes on it. Real hot breath coming out and almost making me lose my balance. So I keep dancing, grinding real close to her face. She starts unbuttoning her blouse, no bra on. She lets her tits fall out, then she starts rubbing and pinching her own nipples.

She's trying to outdo me, I think. I shake my head, that bitch is trying to steal my spotlight. So I reach down by my feet and pick up my prop: a big pink vibrator. I'll give her something to feel herself about, all right. I take the toy and draw it slowly through my mouth, lubing it up. She licks her lips, still staring right into my eyes. I bring the vibrator down and tease my clit with it, knowing it'll pop out hard and full, giving her something to stare at. So I start moving the vibrator around, turning it up a notch and breaking a sweat.

She has her skirt around her waist now, her long legs spread wide. She tilts her hips up, and starts jilling off.

She mimics me, each stroke I make with my vibrator she copies with her finger. It's a masturbation duel, and I'm not sure if the objective is to come first or last. Without missing a beat she puts more quarters in.

I slide the vibrator up inside me. She matches this with her fingers. I'm squatting, using my palm to stick the vibrator up, then releasing my muscles to let it fall back. Her digits are diving in and out, with the same gentle rise and fall. I shake my head; I'm on fire now, this woman is making me hot. Her pretty head is tilted back slightly, her lips parted, her eyes stuck on mine.

Suddenly it hits me. I want to fuck her. I don't usually do customers, but I want her real bad. I get up in her face, my whirring cunt is inches from her mouth, and I say, "You want me."

She smiles, her hand never stops, and she says, "*You want me.*"

"Fuck me," I tell her, and my voice quivers a little with the excitement, even though I'm trying to sound stern.

She takes the vibrator in her mouth, and she starts fucking me with it. I'm squatting above her, and she is fucking me with my own vibrator in her mouth. Meanwhile, her hand never stops moving. She's getting lipstick all over my toy and juices from my dripping slit are sliding down and gathering on the corners of her red lips and she is still staring at me. My legs are trembling, because she is fucking the hell out of me and herself at the same time.

"Yeah, honey, fuck me, fuck me," I pant and I can almost see her smile.

I wrap my hands around her head and push her deeper into me. I'm moving her head and every time I look down those eyes are staring at me. My legs are shaking and my cunt starts to clench and I feel my insides begin to boil and I look down and she winks at me. I can't believe it, I lose my shit. I start to come, shaking and crying I fall over on her.

"Please stop, stop, stop," I cry, but she won't. That vibrator isn't moving, but it's still deep inside me. I reach down to grab her hair but then, the bitch, she starts to come and I get off again, just feeling her shaking and moaning under me. It's too much.

She's done, and finally she pulls out the vibrator. I climb off of her, and she turns off the toy and places it down on the little stage. I'm spent, I feel like I've been fucked for the first time in a long time, and if the floor wasn't covered with spent jizz maybe I could crawl up and go to sleep there.

She's still looking at me, that smile that's more like a smirk on her face, and she's buttoning up her blouse and pulling down her skirt. She stands up, looking like nothing ever happened, and she walks over and you know what she does? She kisses me. Plants a big wet one right on my mouth while she slides a twenty on the stage; then she turns and walks out.

I can't believe her. The nerve of that slut, I know her type, the kind that always needs the last word. I shake my head, some people are just crazy, you know what I mean? I get back on stage and wait for my next show.

Thermal Stress
María Helena Dolan

I'm an ass woman. I can't help it; that's just the way I'm wired. Oh, of course I love the way women look and feel and taste and smell and sound. But I really love the way women sway. Uh-hmm.

And a woman who knows how to work it...whew! A thoroughly religious feeling just comes all over me. When I see a positively heart-stopping ass, it makes me want to get right down on my knees and...say the rosary! Oh yeah!

Especially when they make it sway, honey. Swaying on the street, swaying in the breeze, swaying on the dance floor, swaying like it has a mind of its own, if you please. Any one of those moves can knock me down and roll me over; but you know I'll be right back up for more.

And, truth be told, I should say that I especially love the way *she* sways, my sweet, sweet thing. Uh-hmm.

I must declare, she has got to be the finest work of womankind on the Goddess's green Earth, built with the roundest, sweetest, firmest, ripest, shakinest, succulentist mounds imaginable. I swear, grown women start to weep, and even faint dead away, when they see that garden of delights crossing their paths. Woo.

Now, this kind of thing is a gift you've got to be born with. You can't fake it, you can't acquire it, you can't learn it. There can't be any doubt that my woman started out from toddlerhood with handfuls of the stuff. Hell, when she was just a teen queen, trying to figure out which way to go—you know, whether it'd be boys or girls or both—she already knew that a pair of tight jeans exhibited her best and most stirring calling card.

Oh yeah. And being a southern gal, she liked to strut—even before she knew how to work it. Some innate pool of female knowledge bubbled up to the surface long enough to let her know that punctuating her arrivals and departures with that undiagrammable but definitely declarative sentence was precisely the way to proceed.

Some things just come instinctively to the naturally gifted. It ain't as if anyone put her up to it. In fact, all kinds of folks tried to get her to change her ways.

Shoot, for years, the neighbors could hear her mama hollering out the window, "Come on in here, girl, before you shake yourself all to pieces!"

But thank God that didn't succeed. 'Cuz now I am the happy beneficiary of all that bounty. It's a glory so sweet that sometimes it just about makes my teeth ache....

Just watching her walk is a thrilling, fulfilling thing. But actually making love to her...I can hardly stand it! Sometimes, it just comes upon me, like a veritable force of nature.

Take the other night, for instance. We were lying in bed, just reading. It was late, and I was dog-boned weary from work and meetings and the daily runnings around. The most I could muster was a chaste little peck, which I'd already administered on her Oil-of-Olayed forehead.

She has a lamp on her side of the bed, and I have one on

mine; she held a book, and so did I. Mine was a murder mystery with a dyke dick, and hers was poetry.

So we were content, just laying there together, heads on respective pillows, arms barely touching, bodies relaxed and ready for sleep. Calm, comfortable, homey.

But then, she rolls over to her side of the bed, propping her head with one arm as she continues reading, and her butt is all of a sudden touching my hip. A tornado siren wouldn't have shocked my nerves as much as just registering her firm but oh-so-soft flesh against my suddenly awakened body.

I can't help myself; it's just the way I'm wired.

So I naturally have to roll over too, putting my arms around her and pressing my starting-to-get-bothered-about-it pussy against her butt. She smiles, turning her head toward me for a moment. And then, she keeps on reading!

Well, I'm afraid that my now-discarded *novelus interruptus* won't hold my attention any longer. Not with all this soft warmth blending with my own. "Turn over, baby," I croon. She rotates her head over her shoulder and gives me a pointed "have you lost your mind?" look.

By now, I'm working one hand around to her dark triangle in front. Pressing down, the way she likes, I give her that low, lazy voice: "Ooh baby, you know I just want one little lick. Just one lick, and I can die happy."

"Yeah," she rejoinders. "As if one was ever enough for you."

"Ah now baby, it ain't as if you don't receive some benefit, too."

"I'm reading," she says, not quite dismissively.

"Not any more," I point out. "In fact, I think your butt is having some thoughts of her own."

It's undeniably true; just that small circular pressure at the origin of her clit has got her hips moving in circles, and little explosions set off quivers in various other parts.

"Mmm, baby, I can feel your heat. I want to give you some lovin'."

She doesn't reply; but her hips grind a little faster and a little harder, as I kiss her neck from her ear down to her shoulder.

With one hand working her mound, the other comes around to pleasure the nearest breast; once that preliminary negotiation is established, I part her thighs with my leg. And that lets me feel her slick wetness already beginning to collect there, like some kind of thermal spring, as the temperature rises dramatically.

"Ooh, honey, you better lay on your belly. There's something I've just got to give you."

In an evil voice, she asks, "Jewelry?"

"Uh, huh. Pearls of great price." And then I stop what my hands and leg are doing—which she hates.

"Oh, all right," she grumbles and lays belly down. Which puts her butt right where I can reach it.

At first, I simply have to lean back and admire this natural wonder. I marvel that I can't even span all the way across it with both hands stretched out, like a piano player searching for the last, best chord. But even that attempt sends shudders through her and me.

Kneeling now, I run my hands up and down her mounds, sometimes kneading and sometimes just drawing my fingertips lightly across her puckering skin. Keeping it going, I reposition myself over her and then drag my breasts across her back, just barely touching her skin with them. Slowly, ever so achingly slowly, I trail my now-hardened nipples down her ass to the tops of her thighs. Ah, her hips are really grinding now.

Inspired, I take my right tit in my hand and stuff it up into her crack, so she can feel my flesh all up and down her. Her heat rises higher, and her hips move more furiously, sucking my tit into her.

She protests heartily when I pull out of her, but she quiets as I begin to once more rub my breasts up her back. Reaching her hairline, I stop and hover over her. Then, starting at her neck, this time with my lips, I kiss downward, slow, with deliberate torpor; velvet mating with satin to form a wondrous combination. This delicious mating takes so long because I simply have to cover every inch along her perspiring spine.

As I finally claim the territory of her left cheek with sovereign kisses, I cheat with an unexpected infiltration and cross over to her coccyx with my indefatigably exploratory mouth. That bony tail remnant twitches mightily as I part her mounds with my hands and kiss inside the crack.

Her smell is so sweet and so like her that I can't imagine ever wanting to stop. With my reverential tongue tip, I begin my search of her quivering ring, that delicate, puckered peach pit. I work my assertive tip of tongue flesh against those folds, dispatching trills of sensation that expand into undulating surges of excitement as they spiral through her. She moans out her pleasure into the mattress as I work her more and more feverishly, her asshole clutching and shaking.

But I can't resist the pull of her pussy any longer. My mouth races down to her near-gaping hole, and I lick the outer walls in a circular motion.

Fixing to boil, she blurts out, "Give it to me, honey. Put it in me. I need it now. Tongue-fuck me!" she calls out in an imperious plea.

And I do, thrusting my face against her, my nose seeping into her ass, my tongue charging in and out with a great heat, a ferocity usually seen in people desperately trying to save treasured objects from furiously burning buildings.

She screams, and I keep at it. I can't breathe, but it doesn't matter. I just keep moving my head against her, my hands on her hips, pulling her butt up toward my face with fast, hard strokes. I just keep fucking her with my tongue, as her fingers fly to her now-frantic clit.

When she's just about to come, I somehow pry my head up and out of her. She screams in terrible frustration, but she knows what's coming next. And so, still breathing in the savor of her wetness laying atop my upper lip, I slip the first finger of each hand into her unbelievably hot and seeping pussy, thus simultaneously following both her upward thrust and her downward path. I slide in and out with shuddering ease, letting her really feel the penetration as I move against her wet walls, which begin to lengthen and deepen and open wider. Getting it from two angles at the same time drives her harder and hotter still.

As she thrashes, I withdraw one hand and allow the other hand's forefinger to remain in order to meet up inside the palace walls with the rest of her sister digits. I then ease the withdrawn hand's slickly coated finger into her waiting asshole. Her proprietary folds surround me, hold onto me, demand me. I fuck her ass with gentle force, steady and targeted and continual between her yielding tightness. And I haven't neglected the right hand, which keeps fucking her other, slippery hole, just up to the end of the fingers, which I wiggle against her inner wall at the end of each thrust.

She begins to come as I push first with one hand, then the other, alternating strokes so she and I can both really feel the fiery, thin wall between them. Screaming and clenching, she tightens both of her realms against both of my hands.

"Oh yeah, baby. Give it up. Give it to me," I chant over and over again with mantralike intensity, fucking her for all I'm worth.

And wonder of wonders, she does! She flat out gives it up, wailing and rocking with the force of her orgasms, clenching me tighter and tighter as her limbs thrash and then collapse.

She has me right where she wants me. And I couldn't be

happier, with my fingers still inside her, as I bend down to kiss her ass one more time, feeling the radiating heat flush my awestruck face.

"Mmmmphh," she half sighs as I gently withdraw from her still-holding-tight districts. "You know what you do to me is a sin and a crime," she chides in a voice that reverberates low and nastylike, accompanied by that slow and slight smile.

Holding my expatriate fingers against my nose and inhaling deeply, I reply, "Well, it certainly is in most of these contiguous southern states. But not, apparently, in your sovereign territories."

Used to me and my ways, she smiles again, touches my face, and reaches up for a last little kiss. Then, she curls against me, her ass snuggling up to my pulsating pussy. Ah, there she is again, her ass abutting me as it had over an hour ago.

After a moment of luscious silence, I ask, "Isn't this how we got started in the first place?"

"No. Actually honey, I think it was when you said something about giving me jewelry."

At that, we have to laugh.

These southern gals—they sure know how to work it.

sex hall
MR Daniel

The hallway is narrow. I had expected it to be less bare—there are no pictures on the walls, which have all been painted dark reds, slick mahoganies, and purples. I laugh to myself. The colored girls must have had fun checking out swollen pussies when they were painting this. The lights are sunk deep into the ceiling and turned down low so it's lit like a club. A house diva is wailing through the PA system, backed up by an insistent fuck-me-baby, fuck-me-baby tempo. I feel as though I'm in a peep show.

Brown, bronze, and various sun-kissed women move past me, some with their eyes straight forward, nervous, others whose eyes seem to burn a path before them. I can feel their heat as they pass. There is a steady pulsing below my skin as I move forward, the current stopping and starting and me feeling the blood push-flow push-flow through my neck and fingers, my heart growing, forcing blood into my breasts. I pass the first doorway and hesitate. The door is open but I am suddenly afraid to be caught looking.

Someone behind me stops to look over my shoulder, and

her fingers inquire at my leg. I can feel her questions all the way up my thigh into my stomach. I almost jump into the room, and there is laughter behind me. I catch my breath, surprised at my confusion. This morning I was so sure of what I wanted, what I felt, but now...Excitement? Pleasure? Fear?

Didn't I want to be fucked from behind, anonymous?

A voice in my ear is saying, "Look forward, baby, or I'll leave."

And, "I know you're wet."

And, "When I remember how you look I'm going to think about parting your bush, how you *almost* reached behind to guide my hands. But I told you not to move. *Don't move.*"

Hiking up skirt, pulling down panties, the snap of a glove, and a hand between my legs. Fucked in a doorway. Fingers up my cunt, feeling the space in my flesh, pushing deeper and rubbing 'til there's this cross between a sharpness and pleasure, my muscles filled with blood, taut, filling and pressing until I think I'm going to pee on the floor.

My mouth is filled with stars and they're burning their way through my vagina. They hurl through my chest and I can't breathe; sweat collects in the band of my skirt. They light up nerves, sending shocks to my clit and behind my eyelids. I hear myself salivate as she works her hand in further, I pant, my cunt pants for her and the feeling of stars.

I am high, nipples sharp from the sound of her inside me. I am straining against damp fabric, pores fucked alert, open, wanting to feel air on sweat-and-oil-steeped skin, as I brace myself in the doorway.

Bodies passing by us go quiet as another finger goes in my puckering ass, tilted to receive, and lips circle my neck, her tongue leaving a trail that ends with a mouth clamped on the back of my throat, kissing, sucking hard, until a half-moon appears. I wanna come bad, but I could stay here forever.

Can you fuck too much? Can you feel too good? Can you

be so ripe that you keep bursting and swelling, bursting and swelling until a mouth bites you open again? Her teeth burn into my ass, she whips the hand out of my cunt and I feel the air leave my chest, my breasts suddenly get heavy and full. Her hand spanks my ass, my skin wet and hot, and enters me again like horses. I swear I'm gonna drop to my knees as the finger in my ass moves back and forth, teasing the rim of my anus. I feel myself coming, raging against the horses, grasping them expelling-thrusting them out as they lunge, push further inside. She holds onto me. "That hand isn't going anywhere," she says.

I feel come like hushed spurts, warm like blood, flowing out of me. I'm on my knees, my unconscious fingers take her horse hand, arching as I pull her out of me and rub her against my lips and clit. I feel like a dog, mouth open and bent over, writhing against her hand, I'm not thinking anymore, just doing what feels good. She doesn't pull away. I come again, air passes through my throat and I hear a sound like the last breath as you break the surface of water. Doubled over, breathing hard, I pull away from the finger in my ass and push her other hand from between my legs. I lick my juice from her glove, and pull the latex off. My tongue dives for the skin in between her fingers. This is how I will remember her, by her hands. She helps me up from behind, pulling up my panties stretched and tangled in my boots, her fingers spread wide feeling me up as she pulls my skirt down.

She bites my neck and says, "It's too bad you came so soon," and rubs her pelvis against the crack of my behind. I can feel her packing. Well, I'm sorry, too.

"Next time," she says, her hands firm on my hips, teasing, pressing into, circling against me, slowly. "It's underneath my black vinyl shorts, it peeks through a little 'cause they're short-shorts like the ones the reggae dancehall queens wear. Zippers up the sides. I only wear them here."

"How do you know you're the only one?" I ask. She can't see me smile.

"Well, if I'm not, we'll find out soon enough," she laughs, and bites the half-moon she left before. I listen to her walking away.

Boots, I guess, with heavy soles.

Sometimes She Lets Me
Alison L. Smith

Last night her back was sore, spasms from the past, a high school injury, and I said that I'd rub it and then we could just go to sleep, and when I finished she asked me to massage her ass and I said yes but I could not do without kissing it, licking that white moon. I ran my teeth along the arc of it, biting, and her ass started to move under me.

Then she rolled over and I pulled off her shirt and she let me touch them. They are secrets she holds separate from me, their roundness flattened against her chest all day. She does not like them, but I do. And sometimes, when she lets me, I fall between them and I breathe in. The tip of my nose measures their softness and the fine, white hair rises and she gets goose bumps.

I took one of them in my mouth last night and the dark snail of her nipple grew under my tongue. Her pelvis moved beneath me, moved up toward mine when she let me. The moon was gone and the river lights outside her window reflected like stars, as if the sky moved beneath us and she lay on her back for me.

Her hipbones cut the air in thin circles and she tightened under me. She let me unbutton her boxer shorts. She let me take her in my mouth, press my face into her. I cupped her ass in my palms and she got hard for me. She dug her hands into my hair and shivered in the heat-soaked room and I watched her through the keyhole of her thighs.

Sometimes she lets me and when she does she talks to herself. In a low voice, she talks the fear away. Like last night when her ass was cupped in my hands and she was in my mouth and she whispered and her hips circled faster and her voice began to rise.

The dog woke, his pink tongue curling. He yawned. He circled once, twice, spread out beside us again and he watched his master's face change. He watched her call out to the ceiling, watched her back arch, watched her reach over her head, her fisted hands knocking the headboard until her long body tightened and her voice grew hoarse.

Then she begged me. She said *don't stop don't stop don't stop don't stop* and she trembled under me and her hips pitched and I almost lost her and I pressed my hands into her ass to steady her until she came in my mouth.

Afterward, she pulled the covers up around her. She curled into their soft protection and rolled away from me. She hid. The dog burrowed under the comforter, panting into the darkness. After she let me and she fell asleep on her sore back, the sound of her voice stayed in my ears. I watched her as she kicked the covers off in the night's long heat. First her shoulders appeared, then her breasts, then the damp stain on her boxers where I had put my mouth. And I wanted to put my hands on her again, but I didn't. I just watched. The old radiator cracked and pinged in the corner and light from a street lamp bled in through the tall window and she slept and I watched and she let me.

Grand Jeté
Toni Amato

You ask for a kiss and I refuse. You ask for a kiss and I say no for all the right reasons, and come morning I wait for your sleep-soft face and a chance to say yes, oh god yes please. That evening, the thick smell of paint and a worn mattress in your studio and as your hand leads mine toward your breasts, I become harder than ever before. I become a drowning man as your hand urges mine into a salt-slick sea, and I come harder than ever before.

The first time I dress for you, I am a teenage boy on his first date and I want to be a man for you, I want to be a man who can hold your arm there at the elbow and make you feel safe and cherished and adored. You reach out to straighten my tie and although you don't know all of what you are doing, I am undone.

You reach out to straighten my tie, there, in the hallway, and you have no idea what you have done. And neither, despite my butch-dyke cool, do I. The music is playing softly and you think I am leading as you clap out a rhythm I ache to move my hips to as I watch your woman's hands.

"Can I see it?" you ask, and I am twelve, thirteen, maybe, and suddenly embarrassed and unsure like I have not been in decades. Yes, decades, and for all my boyish ways, for all my teenage charm, I feel as though I may be falling in love again for the very first time, I feel like a baby-faced virgin boy, and I want to disappear as you handle what I have never shown outside my pants, what I have worshipped with and delivered with and sang hallelujahs with, but always from my trousers, always strapped and bound and covered by cotton and darkness.

You sit blindfolded and bound in a plush chair, a woman who has seen more of me than I knew I wanted to show. You sit willing and open for me and I begin the dance that I have mastered, and I watch. I watch the flush and the sheen and the motions of desire. I have become accustomed to knowing that I am wanted, but this time, this time I beg with hands and tongue, and everything I am and yes I pray, I pray to you and what I pray is please, please want this. Oh please want me. And you do. And here begins the dance. A dance interrupted by too many miles and too little time.

I tell myself stories, at night. I tell myself stories, now, to help me get to sleep.

It's hotter than hell here. Can't stand my own skin touching itself, can't stand the weight of even a thin sheet. I'm sweating and twisting and searching for a cool spot on the pillow and there isn't any and the truth is I'm getting restless and cranky and it's too hot even to jerk off.

The truth is, I'm desperate to fuck you. No. That's not the truth, either. The truth is, I need your body. Need your shoulders and your thighs and your belly and your back. Truth is it's very difficult for an animal to talk and what I am right now is a lust-maddened beast and I am trying to make this make sense, to make this something more than guttural noises and deep-throated grunts, trying to be a civilized human being despite the unconscious baring of my teeth. And you think it a lopsided grin, this hungry thing you bring out in me.

I have told you. I have tried to tell you that the veins beneath the skin of your breasts, the blue pulsing of your wrists and neck are a torment to me. But what I can find words to say is only a phantom of what lies down hot and heavy in my own veins and all I can do is show you and there is not space, in this configuration of our lives, there is not time for a complete showing and so the caged animal paces and occasionally growls and so here I am, working words and grinding my teeth and maybe I'll catch it this time.

It's not all sweet romance, it's not all soft and you play with fire when you tell me you remember being dragged into that bathroom.

You play with fire that I want you to swallow, entire and whole, so that I can watch the flush of flame creep across your ribs, along your collarbones. So I can see you burn the way my fingers scorch and sear at the touch of you.

It's not all tender words and longing glances, and the place you have never been to before is a place I have prowled for years but never, not once, has there been a creature like you here. You say you want to have jungle sex with me and oh yes, the jungle, and there I wait, slinking yellow-eyed through vines full of exotic birds and I will hear you coming, yes I will hear you coming again and again.

Nocturnal beast. I am losing sleep over this. Losing sleep and losing rest because when my eyes shut the dreams come and it is difficult to translate dreams into waking words but I will try because you have asked and sometimes, indeed, the hunter gets captured by the prey.

"You have no idea what you do to me," I say, later and from a distance. Wide-eyed wonder across the telephone lines. "What? Tell me what. Go on, give me words."

I am a poor poet deprived of words, a tongue-tied Romeo—I am a woman struck speechless by desire and all the words I know to describe this loosening of muscle, this rhythmic tremolo—all these words are not enough. And these words are all I have.

"Tell me."

All my years of pursuing the one who could take my defiant self and create a safe place for the bended knee I am desperate to offer—all those years of dark and mysterious places, actors so sure of their lines, carefully orchestrated scripts and now, here, this. Your voice. All right. I'll try to tell you.

What would I use to say the unspeakable, to tell you the things that lay heavy on my tongue? The things that I wish had not ever been said before and I want to make a new language, then. A language all ours, a set of sighs and murmurs and exultant shouts. Soft groans of deep surprise and loud, loud earsplitting shrieks of hearts torn wide open. I want a series of clicks and tooth chatters and gusts of breath that will tell you the particulars that are so particular. The peculiar and the personal and I do indeed believe that this can only be said by speaking in tongues. Strange language and insane gesticulation.

In my dreams we have days and nights. Yes, long nights, hot like these I suffer through. In my dreams there are as many hours to the darkness as passion can create, and there is enough of it, of passion and all its attendant desire and hunger and need, enough to make for an eternity.

You lie on a bed of fur, soft and caressing, dark beneath you. You lie on the skin of an animal and this reminds me of what I become for you. More than that—helps me remember what you need from me. Soft despite the hard wanting, the way my muscles tense and flex with needing you. You lie on a bed of fur and look at me, and there are myriad women gazing through eyes I watch go large and dark with the same

45

fierce need that moves me. You are a playful, impetuous child, a young woman discovering what your body can do for you, a temptress who knows quite well what she does to me. That one, the one who taunts and provokes and most certainly dares me. And I am desperate to please them all.

I can smell you from across the room. It's the scent of metal and blood and deep, secret places. Salt of the ocean and tang of pine needles on an ancient forest floor. My teeth ache with it, my mouth waters, and something old behind my eyes drops down. I can smell you and the memory of everything pleasurable lies just beneath that scent. I close my eyes and pull molecules of you deeply into me, the way I long to be pulled into you. Let the capillaries in my chest pass this on to every blood cell and so to the very fibers of my body. This is the first sweet step toward losing track of the boundary between us, toward forgetting where I let off and you begin.

Flooded, saturated, I open my eyes. The arch of your foot. The long curve of calf. The most succulent of all tender places resting beneath a gathering of your own fur. I need to see your belly rise and arch, need to feel your muscles tense and release. Already I can see your pulse lifting the intricacies of your veins closer to that skin, that smooth and supple skin I burn with the heat of, even here across the room.

I need this more than you can possibly imagine. Like a starved thing, too long alone and unfed, and no matter how much you give me, I know this hunger will not be abated.

I need this and I pray for self-control, for the presence of mind to treat you like a precious thing even as I lose my mind in animal ecstasy. Pray for strength and pray in thanksgiving and the words of the prayer fade away into gibberish when I reach you, when I reach down to you, kneel down before you and begin a long night of supplication and speaking in tongues.

Where to begin? A kiss, just one kiss and the fullness of

your lips, the taste of your breath are enough to make me shudder. I want to kiss you until your lips bleed, until you come up gasping for air—and even this only once I've had enough. There is danger in this wanting. The continually present danger of the bottomless hungers I suffer in your absence. The hungers that are only sharpened by your physical presence.

A kiss, then. Or more like a thousand kisses in one extreme lingering. I want to feel you move for me. Feel the tip of your tongue and the smooth coolness of your teeth. I want to eat your mouth as though it were a fine, sweet fruit. Crush it and let the juices run down my chin. So easy to slip from mouth to cheek and follow that first downy caress to your ear. To that place which brings from you the shy turning of your head, the quick intake of breath.

And once my lips have made that journey, once I have mouthed a trail of desire across the delicate bones and bitten more gently than is imaginable, then I exhale. Allow the deepest of sighs to escape my lips and enter the echo chamber of your ear. Imagine the hot, wet wind before a storm, imagine the force of murmured words—"Jesus god I want you"—able to course the distance to a place I long to be but will not go for a long, long while.

Instead, I caress the delicate contours with my tongue, the ridges and folds and the astounding contradiction of soft skin over cartilage. Between my teeth a fragile thing. Instead I burrow into a small indentation, an almost secret tender place, and drink deeply.

There is a shift, then. The last vestiges of control shatter, and my hands are creatures unto themselves. My hands that knew their way across your body from the very beginning. I want to cup the weight of your head in my palm, push my fingers through the fineness of your hair. Want to place the full grip of my desire on either of your strong and freckled shoulders, pushing into you all my want and need. Here I can feel the first soft surrendering, the first relaxation of your muscles. The giving in and letting go. If I close my eyes, I see you naked in the cool reflection of water, see the way you could float on the surface, with your body this loose, and I will myself to be the ocean, to be the steady beat of waves on a roundly pebbled shore.

Trace your collarbones with trembling fingers, run my palms over the plane of your chest, the mound of your belly, the long smooth glide of your sides and across the curve of your breasts. Undone, I am undone and there is no restraint, now. I am beyond lingering, beyond savoring, and the time has come for abandon, for high winds and torrential downpour.

Monica and Me
Rachel Kramer Bussel

I think I've found a way to convince the ever-luscious Monica
Lewinsky to come back to my hotel room with me—at least,
I'm counting on it.

I've been fascinated with her ever since the news of her
affair with Clinton first broke. I mean, he's the president—it's
not just the everyday person who can get access to being in
the same building as him, let alone down-and-dirty under his
desk.

In all the hubbub over the legal maneuverings and the
moral outcry, it seemed like everyone had forgotten that
Monica is indeed, despite it all, just a young woman, and one
who obviously has a very sensual side. But that's obvious, not
only from her actions with Clinton and whoever else, but by
looking at her and hearing her talk. Her lust extends to life—
she's lively and excited, girlish and sweet.

I'd followed all the drama and the minor tabloid stories,
collecting Monica facts in my head, trying to piece them all
together to create a whole person. But I needed more—I
needed to see for myself what she and I had in common,

whether the sparks I envisioned in my head would truly explode when we met.

I booked a room at the Paradise Hotel as soon as I knew that she would be coming to town for a book-signing. The only really fancy hotel in town, this will provide me with extra chances to casually "bump" into her. Of course this will require lots of preparation and a bit of luck, because I'm sure, with her looks and fame, she has people trying to get close to her every day.

The day of the book-signing, I go to the store as soon as it opens and browse for a little while, thinking I would look too much like a stalker if I were the first person seated in the audience, but also wanting to get a seat up front. I've primped myself into a sexy but not overpowering outfit: a low-cut blouse with a tight silver jacket over it, short black skirt, and sexy black stockings with glittery silver lines sparkling here and there. I also added some shiny silver eye shadow and applied enough black eyeliner and mascara so it actually looks like I have eyelashes.

Completing the outfit is my recent indulgence purchase: open-toed maroon high heels with a patterned design. I don't want to scare her away, but I need her to notice me.

She reads briefly from her autobiography, tearing up once or twice, but more often looking coyly at her audience, knowing that most of them are here because she has captivated their libidos even more than their need to gossip. She licks her carefully painted lips, every action carefully constructed to make us pay nonstop attention to her body. She's flirting en masse, and I'm ready to seduce her right then, but I bide my time.

As she finishes and people line up for autographs, I graciously allow the other attendees to go ahead of me. After all, I'm not *really* here to get my book signed. She looks up and I pierce her with my gaze, brown eyes on brown, not letting her look away until she must turn to the man in front of me.

"Miss Lewinsky, I have great faith in you and am behind you all the way," he says as she smiles and asks his name.

I bet he'd like to be right behind her, but that will be my position later tonight. He steps away and she gazes up at me, looking around for my book.

"Hi. I left my book back at the hotel, but it's very important that I get it autographed."

She looks at me, not saying anything, but a slight smile hovers around her lips. "So, are you going to go back and get it?" she asks with a bit of a smirk.

I stare right back at her, letting her know that I'm open to whatever lascivious scenario she's concocting. "Well, I can't go get it right now, I have a few appointments, but, well—I just *need* to get it signed," I end up whining, desperation making my voice climb. All my acting lessons have been distilled into this moment.

She tells me that she'll be signing for a little while longer, and that if I come back in half an hour maybe she can arrange to meet me later. I have no choice but to trust her. I wink at her and head out the door.

I breathe a large sigh of relief at having actually made contact, and stroll around the block, frantically trying to come up with a plan B to get her up to my room. I walk a few blocks and then head back, realizing that my half hour is almost up.

Despite twinges of uncertainty, I have a feeling she'll still be there and will talk to me.

I see how starved she is not just for good sex but for some real attention to Monica the person, not just Monica the intern. Yes, like everyone else I follow the stories on her in the tabloids, but I'm more than just a groupie. I sense in Monica a kinship, a kind of sisterhood, if you will, that will make our union tonight special beyond either of our dreams.

I reenter the store and see her in the back, talking to the manager. As I walk toward her she turns around and smiles, beckoning me to where she's standing.

I wait a few steps away, not wanting to intrude on her conversation.

She finishes talking and takes my hand in hers and leads me into a back room. We sit down at a little table where she's stored her bag.

"So, what hotel are you staying at?" she asks me.

I stare at her, so caught up in being close to her that I can barely answer.

"Well?" she teasingly persists.

"The Paradise."

"Oh great—that's my hotel too."

I'm still gazing back at her, starstruck, awestruck, and lust-struck all at once.

"Come on, let's go," she says rather matter-of-factly, standing and grabbing my hand.

"What do you mean? You're just going to go off with some stranger? I could be anyone!" I halfheartedly protest.

"Well, then tell me your name."

"Rachel," I say.

"So now I know you—let's go!" she repeats, this time more forcefully.

We walk out of the store and toward the hotel.

"Don't you have, like, people who are traveling with you? A chaperone?" I ask.

"Usually, but this time I wanted to be on my own. I've gotten used to the crowds and I can pretty much handle it. I don't usually attract people like you, who are sweet and normal."

"Thanks," I reply.

We walk the rest of the way in a comfortable silence, each of us surreptitiously trying to sneak looks at the other.

When we get to the hotel we both pause, staring at the ground and then at each other, not sure how to approach the topic of where to go. Finally, after an absolutely interminable silence, I say, "Do you want to come to my room for a bit?"

"Yeah, I do," she says softly, suddenly growing shy.

Alone in the elevator, I take her hand, holding its soft flesh in my own rough one. I squeeze her hand and she squeezes back.

I open the door to my room and we're greeted by the many offerings I've brought here to tempt her. I've arranged for the room service carefully, noting her likes and dislikes: champagne, strawberries, and chocolate have been delivered on elegant silver trays that show she's worth it. I don't want this to be like the Clinton affair for her. Despite her protestations that she had the first orgasm of that relationship, I'd venture to guess that her pleasure wasn't at the forefront of Clinton's mind.

I, on the other hand, have her delight as the goal of my evening. I know that Monica is really a bad girl lurking in the fancy outfits of her richer, more genteel peers. I want to unleash that bad girl, let her show her true colors.

She looks a bit stunned, but then takes it in stride. I don't know if this exactly meets her expectations, but I do know that she wanted to come back here with me.

"This is a nice place, isn't it?" she comments, sitting down on the bed.

I give her a glass of champagne. She takes it and giggles as she slips out of her heels. I'm trying to figure out how I should play this: slow and languid or rough and dirty.

Maybe a little bit of both would work.

We talk about her day and the book-signing, and she tells me how tough it's been for her. "People always want, want, want from me—they want my time, my name, my money.

They act like I'm some superhuman force rather than just a normal girl."

She looks as if she could cry, and while I do want to get to know her better, I don't want her to dissolve into misery. I motion for her to scoot closer to me and I start massaging her shoulders and back. She sighs and relaxes her muscles, letting me squeeze and shape them, vigorously tending to all the places that feel too burdened, too knotty. I reach under her shirt and work my hands into her skin, manually telling her that I want to please her, to do for her.

As I knead harder and harder, digging my knuckles into her shoulders, pushing my thumbs into her back, she releases an "mmmm" and starts to lean into me.

"More," she says, and I squeeze as hard as I can.

Now I'm giving her skin little pinches, knowing their sting will stay with her for a few seconds. I can tell she's getting excited by the way she's squirming around, like she wants to take her clothes off but doesn't quite know how to go about it. I move over and she lies down across the bed. I run my fingers across her lips and she kisses them.

"You are so gorgeous, do you know that?" I ask her.

She responds by taking my index finger and biting it gently.

"I guess you do," I say as I start to take off her top. As I lift her shirt, I see a gleaming lacy-black bra underneath. Her full breasts are cozily couched there.

"Touch me," she says, opening her eyes and staring back at me as she had at the bookstore.

Her eyes bore into me, giving me a taste of her soul, her passion, the things that she now has to hide behind a steely gaze to protect her media reputation. For whatever wondrous reason, she is letting herself go with me.

Instead of complying with her request, I tell her to get comfortable in the nice, soft queen-size bed, and that I'll be right back. I sneak off to the bathroom, where I've hidden my stash of sex toys. I'll bring only one of them back to her; my purpose in leaving is mostly so that she'll get nervous and question my next move.

I want her on edge, unsure, my actions unreadable.

I walk back in and dim the lights. She is sitting up in bed, eyes closed, sipping her champagne, a dreamy smile on her face. I wonder what she's thinking about.

I walk over and kneel on the floor in front of her. She turns her brooding gaze toward me, her mouth hovering over the champagne glass without drinking. She dips her tongue into the champagne, then leans down and slowly slips her tongue into my mouth. She teases me, lingering around my lips and then slipping away.

"I know how much you want me," she says wickedly.

Of course she knows; I'm kneeling in front of her, practically panting with lust.

"You can have me...I just want to have a little fun first," she says.

I give her a quizzical look.

She spreads her legs and brings them around me, pulling me closer to the bed. Then she leans down again, places her glass on the floor, and kisses me. When I say kissing, I mean really, deeply *kissing* me, as if kissing alone were the entirety of sex. She puts her hands on the back of my head and positions me to her liking, then somehow slides her mouth to mine and does the most amazing things with her luscious soft lips.

She feels like a pillow, like silk, like pure sweetness.

She tastes gorgeous, and her aggressive side is a complete turn-on.

She swirls her tongue around mine, gently licking and stroking, turning her head this way and that.

We kiss like that, frantic and needy, consumed by our mouths, for a long time—twenty minutes or so—before we both stop to catch our breath. She sits up with her eyes closed, still in that blissful desire-soaked world. I choose that moment to take advantage of her position, tying a silky black blindfold around her head. I see the look on her face as she realizes what I've done: startled, surprised, a tiny bit scared, but even more excited. She knows that finally someone is unlocking her deepest fantasies, and that she doesn't have to pretend anything with me.

"How does that feel?" I whisper in her ear.

As she starts to answer me, I slip two fingers into her mouth and she sucks on them. "Shh...you don't have to answer that; I just wanted you to think about how the blindfold feels covering your eyes. You're going to have a really delicious time tonight if you do what I tell you to, OK?"

She nods her head and makes a small whimpering noise.

I decide to tease her a little by making her guess what I'm doing. In preparation for tonight, I've bought some of her infamous *Barbara Walters* lipstick, "Glaze" by Club Monaco—I got one as a gift for her and one as a gift for me. I open mine and start decorating her lovely body, swirling the plum-colored makeup onto her nipples.

"What are you doing?" she asks, not really expecting an answer. Her nipples harden.

"You're my canvas and I'm painting you, all of this gorgeous pale skin of yours, and your pretty nipples," I tell her. I make them nice and dark, juicy-looking, then snap a Polaroid to show her later. Then I lean down and rub my lips against her nipples, giving new meaning to the words *lipstick lesbian*. I squeeze her round, bulging nipples between my fingers, pulling them tightly until I hear her gasp.

"Do you want me to stop?" I say in my most teasing voice.

She shakes her head no.

"What was that? You have to speak if you want me to hear you."

"No, please, don't stop," she begs me.

I keep pulling, drawing her nipples toward me, squeezing them just about as hard as I can for a second or two. By now she's frantic; her nipples have become gateways to her cunt. She reaches up to touch them and I observe her technique. She rubs the edges of her short nails against them, scraping and pushing, giving a little jolt each time her hard nail rubs against the even harder surface of her nipple.

With the lipstick I draw a line down her cleavage, down over her stomach and toward her pussy. I replace the cap and then rub the slim tube up against her panty hose. I lay it flat against her and rub it back and forth over her clit, getting her even more worked up. I keep pushing the lipstick against her, wanting to touch her for real. She pushes back in rhythm, already aroused despite still being dressed. When she seems on the brink of coming, I stop.

I walk over to the counter where the champagne is chilling, picking up the bottle in one hand and palming a few ice cubes in the other. "Open your mouth, sweetheart," I tell her, then slip a cube into that sexy pink hole.

By now her lipstick has almost all worn off, but I can still detect its traces on her soft lips, which are getting flushed and big in her excitement. "Now spread your legs for me, Monica," I instruct her, liking the way she instantly obeys me.

I lift up her dress and press my fingers against the fabric that encloses her pussy—it's wet and thick. I push the fabric against her, making her feel her own dampness, making her even wetter. She wants to talk but has to finish with her ice cube first. She sucks it greedily, eager to tell me all the naughty things she wants me to do to her.

I don't let her, though, since I already have enough naughty ideas in my head to last all night. I give her another cube to suck and tell her she's being a very good girl and will be rewarded for her patience. With that I climb over her and push my knee hard up against her cunt. She pushes back with all her strength, needing as much contact as I can give her—and then some.

I take her wrists and hold them above her head, leveraging myself against her body, rocking softly against her stocking-covered pussy, on the edge myself. If I don't pause for a moment to regroup, my carefully formed plans will go out the window.

I take off the blindfold and she looks at me quizzically. I tell her we're going to play show-and-tell. She knows what I want to see first. Now it's my turn to sit up against the nice fluffy pillows and relax.

I tell her to bring me a glass of champagne and then to stand by the bed. "Lean over," I say gruffly, wanting to make sure she knows that there are no other options. "Lift up your skirt for me, honey," I tell her, wanting my own glimpse of the Monica-thong. But Miss Lewinsky has her own plans—she pulls her dress up and slowly starts to peel down her stockings to show me that she is, alas, not wearing a thong.

And she's not wearing any other undies either!

No, the only thing I'm seeing now is her round white ass, looking so fucking gorgeous that it's all I can do not to grab for it right away. I let her finish her little show for me.

She pulls the black stockings all the way down to her ankles and leans over farther so that I can also see a little bit of her bright pink cunt poking out underneath. By now I've forgotten all about my champagne and I'm staring breathlessly at Monica's ass, wondering what she'll do next.

Now she moves around and spreads her legs even farther apart. I can see the way her ankles are stretching the elastic of her stockings, the contrast between their darkness and her pale skin. I can't contain myself any longer and I reach up and bring her ass closer to me. Her skin is cold and beautiful, tender, soft.

I kiss her ass softly at first, then take a little bite and hear her intake of breath. I bite harder, knowing that she's eager for me to get to the heart of who she is. Knowing that I'm so near to her warm pussy is driving me crazy. I lean back and push her forward a little, then give her a nice slap on the ass.

I can see my bite marks and the red stain left by my hand. I tell her how sexy her ass looks. She doesn't say anything, but turns her head to look at me with deep longing in her eyes. I lift her up and pull her on top of me.

"Hmmm, you're so beautiful. I love how full and soft your body is. I've dreamed of being with you and here you are. What do you want me to do, Monica?"

She closes her eyes and turns over onto her back. "I want you to fuck me," she says, surprising me with her language. Even though it's been obvious all night that that's what she wants, I'm still a bit taken aback.

"With what?" I ask her.

She takes my hand, licks the palm, and says, "With this."

I put two fingers in her mouth before moving down to her pussy, covered with its dark, curly pubic hair. "I'm gonna give you what you want now," I say as I slide my fingers into her warm, soft cunt.

She moans as I enter her and she pushes herself up off the bed. "How many fingers are you using?" she asks me, so caught up in her heat and my hand that she's almost talking to herself.

"What do you think?" I counter.

"I don't know," she pants, barely able to speak.

"Two," I whisper into her ear, and I like how she squeezes me even more tightly as I say the word. I push and push, wanting to go as deep as I can, wanting to fill all of her. I press my stomach and hips into her, pushing her against the bed, and put two fingers of my other hand into her mouth.

I want to feel all of her reactions to my touch. I slide

another finger inside her and she moans. "Three," I say directly into her ear. She is pushing against me, wanting to turn over so she can look at me. She's so beautiful, so big and lustful and open and soft, I can't resist her request. I let her turn over and I gaze into her eyes, letting her know that I'm enjoying myself as much as she is.

I push harder, faster, deeper than I think is possible, and she is ready for me. Now I have four fingers inside her.

Her breathing quickens, her eyes close, and she is pulling at her skin, her hair, the sheets, the bed, anything to hold on, to try to prolong the ecstatic agony of her orgasm, but she can't resist. The shudders start inside her and her thighs shake and her pussy gets even tighter around my fingers.

I coax her on, whisper to her, brush a finger over her G-spot, make it last as long as I can. After about twenty minutes, she's done, and she looks at me with such sexy tiredness, relief, and delight that I want to stay with her forever. I hug her and lie down next to her on the bed, taking in her warmth and her scent.

We lie there for a while, holding each other, drifting in and out of luscious sleep. I get some of my energy back and decide it's time to test her infamous skills. Telling her to touch herself and wait for me, I get up and go into the bathroom and come back festooned with a nice sturdy harness and a rather large cock. I've never really been much for strap-ons, from either side, but this seems like a moment to just go with the impulse.

As I walk toward her, her eyes seem to bulge—I'm not sure if it's anticipation, trepidation, or a little of both. I smile reassuringly at her, letting her know that I really mean all this in fun, even if it won't seem that way in a few minutes. I pull her head toward mine and kiss her roughly, then push her down toward my bulging red cock and tell her to swallow it.

"Yeah, baby, I know you're good at it, I know you'll give

me what I want," I tell her as I see her lips part and start to take in the tip of my silicone extension. I start to understand why so many dykes are into strap-ons. The sheer power of standing against the bed while she kneels in front of me, doing my bidding, letting my cock go deeper and deeper down her throat until it starts to cause her discomfort, makes me feel special—high almost.

Her lips suck and then push down against my dick, practically causing my clit to spark. When it seems just unbearable, I pull her off me, get rid of the strap-on, and push her back into place, needing her tongue on my clit that very instant. She seems startled at first, unsure, but I think she picks up on the fact that she doesn't have to be all that proficient to satisfy me once I'm so worked up. Her tongue takes to my cunt in a pleasantly unexpected way, lapping and licking and discovering all its contours and crevices.

After the pressure from the cock her soft tongue is such a delightful contrast that my come is soon dripping down my legs. She licks some of my juices off me and kisses me, then curls up against the pillows and falls asleep.

I know that I could treat her better than the Bill Clintons and Andy Bleilers of the world. They were married men full of their own concerns, out to use and discard her without taking a moment to notice who she was beyond what she could do for them. I want to give her back a sense of joy in her sexuality—the joy that exudes from her every pore when she's with me. I knew when I first heard her story that not only does she have a lot to give as a lover but she can take pleasure as well.

I envision the two of us living together and gallivanting all over the world, taunting everyone with our sensuous escapades, shoving the media's hypocrisy back in its face. I picture her happy, glowing, free to pursue her own interests and desires. And most of all, I picture her next to me, just like she is now. She sleeps through the night, occasionally reaching for me, once even waking up and touching me, knowing right where to put her fingers to make me instantly wet. I grind against her and come on her fingers, unsure if she is asleep or awake.

In the morning she wakes up and grins at me slyly. I've seen a side of her that few people have. She gets up and puts her clothes back on, telling me she has to go to some meetings and that we should stay in touch. I give her my card, walk her to the door, and kiss her lingeringly, almost pinning her to the wall. Then I realize I have to let her leave.

If she wants to call me, she will.

I haven't heard from Monica since then, but I think about her often. When I see that she's going to be on TV, some big interview, I smile to myself, because I know more of her secrets than will ever be told to some reporter. I wonder whether she thinks of me, if she'll give me some secret signal during the broadcast, if when they ask about her sexual appetites she'll remember our wild night together. I hope so, because I certainly do.

If you're reading this, Monica, I have more tricks up my sleeve.

Lots of them.

Blood and Silver
Patrick Califia

Once upon a time (and still), there was a young woman who was very tired of being treated like a little girl. Her name was Sylvia Rufina. Like most female persons in her predicament, the only available avenue of rebellion was for her to pretend to obey the commandments of others while protecting a secret world within which she was both empress and impresario. Having frequently been told, "Go out and play," more and more, that was what she did. Her family lived in a small farmhouse that felt smaller still because of the vast wilderness that surrounded it. She was at home in this untamed and complex landscape, if only because there was nothing false or sentimental about it.

One of the games she played was "holding still." This was a game learned under confusing and painful circumstances at home. But hidden within a stand of birches or scrub oak, she was not molested. Instead, if she learned to let her thoughts turn green and her breath slow to the pace of sap, she became privy to an endless variety of fascinating events: how beavers felled trees, how mice raised their children, the way a fox twitched its nose when it spotted a vole.

One day, when she was studying the spots on a fawn that dozed in a copse just a few dozen yards from where she held her breath, the wolf appeared. He (for there was no mistaking the meaning of his big face, thick shoulders, and long legs, even if she had not espied his genitals) was an amazing silver color, with dark black at the root of his stippled fur. His teeth were as white as the moon, and his eyes were an intelligent and fearless brown. They studied each other for long minutes, wolf and woman, until he lost interest in her silence and relaxed limbs, and went away.

The next time he came, he walked right up to her and put his nose up, making it clear that he expected a greeting of some sort. So she carefully, slowly, bonelessly lowered her body and allowed him to examine her face and breasts. His breath was very hot, perhaps because it was autumn and the day was chilly. His fur smelled of earth and the snow that was to come, and the air he expelled was slightly rank, an aroma she finally identified as blood.

Satisfied with her obeisance, he went away again, tail wagging a little, as if he were pleased with himself. This was the only undignified thing she had seen him do, but it did not make her think less of him. She appreciated the fact that the wolf did not caper, bow down, yelp, or slaver on her, in the slavish and inconsiderate way of dogs. The wolf was no whore for man's approval. He fed himself.

She did not see the wolf again for nearly a week. But when he returned, he brought the others: two males and three females, one of them his mate. This female was nearly as large as her spouse and as dark as he was metallic, the eclipse to his moon. Some instinct told Sylvia Rufina that she must greet them on all fours and then roll over upon her back. This seemed to excite everyone to no end. She was nosed a good deal, fairly hard, licked three or four times, and nipped once. The surprisingly painful little bite came from the leader of the pack, who was letting her know it was time to get up and come away with them. It was later in the day than she usually stayed out-of-doors, and as she fled, lights came on in the little house, dimming the prettier lights that bloomed in the deep black sky.

Racing with the wolves was like a dream, or perhaps it was normal life that was a dream, for the long run with the wolf pack was a flight through vivid sensations that made everything that had happened to her indoors seem drained of color and meaning. She never questioned her ability to keep up with them any more than she questioned the new shape she seemed to wear. Her legs were tireless; running was a joy. Even hunger was a song in her belly. And when the group cut off and cornered a deer, she knew her place in the attack as if she had read and memorized a part in a play.

After they ate, most of them slept, yawning from the effort it took to digest that much raw, red meat. Unaccustomed to so much exercise and the rich diet, she slept also.

And woke up miles from home, alone, in harsh daylight. Every muscle in her body hurt, and her clothing was ripped, her hair full of twigs, leaves, and burrs. Her shoes were gone and her stockings a ruin. Somehow she made her way home, hobbling painfully, trying to think of a story that would excuse her absence without triggering a proscription against hikes in the mountains.

There was no need for an alibi. Her family had already decided what must have happened to her. She had followed a butterfly or a blue jay or a white hart and gotten lost in the woods. When she crossed the threshold and heard inklings of this story, she saw that each of her family members had picked a role, just as the wolves had memorized their dance of death with one another. And she gave herself up, too exhausted to fight back, letting them exclaim over and handle and hurt her with their stupidity and melodrama. Though a part of her sputtered indignantly, silently: Lost! In the woods! Where I've roamed for three-and-twenty years? I'm more likely to get lost on my way to the privy!

Unfortunately, when she had gone missing they had called upon the Hunter and asked him to search for her. He was someone she avoided. His barn was covered with the nailed-up, tanning hides of animals, and thatched with the antlers of deer he had slain. Sylvia Rufina thought it grotesque. Her father had taught her to recognize certain signals of an unhealthy interest. After having finally grown old enough to no longer be doted upon by her incestuous sire, she could not tolerate a stranger whose appetites felt revoltingly familiar. When the Hunter lit his pipe, waved his hand, and put a stop to the whining voices so glad of their opportunity to rein her in, she gaped at him, hoping against her own judgment that he would have something sensible to say.

He had brought something that would solve the problem. No need to restrict the young woman's love of nature, her little hobbies. No doubt it gave her much pleasure to add new leaves and ferns to her collection. (In fact, she did not have such a collection, but she was aware that many proper young ladies did, and so she bit her tongue, thinking it would make a good excuse for future rambling.) The Hunter shook out a red garment and handed it to her.

It was a scarlet sueded-leather cloak with a hood, heavy enough to keep her warm well into winter. The lining was a slippery fabric that made her slightly sick to touch it. He had kept hold of the garment as he handed it to her, so their hands touched when she took it from him, and her eyes involuntarily met his. The predatory desire she saw there made her bow her head as if in modesty, but in fact to hide her rage. Even during a killing strike, the wolves knew nothing as shameful and destructive as the Hunter's desire. She knew, then, that he had bought this red-hooded cloak for her some time ago and often sat studying it, dreaming of how she would look laid down upon it. If she wore it in the forest, she would be visible for miles. It would be easy for a hunter, this Hunter, to target and track her then.

She was poked and prodded and prompted to say thank you, but would not. Instead she feigned sleep, or a faint. And so she was borne up to bed, feeling the Hunter's hard-done-by scowl following her supine body up the stairs like an oft-refused man on his wedding night.

It was weeks before she was deemed well enough to let out of the house. The red cloak hung in her closet in the meantime, its shout of color reducing all her other clothes to drab rags. It would snow soon, and she did not think she would survive being stranded behind the pack, in human form, to find her way home in a winter storm. But she must encounter them again, if only to prove to herself that the entire adventure had not been a fevered dream.

Her chance finally came. A neighbor whom nobody liked much, a widowed old woman with much knowledge about the right way to do everything, was in bed with a broken leg. This was Granny Gosling. As a little girl, Sylvia Rufina had gone to Granny Gosling with her secret troubles, mistaking gray hair and myopia for signs of kindness and wisdom. Her hope to be rescued or at least comforted was scalded out of existence when the old woman called her many of the same names she had heard in a deeper voice, with a mustache and tongue scouring her ear and her long flannel nightgown bunched up painfully in her armpits. The child's hot sense of betrayal was quickly replaced with stoicism. We can bear the things that cannot be altered, and now she knew better than to struggle against the inevitable.

Other neighbors, a prosperous married couple with a bumper crop of daughters overripe for the harvest of marriage, were hosting a dance with an orchestra. People were to come early to an afternoon supper, dance in the evening, and spend the night. Mother and father had their own marketing of nubile damsels to attend to, but their house stood closer to Granny Gosling's than anyone else's. They were expected to go and lend a hand. What a relief it was to everyone when Sylvia Rufina said quietly at breakfast that she thought it might do her soul a great deal of good to visit the sick and unfortunate that day. She was young. There would be other cotillions.

As the other women in the household bustled around, curling their hair and pressing the ruffles on their dresses, she made up a basket of victuals. She picked things she herself was especially fond of because she knew anything she brought would be found unpalatable by the injured granny. She helped everyone into their frocks, found missing evening bags and hair ribbons, sewed a buckle on a patent-leather shoe, and kissed her mother and her sisters as they went off, consciences relieved, to the dance. Her father, realizing no embrace would be offered, avoided the opportunity to receive one. As soon as their carriage disappeared around a bend in the road, she set off in the red cloak and kept the hateful thing on until she had gone over a rise and down the other side and was out of her family's sight.

Then she took off the cloak, bundled it up as small as she could, and put it inside a hollow tree, heartily hoping that birds and squirrels would find it, rip it to shreds, and use it to make their winter nests. At the foot of this tree she sat, snug in the nut-brown cloak she had worn underneath the Hunter's gift, and ate every single thing she had packed into the basket. By the time she finished her feast, it was nearly dark. Cheerful beyond measure to be free at last from human society, she went rambling in quest of her soul mates, the four-footed brothers and sisters of the wind.

Faster and faster she went as her need for them became more desperate, and the world streamed by in a blur of gaudy fall colors. The cold air cut her lungs like a knife, and she found herself pressing the little scar the wolf had left on her collarbone, using that pang to keep herself moving forward. The sun plunged below the hills, and she ran on four legs now, chasing hints among the delicious odors that flooded her nose and mouth. At last she found a place where they had been, a trail that led to their present whereabouts, and the reunion was a glad occasion. There was a happy but orderly circle of obeisances and blessings—smelling, licking, and tail wagging—and favorite sticks and bones were tossed into the air and tugged back and forth.

Then they hunted, and all was right with the world. She was happy to be the least among them, the anchor of their hierarchy. Despite her status as a novice, she knew a thing or two that could be of value to the pack. The crotchety neighbor would never be in pain again nor have occasion to complain about the disrespect of young folk or the indecency of current ladies' fashions.

But this time, forewarned that dawn would put an end to her four-footed guise, the young woman took precautions. While everyone else turned in the direction of the den, where they could doze, meat-drunk, she bid them farewell with heartbroken nudges of her nose, and retraced her footsteps back to the hollow tree. There, she slept a little, until dawn forced her to put on the hateful red cloak again and return home. She was lucky this time and arrived well before her hungover, overfed, and overheated relations.

She thought that perhaps, with what she now knew, she could endure the rest of her life. She would have two lives, one within this cottage and the other in the rest of the world. Knowing herself to be dangerous, she could perhaps tolerate infantilization. And so she made herself agreeable to her mother and her sisters, helped them divest themselves of their ballroom finery, and put out a cold lunch for them. She herself was not hungry. The smell of cooked meat made her nauseous.

She had not planned to go out again that night. She knew that if her excursions became too frequent, she would risk being discovered missing from her bed. But when the moon came up, it was as if a fever possessed her. She could not stay indoors. She pined for the soothing sensation of earth beneath clawed toes, the gallop after game, the sweet reassuring smell of her pack mates as they acknowledged her place among them. And so she slipped out, knowing it was unwise. The only concession she made to human notions of decorum was to take the hated red cloak with her.

And that was how he found her, in the full moon, catching her just before she took off the red leather garment. "Quite the little woodsman, aren't you?" he drawled, toying with his knife.

Sylvia Rufina would not answer him.

"Cat got your tongue? Or is it perhaps a wolf that has it, I wonder? Damn your cold looks. I have something that will melt your ice, you arrogant and unnatural bitch." He took her by the wrist and forced her, struggling, to go with him along the path that led to his house. She could have slipped his grasp if she had taken her wolf form, but something told her she must keep her human wits to deal with what he had to show her.

There was something new nailed up to his barn, a huge pelt that shone in the full moonlight like a well-polished curse. It was the skin of her master, the lord of her nighttime world, the blessed creature whose nip had transformed her into something that could not be contained by human expectations. The Hunter was sneering and gloating, telling her about the murder, how easy she had made it for him to find their den, and he was promising to return and take another wolf's life for every night that she withheld her favors.

His lewd fantasies about her wolfish activities showed, she thought, considerable ignorance of both wolves and women.

The wolves were lusty only once a year. The king and queen of the pack would mate; no others. The big silver male had loved her, but there was nothing sexual in his passion. He had been drawn by her misery and decided out of his animal generosity to set her wild heart free. And her desire had been for the wilderness, for running as hard and fast and long as she could, for thirst slaked in a cold mountain stream, and hunger appeased nose-down in the hot red mess of another, weaker creature's belly. She craved autonomy, not the sweaty invasion of her offended and violated womanhood. But the Hunter slurred on with his coarse fancies of bestial orgies, concluding, "After all this time I pined for you, and thought you were above me. Too refined and delicate and sensitive to notice my mean self. Now I find you're just another bitch in heat. How dare you refuse me?"

"Refuse you?" she cried, finding her voice at last. "Why, all you had to do was ask me. It never occurred to me that such a clever and handsome man would take an interest in someone as inexperienced and plain as me. I am only a simple girl, a farmer's daughter, but you are a man of the world." Where this nonsense came from, she did not know, but he lifted his hands from his belt to wrap his arms around her, and that was when she yanked his knife from his belt and buried it to the hilt in the middle of his back.

He died astonished, dribbling blood. She thought it was a small enough penance for the many lives he had taken in his manly pride and hatred of the feral. She took back the knife, planning to keep it, and let him fall.

By his heels, she dragged him back into his own house. Then she took the hide of her beloved down from the barn wall, shivering as she did so. It fell into her arms like a lover and she wept to catch traces of his scent, which lingered still upon his lifeless fur like a memory of pine trees and sagebrush, rabbit-fear and the froth from the muzzle of a red-tailed deer, the perfume of snow shaken off a raven's back. It was easy to saddle the Hunter's horse, take food and money from his house, and then set fire to what remained. The horse did not like her mounting up with a wolf's skin clasped to her bosom, but with knees and heels she made it mind, and turned its nose to the city.

Since a human male had taken what was dearest to her, she determined, the rest of the Hunter's kind now owed her reparations. She would no longer suffer under a mother's dictates about propriety and virtue. She would no longer keep silence and let a man, too sure of his strength, back her into a corner. The wolves had taught her much about wildness, about hunters and prey, power and pursuit. One human or a thousand, she hated them all equally, so she would go where they clustered together in fear of the forest, and take them for all they were worth.

In the city, the Hunter's coins obtained lodging in a once-fashionable quarter of town. Down the street, she had the red cloak made into a whip with an obscene handle, cuffs, and a close-fitting hood. For herself, she had tall red boots and a corset fashioned. The next day, she placed an advertisement for riding lessons in the daily newspaper. Soon, a man rang her bell to see if she had anything to teach him. He wore a gray suit instead of the Hunter's doeskin and bear fur, but he had the same aura of barely controlled fury. He was wealthy, but his privilege had not set him free. It had instead deepened his resentment of anything he did not own and made him a harsh master over the things that he did possess.

Since he despised the animal within himself, she forced him to manifest it: stripped of anything but his own hide, on all fours, forbidden to utter anything other than a wordless howl. He could not be trusted to govern himself, beast that he was, so she fettered him. And because he believed the animal was inferior to the man, made to be used violently, she beat him the way a drunkard who has lost at cards will beat his own dog. He forgot her injunction against speech when it became clear how the "riding lesson" was to proceed, but she had no mercy. Like most men, he thought of women as cows or broodmares, so if he wanted to experience servitude and degradation, he would have to experience sexual violation as well as bondage and the lash. Bent over a chair, wrists lashed to ankles, he bellowed like a gored bull when the wooden handle of the whip took his male maidenhead.

In the end, he proved her judgment of his character was correct—he knelt, swore his allegiance to her, and tried to lick her, like a servile mutt who wants a table scrap. She took his money and kicked him out with a warning to avoid attempts to sully her in the future. He went away happy, his anger temporarily at bay, his soul a little lighter for the silver that he discarded in a bowl on the foyer table.

Soon Sylvia Rufina's sitting room was occupied by a series of men who arrived full of lust and shame and left poorer but wiser about their own natures. But their pain was no balm for the wounds the Red Mistress, as she came to be called, carried in her psyche. Her self-styled slaves might prate about worship and call her a goddess, but the only thing they worshiped was their own pleasure. She knew, even as she crushed their balls, that they remained the real masters of the world.

Her consolations were private: the occasional meal of raw meat, and nightly slumber beneath a blanket of silver fur. For one whole year, she tolerated the overcrowding, bad smells, and disgusting scorched food of the city. Her fame spread, and gossip about her imperious beauty and cruelty brought her paying customers from as far away as other countries. The notion that one could buy a little freedom, pay for only a limited amount of wildness, bored and amused the Red Mistress. But she kept her thoughts to herself and kept her money in an ironbound chest. She lived like a monk, but the tools of her trade were not cheap, and she chafed to see how long it took for her hoard of wealth simply to cover the bottom of the box, then inch toward its lid.

When spring came, at first it simply made the city stink even worse than usual, as thawing snow deposited a season's worth of offal upon the streets. There was a tree near Sylvia Rufina's house, and she was painfully reminded of how beautiful and busy the forest would seem now, with sap rising and pushing new green leaves into the warming air. Her own blood seemed to have heated as well, and it grew more difficult to curb her temper with the pretense of submission that fed her treasure chest. An inhuman strength would come upon her without warning. More than one of her slaves left with the unwanted mark of her teeth upon their aging bodies and thought perhaps they should consider visiting a riding mistress who did not take her craft quite so seriously.

The full moon of April caught her unawares, standing naked by her bedroom window, and before she willed it she was herself again, four-footed and calm. After so many months of despicable hard work and monkish living, she was unable to deny herself the pleasure of keeping this form for just a little while. The wolf was fearless and went out the front door as if she owned it. Prowling packs of stray dogs were just one of the many hazards on this city's nighttime streets. Few pedestrians would be bold enough to confront a canid of her size and apparent ferocity. When she heard the sound of a conflict, she went toward it, unfettered by a woman's timidity, ruled by the wolf's confident assumption that wherever there is battle, there may be victuals.

Down a street more racked by poverty than the one on which the Red Mistress plied her trade, outside a tenement, a man in a moth-eaten overcoat and a shabby top hat held a woman by the upper arms and shook her like a rattle. She was being handled so roughly that her hair had begun to come down from where it was pinned on top of her head, so her face and chest were surrounded by a blonde cloud. She wore a low-cut black dress that left her arms indecently bare, and it was slit up the back to display her calves and even a glimpse of her thighs. "Damn you!" the man screamed. "Where's my money?"

The wolf did not like his grating, hysterical voice, and her appetite was piqued by the fat tips of the man's fingers, which protruded from his ruined gloves, white as veal sausages. He smelled like gin and mothballs, like something that ought never to have lived. When he let go of one of the woman's arms so he could take out a pocket handkerchief and mop his brow, the wolf came out of the shadows and greeted him with a barely audible warning and a peek at the teeth for which her kind was named. He was astonished and frightened. The same pocket that had held his handkerchief also contained a straight razor, but before he could fumble it out, the wolf landed in the center of his chest and planted him on his back in the mud. A yellow silk cravat, darned and stained, outlined his throat and was no obstacle.

The wolf disdained to devour him. He was more tender than the querulous granny, but dissolute living had contaminated his flesh. She did not want to digest his sickness. Licking her muzzle clean, she was surprised to see the disheveled woman waiting calmly downwind, her bosom and face marked by the pimp's assault. "Thank you," the woman said softly. She knew her savior was no domesticated pet that had slipped its leash. Her life had been very hard, but she would not have lived at all had she not been able to see what was actually in front of her and work with the truth.

Human speech made the wolf uneasy. She did not want to be reminded of her other form, her other life. She brushed past the woman, eager to sample the evening air and determine if this city held a park where she could ramble.

"Wild thing," said the woman, "let me come with you," and ardent footsteps pattered in the wake of the wolf's silent tread. The wolf could have left her behind in a second but perversely chose not to do so. They came to the outskirts of a wealthy man's estate. His mansion was in the center of a tract of land that was huge by the city's standards and stocked with game birds and deer. A tall wrought-iron fence surrounded this land, and the golden one made herself useful, discovering a place where the rivets holding several spears of iron in place had rusted through. She bent three of them upward so the two of them could squeeze beneath the metal barrier. The scent of crushed vegetation and freshly disturbed earth made the wolf delirious with joy.

Through the park they chased one another, faster and faster, until the girl's shoddy shoes were worn paper-thin and had to be discarded. The game of tag got rougher and rougher until the wolf forgot it was not tumbling about with one of its own and nipped the girl on her forearm. The triangular wound bled enough to be visible even by moonlight, scarlet and silver. Then there were two of a kind, one with fur tinged auburn, another with underfur of gold, and what would be more delicious than a hunt for a brace of hares? One hid while the other flushed out their quarry.

Knowing the potentially deadly sleep that would attack after feeding, Sylvia Rufina urged her new changeling to keep moving, back to the fence and under it. The two of them approached her house from the rear, entering through the garden. The golden one was loath to go back, did not want to take up human ways again. But Sylvia Rufina herded her relentlessly, forced her up the stairs and into the chamber where they both became mud-spattered women howling with laughter.

"You are a strange dream," the child of the streets murmured as the Red Mistress drew her to the bed.

"No dream except a dream of freedom," Sylvia Rufina replied, and pinned her prey to the sheets just as she had taken down the hapless male bawd. The wolf-strength was still vibrant within her, and she ravished the girl with her mouth and hand, her kisses flavored with the heart's blood of the feast they had shared. Goldie was no stranger to the comfort of another woman's caresses, but this was no melancholy gentle solace. This was the pain of hope and need. She struggled against this new knowledge, but the Red Mistress was relentless and showed her so much happiness and pleasure that she knew her life was ruined and changed forever.

The bruised girl could not remember how many times she had relied on the stupor that disarms a man who has emptied his loins. No matter how bitterly they complained about the price she demanded for her attentions, there was always ten times that amount or more in their purses. But instead of falling into a snoring deaf-and-blind state, she felt as awake as she had during the change, when a wolf's keen senses had supplanted her poor, blunted human perceptions. The hunger to be tongued, bitten, kissed, and fucked by Sylvia Rufina had not been appeased; it drove her toward the small perfect breasts and well-muscled thighs of her assailant and initiator.

Goldie did not rest until she had claimed a place for herself in the core of her lover's being. It was the first time in her life that Sylvia Rufina had known anything but humiliation and disgust from another human being's touch. Her capacity to take pleasure was shocking, and yet nothing in the world seemed more natural than seizing this cherub by her gold locks and demanding another kiss, on one mouth and then upon and within the other. They fell asleep on top of the covers, with nothing but a shared mantle of sweat to keep them warm. But that was sufficient.

Dawn brought a less forgiving mood. The Red Mistress was angry that someone had breached her solitude. She had not planned to share her secret with another living soul, and now she had not only revealed her alter ego but made herself a shape-shifting sister.

Goldie would not take money. She would not be sent away. And so the Red Mistress put her suitor to the severest of tests. Rather than imprisoning her with irons or cordage, Sylvia Rufina bade the blonde postulant to pick up her skirts, assume a vulnerable position bent well over, and keep it until she was ordered to rise. With birch, tawse, and cane, she meted out the harshest treatment possible, unwilling to believe the golden one's fealty until it was written in welts upon her body. The severest blows were accepted without a murmur, with no response other than silent weeping. When her rage was vented, Sylvia Rufina made the girl kiss the scarlet proof of her ambition that lingered upon the cane. And the two of them wept together until they were empty of grief and could feel only the quiet reassurance of the other's presence.

That night the refugee from the streets who had been put to sleep upon the floor crept into the bed and under the wolf hide that covered the Red Mistress, and made love to her so slowly and carefully that she did not fully awaken until her moment of ultimate pleasure. It was clear that they would never sleep apart again as long as either one of them should live.

They became mates, a pack of two, hunter and prey with one another, paired predators with the customers who were prepared to pay extra. With the comfort and challenge of one another's company, the work was much less onerous. The Red Mistress's income doubled, and by the time another year had gone by, she had enough money to proceed with her plan.

On a day in the autumn, a month or so before the fall of snow was certain, she locked up her house for the last time, leaving everything behind except the trunk of coins and gems, the maid, and warm clothing for their journey. They went off in a coach, a large silver fur thrown across their knees, and headed toward the mountains. No one in the city ever saw them again. On the way out of the city, they stopped to take a few things with them: a raven that had been chained to a post in front of an inn; a bear that was dancing, muzzled, for a gypsy fiddler; a caged pair of otters that were about to be sold to a furrier.

They had purchased wild and mountainous country, land no sane person would ever have a use for, too steep and rocky to farm, and so it was very cheap. There was plenty of money left to mark the boundaries of their territory, warning hunters away. There was a cabin, suitable for primitive living, and a stable that had already been stocked with a season's worth of feed for the horses. Once safe upon their own precincts, they let the raven loose in the shade of an oak tree, freed the old bear from his cumbersome and painful muzzle in a patch of blackberries, and turned the otters out into the nearest minnow-purling stream.

And that night, amid the trees, with a benevolent round-faced moon to keep their secrets, Sylvia Rufina took the form she had longed for during two impossible years of bondage to human society. The golden-haired girl she loved set her wild (and wise) self free as well. Then they were off to meet the ambassadors of their own kind.

They lived ever after more happily than you or me.

I've told you this story for a reason. If your woman has gone missing, and you go walking in dark places to try to find her, you may find Sylvia and Goldie instead. If they ask you a question, be sure to tell them the truth. And do not make the mistake of assuming that the wolf is more dangerous than the woman.

Business Casual
Lauren Sanders

There is time for work, and there is time for love.
That leaves no other time.

—Coco Chanel

She was mine in the conference room on the thirty-sixth floor. Two leather chairs jammed the door, the lights were turned down low. Easing her onto the mahogany table, I ran my hands along the length of her fully clothed body before turning her head toward the windows, unveiling a theater of buildings by night, charcoal glass checkerboards with brightly lit squares. Between the cracks was the river, a sliver of bridge, the outer boroughs glimmering like an old-fashioned movie marquee. I wanted her to know how high up we were, to feel the risk in my hands, breathe the fear through my lips. I'd become obsessed with the spotlights on rippled black water, the crystalline buildings wrapping their legs around us. It was as much of a rush as our frenzy for quick, muted orgasms. She smelled like rosemary-mint conditioner from the corporate gym.

On good days, she escaped to the gym at twilight, just as I was beginning my day, and practically met me at the door when I came in at eleven. Other times, when I casually passed her cubicle she was buried in the corner, headphones crushing her wavy brown hair and eyes strained on her computer screen, adrift in a haze of high-stakes numerical analysis. I knew not to approach her then. She became irascible when anyone broke her spell, and there were still too many people around. We had to be discreet.

She was an investment banker at a large financial institution. I was a painter with a night job in the word-processing department there. In a manner of speaking, I worked for her.

For someone so young she had so many words. Hundreds of sentence fragments attached to bar graphs and pie charts, and she had strong opinions about how they should appear on the page. She was a perfectionist, she said, but open to suggestions. She listened when we told her what was not possible and she trusted our deadlines. Sometimes she lingered after dropping off a job, joining a conversation about a movie, play, or the political drama of the week. Nobody talks out there, she said, meaning the other bankers, her colleagues. It was important for her to separate herself. To prove she didn't belong *out there*.

Over time, I learned that she hated investment banking. She'd resigned herself to the training program to please her parents, immigrants who'd shoveled the bulk of their hard-earned salaries into the Ivy League playground she'd recently left behind. She knew how they gloated whenever they told anyone where she worked. I said I understood. My parents lived in the same rural town I'd escaped almost two decades earlier, and had always hated telling people there that I was an artist. Even the painting class I taught seemed intangible to them. But when I started working at the investment bank they suddenly had a name people recognized. Something to talk about. They never mentioned that I was a glorified typist.

She laughed at this the way she always laughed at my jokes. She engaged me in conversations about art—not in the aggressive manner of my students, particularly the little dykes with big baggy pants who followed me to the subway, demanding to know about the art world, who'd been included and excluded, what was the dominant style, how could they possibly work themselves in. No, she wanted to talk about the paintings she'd seen in museums, whether her interpretations had been correct. When I told her there was no right or wrong and offered to give her an art tour of our building, which incidentally had the most expensive collection of twentieth-century paintings and prints I'd seen outside of a museum, she said *cool*. Then she asked me if I had always known that I was an artist. Although I hadn't picked up a brush in months and was even considering dumping my studio, I said yes. This was very cool, too.

I liked her enthusiasm. Her words. The flicker in her eyes when she said *cool*, electric-green chewing gum jutting in and out of her mouth like a serpent's tongue. How eager she was to gobble up the world. I started looking forward to her emails and thought about her on my days off. In short, as the months passed and she marked her first year on the calendar, I developed a bit of a crush on the kid—nothing serious, really—the kind of amorous affection that occasionally crept into a relationship with one of my students and that I'd learned to keep at bay.

Until one night her presentation made the "hot jobs" board, and I spent half my shift with my forefinger buffing the mouse to create a graphic of an archer with his bow pointed at a reindeer to *imagize*—company term—a hostile raid she and a few other bankers were shoveling through the pipeline. I tried telling her there probably weren't too many hunters equipped with bow and arrow in subarctic climates, where the reindeer roam, and besides it was a cruel image. She smiled and I thought, what a beautiful mouth she has, curvaceous purple lips that seem almost heart-shaped, and commanding white teeth. What was it about cruelty that in the right face could become so alluring?

Before I began fantasizing her cultured sadism, she confessed a similar conversation she'd had with the partner who was spearheading the takeover, her boss. Apparently, she'd told him the image was a mixed metaphor. Repeating this, she shifted her weight to her left leg so her hip jutted sideways. She rested her hand upon it, giggling a bit as she revealed the balance of their conversation: naïvely, she'd informed her boss that a bow and arrow would hardly slay a reindeer, and she was treated to the following pabulum: "A hunter never questions his weapons." Her boss walked off, and that was the word.

"I was embarrassed bringing in the job before," she said. "I wanted you to do it."

"But you could have been home already."

"I'm like you, a night owl," she said, hand still on her hip, snugly encased in tight gray trousers. Ever since the company went business-casual, her clothing had been shrinking. While the men dressed down to comfortable khakis and polo shirts, and the women into flat loafers, she'd gone more contemporary—synthetic skins and form-fitting blouses, patent-leather platform shoes, as if she'd walked off the pages of a fashion magazine. It was her battle against the corporate culture and she waged it valiantly.

I told her not to worry. We would give her boss what he wanted.

When she came back a few hours later, I handed her the page and she burst out laughing. In her absence, I'd dug up an image of a U.S. army tank and pointed the cannon directly at the reindeer.

"Poor bastard," she said.

"A hunter never questions his weapons," I responded.

"I meant the reindeer."

"It's a she."

"But it's got antlers. Only males have antlers."

"Reindeer aren't like other deer, they both have them."

"Cool," she smiled. "I wonder if it makes them any less sexist."

I laughed, bemused by her twisted-rebel stance and ruthless determination. My students were usually shy in their flirtations, stammering bunnies afraid to stand too close or look me in the eye. But this kid was unflinching. She smiled as if she had me where she wanted me, and what killed me was we both knew it was true. I wanted to pin her down right there on my desk in the awful fluorescent lighting with an annoying pop song playing and make her put up or shut up. But my two colleagues were tapping away at their computers and there were other jobs in the rack. I handed her the real document with the bow and arrow, and when she took it her hand brushed against mine. As she left the word-processing center, the hand she'd touched started stinging. I looked down and saw my forefinger was bleeding. The little raider had given me a paper cut.

In the bathroom, I ran my finger under the tap. The warm water was soothing, but I couldn't stop laughing at myself. Flirting was an occupational hazard.

I never heard the door click open, had no idea I wasn't alone until I saw her face materialize in the mirror in front of me. She asked what happened and I told her she'd wounded me. I moved my finger from the water and held it in front of her. A few drops of blood seeped through the scratch.

"A paper cut," she said.

I nodded.

She took my hand in hers, and I felt as if I were being submerged in the gushing warm tap. Slowly, without taking her eyes from mine, she lifted my finger and kissed it lightly before opening her lips around the cut and sucking as if I'd been bitten by a snake. I slipped back against the sink, letting my skin melt with every stroke of her tongue on my finger. She kept her eyes open, staring at me.

I took a deep breath. "Do they know about you out there?"

For a second, she stopped sucking and shook her head, then took my entire finger in her mouth. "Oh fuck," I said. "Fuck."

I grabbed her by the cheeks and pulled up her head. My wounded finger throbbed against her skin. She cupped her hands over mine and we stared in the rushed and inexorable manner of lovers on the precipice. Her eyes were engorged, pitch-black catacombs of desire. A reflection of my own. I pressed her back against the tiles and kissed her in the bright light. She grabbed my neck. I slid my hands down to her breasts, felt her squirm beneath me. Our kissing was ferocious.

Suddenly she pulled away. "Not here," she said.

"Then where?"

"I know a place."

Ours was a sick building. With its windows sealed shut, the same fetid air circulated through every crevice day in and day out. She got colds all winter long. I brought her echinacea tea and zinc drops, held her head in my lap in the secret room we found off the foyer on the eighteenth floor. It was like something out of an old movie. You pushed the wall and it revolved backward. Inside was a metal desk with a small painting above it. The painting was by one of my favorite artists, an innovator of the New York school. It was pristine in its simplicity. A few colored boxes—red, yellow, blue, nothing exotic—with frayed edges bouncing off each other, as if energized by the magnetic fields between them. She said someone had left it there for us.

At last unfettered, she cried about not sleeping, about missing the gym, traveling too much, and not seeing me for days. She was being pressured to take on more clients, and with every deal she grew sicker of her own deferential conformity, her uncanny ability to make money for a system she despised. I found her moral conflict absurd, if not a bit youthful. She was playing dress-up in the last bastion of white-collar patriarchy. Though the collars were less constricting, the roles were still clearly defined. You couldn't get any further from the reindeer, I said. She cried harder.

I told her she was my baby, promising everything would be okay, and although the banalities slipping from my lips alarmed me, I knew it was what she wanted to hear. I knew it as instinctively as if she were my child. We rocked gently, her face against my breasts until longing usurped comfort and I wanted to fuck her as much as I needed to protect her. I didn't have to say it. She'd learned to read my rhythm, my body, my breath, and she was a quick study. She ripped open my shirt and played with my nipples. She adored my nipples, loved burying her face between my breasts, which made me feel more maternal and at the same time brought me to my knees in delirium, if only for a few minutes in our hidden cavern before we returned unsuspected, though a bit rumpled, to our desks.

My supervisor never questioned me. Those of us who worked grave had a tacit understanding that anyone might disappear for a while. Some people paced the halls or hiked up and down the carpeted stairwells; others, swamped by their circadian clocks, napped on the plush couches in one of the more deserted lobbies. Whatever it took to make it to sunrise.

She left before the sun came up, often skipping out just after we parted as if our assignation had been her reward for making it through another sixteen-hour day, but not without an email saying, "goodnight" or "miss you." In her emails she called me Rembrandt. She said I was the only person she could talk to. The only one who understood her. She never used the word *love*.

After being together, I was bombarded by the adrenaline of our interlocked bodies, her teeth on my nipples as she shoved her entire hand inside me. You take so much so fast, she said, as amazed by the dexterity of my cunt as I was by her ability to get me there so quickly. I never told her how good she was. I didn't have to. With her hand inside me we were both acutely aware of her cutthroat ambition. "Did you come?" she asked. "Did you really?"

"You were here."

"We can do better."

"I have to get back."

"Please, one more time. I really want to see you."

She would arrive even earlier the next morning to finish the work she'd forsaken. I would claim another migraine had kept me from my desk. Never in my life had I been such a bottom, and without an ounce of guilt.

What can I say? The kid knew how to fuck.

I blushed remembering every twist and permutation of her hand as if it were still there, like a severed limb that leaves its ghosted particles behind. The energy could remain for hours, days, even weeks.

Occasionally I went to the bathroom, turned on all the taps, and masturbated in one of the stalls, but mostly after she left I became so morose I put on my headphones and listened to country music until I cried.

At dawn I stumbled out into the cold quiet mornings and by rote ambled to the subway station. Staring at the freshly scrubbed faces, I wanted to embrace them for their tenacity. Up so early pursuing their dreams. Like her parents. I became an ethnic detective, dissecting skin color and bone structure to determine if anyone was from her country, desperate to see how she might look in daylight. I imagined her at home in bed, buried beneath the pale orange comforter she talked about. We romanticized her bed with its billowing canopy, the hotels she frequented that had two king-size beds and cable TV. She said she always ordered a porno film and charged it to the company because she knew it was what guys did on the road.

I saw her in a hotel room, lights dimmed, misty blue streams of television caressing her limbs. I saw her in the boardroom, the only woman at a table full of suits as titillated by her professional machinations as I was by her hand inside me. I saw her next to me on the walk from the subway to my apartment, promising to make me scrambled eggs with avocado slices for breakfast.

Alone in my apartment I poured a bowl of cold cereal and realized I didn't even know her phone number.

Before her I had a girlfriend. We had been dating almost a year when my affair with the investment banker began. My girlfriend was kind, beautiful, and wildly intelligent. She was a serial monogamist who fell in love with people the way she fell in love with authors, deeply and chauvinistically, devouring every sentence she could find by and about the enamored scribe, her fingers smeared with ink from rare books, diaries, and Xeroxes of academic journals. But unlike scholars who could make a life's work out of one writer, my girlfriend eventually got bored. The signs were subtle. She carried fewer titles to work, kept a bookmark on the same page for weeks, stopped visiting the library, and eventually found some nugget of betrayal she could not overlook.

The email had been on my night table. It wasn't incriminating, but would have been enough to rouse the dander of any lover. When she asked who, it seemed pointless to lie.

My girlfriend had fallen out of love; I'd never really been there. She called me a cheater, said I had no respect for her, and questioned my sanity in having an affair with someone at work—someone so young and wrongfully employed. I stopped listening, and instead remembered my girlfriend's wet tongue traveling from my hipbone to that spot in the back of my neck where all the nerves met, and kissing me there as if I'd grown another set of lips. We'd spent hours on her couch making out like teenagers before ever touching a button, waistband, or zipper where underneath lay another treat. My bookish girlfriend had wonderful taste in lingerie. How she could wear corsets, garters, red stockings, and lacy bras without ever looking tacky amazed me. Then again, she was the first lover whom I let light candles and rub scented oils into the crevices behind my kneecaps, the first whose pussy I lapped wholeheartedly as she mimicked on mine and somehow it never felt stereotypical. She knew how sexy tenderness could be in the right hands. She also knew how easily it could evaporate.

After my confession, she saw me as she saw her once-revered politically oppressed writer who left his wife and children for a woman half his age, moved to another country, and had cosmetic surgery, becoming a painful joke to those who believed the intellect should rule matters of the heart. Those like my girlfriend. I let her believe my moral failings had sunk our relationship. A few months later, I heard she'd moved on to her next lover. The news made me neither happy nor sad.

I stopped seeing most of my friends and started picking up extra shifts at work to increase the odds of bumping into my little banker. Insomnia set in. Even the eye masks and sandalwood I burned no longer worked. I drank red wine and watched morning talk shows, the soaps, cooking shows, and reruns of old cartoons—whatever it took to disappear inside the screen.

Then one day at the onset of spring, when sun-drenched mornings brought the rush of children lining up outside before school and dogs dragging their heavy-eyed owners through the streets, after work I went to my studio instead of going home. The last time I'd been there I was so frustrated that I hadn't cleaned anything. Most of my brushes had hardened. Paint was splattered on the walls and floor. The sink was clogged. I dug up an old canvas and whitewashed it with a roller. Then I mopped, wiped down the walls, opened all the windows, and sat silently while the canvas dried, thinking about suspended color boxes, prisms of static, and the electrified fields sustaining us.

I thought I was sick with love, sleeping as little as she did so we'd be on the same time clock. It took me weeks to see it wasn't only her cycle I was emulating. I had begun to worship productivity, becoming devout in my routine, unflagging in my work ethic, greedy in my pleasures. Unlike her, I was pleased with the fruits of my labor.

Each night in the car on the way to work I wondered whether it was a good day or a bad day, or if she'd be there at all when I arrived at the office. Her career was blossoming. Throughout the spring, they sent her on whirlwind road shows that kept her out of town for weeks, and spoke about transferring her to one of the firm's European satellites in June. When she returned, often for one or two nights before they shipped her off again, she was so worn out she could barely wheel her suitcase down the hall. She set the alarm on her watch to remind her what time it was, and swallowed antihistamines by the handful, craving the speediness as much as relief from her allergies.

One night she begged me three times to meet her in the anemic yellow stairwell, where she clung to me as if we might never see each other again. The next night she simply nodded hello, as if I were just another company perk like the twenty-dollar dinner allowances or strip clubs her male colleagues frequented on expense accounts. It amazed me how readily she could liquidate her sexuality, and how obsequiously I'd relinquished mine to the vagaries of her profession.

When she was away, I sulked through my shift, drinking stale coffee in big Styrofoam cups until I fled in the mornings, pumped-up and aggressive, ready to attack the canvases I'd carted to my studio. I was monopolized by huge territories of color, returning to the most primary forms to see how I'd slipped so far away. It had been years since I'd felt so unburdened.

At night I was still chained to her. My mind oscillated between rapturous sparks of memory and the most painful longing I'd ever experienced. Did she really stop the elevator midstream and drop to her knees in front of me with the security guard intoning through speakers *Hello, is there anybody in there? What's going on?* Did she come up behind me at the printer bay, sink her entire body into mine, hands on my tits and cunt grinding to the beat of the lasers? Did she whimper and call out my name as if our meeting were a hallowed exercise? Did she say I was the only one? Grieve in anticipation? Make me shudder with joy? The night she flew in from Tokyo, her voice cracked as she carted an armful of documents into the word-processing center and pleaded that all work be done immediately. She had to catch the shuttle to D.C. the next day. She kept her head down as she spoke and her voice in its professional guise made me cringe, her breakneck itinerary a personal rejection. My heart collapsed, at the same time increasing its missionary task, and I wondered if that was what a heart attack felt like—that sinking, speeding feeling. I brushed past her and smelled her unkempt scent, less perfumed, more doughy. She stepped one leg back as if she were trying to trip me. I wanted to smack her.

She found me in the bathroom and told me she missed me.

I didn't respond. Through a series of yawns, she said she was totally spent. That earlier she'd fallen asleep on the toilet seat, and her allergies were raging. She hadn't even been home to shower or change clothes, although she'd substituted for her silk blouse an oversized company T-shirt that tucked into her skirt in the front and made her look like a feminized Minotaur, half bull, half sorority girl. I wondered how many before me had been sacrificed at her profiteering hands.

Though I knew she craved the warmth of our secret room, I took her to the thirty-sixth floor, and without a word shoved her face against the windowpane. I ran my hand along the backs of her thighs, finding the rim of her hose beneath her skirt and pulling it down, my mouth next to her ear, hers open against the window steamed up in front of us, obscuring the buildings with their insolent white lights. I whispered in her ear, "Tell me you missed me, tell me," and she moaned, thrusting her head sideways. I pushed it back to the window so she could see the dark alleyways and slick buildings, the toxic black river beneath us. I wanted her to imagine what it might be like to fall.

She tried to break free and turn around. I pinned all of my weight against her, spreading her legs from behind with one hand and rimming her with my thumb. I talked into her ear, called her a horny little fuck, a capitalist tool, a spy. She slipped back against me, and sighed. I knew she'd shut her eyes. "That's it, baby," I whispered. "Come to me. Come home."

"I'm yours."

"Tell me again." I slipped a couple of fingers inside her cunt, still massaging her asshole with my thumb. By that time, having given over completely, she'd thrown her weight against the window, eyes tightly shut as I brought my other hand to her clit. She moaned again, said she was all mine. Told me to do whatever I wanted.

I fucked her harder than she'd ever fucked me, so forcefully she fell into a trance, enveloped by the field between us, the streaming lights against the windowpane. She wailed, cursing as she writhed beneath me, and with her every word I grew larger, more powerful. Her screams echoed in the steely canyons beneath us. I quickly covered her mouth as we fell to the floor, and, more determined than ever—as if my taking her demanded she come back with full force—she climbed on top of me and kissed all the way down my stomach, undoing my zipper with her teeth.

It was a careless move after her scream, but I didn't care. My body had disintegrated into the resistance of our rhythm, the energy of her tongue in my cunt, and I saw myself suspended above the city with its millions of colored boxes and white lights, the iron claw of her mouth beneath me. I leaned my head back into the carpet and came quietly, pushing her head away. She slithered up my body and was about to speak when I covered her mouth again. I wanted to remember her without words.

Splitting the Infinitive
Jean Roberta

I'm standing in my office waiting for Didrick Bent, the one I think of as Dim Bulb. I don't like to be kept waiting. As long as I have nothing better to do, I glance at myself in the mirror on the back of my office door. I am only 5'3", and I have placed my mirror so that my face is perfectly centered in it and taller people must duck to see themselves in my domain. I would rather stand than sit, and I prefer to see other people below me—I suppose I picked up this preference when I began teaching English at the university ten years ago. I like the legend that Emily Brontë died standing up. Like any great work of fiction, this story probably contains more truth than fact.

I am not a vain woman, but I find comfort in my own reflection. I like to know how I appear to my audience. My long chestnut hair, turning to gray, is coiled and pinned at the back of my head. The overhead light picks up the silver at my temples and gives depth to my large brown eyes. I reapply the burgundy lipstick that dramatizes my full lips, and powder my small nose to cover the shine.

I am wearing my white silk blouse without a bra because I see no need for it; my breasts are still "assertive," as my first woman lover used to say. When I dressed this way as a teenager in the 1960s, the men who called themselves my brothers treated me like meat. Now my students are disconcerted when they realize that they can see my nipples, but they must control their tongues as well as their hands. A tenured position is better than a suit of armor.

My black wool skirt and the cotton petticoat under it brush against my boots as I pace. My wide leather belt emphasizes the contrast between my small waist and my full hips, and it can also be used for other purposes. I am beginning to simmer with anger at Didrick's lateness, which is not surprising. She is the spoiled child of misguided professionals who have always given her expensive toys to substitute for their attention. I suppose they think that a university education is equivalent to the sports car they gave her for giving up her post–high school slacker life and moving back in with them. They, and she, have no idea with whom they are trifling.

The hesitant knock on my door may be meant to appease me, but it's the last straw. The purpose of a knock is to attract the hearer's attention, is it not? Brushing one's oversized knuckles lightly against the wood as if testing it for splinters seems as pointless as daydreaming in class.

When I pull the door open Didrick is already blushing. "I'm sorry I'm late, Doctor Chalkdust," she gasps, seeing my look. She lowers her head in my presence, which somewhat compensates for the fact that she is a good six inches taller than I am. At age nineteen, she could be called a baby butch or a tomboy brat. Her short sandy hair always looks like it's just come out of a wind tunnel. Like most young women, she is a bundle of contradictions. She obviously spends too much time trying to look as if appearance doesn't matter to her; she desperately wants other people to accept her as a cool dyke who knows the score. In her own language: *as if.*

"Didrick," I intone, trying to keep my temper on a leash, "you're in serious danger of failing this course. Do you know that? I've gone out of my way to help you pull up your socks and start learning how to express yourself, and you respond by wasting my time." I could drive her away from me forever, and she knows it. Perhaps this would be the ultimate way of hurting her.

She doesn't know how to start apologizing or explaining herself so she begins to stutter. "I thought—I thought, I mean I used the Spell Check on my last essay, and I thought it looked all right—" This kid is not a cyberpunk or cyberslut; she is a cyberfool who expects a machine to do the thinking for her. Her words make my hands itch.

I sigh. "I thought we could start by discussing that wretched essay, but I see how badly you need a reality check." She knows what this means, and she is already breathing hard. Her large hands are shaking and in another minute the crotch of her jeans will become visibly wet. I'm not willing to wait that long. "Take off your pants, Didrick," I tell her, "and keep my name in mind."

"Yes, Doctor Chalkdust," she answers, not daring to look me in the eyes. She has seen the diplomas on my office wall often enough to know that my first name is Athena. She also knows that for her, that name is unspeakable.

She steps out of her bunched jeans and man-styled underpants. Her long, muscular thighs and firm young ass gleam pearly in the office light. I know that she is embarrassed when anyone sees the triangle of curly light-brown hair at her crotch, and this knowledge makes me smile. "You know what to do," I warn. She is as slow as molasses today.

Quivering slightly in fear or anticipation, she bends over my desk and rests her head on her folded arms. I've decided to use my eighteen-inch wooden ruler because she finds it more humiliating than other means of correction. I will have trouble resisting the urge to break it over her lazy butt.

The first smack makes a satisfying sound and she jumps. The second and third dangerously stimulate my temper instead of soothing it. Against my better judgment, I want to see blood and hear the unwilling scream of a young rebel who has lost her mask. She is already whimpering, probably more from fear than from pain. For a slow learner, she has an uncanny ability to read my moods.

She also seems able to send the heat from her swollen clit into mine, and I can't (or won't?) block it out. Like everything else about this big colt, her reactions to me seem beyond reason. I would rather die than tell her this aloud, but her energy slams into me with a force that I can barely contain. In Portia's words: "my little body is aweary of this great world." When I was growing into womanhood, we were never told that we could channel the tides.

I'm not satisfied, not even close to it, but I know how dangerous it would be to go as far as I want to. In reality, I am at her mercy. I can see that the edges of my ruler have raised some little welts on her very red cheeks. She will heal from these minor wounds much sooner than my career would heal from the coup de grâce she could give me by telling someone over my head what takes place in this room. Too many of my colleagues have heard about the office renovations I had done last summer. Does anyone know that I had soundproof insulation put in, or why? Didrick can afford exposure no more than I can, but whether she can carry our little secret to the grave is another matter. After all, she told me her whole life story (admittedly not a long epic) during our first session.

I slide the ruler back into my desk, but she knows better than to move without permission. I can't resist running my right hand gently, slowly, over her hot cheeks while my left holds her hips in place. She flinches from my compassion as much as from my discipline. "You stubborn little girl," I murmur into one of her freckled ears. "How long do you think you can keep this up?"

I put my hand firmly on her neck to keep her down and to let her know that I'm here, I'm not going away, and I'm not going to lose faith or let her lose hers. A humble pencil on my desk attracts my attention. I reach for it as if I were planning to write a list of her grammatical sins on her back with its sharp little point. I withdraw from her just long enough to anoint the pencil with baby oil from a bottle on my desk. Then I find the small, puckered mouth between her butt cheeks and slide the eraser in until four inches of wood are embedded in the site of her punishment. She groans, and an uncontrollable shiver of pleasure seems to run all through her. Reaching between her legs, I find her cunt lips so wet that a little more attention will probably make the juice run down her legs.

The pointed end of the pencil looks like a little tail, and I wield it so that it dances in spirals and figure eights inside her, stroking walls of flesh that were never explored this way before I touched them. When I draw the pencil out it will be smeared with her shit, and she will blush to see it. I imagine running a steel pole into her hot, pulsing guts and raising her off the floor with it. I imagine her bleeding and crying—but never, never resisting me, even in her innermost core.

"Doctor Chalkdust," she whispers, begging. She needs to come soon, but she will hold off until I give her my blessing. I am tempted to find out how long she can last, but that test can wait for another day.

"Come for me, baby," I tell her, running the sharp burgundy fingernails of my right hand over her bursting clit. She jerks violently, trying to suppress a childish yell as the pencil probes her at an unexpected angle. Her thin veneer of machisma has melted away, leaving her face covered with tears. She convulses helplessly as I draw the pencil out of her and pull her down to the floor.

While she is still open and panting I pour oil into my left hand. Then I push each of my small, slick, well-manicured fingers into a cunt as wet and heaving as an ocean cave. I form a fist inside her and let it rock her the way it wants to.

She is afraid of exploding out of her skin. I know that she is ashamed of her needs and her ignorance but she is terrified of the possibility that in an instant I can change her into someone she doesn't recognize. Education is about transformation, and she feels as confused about that as all my other students do. I wonder if any of the others have dreamed of writhing on my fist in anguish and relief, screaming my name in the silence of their half-formed minds.

"Didrick," I call her, almost singing her name to the rhythm of my fist and her hips. "You have to give me more. I know you can." Her heat is rising up my arm, which is aching. Nonetheless, I won't stop until I'm finished. I know that this strong young animal plays on the women's basketball team. I picture myself fucking her in the gym, surrounded by her amused teammates. That would be a suitable penalty for writing another essay like her latest masterpiece.

She is crying, shaking, and gasping louder and louder, as if she is about to start howling like a wolf. I know that she wants to please me and is terrified of failing. In class she watches me when I call on my most articulate students for answers, and her face is an open book. I suspect that she wants to kill Reginald, my wannabe pet, who keeps inviting me to watch him rehearse with the other young Hamlets in the Shakespeare Club. Alas, poor Didrick—know ye not a budding queen when he poses before ye?

I am kneeling over my hapless pupil, who hasn't had a chance to catch her breath since her last climax. Now she seems about to erupt like a volcano. "Not yet," I warn her, pressing her cervix. "I'll be very angry if you come now."

My threat comes too late. Her hot cunt clutches my fist over and over, and the more she tries to control this greedy mouth, the more it talks back in its own way. My right hand checks out her clit and my gentlest stroke sets off a new wave of contractions. I suddenly wonder what she would look like giving birth.

She is soggy with spent energy, gratitude, shame, and guilt. I can see her bracing herself for a few strokes of my belt. I usually give six for disobeying an order. "I—I'm s—sorry," she snivels. "I couldn't help it, Doctor Chalkdust."

I feel generous. "Ssh," I soothe her, petting her head. She reminds me of a racehorse colt in training. I feel blessed to have such a powerful female creature under my control. "This time I'll let you make it up to me instead of punishing you, Didrick," I offer, "but stop blubbering or I'll change my mind."

She glows, and her blue eyes almost reflect an image of my body under my clothes. I want to shed all of them, but I can't allow her to be covered more modestly than I am. "Take your shirt off," I tell her. I know that she takes pride in her muscular arms, but the heat of my gaze on her small breasts makes her uncomfortable, so she grabs the hem of her T-shirt and pulls it roughly over her head as if to get the process over with as quickly as possible. Her pungent sports bra soon joins the pile of her clothing on the floor. I smile at her innocent pink nipples and she forces herself to seek approval in my eyes.

Without a word, I walk to the antique chaise longue that stands in a corner of my office near the floor lamp with the ivory silk shade. I turn on the lamp and it casts amber light on the midnight-blue velvet that will soon receive my bare skin. "Turn off the overhead, Didrick," I tell her casually. She rushes to obey, and we are left in an intimate circle of light. The books on my shelves watch us from the darkness like discreet mentors.

I sit. "You may undress me," I offer, "beginning with my boots." She kneels at my feet and studies one small, creased leather boot as she carefully pulls the laces out of their holes.

After my boots are neatly placed, side by side, under my desk, Didrick raises her head and gasps as she sees my hair flowing over my shoulders, released from its pins. "You may bury your face in it when you get there," I tease. She blushes, and looks flustered as I stand up and slowly, deliberately, unbuckle my belt. She looks relieved when I hand it to her in a coil, like a sleeping snake, to place on my desk.

I turn my back to her, shaking my hair over my shoulders. She reverently unbuttons and unzips the back of my skirt as if it could easily tear. She is moving too slowly. "Hurry up, brat," I warn her. Her fumbling fingers pull the skirt downward and I must remind her to pull the petticoat down with it to save time. As I step out of the fabric at my feet, she waits awkwardly.

I remain standing for a moment so that she can take in my black satin panties and the matching garter belt that holds up my stockings. When I sit down, I gesture impatiently. She begins shakily unbuttoning my blouse. She removes the sleeves from my arms as gently as a loyal maid, but as she glances at my breasts, she can't keep the predatory gleam out of her eyes. I am reminded that I am making myself vulnerable to a newly ripened incarnation of the Amazons of old, a novice warrior who doesn't yet know her own strength. As I watch her, she drops her eyes as if sheathing a weapon that might give nightmares to a sheltered soul. Her chivalry pleases me even as it makes me see red.

"Sometimes you want to take me hard, don't you, honey?" I demand. As usual, she doesn't know what to say. "You can tell the truth, baby," I whisper in her ear as she kneels at my stockinged feet. She mumbles something and I tell her to repeat her answer.

"I want to satisfy you," she says bravely to my face. "If you'll let me, Doctor Chalkdust," she adds quickly.

I chuckle as I slide my panties down with one hand then kick them off. I gesture in a way she recognizes. She fastens her mouth on my left breast like a leech, sucking steadily as if she could pull the milk of knowledge out of my hard nipple. "Ahh," I sigh as one of her big hands envelops my right breast. Her mouth and her hand speak to my hungry pussy, and I can hardly sit still.

"I want your fingers, Didrick," I insist. "Now." I seem to be filled with boiling lava. I am so close to coming that my touchy clit could not stand any direct attention. I don't want to be tickled now. I want to be plowed.

She pushes two long fingers into me and begins to pump, slowly at first and then faster. A third finger, not wanting to be left out, finds room inside me. With her head against my heart, she fucks me tirelessly. Like a devoted knight in service to her queen, this child strokes me harder and deeper than anyone else I can remember.

Didrick, Baby Dyke, you move me more than I'm willing to tell you. I don't expect my heart and my mind to change much in the future. Why must yours?

Thank the Goddess for soundproof walls. I hear my own animal sound as if from a distance while large quakes and smaller tremors run all through me in quick succession. She stays deep inside me until my breathing has steadied.

I kiss the top of her head. "I have to be home soon, baby," I murmur into one of her protruding ears, "and so do you." Penelope is usually too tired for what she calls "lovemaking," but she is a good cook, and she no longer asks me to explain my absences in detail. After twelve years together, we are probably getting as much from each other as we can reasonably expect.

Didrick doesn't want to move. "Doctor Chalkdust," she

asks, desperate to hold my attention for a moment longer, "did I split a lot of infinitives?"

The child can be trusted to screw up her priorities. Luckily for her, this topic no longer makes me feel rabid. "Yes," I laugh, "but that's one of your minor problems. I'm more concerned about your dangling modifiers and misplaced punctuation, paragraphs that are all over the map, and your argument as a whole." I sigh. "Didrick," I advise her as patiently as I can, "you need to learn how to think." I can't keep the sarcasm out of my voice.

She can't look at me because I have hurt her. She tries to hide her tears from me, and the sight of her wet gaze makes my cunt tighten. "You're so smart," she gushes. "I don't think I can ever—"

"Sshh," I silence her. "Never say never. I'll let you rewrite that essay. If it's still not clear, you'll rewrite it as many times as you need to. Until your logic would persuade the devil to change his mind."

Didrick's smile is part hopeful, part skeptical, and part sassy. "I've never been good at putting words down," she confesses. As her friends would say: duh. "Do you really think I can fix it that good?"

"You'll fix it *well,* honey," I threaten, "or you'll face the consequences."

She looks dangerously close to the psychic state I think of as her bottom trance. I stand up at once. "Turn on the overhead, Didrick," I remind her briskly. The circle has been opened.

As we both put on our clothes and prepare to face the outside world, split infinitives strut through my mind: to soundly thrash, to thoroughly fuck, to helplessly wriggle, to sweetly beg, to piercingly scream, to stubbornly love, to boldly go where few (or many) have gone before. I remember that rules were made to be broken, and that to fully live is to dance on the edge of a knife.

Didrick, you are my offering to the Goddess I serve. Don't bring my judgment into disrepute by messing up. "You have to come in again this week," I tell her. "Come here at one o'clock sharp on Wednesday to work on your essay. You'll be here all afternoon."

The brat can't hide her pleasure. "Cool," she grins. "I mean, yes, Doctor C."

The Word Nebraska
Tennessee Jones

The men in Vermont usually thought we were boys when they picked us up. A stone mason stopped for us on Route 5, a two-ton slab of marble in the back of his truck, the big wheels almost as tall as my chest. He was thin and dark, his torso covered by a bulky stained jacket, his hands so huge the steering wheel seemed to disappear between them. His eyes were dark brown, half hidden by heavy brows. I smelled tobacco and sweat when Jake opened the passenger door, but when we climbed into the cab of the truck he yelled, "Jesus fuck! You guys smell like shit; roll down the window!" as I extended my hand to him. The introduction froze on my lips. As the truck accelerated he said, "It's all right. I know what it's like. I started hitchhiking when I was fifteen. I didn't like riding the bus so that's how I got to school. I grew up around here and after a while people start to get to know you and they don't mind picking you up. Then when I got out of school I didn't stop for a while. I went all the way to the West Coast." He stopped for a moment. "What are you guys doing?"

"We're going out west too," Jake said to him.

"There's nothing much out there. That's why I came back here. I was tired of being broke, tired of having long hair, tired of being nobody. I guess I was still nobody for a few months even after I came back. I used to terrorize the cops here, come around the curves at seventy miles an hour and then when one of them would get behind me and flash his lights I'd speed up even more. I'd race the fucker until I was in New Hampshire and there was nothing he could do to me.

"I came back here because I knew someone who could teach me a trade and I knew I could make a lot of money at it. I apprenticed for a few months laying brick and restoring old buildings and then I went off on my own."

He talked about rocks for the next half hour like he was almost crazy. He talked about them like he was in love with them, pointing at old brick farmhouses as we passed by them, telling us how much money each would be worth. "You can charge a dollar apiece for vintage bricks and people will pay it," he said. "That old house over there's got at least a hundred thousand on it." I closed my eyes briefly and saw the building demolished, the burnt orange of the trees rising around nothing.

I noticed him looking at me closely as he talked as if he was starting to sense that I wasn't a man. Did he notice the absence of a beard or Adam's apple? Was it something in the scent my body gave off, not as spicy and dark as his own? "I wanna pull over for a second and show you part of a wall I restored. I don't want you all getting nervous, it's just off the side of the road here." He pointed to a gravel parking lot and an old brick building. We got out of the truck and walked over to it, close enough so that he could lay his hands on the rough surface of the bricks. "I matched up bricks over here," he said. "Pulled out the old crumbling ones and replaced them. You can hardly tell, can you?" I noticed his fingers were long and thin, the knuckles brushed with hair. He touched the wall gingerly, as if feeling for the pulse of the person who had originally laid the brick.

After the stone mason dropped us off on the side of the road in Massachusetts, Jake and I talked about dragging him off into the woods, looking into his big brown eyes, and forcing him to suck both of our cocks, feeling his white teeth brush up against our pubic hair. It's funny how queerness seems to spread as our lovers take on other genders, how behaviors like sucking cock become desirable and transgressive. We talked about fucking his ass and leaving him in the dry leaves with his pants down around his boots. Maybe we thought about these things because we were terrified of being discovered, terrified of being beaten by small-town boys because we had pussies instead of dicks.

Jake collars me for the first time in a basement in Louisville, Kentucky. I am skeptical. "After I put this on you," he says to me, "I don't want you to make another sound." I face the gray basement wall and he steps behind me, so close that I can feel his broad chest pressing against my shoulder blades. He places the piece of leather across my throat, drawing it so tight against my trachea that it is a little difficult for me to breathe. I close my eyes as he puts it on, trying to process how I feel about it and what I think it means. He grabs my shoulders and turns me around to face him. "I'm going to tie you up now, darlin'," he breathes in my ear. He has a long length of white rope in his hand. He pulls my wrists behind my back and wraps rope around each of them separately, so that my forearms are tightly encased almost to my elbows. He ties a knot to draw my wrists together and with the same piece of rope ties my feet. "I want to make sure you don't talk," he says, drawing a leather gag through my teeth. "Stand here and wait for me."

He starts walking up the stairs and I feel panic spread in

my chest, tightening the ventricles of my heart, shrinking my lungs. My breath turns hot, as if I've inhaled glass. When he reaches the top of the stairs, he flicks off the light switch and I am left in darkness. My feet turn cold and then my shins. I discover that boredom is my greatest fear. I can hear him pacing upstairs and then I hear the electric pop of the TV being turned on. White-hot anger flares up in me. The cold spreads to my hands and then stops. I try to move and I cannot. This is a curious feeling. I strain against the ropes and they remain tight. I try to expel the gag from my mouth. I stand for a few moments, long enough to forget that I cannot walk, and almost fall over when I try. I discover I am terrified of falling, terrified of what he would do to me if he found me lying on the dirty concrete of the floor instead of standing.

After a while I feel myself becoming someone else. I am no longer angry. I want him to come back. That desire shuts everything else up. I stop thinking about getting to the interstate the next morning and the novel I'm writing. I stop thinking about myself. I think only about whether or not I will be able to do the things he will demand of me.

Relief mixes with terror when I hear the heavy clunk of his boots on the stairs again. The light flickers on and I discover I cannot look at him. He is tender when he comes to me, holding my cheeks, whispering "honey" again and again softly. He removes the gag and wipes away the drool that is running down my chin. He kisses me slowly, his tongue filling up my mouth completely, my face in his hands, his thumbs digging into my cheeks.

He breaks the kiss and sits down in a gray folding chair. He says, "Come over here, honey." Ashamed, I hop clumsily to where he sits. "Get down on your knees," he says in the same sweet voice. He spreads his legs wide and I see the outline of his cock underneath the thick fabric of his work pants. I press my face into his crotch, the spit from my open mouth staining his pants darker. He grabs my hair and jerks my head back. "Don't fucking touch me until I say you're allowed to." He slaps my face hard, the sting of it spreading to my neck and lips. His gray eyes spark. "You fucking bitch. If you want my cock so much, I'm gonna make you swallow it." He unzips his pants and the big black dick he won in a drag king contest spills out.

I turn into a faggot when I'm sucking his cock. I can envision my eyes closed, my cheeks hollowed out, the perfect curls of my lashes almost disappearing. I look sixteen, dark-haired, some young boy he's picked up off the street. I gag when he puts his dick in my mouth. This makes him impatient. He grabs my head in his big hands and thrusts his hips so that his cock is hitting the back of my throat. It slams into my throat until I finally open up and let it slide in toward my gut. He has his hands squeeze tighter at my temples to let me know I'm not getting away, that I'm not allowed to breathe until he's done. It becomes a meditation: sneaking in bits of air, finding a way to adjust to the thing that is filling up my mouth completely. I suck him off as hard and fast as I can, the muscles in my jaws and neck aching, the ligaments screaming. I lose who I am while I am doing this.

I come back to earth after he has pulled my head away. He zips his pants and stares at me. I'm still on my knees, the collar tight around my throat. "You're so fucking pretty," he says to me and takes out his knife. He bends down and cuts the rope off my ankles. "Get up," he says and leads me closer to one of the cinder block walls. He unbuttons my shirt, the knife clenched in his teeth. He pushes the cloth down to my tied wrists. They tingle with the motion. He rubs his dick against my ass and pushes my naked torso against the wall. My nipples and cheek grind against the rough block. He puts the knife against my throat and whispers again, "Don't make a sound." I feel his other hand loosening my belt and then my jeans drop down to my ankles. He touches my ass and his hand is slippery with grease. The knife presses tighter against my throat so that I am sure there must be a thin line of blood trickling down my throat and across my collarbone.

He presses the big dick against my asshole and I shudder; my body bucks against him. The cinder blocks tear at my nipples. He is rough with me, sliding the first half-inch into me viciously. It stops when it hits the tighter ring of muscle inside my ass. He moves his hips in short strokes against me, thrusting a little harder each time. He does this until he stretches out my asshole. I sense the rest of the dick before he puts it inside me, feel him drawing back before he slams into me. I feel like I am losing consciousness when I am being fucked in the ass, the pleasure so great that all I can do is open my throat and howl. I forget about the knife against my throat. He fucks me until my tits are bloody and I cannot speak.

The clouds in Nebraska almost made me believe in God again. Plains wide and endless, the skeletal bodies of electric windmills, the sky tumultuous and silver. The snow had almost stopped, a few dry flakes snaking across the asphalt. It must be wretched to live in the Midwest during the winter, I thought, cut off from the rest of the world, land fallow, crops plowed under. The clouds were as large as the earth.

Jake and I slept not a hundred yards from the interstate in Des Moines the night before in a dry ditch covered with leaves. Tall reedy plants grew all around, stalks brown and thin as paper. We stamped out a place to lie down, hard winter stars sparkling above us. We lay half awake and freezing all night, until the sun began to turn the cloudy sky gray. I felt as if I'd never get warm again as we trudged up the on ramp when a woman driving all the way to Denver pulled over and gave us a ride.

After a while landscape becomes conversation. Landscape

becomes impetus and reason. It becomes home. Months before, we stood on a bridge over the Penobscot River in Bangor, Maine, the clear sun creeping up toward noon, the town to the left of us, a conglomeration of church steeples, doorways, and streets. The view from the bridge was enough to justify every step I had taken in my life up to that moment, enough to make up for the hot sun, the highway police, the miles we had walked. New England is mountainous and complicated, Maine filled with people who have gray hands from fishing, from trying to support themselves in small towns with no economy. The silvery timber, Interstate 95 dark and silent but for the occasionally roar of a semi, sea water slamming against beaten faces of rocks so hard that the foam surprised us, wet the lenses of our cameras, the cotton of our shirts— these things are a part of me now.

Cutting across these desolate landscapes, I began to remember the desires I had when I was twelve, I began to dig through the dark earth that existed before I became a teenager, before I turned twenty. I used to dream of being cut, of being beaten. I shoved ice cubes into my cunt on summer nights, tied my feet together and dreamt of being left for dead, made molds of my nipples with hot wax.

It was a surprise when these things began surfacing again, when the touch of him suddenly made me drop to my knees and remember all of the things I used to be. Dreams of stalking through Egyptian tombs, being buried in the hot sand, picking my way through the jagged tops of mountains.

My head is clear when he beats me. Fear supersedes everything else. I sink into myself, dig through layers until I hit bedrock, travel with the rush that is flowing all through me until it emerges, rocket-like, from the side of the mountain. Ancient sediment blasts out over the road and I remember a thousand things I thought I had forgotten.

Jake calls me from Texas after we stop traveling together. He calls me around midnight, his voice tremulous. "Hello," he says to me, half hoarse. The sound hangs in the air between us, passing over hundreds of miles of dark highway. There is no conversation for us to have. I close my eyes and see his body spread across the floor, breath ragged, hands splayed out against the carpet. Standing over him I feel that I am six and a half feet tall, the muscles in my arms and shoulders huge and full of venom, as if parts of me are ready to explode. I grab him by the scruff of his neck and pull him up on his knees, my forearm a thick bar across his chest, pressing against his collarbone. I take my dick out so that he can feel it between his thighs. He moans and arches toward me more. My arm slides up and presses against his neck. His throat caves in slightly and he goes limp against me, his labored breath becoming so loud that it clogs my hearing. We sink into this silence together; memories flash across our field of vision that we have never had before: ships sailing, the fear of falling off the edge of a flat world, discovery of new lands. I touch a space that exists in his chest only in these moments. It is just as wide as the plains in Nebraska.

When I let him go he falls back to the floor, his arms wrapped around his head and neck. I loosen my belt and fold the soft leather around my fist three times. The first blow is soft, hardly making a noise against his shoulder blades. I am careful to build the intensity of how I hit him, layering the blows to cover every inch of his wide shoulders. He is whining softly now, begging me to hit him harder. I want to hit him until I am hoarse, until my voice disappears, until there is nothing but sensation between us. I raise the belt high above my head and bring it whistling down. He screams and I hit him again and again. I follow the movements of his body and strike him in the places that sting the most. I watch his jaws clench and unclench, his eyes closed tightly. I can tell that he has reached a place of absolute trust, that he has given me the right to do anything to him that I want to with the faith that I will not ask too much. I hit him until I am exhausted, until his back is covered with splotches, until his shoulders are black and blue. I collapse onto him, unable to move.

I do not come to the sound of his voice and the insistent pressure of my finger on my clit. I am left full of desire for him; the thick timbre of his voice is not enough. I think of the places we passed through together, the valleys of Tennessee, the tenement buildings in Manhattan, how our bodies claimed these places and made them a part of our interior. I traced the contours of who I was becoming out of the negative space of what our bodies did. I think of this when I look at my hands, the blue veins raised under the skin and curving like the line of Route 5 across Vermont.

Anonymous
Amie M. Evans

She grabs a fistful of my hair before the door closes behind us. She locks the bolt and pulls me over to the bed. "I'll call you Dee and you call me Jimmy. Get on your knees."

As she unzips her pants, the cock I felt on the ride pops out. She pulls my head toward it and hisses, "Suck it, bitch."

It is almost impossible to find anonymous lesbian sex. Maybe in San Francisco or possibly New York City you can find it at an upscale women's club or cutting-edge cruising spots, but not in Boston. Not proper New England Boston. The mixture of Puritan values and lesbian ethics deters casual lesbian anything. But I like a challenge, so I was determined to engage in anonymous lesbian sex in Boston. Anonymous sex with real live lesbians. No exchange of numbers or first-date sex; but rough, hard, no-name sex: the stuff of gay boy novels and urban myths.

It is good to have goals.

I considered personal ads for a while. I read through them, studied them for content and form, and ruled out useless information about beaches, smoking, and cats. Then I wrote my own ad:

Hot, femme dyke bottom (should I hyphenate or not?) seeks sexy butch top (again to hyphenate or not?) for anonymous kinky sexual encounter.

She would call and leave her name and number and we would set up a time and date and I smelled the U-Haul—parked just around the corner.

The second ad I composed reads like this:

Hot femme-dyke-bottom seeks sexy butch-top for anonymous kinky sexual encounter. (At this point I thought hyphens were the way to go. They showed the connection of the identity markers I was using to solicit a sexual partner.) Meet me at the Duck Statue in the Common Gardens on Saturday at 9 P.M. I'll wear a red silk scarf around my neck; you wear a red bandanna on your wrist.

This ad eliminated the phone calls, the messages, the number exchanges. It created the fantasy of being picked up blindly in the park—something I've envied in gay boys since I was first introduced to their culture. But the problem with this ad was that every horny straight guy with a lesbian fantasy who reads the women-seeking-women classifieds would show up with a hard-on. A male gang-bang was not what I had in mind. Not to mention, what if no one showed up? New England dykes—dykes in general, but especially New England dykes—aren't known for their sexual abandon. How many Saturday nights would I have to spend wearing a red silk scarf and standing by the Make Way for Ducklings Statue waiting for Ms. Butch-Top? The Boston Mounted Police would speculate about what I was doing there. An investigation into possible drug trafficking or prostitution would ensue and countless taxpayer dollars would be wasted before they discovered I was just after a cheap lesbian-sexual thrill. Of course, a whole series of newspaper articles on lesbian sexual habits would appear, and the Boston Pride Committee would have to do more than ban a lesbian float featuring an empty bed to prove to mainstream corporate sponsors and the general public that queers don't really have sex. No, the classifieds, as always, were a bust.

What I really wanted was to cruise lesbians. But as a gay male friend pointed out in the 1980s when I first came out: Lesbians don't cruise each other. Then whom do they cruise? I wanted to know. Imagine a place where bunches of lesbians gathered for no other reason than to have sex—anonymous sex. We could have our own system of identifying sexual desires like the boys had with their hankies in the heyday of gay male cruising. Displays on the right for tops and on the left for bottoms carries over into lesbian sex. In fact, a lot of the boys' codes would work for lesbians. Black for leather sex and yellow for golden showers. New colors could be added for lesbian-specific sexual acts. We'd need one for vaginal penetration and one for those who were opposed to penetration. And, of course, a color for the lesbian sexual staple: 69. We could use ribbons instead of those bulky hankies, or colored rope for those in the butchier set.

I'm sure a committee would have to be set up to determine which colors would represent which sex acts. The committee would be charged with making sure the color selections in relation to the sex acts and any social or cultural baggage offended no one. Then they'd want to separate the cruising area by color selections so the antipenetrators didn't have to look at the penetrators while they cruised. Maps of the approved cruising zones divided into plots by activity would be distributed. The zones closest to the bathrooms, center hub, and public transportation would be randomly assigned to the sexual activities the committee members engaged in, and a central, sex-free plot would offer peer counseling for those lesbians experiencing cruising distress. A group of volunteers would patrol to make sure penetrators stayed out of the nonpenetrating plots and that the golden showers didn't venture into the oral sex–only zones. A statement on diversity and respect would emphasize the needs of sexual assault survivors, but exclude the needs of sexual assault survivors who participate in S/M activities. Before long the committee would make the leatherdykes wear signs announcing that they may cause flashbacks and that lesbian-identified MTFs would be picketing the area. No, this wouldn't work—not for lesbians.

I decided to go to a lesbian bar. There aren't any real lesbian bars in Boston, but there are a number of ever-changing one-night-a-week lesbian clubs. The problem with lesbian bars is the music. For some reason the DJs don't seem to keep up with the new dance music hits. No matter how hip the DJ looks, the music always sucks. But I wasn't going to dance; I was going to find a fuck. The clubs were my only option if I was ever going to have anonymous lesbian sex. I went alone, since taking a femme support group with me would turn the covert sexual mission into a giggle feast, and taking a butch friend would mark us as a couple. Since you can never tell who is sleeping with whom, no matter who I took with me for support, my chances of finding a sex partner would be reduced. Alone was the best choice. If I failed, I could wallow without sharing the details with any of my friends, and if I succeeded I would have one hell of a story to share over brunch.

I slipped into a short, clingy black skirt with thigh-highs and a black garter belt with purple trim. I put on a black lace bra with a long-sleeved fishnet shirt. I finished the outfit with a pair of knee-high platform black-leather boots, and a silver dagger necklace that hung just above my cleavage. A little mascara, red lipstick, and a spray of perfume and I was out the door to the club.

The bar was crowded when I arrived at eleven-thirty. Bad dance music was blasting, spun by the very punk-looking May, a local lesbian DJ, so wrapped up in herself that she is unable to play requests even if you are the only one dancing. A handful of dykes in groups of twos and threes were on the dance floor. I scanned for potential sex partners. The spectator crowd on the perimeter of the dance floor was a mix of nondescript andro-lesbians in jeans and button-downs over T-shirts, punky Lesbian Avenger–type college students, and sports dykes in athletic tops. I even noticed one or two femmes in skirts. No one caught my eye, but I made a mental note that a few of the women-watchers were kind of cute.

I walked through the table area on my way to the bar and spotted a really sexy blonde, punk-dyke, but she was with five other punk-dykes talking and drinking beers. Any one of those hot dykes would have done, and since there were five, there had to be at least one single girl among them. I noted the table location and continued to the bar for a drink.

I bumped into the hottest African American butch I have ever seen. She was wearing black dress pants, a pressed white shirt, and a buttoned vest. Her hair was cut Grace Jones style, and she had a pocket watch in her vest pocket attached to a thin silver chain. Her dark skin was flawless. I smiled and mouthed, "Excuse me." She put her hand on mine and mouthed, "No, excuse me." Hmm. She stepped to the side to allow me to pass, and I saw a royal femme in a red dress move in close behind the butch. The femme placed her hand on the butch's back. So much for that. I smiled at them both and made my way to the bar. It felt good to be in a room full of women.

The bar was lined with an assortment of sitting and standing lesbians. Among them I spotted a dark-haired woman in a pair of blue jeans rolled up at the bottom to expose her biker boots. She had on a bowling shirt with cut-off sleeves and sported a chain wallet. Her dark short hair was slicked back, and she looked like a dyke version of a greaser. I watched her swig her beer from a bottle and light a cigarette as she watched the dance floor from afar. Leaning on the bar, she had one foot hooked on the bottom bar rail. She was tight and lean, though she wasn't my usual type—a bit too much James Dean and not enough Sid Vicious—but she was alone, and James Dean beats early Cris Williamson hands down every time.

Approach was everything, since too much chitchat would ruin the cruising feeling I was trying to create against all odds. There were other factors I had to consider: *I might scare her, since lesbians don't act this way as a rule. Or she might think I'm a straight woman trying to pick up a third since lesbians don't look this way as a rule either. She might get outraged since sexual outrage runs close to the skin of my lesbian sisters.* Even if everything went off and she agreed to do this, she might have been one of those oral-sex-only-please lesbians, or worse yet, a bottom.

I put my faith in the fact that she had her wallet chain on the right and that maybe that tattoo on her arm of the busty Betty Page meant more than that she felt pressured to pick a cool image in the tattoo parlor. Not much to put your faith in, but more than a tale of fish and loaves written by an unknown author. I walked straight up to her and looked into her eyes. She held my gaze, a good sign since lesbians seem unable to make eye contact with each other. I leaned into her, almost touching, and put my mouth close to her ear so that she could hear me over the music.

"Are you alone?" I asked.

"Yes." She slipped her arm around my waist and pulled me closer to her, perhaps to ensure we weren't pulled apart by the motion of the crowd.

"Don't tell me your name. Just listen and a simple yes or no answer will be fine."

"OK, talk."

I placed my hand on her upper arm near Betty Page and felt the bulge of a well-developed muscle. "I want to have sex with you. Anonymous, rough sex in a sleazy motel room."

She shifted her weight against the bar, and I leaned into her. I thought I felt the bulge of a strap-on, but I was nervous so I didn't pursue the hunch. "No names, no numbers. Are you up to it?"

She pushed me away and looked at me from head to toe, then pulled me back against her. "Are you a dyke?"

"If you are asking me if I fuck boys or if I am a closet case, no to both. I'm a dyke."

"Let's go, then."

I stepped away from her as she took my hand and led me out of the bar. My heart was racing, and I was wet. My head spun since I never thought I would get this far. Outside, the cooler fresh air hit us and we stopped.

"My car's over there," I said.

"Yeah, my bike's right here." She gestured with her chin to a black Triumph with chrome shined for a Saturday night and fire blazing on either side of the gas tank. She really *was* James Dean.

"Your bike it is."

She handed me a helmet and got on. I situated myself behind her and wrapped my arms around her waist. She pulled onto the road, seemingly knowing where she was going. At the first stoplight she reached back and ran her hand up my leg and under my short skirt. "Tell me what you mean by rough sex."

She pulled the bike into traffic before I could answer.

At the next light I said, "I want you to take me, use my body. I want to have my 'no' ignored." I ran my hand down her hip into her crotch, verifying the existence of the dildo I had thought I felt in the bar. I started to think about the implications of this woman alone in a dyke bar packing, but before I got far the bike stopped at another light.

"Do you have panties on and what's your safeword?" Again she pulled out before I could answer.

"No and 'ice cream,' " I said as she parked in front of a rundown wooden building that at one time was painted gray. A neon sign in the window flashed OPEN in red, and a battered metal sign said MOTEL BY THE SEA. A number of small cottages in various states of disrepair all were in need of paint. The landscaping consisted of white rock paths and clumps of weeds. A few bushes growing unattended dotted the muddy area around the Motel by the Sea. The sea was miles from here. This was definitely sleazy.

I waited outside while she went into the office and paid for a cabin. My skin felt cold from the open ride in the night air. Our cabin was number 3—my lucky number—and I felt like a high-school girl as we walked over to it. I was bursting with excitement but maintained a cool, calm exterior like I'd done this a million times. I followed her to the cabin, watching the slight wiggle in her walk. She had a tight little butt, and I could not wait to get my hands on it.

That's how I got here on my knees in front of this butch I don't even know. I take it into my mouth. It isn't the biggest dildo I've ever had, but it was the first I've ever had in my mouth. I take as much of it in as I think I can handle—about half. My mouth slides up and down the shaft that feels bigger than it looked. I moan an "umm" as it eases in and out. This isn't what I had in mind. I release it from my mouth and hold it in my hand, flicking my tongue on the tip and licking the crown. Jimmy D. puts her hands on the back of my head. I look up at her, not raising my head. She intently watches my tongue work on her dildo. The look in her eyes excites me, makes me eager to please her despite the fact that her cock is made of silicone.

I take it back into my mouth, this time relaxing my throat like the drag queens and gay boys I hung out with in college described. I am able to get more of her cock into my mouth, but not all of it. It slides in and out, and she begins to meet my strokes with her hips, her hands clamping into my hair.

After a few moments of deep thrusting, she pulls me off her cock and tosses me next to her on the bed onto my stomach.

"Get on your knees, Dee." I get up on my knees and lean onto my elbows, my ass in the air.

"No panties. You are a bad girl." I hear her unwrapping a condom. Her hand caresses my bare ass as she gets into position with her knees behind me.

"Such a pretty white ass." Her hand comes down on my cheek in a quick slap, then another. Her strokes are hard and stinging.

"I'm going to put my cock in your cunt and fuck you. Would you like that?"

"Yes," I say and thrust my hips back in anticipation. This is more like it. This is what I had in mind—none of that sucking on silicone; a good fucking is what I want.

She does exactly what she promised, pushing the head of the dildo into my wet cunt and slowly thrusting forward. When the whole cock is inside me she rotates her hips so that the cock bumps against the perimeter of my cunt. She thrusts, slow and easy at first, working up my excitement and feeling out my insides. In and out the cock slides, building up speed and strength with each stroke until she is clasping my ass and pounding into me.

It feels good. Really good. She knows how to use that dildo. My body tingles and my cunt feels excited and full. I want her to make me come. She stops buried deep inside me. For one second there is no movement; I can hear her heavy breathing then a popping as she pulls out. She grabs my thighs and flips me onto my back, positioning herself on top of me and reinserting her cock into my pussy. No hip movement as she pulls my shirt and bra up exposing my breasts but not removing my clothes. Her hands grasp my breasts hard. She rubs them, then brings them together.

"Does it feel good to have me fuck you?"

"Yes. I want to come. Make me come." I squirm under her, trying to get her to start fucking me again.

She pinches my nipples tightly, prodding a moan from me. "I won't make you come unless I can hear how good my fucking you makes you feel."

She takes one nipple into her mouth, working it with her tongue, sucking on it, then biting into the flesh. I moan and push against her with my hips. She groans in response and strokes in and out with her cock.

"No one can hear us, Dee, and anyone who can is doing the same thing we are."

I moan again louder and lift my legs so that she can get deeper inside me.

She pins my arms down with her hands and holds her upper body over me. Our eyes lock for a moment as she fucks me harder. I moan and push against her arms, feel her fingers tighten on my wrists. I groan louder as she fucks me harder and faster. Her strokes are even in and out. She is slamming into my cunt. Her upper body comes down on top of me, and she grabs my shoulders for leverage. I lock my legs at the ankles around her back. She slides in and out, fucking me like a wildcat.

I scream, "Fuck me, Jimmy! It feels so good! Make me come!"

She slips one hand between us and strokes my already swollen clit with two fingers.

"Harder," I gasp.

She strokes my clit in hard tight circles and pounds me with her dildo. I grab her upper arm with one hand and her tiny ass with the other as the shock waves of orgasm rip through me. My hips jerk forward, and my nails sink into her flesh. She stops fucking but stays inside me. Our faces are cheek to cheek, we are covered in sweat, our breathing is rapid. I roll her onto her back. I'm on top now and take a few slow strokes on her cock. She groans low.

"Can I touch you?" I ask, looking into her eyes.

"Yeah," she says, reaching up and pinching my nipple.

I dismount and undo her belt and jeans, pulling them to her ankles. She unbuckles the harness and slips it off. I slide to the floor, and she moves to the edge of the bed as she opens her legs. I spread her outer lips, noticing the soft blonde pubic hair wet with her juices and sweat. I plunge my tongue into her opening then lick straight up from her wet cunt to her clit. Her body involuntarily jerks and she moans. She is so wet. I slip my finger inside her then lightly lick her clit. I move my finger in and out, increasing the speed of my licking and my finger fucking until she groans and her hand rests on top of my head. Her cunt tastes sweet, and I want to tease her, but I don't stop to pursue that course of action.

She grabs my hair as she comes. Her legs twitch, her hips buck, and her other hand grabs my upper arm. I rest my head on her stomach and push my finger deep inside her as an orgasm rips through her.

Jimmy pulls me onto the bed next to her and kicks off her boots and jeans. We lie there a few minutes before she puts her arm around me and pulls me over to her. I put my head on her shoulder and close my eyes to catch my breath. I am exhausted and content, thrilled with the results of my hunt.

I wake up with a start. The sun shines through the blinds. The clock next to the bed says 9:00 A.M. I am angry for having allowed myself to fall asleep. I had just planned on closing my eyes for a few minutes, then calling a cab to take me back to my car at the club. I wonder if I can sneak out and call a cab from the lobby without waking her. I move slowly, dis-entangling my limbs from hers, but she stirs and looks at me groggily, then smiles.

"Hi," I say and smile back as I stand up. So much for that plan.

"Morning," she says as she stretches and yawns.

I'm not sure what to do. I am not supposed to be here. I didn't plan this part. We stare at each other for an uncomfortably long time.

"Do this often?" she says, smiling broadly and scratching her head.

"No. You?"

"No." She gets up. She has a really hot lean body with a cute small ass and piercing blue eyes—a little white-blonde hair color would bring out those baby blues. What am I thinking? This is anonymous sex, not a relationship.

"I've been going to that dyke bar for months. I had this fantasy...." She stops short, blushes a little. "Oh, I forgot. You don't want to hear anything about me."

"No, go ahead." I am interested in her fantasy and that she has been thinking about it and trying to act on it for months.

"OK," she says, walking into the bathroom and not closing the door. I hear her pee as she talks. "So I wanted to have a girl come on to me for sex—just sex."

I giggle, catch a glimpse of myself in the mirror across from the bed, and stop.

"Last night," she says as she emerges from the bathroom and sits on the bed, "it happened."

"I'd been planning this for a long time but never found the right pickup or the right way to find the right pickup." I smile, "Until last night." We start to get dressed.

"Do you have other fantasies?" she asks as she buckles her belt.

"Yeah, tons of them," I say, feeling unusually flat as I go

into the bathroom and close the door. She's not really ruining the fantasy. Last night I knew nothing about her. It's over, and I still know next to nothing about her. What harm is there in sharing our fantasies with each other?

When I come out of the bathroom she is dressed and smoking a cigarette on the bed. I pause for a moment, standing with my hand on my hip, then say, "I want to be paid for sex."

She raises an eyebrow.

"You know: picked up on a street corner dressed like a hooker; negotiate the cost of services; get paid; fucked in the john's car; then dropped off on the corner again."

"Hmm," she says, staring at me, then stands up. "Ready? I'll drive you back to your car."

I nod.

The ride back is uneventful. I am lost in my thoughts and she is quiet. I wonder if I made a mistake telling her my hooker fantasy. I wonder if I'll tell my friends this story or keep it for myself. I wonder about the significance of her packing and if I can go to a restaurant for breakfast on a Sunday morning alone dressed like I am. We pull into the almost empty parking lot of the club, and I point out the blue car as mine. She stops next to it and puts her hand on my inner thigh as I stand between her bike and my car, not knowing what to say.

"What's your name?" she asks.

"Sandy," I say, unusually timid and self-conscious.

"Karen." We both laugh.

"Bye," I say as I walk the two steps to my car and unlock the door.

"Sandy, eight o'clock Saturday night on the corner of Fifth and Washington in Chinatown." She revs her engine.

"What?" I turn toward her, confused.

"Fifth and Washington in Chinatown, Saturday at eight. I have a red '56 Chevy and a dildo twice the size of this." She indicates her crotch with her hand. My mouth drops open at her boldness. "I like my whores in push-up bras and low-cut tops."

She pulls away before I can answer her. My mouth is still hanging open as I get into the car. Cocky butch, what nerve!

I pull the car out of the spot and head for the street. Before I merge into the light Sunday morning traffic I write "5th and Washington, Chinatown" on a scrap of paper. Then under it I write "Karen, 8:00 P.M., Saturday, push-up bra, red '56 Chevy."

Symphony in Blue
Betty Blue

*I spent a lot of my time looking at blue, the color of
my room and my mood: Blue on the walls, blue out
of my mouth....*
—KATE BUSH, "SYMPHONY IN BLUE"

I watched a stripe of sun on the bare wood floor as it traversed
the room over time, a sextant marking invisible stars, while
my fingers wandered idly through the valley between my legs.
Liss used to call me at work and tease me while "jayin' it," as
she liked to call it, lying in just such a patch of cat-gratifying
sun as this.

There was a sort of blue, somewhere between periwinkle
and cornflower, that seemed to permeate the room as the
sun rode over it, though there was no true blue in it, only
cool white walls and the dark stain of the wood. The blue
came from the varying shade and light of trees through the
window, perhaps magnifying a hue of the glass that wasn't
noticeable to the naked eye. Depending on the time of day, it
might be a faded Victorian blue, or a soft, breakable, Asian

blue—like silk, or a delicate egg.

Lying here, looking up into the discolored light, I felt as if I were under water, eyes open, looking up through the crystal-cordial distortion of waves. With both eyes open, the light was merely shifting from white to gray, but if I alternately closed one eye and then the other, it was bluebottle-fly blue, then China-egg blue, then broken-windshield-blue bits scattered across the ground like chips of ice melting in the sun.

And then Liss danced through the aqueous vision, her ice-chip pale eyes smiling that veiled smile that promised passion and loyalty but that fled like a wild and not entirely friendly animal when looked into too deeply, as though love was a challenge or an act of war. That was a blue I would not see again. Liss had taken off for warmer climes at the first sign of love (ergo, trouble), promising to write to try to work things out when she'd gotten them settled in her head—and did not, as both of us had known she would not.

I sighed, my fingers moving more insistently and with more intent. Liss's eyes—they were integral to the image that spurred my fingers on, but what if they were closed? What if Liss had been unable to look into the reflection of her desire as I straddled her hips—those soft and generous hips that felt like a cloud in my palms, so surprising, so soft and ethereal, as if these, too, were ready to fly? What if I had lifted the sash from my robe over the door and slipped it across the ice-pale doubt, tying off Liss's promises and fears, allowing only the midnight blue of the rain and discovery?

Tempo building at my cunt, I conjured it: the slivered outline of Liss's ghostly pale body under the shadow of water-on-glass—a swift-moving rivulet of rain painting her in silver; eyes muted by the rose-patterned sash; skin the color of bone in the monochrome of night. Where I stroked the soft skin between my own thighs, it was the breast of Liss beneath my fingers, hot yet shivering under my touch. I traced the slope, the gentle curvature, seized and pinched the firm, rose center, and *"oh, god, yes,"* my fingers against my clit were Liss's fingers, prodding, tugging, stroking harshly and then easing up, teasing until they became her mouth.

With the eyes silenced, the tongue was forced to say it all. She let it burrow into me, my thumb doing that job for the Liss of my imagination, and *"oh, fuck!"* I was coming before I was ready to, a sort of quick and angry climax, remembering how she would tell me about teasing herself, " 'jayin' it" to the bare tingling edge of her orgasm and then stopping, making herself wait, maybe for days—until the frustration and sheer saturation of her cunt sent her tumbling over into the ecstatic abyss. She would have made, I thought, a fabulous sadist.

I pulled my shorts back over my hips, wiggling into them and buttoning the fly, rubbing my hand once more across the warm and comfortable swell beneath the denim. The sun had gone completely, now, leaving the late-afternoon dusk of the room an ordinary gray.

"Annie?" The door, half shut, swung inward and I scrambled to my feet, guilty and hot faced like a twelve-year-old. "I found the tarp—" Alyn paused, eyeing me quizzically, suspiciously. "What are you doing?"

"Nothing," I said sharply, annoyed at her for the way I was behaving. "Let's just do it."

Alyn scowled, tucking the canvas tarp under her arm. "Are you pissed at me about something? If you don't want to paint it—I mean, it was your idea." A lone, dark curl over one eye gave weight to her scowl and I smiled in spite of myself.

"No, really, let's do it. I was just—wallowing."

Her eyes flickered briefly, regarding me with a moment's more suspicion, and then she shrugged and held out the tarp.

I took one end of the canvas and we stretched it across the room, covering the wood, changing the brooding shadows to a dull backdrop. Alyn pulled the masking tape gun from the back pocket of her overalls and bent down to secure the tarp at the baseboard, the buzzed nape beneath her short curls (soft, fine hair she called "puppy tummy") showing off the long slope of her neck. I began to wish I hadn't wasted that orgasm.

We started on opposite sides of the room with our rollers, spreading the pleasant smell of latex paint. I loved the texture and sound of it as it went on, the soft squish and satisfying gloss of it covering the dimpled landscape of the wall, making it look almost like skin. We had chosen a soft turquoise, a shade just shy of the blue I had invoked, and again it turned my thoughts toward Liss.

It was in this room that we had discovered each other, fumbled in the dark to learn each other's secrets. I had been afraid that she would find my shape too plain and boyish, with a waist and hip that were nearly even; I had always longed for curves. But she had peeled off my panties and pushed up my bra and called me *beautiful,* in a voice that made me want to cling to her and cry. She had touched me with a sense of fascination, as though she had never seen a woman before, hands smoothing over me to read me like Braille. She had placed her lips against my pussy, almost whispering to it—all of her touch was cloud-like.

"You're wallowing again," said Alyn behind me.

I stopped my roller on the single strip of wall that I had been painting, absently repeating the same stroke without moving on. I turned and looked at Alyn, paint on her nose, and deep, dark eyes regarding me. The entire wall was finished behind her.

"Maybe this was a bad idea," said Alyn quietly.

"No, it's great," I said. "It needs painting. I like it already."

"I mean me, moving in."

I dropped my arm and let the roller slide down the wall. "Alyn—"

"Annie, do you want me here or not? I feel like you're somewhere else all the time. Or with someone else. Are you having an affair?"

"Am I *what?*" I reached out for Alyn's hand, but she jerked her elbow to avoid my touch. Pale turquoise paint splattered across my shirt. "Al—" Another flick of paint hit me, this time in the chin. She was flicking the roller on purpose now. "I'm not having an—" *Flick.* "Will you *stop* that?" *Flick!*

I glared at her and flicked back, smattering her cheek with blue. Alyn shook her head angrily and reached out with her roller, smacking it in a straight and steady stroke down the front of my face. I made a swift, furious swipe across hers and she tackled me, knocking me into the section of wall I had managed to paint. We slipped and slid against the wall and I tripped over my pan, sending blue flying. Alyn was covered and she smacked her body against me, sharing the paint, and took me down. We rolled and tumbled on the canvas like pigs in mud, Alyn still trying to wield her roller. I climbed over her and grabbed for the open can.

"Don't you *dare!*" Alyn ordered, barely managing to close her mouth before the full gallon of paint slapped her head-on. She stood astonished, arms spread at her sides in sticky disbelief, entirely turquoise and devastatingly beautiful. I kissed her before she could hurt me.

"Go away!" she protested, trying to fight with me, but she was laughing and pissed all at once, and we hit the floor once more. I rolled with her and climbed on top of her, pinning her arms down as she continued to laugh furiously.

Here beneath me was the warm, flesh-and-blood beauty who had agreed to share my life with me, who hadn't run away at the threat of love. What candle could a ghost-girl hold to that?

"You're a mess," I said, pulling the straps of her overalls down. Paint had dripped down her face and into her once-white ribbed tank, and I lowered it, tucking it below her blue-smeared breasts. "And you're a slut," I teased. "Traipsing around without a bra."

"Shut up," she said, half-heartedly, trying to wipe the paint from her eyes as I freed her arms.

I pressed my hands into the paint on her tits and cupped them, watching the blue squish up between my fingers.

"Don't," she said softly, petulantly, and poked me in the breastbone, one dark-satin eye peeking at me from out of the ocean of turquoise. "You're a jerk."

"I *am* a jerk," I agreed, peeling off my own ruined shirt and unhooking my bra to let our breasts touch. The paint felt like cool velvet.

"And you wallow," she pouted, arching up slightly.

"I'll stop," I said, slipping one hand into the overalls.

"And don't get paint in my pussy," she murmured, pulling the overalls down.

I unbuttoned my shorts and kicked them off, peeling out of my underwear. Alyn bared herself conveniently, with the overalls shoved down just far enough so that I could straddle her, skin to skin.

"You're a slut," I whispered into her ear as I pressed myself against her, paint sliding between us. "Can't even bother to take off your clothes."

"And you're wearing socks," she murmured, hips undulating beneath me. "You're just weird."

I rocked against her slippery pussy, clutching her breast and pinching the nipple, which kept sliding away from me in the paint as she met my motion. Alyn slipped her hands behind my ass and poked one relatively paint-free finger into my cunt and one into hers as she began to thrust harder, making the little sound in her throat, like a pigeon cooing, that drove me wild.

I braced my hands in her paint-slicked curls and drove

my cunt back against her finger, the apexes of our mons still pumping together. Alyn went motionless for a moment, the sign of her impending burst, and then began to pant, her shallow, breathless noises and her finger in my pussy pushing me toward my own climax. Her high, delighted squeal put me over and I wrapped myself around her and came, waves of desire and release fluttering through my cunt as I felt her paint-smeared lips throbbing against mine.

Aqua-eyed Liss, even before she was a memory, had always been a ghost-girl, slightly out of phase. But Alyn was solid, deeply real. I could see growing old with Alyn, without fear. Her heart, beneath layers of paint still slicking between us, was pounding steadily, making promises.

I relaxed against her when we had both calmed down, my hands still in her hair, where the paint was starting to feel stiff. "Alyn," I murmured sleepily, happily. "I've changed my mind. Screw the blue. Let's paint it white again."

From the handprint she left on my ass, I think Alyn preferred red.

Good Old Tyme
Linda A. Boulter

Even the old-timers didn't remember the days of mechanical bulls, animatron broncos, and real, honest-to-goodness pinball machines. When the Old Tyme Gaming Saloon opened its doors, the curious wandered in to see the legends they'd only seen in holostreams or read about in vidzines; the realism that wasn't real was like looking into a mirror looking back at yourself into a mirror.

This was the good old-fashioned reality of gaming. The simple slots with flashing lights, rolling symbols, noises, the notorious one-armed bandit...now that was real. The Saloon drew crowds after its first week and three years later you could always expect a wait on the most popular games. And then there was the headliner, The Rage.

Many a cosmic cowboy sauntered into the joint, slapped his ATM card down, cocksure he would win the million-credit nightly prize for riding The Rage the longest that hour. The Rage was a mechanical bull right out of the '80s souped up with a little modern 21st century technology. It could outperform the real thing and didn't need a spiked harness over its privates to do so. A computer chip implanted in the bull sensed the rider's weaknesses and emotional state. Sensors in its side at stirrup level provided extra action not recommended for the faint of heart. Most of the young bucks thought riding The Rage would be like suiting up to battle in one of the many cyberspace killing arenas. But cyber-fitness can't match real physical shape, so just as many had been carried out on a stretcher or braced between buddies to put ice on black-and-blue balls. The macho types that challenged The Rage scoffed that women never rode the bull; they only rode the men who'd won.

The regulars didn't remember when mechanical bulls were all the fashion. But they will likely never forget the day when the petite redhead with fire in her eyes strolled in and demanded a shot of whiskey straight up. Her tooled leather boots replete with spurs jingled as all heads turned, male and female alike, to see a woman dressed like a western warrior. She wore sturdy, button-up blue jeans topped with fringed leather chaps. Her upper body sported a genuine silk western shirt intricately embroidered and unbuttoned down, just so. Slung over her shoulder she carried a studded blue-jean jacket—obviously couture. And on her head she wore a Stetson, as I later found out. Her stride didn't speak of arrogance, it spoke of surety and *don't fuck with me or you'll reap the results*. She walked up to the bar with a cuntsiness that was cultivated by a strong sense of self-esteem. She paid her 1,000-credit entry fee plus the extra 1,000 credits to meet the current champion, then keyed her name—Dale Evans—into the computer to add it to the list of hopefuls ready to risk life and limb and for sure a sore butt riding The Rage. She was ready to ride The Rage with one goal in mind: winning. Winning meant beating the cocky cyber-cowboys who strutted their machismo and scorned the abilities of a woman.

I'm a pretty good-looking lady myself but let me tell you, that woman was gorgeous. I couldn't keep my eyes off her, and the boss had to warn me several times to keep the prattle up pedaling the hooch and the hits. The more we sell, the more credits are spent on the machines and the more exciting the action is in and around The Rage's Ring.

Every hour, twenty-four hours a day, our announcer warms up the crowd with music and sound effects. Then, precisely on the hour, the purple velvet curtain that surrounds The Rage is hoisted up in the air. The massive sound system built into the walls emanates a giant inhale, and everyone unconsciously joins in as the excitement mounts. It was midnight, the Grand Contenders Hour, when regular challengers might take on the current champion or a young upstart might try to dethrone the current king. Jake, our most talented announcer, worked the crowd.

"Are you ready?"

The crowd replied with polite applause.

"What, I can't hear you? Are you 'Rage' ready?" he shouted.

This time the crowd, swept up in the urgency of Jake's voice, yelled as one, counter thumping and foot stomping.

"Rage, Rage."

Calmly sitting at the bar, Dale Evans tightened the buckles on her chaps, pulled her leather gloves on, carefully making sure they fit as tight and close as her skin. Dale's eyes were fixed on The Rage, her concentration steady, unwavering. My eyes were caressing every inch of her perfectly formed body.

Jake's voice boomed over the roar of the crowd, "This hour we have only two riders. The incomparable, current standing ch-am-peeen, The Red Rider."

A burly, red-bearded, bow-legged man rose from the crowd, towering above them, lifted a shot glass, saluted them, downed it, and then raised his arms together, his hands clasped champion fashion as the room exploded with cheers.

Jake played with the crowd, like a cat with a mouse: "The

Red Rider has six wins, including the longest ride ever...ten, that's right folks, ten loonnnng seconds on The Rage."

At that point, the Techie activated The Rage and the bull started to paw and snort, lunging at the crowd, which roared and gasped at the fury soon to be unleashed. Eight seconds technically is a win, unless your opponent goes longer, and anything beyond that is a sweet bonus.

Jake continued, "And I am informed that our second rider is a first-timer."

The crowd was silenced.

Jake pulled out a card and read with a smaller voice, "Our contestant and challenger to The Red Rider."

A feeble cheer went up, everyone anticipating the great Red Rider's next win. In all, it had taken him over a hundred rides to win only six times. The odds were low that he would win. But all wanted to see the win as the greatest or the longest ever. They wanted to be able to say, "I was there when Red Rider rode twelve seconds and won his seventh." Or, "I was there when Red Rider defeated his great rival, The Hood." All knew that the challenger was an unknown, and the best they could hope for was a record-breaking time for Red. The energy in the room dropped a few notches.

Jake could feel the change. He was nonplused. He was ready to play his winning card in a deck that was loaded in the house's favor. He lifted his eyes to the waiting crowd. His voice started low and began to build.

"Ladies and gentlemen...challengers, past, present, and future...this hour's Challenger against the great, incomparable Red Rider is, uh, Dale Evans."

Dale stood up, her long chestnut hair glinting in the colored lights of the Saloon, her gloved hand rose above her head and waved to the crowd. She did a slight toss of her head and her hair rippled over her shoulder like the mane of a beautiful chestnut mare.

A gasp rippled throughout the room.

"A woman."

"She's little."

"She's gonna get slaughtered."

"What a rip!"

Some turned to go, and others, those who anticipated a blood bath, stayed.

Jake let the crowd hang for one helluva long minute. Then he turned to The Red Rider, who was obviously not very happy with his Challenger, and said, "Red, your choice—who rides first tonight?"

Red scowled.

"I might as well get this over with and get back to drinking. I'll go first. I ain't gonna pick up the pieces of that little woman after The Rage is finished with her. Some challenger!"

More than a few in the audience had their hackles raised by this obviously sexist comment. In fact, suddenly the room was split into two camps: For Red and Against Red—which meant For Dale Evans. Interestingly, not one woman in that room placed her bets on The Red Rider. It was unlikely that a win would assure him one or more sexual partners of the female persuasion for the night. Dale Evans, on the other hand, would likely have her pick of bed mates. I wasn't alone in desiring an evening with this very intriguing woman. Win or lose, I would love to kiss her better, all over.

Mr. Red Rider, like the Cock o' the Walk, strode up to The Rage. The Techie slowed the bull down to a roar. All eyes were on Red as he mounted the beast. He fixed his seat. He turned to smirk at Dale. And then, in a flash of the eye and one buck of that raging bull, The Red Rider went flying over the bull's head and landed ass over tea kettle in the most undignified way, flat on his butt. As he rose, he rubbed his cheeks and skulked out the back door to the sounds of hoots and roars of the women. A hero one minute, a goat the next—it would be a long time before The Red Rider would strut back into the Old Tyme Saloon.

Jake's voice broke over the hoopla.

"Well, folks, it's up to Dale Evans to defeat our current champeen and win one million credits. Stay on for over the current best, ten seconds, and take home a bonus one hundred thousand credits."

Dale rose from her barstool and casually walked to the arena. I was beaming a silly little kid ear-to-ear grin, and for the first time she noticed me. She winked and flashed me a little smile. I blew her a kiss and whispered a prayer in my heart. My boss noticed the kiss, saw that I wasn't doing the rounds. But he also knew that the place was so enraptured by what was soon to happen in the arena that he was sure that afterward the hooch was guaranteed to flow, in celebration of a win, or the drowning of sorrows depending on which sex you were. As I whispered my prayers, I'm sure he was counting the cool credits in hooch and hits that a win could bring him.

Dale was now in the arena with Jake. He started to say, "It is my duty to inform you of the rules for riding The Rage."

At this point he attempted to drape an arm around her shoulder in a patronizing way. She simply brushed his arm away and spat, "I know the rules and I'm ready now."

Someone jeered; someone else hooted.

Jake said, "Fine."

Those of us close up could hear him say under his breath, "Die, you bitch."

Dale Evans carefully mounted The Rage. She adjusted the stirrups so that her spurred heels were at the level of the sensors that, when kicked, rocked The Rage into even more fury. She grasped the reins in one hand. Then she plunged her spurs into the animatron's sides, the bull snorted, lurched forward, Dale caught herself, her thighs gripping tight on the big beast's back. The animal bellowed like the ear-splitting sound of a foghorn of old. It bucked, front legs aggressively, jerked onto its back legs, all the while throwing its head from side to side trying to gore off its rider. Sweat beads of concentration dripped down Dale's brow. The bull was shaking its burly head, showering those nearby with foamy saliva. The bull snapped and reeled. Dale only clung tighter. Every muscle in her quads was pumped and straining to keep her seat on the beast. With every violent movement of the bull, the two rode as one. Under her glove, no doubt her hand was white to the knuckle. The Read-o-Graph seemed frozen, the seconds suspended in time.

Dale heard in the background voices yelling, "Five. Six. Seven. Eight. Nine. Ten."

The crowd roared, she'd beaten the Red Rider's best. The counting continued, "Eleven. Twelve. Thirteen...."

And then a simply amazing thing happened at thirteen seconds when time was on Dale's side: The Rage began slowing down. First the bucking stopped, then the bull's big head and tail drooped down, and finally the bellowing became a sick-sounding bawling moan like a baby calf wanting milk from its mommy, and then the machine just stopped. Stopped dead.

Dale slid off the bull onto legs that felt like jelly, but she never hit the ground because I was there to catch her. She simply looked up into my eyes and before she fainted said, "Oh, my."

The boss instructed Big Eddie, the bouncer, to carry her up to his private suite. And then he gave me the night off. I guess he figured he could guarantee his gourmet meal ticket if one of his employees was her lover. I beat off her admirers.

When Dale woke up in the boss's king-sized bed, I was there holding a glass of pure Aqua Gold to her lips. She sipped it gratefully. With the most sultry voice imaginable, she looked into my eyes and said, "I do believe I've died and gone to heaven."

She then drawled, in a sweet southern accent that sounded

like music to my ears, "And who might *you* be, my angel?"

She was as smooth as silk, and now I felt like I was going to faint.

"I work here, I'm Tessie, one of the bar girls."

She toned, "Hmmmm. Well, Tessie, I want to give you a big southern kiss for letting me wake up to an angel."

She put her arms around me, and ever so gently her tongue found its way into my mouth. Before I could come up for air, I was panting.

She reached under my outfit and teasingly said, "I thought it would be me who was a little swollen—you must be a very empathetic person."

I could only nod in pleasure, as she had found my nipples firm and ripe beneath my bodice that was part of the Old Tyme Saloon uniform. Her gentle hands lightly caressed my breasts, my nipples hardening even more. I felt like I was going to come right then under her touch.

She continued, "Help me slip these chaps off. And give me a hand pulling off these boots—but mind the spurs, 'cuz a cowboy may go to bed with his boots on but not this gal."

I unbuckled the chaps, which smelled of leather, and I wondered if they were real or just sleather (synth leather infused with leather scent buds). The spurred boots clunked and jingled to the ground. She pulled off her gloves, finger by finger, and then those slender fingers started to undo my dress hook by hook, punctuated by tongue probing and stroking. She nibbled my ear and I could hear her sultry voice begin to moan and pant. She was as turned on as I. I helped unbuckle her belt and she lifted her butt off the bed as I slid her jeans over her hips and to the floor. I gasped. Underneath she was wearing a black leather strap-on. It was gleaming from a mixture of sweat and cream, for, while the ride had turned the bull off, it had definitely turned Dale on. When the jeans slid to the floor, the dildo stood at attention.

She laughed, "Ahhh yes, meet Dick—at your service and for your pleasure."

I stammered, "How do you ride with that beast between your legs."

She laughed, "Oh, I just kind of tuck it back. It flattens and acts as a cup to protect my privates."

I grasped the head of Dick and it was her turn to gasp. She was obviously wearing the latest sensor-activated strap-on that stimulated clit and cunt with the merest touch of the dildo. I leaned my head down and ran my tongue around the tip of Dick, whose finely shaped contours were not a mimic of a penis but a unique creation. It was warm, soft yet hard. The head was similar to a small tongue and as I sucked, it moved. And she moaned. Dale held my head between her hands. Her hips rocked gently forward as my mouth explored the taste and touch of her Dick.

"Oh girl, that feels so good. Please take all your clothes off. I want to taste you and smell you."

As she spoke, she undid the shiny buttons of her silk shirt, leaving only a bandanna tied around her slender neck. Her small, perky breasts did not need the taming of a constrictive bra. They only needed my lips to nibble and gently pull each brown button to erection. She pulled me down on top of her. Strong arms embraced me, firm hands traced the curves of my body, soft lips suckled my brown nipples. I held her close, my fingers wandering around this new-to-me body, every muscle cut and firm. I love the feel of a woman who wears her muscles well defined. As my fingers touched her, her tongue explored every inch of my flesh. Tracing the soft, downy hair from navel to pubis and beyond, I was trembling when her breath lightly caressed my labia. She did not linger but savored every moment as she moved downward, traced down each leg, licked behind each knee until she sucked and gently bit each toe. Finally, when she ventured back up to the jewel of my desire, I was panting to have her fingers inside me, her tongue lapping up my nectar.

As if she had memscan, she fulfilled my desire. And, then as my body burst into orgasm, I felt the tip of the dildo slip past my labia and fill my pussy. My muscles clenched tightly, drawing her into me, my arms holding her as if I never wanted to let her go. She rode me as gently as the little beast I am. My hips involuntarily bucked as orgasm after orgasm swept over me. Her moaning and quaking were evidence that we were coming and coming and coming together. Our bodies were slick, the bed was wet as our passions overflowed. With a sigh, I lay in her arms, with her still inside me. The little tongue of Dick was gently pulsing inside me, massaging the spot that sent small earthquakes through my body.

Dale smiled at me, sighed, and said, "Now, I know I'm in heaven."

Redemption
Michael M. Hernandez

She parted the heavy leather curtains and entered the bar, one of the oldest on Warmoesstraat, suffering that temporary blindness that accompanies travel from light into darkness. At the moment it was impossible to see without infrared vision. It was easy to believe that it was the bartenders' fault. The fumbling around in the darkness ensured that the power balance remained with those who were serving. Then again, more than likely the reason for keeping the bar so dark was that darkness invited raw sexuality. Light tended to drive out the beast within. The darkness served another purpose than employee entertainment. It allowed those sitting along the bar to feast their eyes upon their future conquests without the potential "victim" receiving the reciprocal benefit.

Ian knew that if she could just stroll up to the bar without tripping over anyone or her own two feet, her eyes would adjust in the amount of time that it would take the bartender to bring her a drink, and that itself would increase her opportunity to score tonight. In this bar, the balance of power was paramount. Appearances were everything.

Anyone who forgot that would soon have the tables turned.

She was the smoothest of operators, clad immaculately in black leather from the Daddy cap on her head, down to her steel-toed motorcycle boots, blending easily with the raw masculinity of the majority of the bar's patrons. She wore faded blue button-down 501s under her chaps revealing a rather large basket. As she approached the bar, she absentmindedly reached down and stroked her cock. Her leathers, while clean, did not radiate that polished gleam that came from the pristine butches or leathermen. While she respected the traditional values of the older generation, such fastidiousness was not her style. She was dependent on her ability to blend into the background. All the good hunters in the animal kingdom depended on good camouflage. The respectable fade of her leathers increased her chances of remaining hidden in the alley, of watching from afar without being spotted, and of disappearing without a second glance. She could move through the Warmoesstraat and be noticed at the time of her choosing.

Tonight she wasn't looking for anything in particular. Butch, femme, either/or, punk, something else. Thrill-seeker tourists from Germany or the United States were always good and hungry. Anyone would do so long as they were a good time. Gender was irrelevant. It was all about a quick thrill, sex in a public place, and her getting her rocks off. She didn't have to go far nor did she have to take her clothes off to bury her cock in some young mouth. The alley behind the bar would do quite nicely for starters. Her dick twitched. She could smell a potential partner within a two-mile radius. A little verbal sparring and the next step was the alley. If "it" sucked well enough, they'd go back to her fuck pad in the Jordaan. Blindfolds were used as a matter of course. The combination of blindfold and her neighborhood, which was less than welcoming at night, also prevented visitors from appearing at her play space uninvited. She'd interrogate a scene out of "it," then play to her heart's content, although her heart was not usually the organ that got the action. Actually the word *play* was too mundane of a description of what she did. It was more like...feeding.

That was it. She consumed her prey. It was the emotional juices that she craved as well as the physical ones. Emotions such as fear, desire, passion—that is what she sought to elicit. That, and the skeletons that everyone hides carefully in the closet.

Barst safe, sane, and consensual! It was the edge of non-consensuality that lured her and in turn lured her victim. No, *victim* was too harsh a word. *Quarry* was more like it. She did not feed often. Prey that proved satisfactory were few and far between, but when found, a veritable pleasure. She, like her cats, played with the mousies before the spilling of guts upon the floor, metaphorically speaking of course. Through her skill, Ian was able to carefully excise and bring the souls of her partners into the light of day where she played until she tired and moved on to the next one.

If her quarry showed enough initiative to stop the scene, she did so promptly, reapplied the blindfold, and drove back to the bar. No looking back, no regrets, no second chances. She played for keeps. Catch and release kept her skill honed. Only once had the prey *really* meant it. The others complained all the way back to the bar about the scene having terminated. Some begged for a second chance, but Ian was resolute. Rules, while bent from time to time, were never broken. In that she was absolutely intolerant. She had no intention of changing a damned thing. That was the way she did things now. No long-term commitments. No mess. No smell. No headaches. No transatlantic phone calls in the middle of the night. No scathing notes pinned to her door with knives. No clothing chopped into tiny bits or personal effects hoarded or destroyed. Oh, her life had drama enough, but it was limited to the drama that she carefully created for herself. She ran the fuck and if the fuck did not want to be run it could go elsewhere. There were plenty of other fucks for the having.

Somehow, she had failed with the last one. Denise. The fact that she remembered a name showed how much that one had gotten to her. It fueled her hunger. A real virgin was a rare find these days. Oh, not that type of virgin. It was innocence that drew her. A clean slate. Fresh, undiscovered, unexplored, untainted by the views of the so-called community. That one filled her thoughts and dreams until she screamed at the walls. She had taken her sweet time and then tossed her out when she had been sated. It had been sweet, but the woman wanted to cling to her for some reason. Unacceptable. It was now a matter of principle. *Verdomme!* "Never go back," she whispered under her breath, and that statement was enough to create the reality for her. She tore herself away, slightly angered at her daydream through the past.

Ian was hungry tonight, very hungry, but she refused to let it show. That would certainly deter her potential candidates for the evening. She slowly unwrapped a cigar and worked it in and out of her mouth, coating the end with saliva. She removed a small silver cigar cutter from the breast pocket of her motorcycle jacket and precisely placed a *V* cut in the cigar. She surveyed the room as she placed the cigar between her lips, rotating it counterclockwise.

Two young punk dykes practically tripped over each other in an effort to light it for her. The cute punk with the jet-black mohawk glared at the shorter skinhead whose scalp was adorned by an elaborate and colorful Celtic knot tattoo. In a split second the room erupted into violence as the mohawk took a swing. Her target deftly removed her face from the fist's trajectory, miraculously causing mohawk to miss. They somehow managed to get into a bear hug and proceeded to knock over several chairs, then fly over a table before crashing to the ground. It was a scene right out of an old Western.

While Ian was enjoying this entertainment, a set of long, perfectly painted red nails came suddenly into view. The thumbnail expertly flicked the head of a safety match, providing the fire for her stogie. *Impressive,* she thought, *very promising, indeed. This one knows that lighters are not for cigars.* Even more impressive was that fact that the femme was not afraid to split a nail or ruin the polish. *Hmm, wonder what she's lookin' for?* Ian flashed a wolfish grin. The *dame* flushed. *Good, good.* This looked promising. Promising indeed.

Ian leaned into the flame and puffed until she was certain that the cigar was lit, then turned her attention to the *dame* attached to the nails. She was struck by the intensity of the eyes. Ian was captivated as surely as a black widow spider's mate. The magical moment was broken by Artie's bellow and his baseball bat hitting the counter. Patrons went scrambling for the corners. "*Wel verdomme!* Cut that crap out, you *rotkoppen,* before I collar your *kutten* and chain you to the goddamned bar. You're gonna get fucked nine ways to Sunday and I guarantee that ya ain't gonna like hot pepper oil being used as a lubricant." The fight stopped mid-punch.

Artie, the bartender, was a force to be reckoned with. Her no-nonsense approach to trouble was well known in Amsterdam and gaining speed throughout the leather bars of Europe. Like any story in the community, it was embellished and passed along from flapping lip to eager ear. The latest rumor flying around was that leatherboys and baby dykes disappeared, never to be seen again. Secretly, Ian believed that Artie enjoyed the artificially created reputation and did everything to continue its embellishment. Artie continued to glare and the baby butches sheepishly looked down at their Doc Martens.

Ian threw her head back and started laughing so hard that

her eyes watered. The new lady, startled at first, was quickly caught up in Ian's contagious laughter. She had a delicate, full-throated laugh that was musical. Artie glowered at them as well. No one was above reproach. They moved away from the bar still chuckling to themselves. No sense tempting fate.

In a better lit corner, Ian sized up the *dame,* taking a puff on her lit cigar in appreciation. The stranger was a tall drink of water, or so Ian thought until she looked down to gaze upon the five-inch spiked stiletto heels. In the heels were a pair of picture-perfect legs enmeshed in black fishnet stockings. Ian's gaze wandered up the legs and just managed to spy the garters underneath the brilliant green velvet dress that the *dame* was l-i-t-e-r-a-l-l-y poured into. Ian's heartbeat doubled. Ample cleavage peeked out from between the sweetheart neckline of the dress. Ian's gaze continued upward across that white porcelain expanse of cleavage to return to the most probing gray-green eyes that she had ever seen. Liquid gold floating in a sea of green. Blazing red hair, and not from a bottle either. Cocksucker red lipstick adorned the full, luscious lips. Where had this woman come from? A tourist, perhaps, visiting the bars in the Red Light District? In for a little action? Ian hoped that was the case.

The *dame* took in Ian's perusal with a smile. There was an impish glee in her eyes. Something said but not quite spoken. Almost as if she had the inside scoop on a private joke. Ian smiled back. This was more than she could hope for. "*Bier?*" she asked, checking to see that Artie had calmed down. The lady smiled and, to Ian's surprise and delight, went to the bar herself, leaning toward Artie to murmur the order. The drinks were produced in record speed. When she returned, the *dame* offered one of the beers to Ian. They clinked their glasses, and Ian downed hers quickly, needing the refreshment badly.

Almost before the glass was set down, the woman wove her fingers into the hair at the back of Ian's neck. Situating her lips upon Ian's, she maneuvered her tongue gracefully and insistently into her mouth, running it slowly and deliberately across her teeth and tongue. The kiss increased in its passion. She gracefully insinuated her leg in between Ian's thighs, finding the dildo resting there. She pressed the base skillfully into and around Ian's clit while continuing to explore Ian's mouth with her own. Ian's responded. A moan was torn from her lips as she encircled the woman in her arms. Passion won out over patience. They both parted breathless and full of desire. A fine sheen of sweat had broken over Ian's brow. She had to have this woman. NOW.

"Let's get out of this pool hall," whispered Ian.

The woman smiled and lifted her glass to Ian, "May you never grow bored and live in interesting times."

"*Dank u,*" responded Ian, and gallantly held her arm out to the woman. The *dame* flashed a perfectly dazzling smile and took the proffered arm. Heads turned as they walked through the bar. There was a fair amount of whispering and, with each step, Ian's ego grew. She was on top of the world and certainly felt it. Pushing the leather curtain aside, she felt as if she were floating on clouds. As they stepped around the corner, Ian noticed that the light emitted by the street lamp had a sharp edge to it, and the canal at the end of the Heintje Hoekssteeg seemed to draw closer, then withdraw. Just then she noticed that she was moving in slow motion.

She tried to mention it to confirm her observations, but her tongue felt thick and dry. The words just would not come. Panic caused adrenaline to flood through her system, but it was not enough to speed the passage of time. Just then she noticed that her legs were jelly. She staggered as the night rushed in to greet her. The last image that she saw was the face of the *dame* above her, bearing the most incredible smile. It looked...perfectly wicked. "*Wel verdomme?...*" was the last thing that she managed to say before she lost consciousness.

Morgan had been *furious* when Denise suddenly dropped out of the program. Denise represented several months' worth of cultivation as potential material for the Marketplace. Morgan, unlike other spotters, employed the services of various under-scouts to do most of the legwork. This ensured that Morgan did not waste all of her time culling through individuals who would never even be considered for training. The job of the scouts was to bring potential property to her attention. If it proved worthy of consideration, the scout received a fee. A scout was given three opportunities to present talent. Three strikes and you were on your way out. Three outs and you were *kapot*. Morgan had developed a nice network that allowed her to present ten to twelve candidates for consideration per year. It was expensive for her, but worth it, if she could keep up that pace.

Denise presented rather unique properties. A novice who had very deep-seated desires plus intelligence, wit, imagination, and a sense of adventure while exuding a naïveté that was unparalleled. A battery of tests had been performed to determine the extent of Denise's potential.

Then, this, *dumkopf*—no, this *kuttenkopf*—had just waltzed in and done as she pleased, ruining months' worth of work, not to mention the lost fees. It was not the first time that Ian had interfered with Morgan's plans, but it would be the last. "Justice, justice shalt thou pursue" ran through her mind, although deep in her heart Morgan knew it was revenge, not justice. She should not take it so personally, but Morgan took everything personally.

She had carved out a reputation for herself for being a fair, but wicked, top. She abhorred femmes who pretended to be stupid or who used their body to manipulate others into doing what they wanted. Morgan's style was more direct. She was the preeminent flirt who was quite able to clearly communicate her needs during the seduction. If the other person was willing to participate, then everyone was happy.

In the past few weeks, she compiled information about Ian, her tactics, her prowling ground, what she smoked and drank. That was another thing that the scouting system did well: compile information. Well, someone had to teach this *kuttenkopf* a lesson. Ian's interference, coincidental or otherwise, just wouldn't do. Morgan should have moved in a little more quickly on Denise, but wanted to make sure that the proper level of desire had been attained. Denise was more than a bottom, she had service in her blood. Clearly, that little delay gave Ian the edge. Denise was ready and was losing patience for the delays and hoops that Morgan was making her jump through to get what she wanted. Well, little Denise got more than she bargained for. It might still be possible to salvage the situation, but only at great effort.

Morgan owed the two punks, but paying off those debts would be more of a pleasure than a chore. The diversion caught Ian off guard, gave her an amusing distraction that allowed for a spectacular entrance and seduction. Such a challenge: to distract another hunter, even an amateur. So delightful to succeed so utterly. Well, enough of those delicious thoughts for now. Justice would be hers and it was time to pay the piper.

Ian opened her eyes and immediately regretted it. What little light illuminated her surroundings had a hazy sort of quality. Her tongue still felt thick and her hip hurt. She tried to wipe the sleep from her eyes, learning then that her wrists were securely fastened by thick leather restraints, the kind that they use in psychiatric wards, to the chair that she was sitting in.

The itchiness around her chest and crotch became more acute as she grew more conscious. Ian saw that a small network of wires crossed her body, disappearing under her shirt, down her jeans, and on her hands and feet. The wires all left her body and ended in a black box that Ian recognized as a machine used by physical therapists to make atrophied muscles jump with small, uncontrollable jerks—making the machine popular with certain fetishists, as well. Ian attempted to pull her wrists out of the restraints, but between their design and the strength of the chair, it was impossible. There was nowhere for her elbows to go. The restraints were tight enough to bind her, yet loose enough to be comfortable if she didn't thrash about. No way out of these at the moment. If only she could get to her belt. She had a long wire taped to the inside of it for emergencies such as these.

She heard the sound of heels on concrete and caught a whiff of perfume before she saw the *dame* appear. "How was your nap, dear?" the redhead queried.

"Whoever you are, I'm sure we can work this out. All you need to do is let me go and...."

"What's the matter," Morgan's voice dripped with sarcasm, "don't you like my hospitality?"

"Hospitality??! Is that what you call it. Look, lady, I asked nicely. Don't make me lose my temper. This is nonconsensual."

Morgan laughed as she approached Ian. "Well, goodness knows that I wouldn't want to do anything like that." Morgan slapped her across the face so hard that Ian's ears rung. She got less than an inch from Ian's nose and whispered in a breathless sexy voice *à la* early Lauren Bacall, "Don't insult my intelligence by mentioning consensuality. That's never stopped you before—or didn't you recognize the recipe for the mickey that was slipped in your drink? Artie told me you should be familiar with it. So then," she lilted mockingly, "you have no idea what this is all about. Do you?"

"*Barst,*" Ian spat through gritted teeth, angry at her situation—and astonished that Artie knew about her little helper. Filing that away to ponder on at a later date, she glared into the startlingly gray-green eyes of her captor and growled. Ian was not a bottom and was not about to be treated as such by the likes of this bitch—*rotwijf,* she growled to herself—or anyone else for that matter.

"Tsk, tsk, tsk," said Morgan shaking her head. "Manners. Manners."

"*Barst!*" Ian spat again. "I demand to be released this instant."

"Released? As you wish." A knife blade immediately materialized under Ian's chin, pricking her ever so slightly. "Ask and ye shall receive. Luke 11:9," the woman said. She deftly began to slice the jeans off her and in the process "accidentally" cut Ian's left thigh. "Oh, dear," cooed Morgan as a thin line of blood started its descent toward Ian's knee, "how clumsy of me. I should tell you that I can be a *dumkopf.* Oh well, it is of no consequence. These things do happen. I suppose that you should be particularly careful if you see any sharp objects in my hands. One never knows," she said as she waved the knife over Ian's thigh, "what may happen." The end of her sentence was punctuated by another rapid slice. Ian felt the burning sting before she saw the knife move and heard a sound escape her lips before she could stop it. "This will never do," smiled Morgan as she wiped her knife off on Ian's face. "I think I must find another way to release you."

The smell of blood assaulted Ian's nostrils. She closed her eyes as a wave of desire washed over her, piqued by the smell of blood, feeling her body dance between fear and desire. Ian had been a blood whore from day one, but this little foray made it clear that, if she was not careful, her passion would betray her in front of this *rotwijf.*

Well, this was certainly going to be fun. Morgan noticed Ian's breath catch during the brief drawing of blood. Morgan continued to cut away the jeans, being particularly careful not to cut her prey anymore. In this case, it just wouldn't do to allow the pleasure to outweigh the fear.

"There is nothing like a virgin bottom," Morgan teased the squirming butch. "I've heard about people who exclusively topped, but I've never believed it, really. It's a simple matter of knowing the territory. Exclusive tops lead a rather one-dimensional life, wouldn't you agree?" She paused, as if for a response, but Ian remained silent and struggled briefly against the bonds.

"I have been waiting patiently for this opportunity," Morgan continued, tapping her knife on Ian's crotch. " 'To me belongeth vengeance and recompense.' Deuteronomy 32:35, or, as they say in Sicily, 'Vengeance is a dish savored cold,' and vengeance shall be mine."

"*Barst,*" Ian answered, spitting a wad of saliva onto Morgan's left cheek.

Morgan knew she could not tolerate Ian's breach of etiquette for even a moment. Sometimes she gave latitude to a person exploring their submission and masochism, as she had with Denise. But, of course, it was this *kuttenkopf* who spoiled it all.

Morgan wiped her face and turned her attention to Ian's jockey shorts, poising her knife over Ian's crotch. Most butches had one major weakness: their dildos. She noted that Ian immediately froze, not even breathing for a moment. Morgan carefully cut away Ian's shorts, allowing her meat to spring free. "And what have we here? A Marty. I thought that they stopped making these years ago."

Even in her panic, Ian was impressed that Morgan recognized her cock. Italian design, produced in America, a "Marty" was the top of the line. The crème de la crème of cocks. It was comfortable yet practical, soft enough for that deep-throat action yet firm enough to fuck with. None of the usual 6, 7, 9, and 13-inch standard sizes. If you wanted one 4 and 3/8's long and 3 inches in diameter, Martino Bagnelli would design it for you. Of course, being the artist that he was, he would try to convince you of what he perceived to be the appropriate size based on your height, weight, body type, and hands. Apparently Bagnelli did not quite understand the concept of *packing* versus *fucking* dicks.

Her romp down memory lane was interrupted as Morgan's knife touched the head of her cock. Ian began to sweat. She was really attached to this dick and could not bear the thought of losing it. There was no replacement for it, and would not be, since Bagnelli had disappeared or retired, depending on which rumor you believed. Clearly, whatever she had said at the bar could not have offended this woman enough to subject her to a castration! She tried to remember the events leading up to this little scene. The concentration required to think and stay still was beginning to give her a headache.

"It is a beautiful piece of work," Morgan said, tapping her knife on Ian's cockhead. "It's a shame to ignore it, no matter who it belongs to." She reached over and embedded the knife in the table next to the black box, then took a condom, opened it, and slipped it into her mouth. She kneeled, placing her hands on Ian's legs. Leaning over she slowly moved her open mouth near the cock. Ian felt the warm moistness as the *dame* blew air onto her lower abdomen, her cock, and legs. Once the mouth came near her cock again, Ian pushed her legs toward Morgan, hoping to shove just the head into that waiting mouth. Her efforts were rewarded by a severe burning sensation when Morgan used her thumbs to stretch open the cuts on Ian's thighs. Morgan rose on her knees and nuzzled Ian's cheek. Lowering her voice to a breathless whisper *à la* Marilyn Monroe, she said, "Thus far I have only corrected your bad manners. Soon enough you will learn that I will hurt you because it gives me pleasure." She leaned back and gazed into Ian's eyes. "Nothing and no one can save you. Remember, you asked for this."

The words shook Ian to the core, making the trickles of

blood on her thighs feel ice cold. How was it that a woman whom she did not know, whom she had not met before, could echo her words so clearly and concisely? It was not exactly a line. Ian did not believe in lines, but she had performed the exact series of moves—that chin nuzzle, the voice inflection, the heightening of the fear factor that could be considered her personal trademarks. Edge players tended not to discuss their techniques. She had declined to teach a number of workshops on edgeplay for the weekend kink crowd, the sexual tourists. Her dialogue tended to change with the reactions of her prey, but these words were too familiar.

And then her cock was deep in the mouth of the *dame,* being worked slowly back and forth. Ian felt the friction of teeth sliding across the shaft, and the throbbing of a tongue against the head that vibrated down the core of the dildo to her clit. All the moves she demanded from her tricks. *Wel verdomme!* That thought cleared Ian's head for a moment, a small part of her brain able to still think as the cocksucking shifted in speed and intensity. This little bar pickup was not a random encounter, but preplanned and perfectly executed. Ian thought back on her previous expeditions. She would have noticed this *dame* at a bar irrespective of how she was dressed. Ian had a photographic memory when it came to faces. She had not met this woman before and had never seen her at a contest or other leather event. But clearly, she was no tourist.

Ian closed her eyes and tried to think of something else, but she could not escape the throbbing and sticky wetness of the blood moving down her thigh and the pulsing of her clit against her dick. She moaned as the woman swiftly buried her mouth all the way onto Ian's cock, taking it to the back of her throat with no effort at all.

Just before Ian was ready to explode, Morgan pulled away, and with a quick flick of the knife she still held in her hand, she cut the dildo harness off of Ian. Removing the Marty, she placed it on the table next to the knife, a bizarrely erotic still life.

Morgan stayed between Ian's thighs, her thumbs resting on the still-fresh cuts. "This is your last chance to apologize, and make amends."

Ian swallowed, her cunt still throbbing from the incomplete orgasm. This bizarre drugging-cum-bondage-cum-fear-and-terror-with-threat-of-electricity scene seemed to be ending. It was clear this *dame* had a few cups missing from her cupboard. Rather than fighting it, Ian figured it would be best to play along, until the bonds were untied. Then she could pull off the electrodes, grab her Marty, and get the fuck out of wherever she was. Later, she would have more than adequate time to revel in the joys of planning and executing an exacting retaliation. "I'm sorry," she said quickly.

"For what?"

"For not pleasing you." Ian hoped that the sarcasm didn't show in her voice.

"Oh, is that the only reason why?"

Ian was confused. *Why should I have to apologize to this rotwijf in the first fucking place? She fucking drugged me and brought me here. What the hell is this all about? If I can just figure that out, maybe I can bargain my way out of this.* Ian had to maintain control at all costs. Buy her time until she could escape.

"Well?" Morgan asked as her thumbs again pressed against cuts, watching Ian's eyes roll back slightly.

"Umm. I don't know what you are talking about."

Morgan slowly leaned over, showing Ian an impressive cleavage, and whispered "Denise" in her ear. Ian's jugular pulsed a little more strongly and that pungent scent of fear emanated from her armpits. "Yes, even *you* remember Denise, don't you?"

"All right, all right, I'm sorry I played with your *kut* Denise, or whoever the fuck she was," Ian growled. "I even admit it was the hottest scene I've have in a long time. But Denise was just a one-time thing." *And she obviously wasn't getting what she wanted from you, rotwijf,* Ian said to herself, forcing her mind away from the scent of the blood and the pleasurable pain of Morgan's thumbs on her cuts.

"That's the problem with you, Ian," Morgan responded. "You are one of those dreadfully shallow people who believes that a hot scene is the highest achievement you can reach. It's a shame, really, because there's so much more possible. Denise knew it, and was working to get there—until you placed yourself like the proverbial stumbling block before her."

"What kind of *bullshit* are you talking about?" Ian snarled. "Denise never said she belonged to anybody, and the hungry little *kut* certainly didn't stumble following me home! In fact, she was pretty near begging me to take her and keep her forever!" Ian smirked, sure now that this was a lover's quarrel, and feeling no need to apologize for being the better top.

Morgan slapped Ian again, following it with a caress across her cheek with her nails, enjoying the involuntary shiver it provoked in her victim. Leaning forward, Morgan purred, "Listen, and listen carefully. You don't seem to understand that you have committed a grave error. You played with the wrong girl. Not yours to do or to choose. You had the ill manners to enjoy it. In fact, you enjoyed it without thought, without doubt, without honor, and without a price."

"Listen, lady, I don't know what your problem is...."

"My problem is you, *kuttenkopf.*" Ian's eyes snapped up in shock at the obscenity, but Morgan continued. "Your interference has cost me a great deal of time and potential...." Morgan stopped, realizing her anger made her say too much. She had almost said "fees."

"What the hell are you talking about?" Ian asked, seeing

that the question made Morgan uneasy, and remembering part of that long-ago conversation with Denise. "Wait. This is about this—this *Marktplaats?*"

Morgan paused, stunned that Ian knew. Half a heartbeat later, she realized Ian didn't know, and was just repeating something heard, no doubt from the traumatized Denise. She needed to turn Ian's mind away from that thought, and quickly.

Moving swiftly, Morgan jerked the knife out of the table. Out of the corner of her eye, Ian saw the *dame* hold her Marty down, and, with horror, saw the knife descend toward it like a guillotine.

Ian's stomach dropped. "What the FUCK are you doing?!" she screamed. There were times when the American curses seemed so much more...intense.

"Language, dear, language," Morgan said, clearing the debris from the table, but Ian continued her multilingual cursing, straining at her bonds until she grew hoarse and bruised, and, finally, sobbing. Her Marty, her favorite dick, her best, irreplaceable.

Morgan stood watching her, quietly, with a smile *à la* the Mona Lisa until Ian finally slumped over, angry tears streaking her face, coughing herself into silence.

"We're back to your need to apologize to me." Morgan didn't even bother to look at Ian, focusing her attention on the black box, instead, knowing that Ian's attention would be drawn there, too.

"Okay, look, lady," Ian said calmly, but through gritted teeth. "So I played with something that belonged to you—so what? Denise never said anything about an owner or mistress or lover or anything else." But there *had* been someone, Ian remembered, her mind racing as Morgan fiddled with the box. Denise seemed to be expecting someone that night—that's right—she asked Ian if she had been sent by someone or sent someplace. Of course Ian had said yes, knowing it would give her access to that delicious little slice of bottom. But now she was frantically trying to remember exactly what Denise had said.

Morgan set the controls. It was easy to overstimulate using electricity. The trick here was to cause pain when she wanted to, not for the convenience of the bottom. Timing was everything. She could dole out pain carefully and concisely for hours, given the right circumstances. The torment would start slowly then build faster and faster until Ian would regret the day that she laid eyes on Denise.

Morgan watched a drop of sweat work its way down Ian's temple. Maintaining a soft and even tone, she said, "You can't just waltz into someone's life, take something that does not belong to you, and then discard it with nary a thought when you are done. People, while they enjoy objectification from time to time, are not objects. It took me a long time to find Denise. I cultivated certain tastes in her. Certain hidden desires were disclosed. Certain tests performed. Then in one fell swoop you snatched her up at the bar, had your way with her, and without so much as a second thought discarded her. You undid in four hours what took my valuable time and effort to discover and arouse...*and* this was not the first time."

"What the hell were you testing for anyway? Cooking? Screwing? Loyalty?" Ian's mind was racing—hadn't Denise said something when they first met, something about a test? "What do you mean, 'not the first time'? Have you been stalking me?"

Morgan ignored Ian's questions and veiled accusations. Threats were easy to make when you were all tied up, but it was a terrible loss of face. It was the beginning of the end for her quarry. Morgan had already wasted several months with the Denise fiasco and hoped that word did not get out into the Marketplace. Trainers were particular in their requirements, tastes, and ethics. She had already lost out twice on preselected clients that Ian had taken and then driven into despair and suspicion. No one liked to work with clients who wondered whether the next master would hurt them as much as the last—and in ways they did not enjoy! And yet, there was nothing she could—or should—do to such a dangerous, cold predator in her world, not according to the guidelines her colleagues agreed upon.

And yet, here she was, her prey attached to her slender, painful leashes, and her hands on the controls. It felt good, like salt in the mouth. She had gone too far not to carry this forth to the end.

"I have been waiting patiently for this opportunity," Morgan informed her adversary. " 'The time has come, the day is near, I will pour out my fury on you and exhaust my anger at you; I will judge you as your conduct deserves.' Ezekiel 7:9."

Ian's eyes flew open as the first dose of current ran through her body. Morgan was somewhere behind her, out of sight, or maybe even out of the room. *Wel verdomme, now what,* Ian thought. Electricity was one of those things that no matter how much you fought the inevitable would happen...you'd get zapped. Each zap increased the stress, which in turn increased the sweat production. Sweat has this marvelous property, salt, which increases conductivity, thereby increasing the severity of the sensation. Just when she thought that it was getting better, the electricity varied. It peaked and pulsed and zapped at unexpected times. Her body jerked and twisted. Her lips were dry, as was her mouth.

Ian tried performing deep breathing exercises. If she could somehow distract her mind it would all work out. She needed to yield to the sensations, as much as she could. She tried to let go as she had seen others do in the past. Having never experienced submission, it was not something that she could simply do. She tried to concentrate on the way Morgan's face looked when she mentioned the Marketplace. But it wasn't enough. The stress of trying prevented the very relaxation that she was seeking. Ian stopped thinking and started screaming. Once she started she could not stop. She screamed to her heart's content. It no longer mattered how she looked or what the woman thought. Survival and pain were all that she thought about. Ian's body finally did the only thing it could to escape, and a smile crossed her lips as the room became black.

A stream of water struck her face, and Ian found herself still seated, but freed from the electrodes. Morgan was standing before her, with a pair of nipple clamps that did not look like anything that she had ever seen before. They had broad tips and large knobs shaped like propane valves. Ian's nipples were quickly trapped in the rubber-coated teeth. Morgan started tightening the knobs until she had the nipple trapped between them, but not hard enough to cause any pain.

"No, no, please—enough, enough, I have learned my lesson, I swear it," Ian tried to say, as Morgan pulled out a cane and tested it in the air before Ian's eyes.

"But I want you to feel what it is that you have subjected others to," Morgan said, stroking the smooth, flexible rod. "You believe yourself to be devoid of feeling. But is that what you really want to be? I will show you a glimpse of your soul. A chance for your redemption. 'The Great Day of Anger has come, and we will see who survives.' Revelations 6:17. Shall we begin?"

In a split second the cane whooshed through the air, embedding itself in Ian's flesh before bouncing back. An intense and fearful shriek was torn from her lips followed by a string of expletives that would make a Swede blush. A reddish welt was already visible across the front of her exposed thighs. Ian had always avoided those damned pieces of rattan. Try as

she might, she had never been able to quite master them. But she had to admit they were effective; this one strike drove all the breath from her and made her see stars.

These momentary thoughts were interrupted by another cane stroke. There was just no way out of this one. It was bizarre to be caned while seated, her body believing that she could just stand up and leave, only to be defeated by the restraints. The caning continued and Ian thrashed about like a fish on a line, able to see each stroke's mark across her thighs, breasts, and stomach. Her flinching and thrashing finally knocked the chair over.

Morgan's strokes did not slow or alter. No attempt was made to place Ian upright, or even in a more comfortable position. New marks appeared on parts of Ian's body that had not been exposed before. Morgan admitted silently that she was enjoying herself. This was about punishment pure and simple. The cane was an instrument that led straight to the soul. Most people could dish out a hell of a lot more than they could take, but that was not the case with Morgan. She had taken a caning just like this before. It was the one thing that separated her spirit from her body and allowed her to soar.

The caning continued until Ian was reduced to a pile of red, bruised, blubbering flesh. She apologized, she confessed, she told the woman that she would never do it again, she begged and promised and cajoled and even made a threat or two in the beginning, Then there was nothing that she could do. She just wanted the caning to stop. She needed to regain her sanity and that was not possible with the flurry of blows she was experiencing.

Then, quite suddenly, Ian no longer cared about appearances. It was no longer possible to think about appearances. All of her defenses, one after another, came crashing down. She had never felt this vulnerable before and yet at the same time she became aware of a humiliating dampness between

her legs. There was a fire of a different sort starting. Even as she begged forgiveness for all manners of sin, she stopped feeling any pain at all. Her eyes were rolling around in her head and howls slowly turned to moans and whimpers.

Morgan, aware of these types of changes in herself, was fascinated that the mighty Ian was not above succumbing to her bodily needs. She slowed and toyed with Ian, giving her a taste—just a small taste—of the peace of mind that comes only when one is stripped of pride and arrogance.

When Morgan stopped, she was covered in sweat and her breathing was labored. Not the type of breathing that comes from a good workout, but the kind that comes from being aroused. She stood over Ian and relished the sensation. Morgan bent down and, with a bunching of her shoulders and arms, righted the chair. With absolute precision, she stepped back, aimed her cane, and then struck the nipple clamps simultaneously, causing them to pop off. Ian was instantly snapped back into her body and the most unearthly sound emanated from between her lips, accompanied by an earth-shattering, body-shaking orgasm. Morgan turned on her heel and left the room.

Ian was kneeling, her body trembling, focusing her attention on Morgan's feet. She wondered if it would be too desperate to lie prostrate, kissing the tips of the black leather boots. She was terrified that she would be sent away now, just as she had found this yawning need in her. She was terrified, because she knew that was exactly what was going to happen.

"You and I differ in an important way, Ian," Morgan was explaining. "You hunt, capture, then discard. I want you to understand—really understand—what it would mean if I sent you away now, with no way to contact me, knowing that you would never see me again." She watched without moving as a tear dropped onto the toe of her polished boot. "This is,

after all, what you do, is it not?" She noted the tears streaking down Ian's face as she nodded yes.

"That is because you are a *player*," Morgan continued, spitting the word out. "I do not play. This work I do is my calling. It is, in fact, my profession. Although," she chuckled, "not in the way you might think.

"Unlike you, I recognize my prey has value beyond the beating and the fucking. Until you learn the same, I do not wish to see you again." Ian choked awkwardly, drawing in a ragged breath, but did not speak. Morgan watched her approvingly.

"I am letting you walk out my front door, so you know where I live, and know how to find me again. I am not, like you, afraid to be found. Indeed, I welcome being found.

"Show me you have been redeemed, demonstrate that you recognize the value of the people around you, bring me proof of your repentance, and I may consider working with you further."

Ian stumbled out the front door, the street noises and scents from the Bloemenmarkt easing through the haze in her mind enough to orient herself, and to ensure that she memorized the address and street of Morgan's house. She wanted to return as soon as she left, but knew she could not. Not without giving her Lady what she required.

She shoved her hands in her pockets, shivering, and felt her fingers brush against a scrap of paper. Pulling it out, she found a torn piece of paper with a phone number scrawled across it, with the note "D—please call." The "please" was underlined twice. Her loins twitched even before her mind recognized who the note was from. Ian sighed. This could be the way back into Morgan's house. A gift. To lay at the feet of her Lady.

Morgan was a jumble of emotions. Her anger was spent and now she was simply excited beyond belief. She entered her bathroom and started the steam shower. Leaning over the sink and popping out the green contacts to show clear blue eyes, she thought about how Ian not only had talent as a potential scout, but also had the makings of a half-way decent piece of property. A bit rough around the edges with a lot to learn, but definitely trainable. She was concerned about her standing as a spotter for the Marketplace, but then again this little adventure had not involved anyone but outsiders. If Ian remained quiet, whether from humiliation or hopeful obedience, no one would be the wiser. She did not think Ian would go to the police with a fantastic tale of drugged beer and electrical torture in a hidden dungeon. Shame on Denise for mentioning the Marketplace to an outsider, to begin with—if she ever regained her confidence and belief in what Morgan had to offer, Morgan would address that issue with her. Perhaps it would all work out in the end.

Morgan removed the red wig, shaking out her raven-black wavy hair before entering the near-scalding hot shower. As her muscles relaxed she thought of the payoff for the punks, then turned her musings to Ian. Mentally, she bet against herself as to how long it would be before Ian returned to her door—to earn back the undamaged Marty that lay on the table in her dungeon. No, Morgan was never one to throw away anything that showed quality. Or to lose something of value without *someone* paying for it.

Farewell to Rain Woman

Thea Hutcheson

Linda is fucking me. Every stroke is designed to invoke Rain Woman. Linda pinches my right nipple and nuzzles me, then the tide is rising, a warm, brimming feeling up from the deepest center of me.

It is warm and inexorable, my gift as the high priestess of bottom pleasure to my lover. I stare at Linda as she fucks, and drink in her clean-cut dyke face. She has a fresh, athletic build, and a soft, but well-defined, handsome face that speaks volumes to my pussy.

My clit feels hot waves of pleasure every time she hits my special fuck spot in my cunt. Will this be gone too? How far below the cervix would they take? The idea combines with or kicks the orgasm over the edge. "Ah," I cry, then "Aah," a notch lower as Rain Woman cometh and the orgasm rises right up, spilling through my thighs in a gush around Linda's dick and she's coming now too, drowning in the flood of hot come that soaks the bed.

Tears flow out too with the thought of such intensity gone, already fading as I'm utterly drained and spent. I lie sobbing in abject sorrow. *Rain Woman, the jewel of my sexual treasure, gone, never to be invoked again.* Farewell, Rain Woman, farewell. And how shall *I* fare?

Linda cradles me, holds me as I mourn. The towel below us is soaked and it turns out that the bed is, too, with the force of my last wet orgasm. *The special ones, I think, the attainable holy grail of my sexual quest.* What use is that patience now if Rain Woman won't be coming, can't be coming because the knife will take my womb along with the large, lumpy tumors that I can trace along the top and center of my belly?

I discovered my little treasure while masturbating one hot afternoon. Even with me doing the manipulating it could take a while to come. Searching for a rhythm I found one completely different than the usual. It was a deep, groaning pleasure that pulled me down into itself. My hips flattened out and I lifted my legs.

My pussy was at once tight and incredibly loose, sucking itself as I inserted one finger and then another. Fucking just a little, teasing, I redoubled my efforts, pressed a little deeper, and my pleasure revealed a new depth, and suddenly welled up out of my center. It reached the top and a hot flood spilled out, between my asscheeks, soaking the bed.

It was different than slick pussy juice and I thought I had peed from the amount, but it was clear. With a little research, I found an abnormal psych. video from the late '70s. That scared me so I asked my doctor, who told me it was normal, although rare because it needed that same long build-up that I did.

How special, I'd thought then. It became my trademark, enhancing my reputation and making me in demand. Suddenly I went from an available bottom to a favored pet under the tutelage of masters and experts who sent me, by varied paths, to subspace, my heaven.

And Linda had, in the six months we'd been together, joined the ranks of those experts, mastering the subtleties of invoking

Rain Woman easily, as if she was made for it. And I thanked the powers that be that she was. Linda is my perfect dyke archetype—muscular and tight, with looks that conjure soft angles and clean breezes. She is solid and competent from her work as a carpenter. I love to be in those arms and love what they offer me. What can I offer her? Where's the prize after this?

The next morning we get up and get ready. Linda picks up the bag, puts it in the car, and drives me to the hospital. We park and she holds my hand as we walk up the drive. The building is new, bright, and shiny in the morning sun like the knife that will cut me, creating the empty space I will have to learn to fill.

"She's a good doctor and she knows what she's doing," says Linda.

Yes, I think. Dr. Dennis is a funny, warm woman and she's been doing this a long time. But all the doctor's warmth doesn't make up for the cold coming out of the open doors. I look at them and beyond to the cold and sterile foyer and I know that I won't be the same when I come back through them. The idea frightens me more than any edge scene ever did. The security guard begins to look at us funny.

I force my legs to move and Linda takes my arm, concerned. "I can get you a chair."

"No, thanks." All the years of learning Rain Woman, using her to get higher, closer, deeper into subspace—no, she's mine and I'll go in under my own power. I owe her that much.

Linda stays with me all the way, holding my hand until the nurse, Janet, comes to lead me to a room with eight beds, four on a side. They're all empty. Janet lifts a gown and a pair of fleece socks with rubber treads on the bottom. "Take everything off and slip these on. Opening to the back, please. I'll be back in few minutes."

I sit on the bed, take off my shoes, and lift my jumper over my head. I lay it all on the bed and slip the gown over my shoulders and reach around to tie the ends together. There isn't really any opening and I am perversely pleased. I'm never modest in play but I'm grateful not to be exposed in the hour of my descent into this unknown. I fold everything carefully before putting it in the bag. The floor is cold and I put on the socks.

Janet comes in and sees that I'm dressed. "Okay. Up on the bed. Make yourself comfortable." She puts a tag around my right wrist. "Let's do the left hand for the IV. I'm just going to give you a little something to numb the area before I do it. Just a little stick, now."

I never notice the IV go in and Janet tapes it down. "I'll get Linda. Be right back."

Linda comes in and sits on the edge of the bed. Janet follows and says, "I almost forgot, you need to take off that necklace and all the earrings."

Linda removes them one by one and puts them in her vest pocket. I feel as if I am being stripped of everything that says who I am or to whom I belong. Linda senses it and leans down to nuzzle me at the base of my neck. The warm tickle turns to sharp pain as she bites. "Just so you don't forget whose collar you wear when you wake up."

"Thank you," I say and she covers my mouth with hers for a long moment.

"Time for you to go now," Janet says the next time she passes through. "Linda, you can wait in the waiting room if you want. It'll be four hours or so. I'll call you on the phone out there when we're finished."

Linda looks at me. "I'll be here when you wake up, Terry. No matter what, it'll be okay. You'll get through this."

I can't speak because of the lump in my throat so I hug her. When she gets up, Linda cocks her head and winks at me. I am undone and I know that's why I'll wake up: to see that cocky smirk pointed at me again.

Dr. Dennis comes in. "Good morning, Terry," she says, reading through the papers on the clipboard at the bottom of my bed. "You ready?"

I guess she can tell, because she sits down on the edge of the bed. "This is a completely normal operation. There are no complications that we know of. There's no reason why this vaginal hysterectomy shouldn't go just like clockwork."

I breathe deeply, not trusting myself to speak, and nod. I realize I'm a little woozy.

"I don't feel right."

Janet laughs. "I gave you a little something. You're going to go on out in a bit and we'll do the epidural."

"A little warning would have been nice," I say, or think I say.

"Terry, Terry, are you awake?"

I open my eyes. Janet is there. "I'm awake."

"How do you feel?"

I check. I feel strange, heavy, pain out there beyond the horizon. "Okay," I say, which surprises me. Then I remember why they are asking.

"Did you do it? How was it?"

"There were complications. You had an abdominal."

I lie there, trying to understand what that meant. One of the reasons I did this now was that I was at the far end of the window Dr. Dennis gave me before the tumors were too big to come out vaginally.

"What kind of complications?"

"They found another tumor, a big one behind your ovary. It was too big to come out so she had to go in abdominally and take it."

"And the ovary?"

"She couldn't save it. But you still have the other one. Otherwise it went fine."

The idea of Dr. Dennis trying to save my ovary strikes me as funny in a comic book, Rex Morgan sort of way.

"Can I see Linda?"

"Not till we move you to your room. That'll be in about an hour."

I try to doze but keep hearing Janet say, "A big one." I try to gauge the size of a big one to the empty space there now, but my waist might as well not exist below the thick bandage covering the lower half of my belly. They finally move me to my room and Linda is there, holding my hand and kissing me while I lie in the bed, bereft, drugged, recovering.

Later, the bandage comes off and she holds the mirror to show me the long, neat slash across my bikini line, punctuated by the thirty or so staples that hold it closed. I have to beg her not to tell jokes to make me feel better because it hurts to laugh. So she brings me flowers and little presents instead.

They let me go home after a few days. I am numb as she and the orderly roll me out the same bright and shiny doors into the cold, gray day. I look back thinking that I'll see what I've left behind, but all I see are people saying good-bye to who they've been.

Juk, the dog, and Bitsy and Almond, the cats, greet me with jumps and leg rubs and distant examinations. Linda lifts the dog out of harm's way while I retire to the recliner sofa. Later Linda shoos the animals off the couch and brings me dinner made from recipes in the cookbook she found in the kitchen. We snuggle together and watch period films, my favorite. They don't make me feel better and neither does the snuggling, because beyond the warm caring of her touch, I feel nothing and I know Rain Woman is no more.

She represented the deepest piece of me that I know, and without her I am unsure of who I am, what path I'm supposed to take now. I begin to be afraid that my remaining ovary has failed to make my body feel pleasure, even though Dr. Dennis said the ovary "never even pouted."

Linda feeds the cats and my little dog and does the chores, while I try to connect with the tattered edges of where my center had been.

I dream that I am being torn to bits. I wake screaming and Linda holds me in the dark. I count the days until my six-week appointment when Dr. Dennis will tell me if Linda can fuck me again.

One morning I go into the back bedroom to look for a notepad. I notice that my Christmas present last year, a poinsettia trained into a three-foot tree, is dying alone in the corner. Linda has forgotten it.

"I know what you're going through," I say to the limp plant. "Dry as a bone and nothing to water your soul," I say as I give it a drink.

Later that day Linda honks in the driveway and I go out to see her truck filled with lumber.

"What's this for?"

Linda smiles at me. "A cat," she says, pausing and looking at Juk perched in his car seat next to her, "and dog tree. You wanna see?"

She takes me into the dining room and unrolls drawings for a tree, seven feet tall, fitted with ramps and perches crowned by a perfect scale model of the porch I wanted on our house.

"And when you're ready, we'll build the full-size model."

"I couldn't."

"You can. It's all scale, direction, Terry. From little to big, from in to out."

"Huh?" I look at her.

"What are you going to do?"

"I don't know. I'm afraid."

Linda hugs me. "What are you afraid of? The surgery is over, you're healing, and you don't have a bloody mess every month."

I stare at her, afraid to say that I'm afraid she won't want me any more, afraid that I don't know how to be anybody but the high bottom, Rain Woman, for her.

"I don't want to lose you."

She stares at me for a moment, puzzled. The she sweeps me into her arms. "Terry, you're mine. Have no doubt that you are until you say otherwise. This was an inconvenience."

"But Rain Woman...," I say into her shoulder.

She pulls me out so that she can look at me sternly and then smiles. "Terry. You always put out this huge energy, being the hungry bottom who knows the brightest center of herself. What about the rest of your life? Coming wet the way you do is cool, but you've been there, done that. There are other bright centers in you, I know it."

She shakes me lightly.

"I want you to be happy, Terry. Let's explore the other side."

"The other side of what?"

"Yourself. It's time to expand your horizons, see what's past Rain Woman. Do things that take you out instead of in. I'll give you all the excuses you need to explore, starting right here. It's all a matter of scale."

I look at the plans, imagine the animals perched on their tiny porch, and look at Linda, thinking how nice it would be to fuck on our porch surrounded by our own secret garden.

That night I dream of being torn to bits, but Linda comes in from a door I never noticed before and begins to sing, "With a knick knack paddy whack, give your dog a bone, this old crone drives away from home," as she puts me back together. When I am finished, she pours water over me. It is warm, almost hot, and I feel my flesh start to twist and bulge in places. The buds open but they don't hurt and all kinds of points and protuberances jut out from my belly, my hands, my heart, my head. I touch them gingerly and they hum eagerly.

The next morning we begin our project. Linda teaches me about scale and new perspectives. I discover that not all play is about finding the center, blown by cosmic breath and watered by Rain Woman, which reminds me of the poinsettia recovering in the bedroom. I give it drinks and fertilizer, grooming it to remove old leaves and stroking the new ones.

The gnawing in my heart about the hole in my belly slides to the background as the tree takes shape. It is perfect, and the animals possess it with a proprietary nonchalance that makes us laugh, and I realize for the first time that it hardly hurts. Linda kisses me then and I feel a tiny familiar flicker of pleasure.

We dance around the living room and dissolve into our recliner, laughing, so that Linda can rub oil across the wide swath of numb flesh below my navel and into the angry red line across the bottom of my belly.

I go with her to buy the materials for the porch and she guides my hands as we pour the pad and float the concrete to a fine brushed surface, cut the studs and nail them together, felt the roof and lay the shingles.

I feel echoes of desire whenever she stands behind me, demonstrating some procedure or trick. She knows what she does on every level and cultivates the moments, drawing them out with little strokes, soft kisses on my neck, and whispered promises for later. By the time our porch is finished, I am hungry for her and she laughs at my need.

We celebrate the completion of our porch with a dinner. While Linda starts a leg of lamb barbequing we put our furniture and the futon we bought at a garage sale onto it. The patio needs a border and I try to think of what I would plant while I pick mint for garnish from the patch that grows wild at the back of the yard.

By an unspoken agreement we let dinner pass amiably and

not until everything is cleaned up and put away do I stand in front of her in the flicker light of the citronella candles. She takes me in her arms slowly and gently begins to kiss me, bringing back up the heat we'd tacitly banked for dinner. I moan into her teeth at the warmth she is coaxing back to life and she laughs against my mouth.

"Take it off," Linda whispers. I unzip the summer dress and let it slide down in a soft susurration that makes me shiver. I fold it and lay it over the back of the chair.

"Come back to me."

She opens her arms and I flow into them. Her leather against my skin is electric smooth and I moan. She wraps her arms around me and down we go, rolling onto the futon, and she's feeling me up from every angle. "God, I've missed this," she says in my ear.

I had volunteered to give her pleasure a few times before I could fuck, but she'd said no, and we'd stayed celibate, waiting for this moment. I feel her release the self-restraint that went into the no-pressure, loving care I had received these last six weeks.

She is kissing me as if she'll never get enough and I answer it, feeling pangs and shifts down there, like things are turning on, gearing up.

The bra comes off and the panties follow between bits of her clothing. Her fingers go slowly, gently, rediscovering the hard bump of my clit. She teases that into a peg and then moves down to slip a finger between my lips and tip up, a little into my hole, reacquainting them.

I gingerly ride her, feeling the difference. Was it from the surgery or just a long time?

She gives me her finger for a while, then she slips two in a little more assertively. I can feel both fingers, their fingertips. The angle is wrong or the lube isn't uniform. *What will it feel like when she puts her dick in?*

She sighs and rolls on top of me. I lift my legs and she kneels up between them. Her dick is pointed straight at me and I know my memory of it, smooth and slippery as an electric greased pig when it's wet from my juice. She meets my eyes and I know that she wants to shove it in hard, the way we both like.

I cringe, wondering whether what's left inside can take her. I am afraid and she sees it. She smiles and cocks her head so I melt a little, letting my eyes trail down across her chest and the strong arms that frame it, down her belly, just beginning to paunch, and the strong legs that offer her dick to me.

She fits the head of it to my pussy mouth and holds it there. Habit makes me purse, and start to draw it in, and then I realize she is going to let me take her this first time. I put my hands on her hips and draw her in slowly, staring into those beautiful gray eyes. A faint smile plays about her mouth, and caution about her eyes.

It fits just like always and I settle around its solid shape and my clit stands up in anticipation of contact. My belly feels the pull a little but it doesn't hurt so I roll up and she slides in quickly, almost totally in before she can pull back in case the sutured end of my vagina is still tender.

I moan as the ghost of that electricity we always share begins to play about her dick, shooting phantom zigzags into my clit. I can almost feel it and my pussy swells a little at the memory.

"No different. It feels the same to me." She smiles and falls to her elbows while she fucks gingerly. "Yep, absolutely the same sweet, tight pussy as ever."

I blush in spite of myself and feel the tension in her arms as she holds back. Suddenly she rolls off me onto her side, and pulls my legs up over her thighs. It slides into my cunt again and my ass is seated against the tops of her thighs.

"Jerk off."

I shiver at the hoarseness in her voice. Nothing has changed for her. For her it was just six weeks of celibacy. For me it was the death of a loved one, my guide, my ticket to success.

She pinches my nipple savagely and I put my finger to my clit. It's dry for all its hope and I slip my finger down along her cock to pull up a little juice and swirl it around that nub, trying to concentrate on her cock.

She plays my nipple gently and fucks a little. I slide my finger around my clit, hoping to hit the spot that would find the eager humming we used to create, her in her slot, me in my slit.

When she slaps the back of my thigh, I scream and the pain shoots its accustomed warmth right to my pussy while she ups the ante and my finger finds the hum of pleasure and we ride it to the crest.

When I am ready to slip over the edge, we both feel it—just the tiniest welling from my center, but unmistakably Rain Woman. Linda smirks and then I am coming, a shuddering pleasure that wriggles across my numb belly and pulls its tender muscles.

"Aighh" becomes a groan as I come, satisfied in body and spirit. She's there, recovering. I am not maimed. I can still feel and I have not lost her, either of them. I am chagrined to think of how much time I have wasted fretting over a possibility blown over into nothing.

A little while later Linda tweaks my nipple and says, "Wanna go to the play party at The Zone tomorrow?"

I consider playing as I relax in the glow of pleasure and of Linda, the opener of my ways, next to me, watching me, eyebrow lifted just that littlest bit, waiting.

"Next time. I'd rather we put in a pool that waters a garden, a really nice one like we saw on that show last week."

Farewell, Rain Woman, fare well, for I shall.

Etched in the Flesh
Sacchi Green

The lonely wail of the train whistle echoed through the empty place inside me as we pulled into Brattleboro. I needed Kaitlin so badly I couldn't think straight. Long train rides always get me horny—the vibration, the swaying undulation—and that wasn't even the half of it. This trip, the first without her in years, had stirred up emotions I just couldn't handle alone.

But Kait wasn't there to meet me. Instead, it was Jenna standing beside the station wagon holding out the keys.

"Where the hell's Kaitlin?" I asked, and Jenna winced. Why did she have to be so damned jumpy around me? With anybody else, customers, suppliers, even Kait—and I knew she had a thing for Kait; who wouldn't?—Jenna was all common sense and competence.

I tried to tone down my irritation. "Everything all right?" Nothing I'd just been through was her fault.

Funerals are such damned, surreal blips in time. Trying to play the dutiful daughter I'd never been, moving ghostlike among people and places so familiar I'd had to block the pain with distance, sensing my grandmother's emanations of love and hate as intensely as when she'd been alive...I was so disoriented that only Kait's warm, abundant flesh could anchor me in my own.

So maybe horniness *was* at least half of it. I even found myself eyeing Jenna. Not bad, but too young, too raw, marginally pert. Pert bores me. In Kaitlin's generous mysteries I could lose myself. In Kaitlin's generous mysteries....

Dammit, where was Kait?

"Everything's fine," Jenna said in a rush. "The shop's been really busy, and then that sales rep for the card company was late for her appointment, so Kait couldn't get away in time."

Made sense, but I still brooded. Kait knows what train rides do to me. Did she think I'd jump her right on the platform? Would she have minded? She didn't mind that time I demonstrated how really roomy the handicapped restrooms on Amtrak are. That's the kind of thing it's a kick to have done once, without wanting a repeat performance. She'd had striped bruises on her lower back for a week from the safety handrail on the wall. Flaunted them, too, in a backless halter-top.

Kait in a backless top. Or out of one. I hurled my bags into the station wagon with unnecessary force, turned to grab the keys from Jenna, and changed my mind. "Go ahead. You drive."

She stared in amazement. I can't stand letting anybody else drive, except maybe Kaitlin. I won't even take a bus. A train is about as much as I can handle; at least I don't have to see who's in control.

"Are you OK, Andri?" Jenna asked when I was settled uneasily in the passenger seat.

"Fine. Just tired." And just wanting to give you a vote of confidence, I thought, with the added attraction of being able to close my eyes and visualize Kaitlin. "She could have let you handle the card order on your own. You have a good sense of what will sell."

The extra bit of reinforcement made her pale, freckled face light up. I watched her through half-closed eyes, since riding blind turned out to be more than I could manage, not to mention the fact that half an hour of visualizing Kait would make me so wet I'd be lucky to be able to walk without getting sore. And not to mention the tension that seemed to radiate from the paper-wrapped packet in my jacket pocket. "For Andrea's Woman" was scrawled across it in my grandmother's slashing handwriting. She'd left little bundles all over with people's names on them, declaring them sealed with curses so that nobody else would open them.

"Andrea's Woman." But she'd known Kaitlin's name perfectly well. I was tempted to risk a curse I didn't quite believe in, to make sure Kait wasn't in for some unpleasant surprise. The one time they'd met, the old termagant had pronounced that, since I'd damned sure never find a man who'd put up with me, it was just as well I'd found a good woman. That had seemed close enough to approval. I forced myself to stop fingering the packet and allowed myself to think instead about touching Kait, just a little, just the curve of her cheek, maybe down to the base of her throat, maybe just down to where her breasts begin to well…maybe to….

I sprinted for the back door of the shop before the car had quite stopped. The bedlam inside was intense. Tourists seem to descend on Vermont earlier and earlier every fall; there'd been no way we could both be gone at this time of year. It wasn't even the weekend yet, and peak color was at least a week off, but you'd have thought it was Provincetown in August the way they were milling around. And buying, too—books, crafts, cards, toys; at this rate we should make it through the rest of the year okay. I would have been elated if there hadn't been so much else on my mind, and if I hadn't seen the exhaustion on Kaitlin's face, in spite of her smooth handling of customers.

I slid behind the counter. "Take a break, Love," I said into her ear as I pressed my crotch against her magnificent posterior. She moved ever so slightly backward into my heat without missing a beat of making change.

"You must be tired after the long trip," she said, her voice doing that number on me it always does.

"You know damned well how I am after the long trip," I murmured, and smiled blandly at the harried father trying to get his kids to settle on their purchases. I massaged the nape of Kait's neck under her thick, russet braid. The muscles were tight. "You have a headache. Go get rid of it before I get home."

"Where's Jenna?" Kait glanced around, but Jenna was already forging order out of the chaos at the other cash register. Ricky, our new part-time clerk, hadn't handled a foliage season before.

"I'm on it," I said. "You go get some rest. Plenty of rest." I edged around and nudged her away from the register with my hip. She copped a substantial feel as she departed, leaving my ass tingling.

"See, guys," I said to the two squabbling boys, camouflaging my private grin in professional affability, "this model rocket goes higher, this one goes farther. But what matters most is skill. You want separate bags?"

Their father looked at me with relief, then added one of Kait's CD's to the pile. "Does this ever take me back!" he said. "I used to see you two at folk festivals, way back when. You wrote most of the lyrics, right? Really dug 'em. And Kaitlin...what a voice!"

"She's still got it," I said with feeling, and his knowing grin answered mine as he shooed the kids onward.

There are worse ways for folks to make you feel old.

A tour bus spilled its load outside just then, and we went into overdrive. Kait tried to come back to help, but I scrawled a note and shoved it at her. When she read it, she laughed and almost challenged me, but changed her mind.

"If you don't get your sweet ass out of here, I'm going to fuck it right across the counter," I'd written. And meant it, too.

Kait was in the garden when I got home, gleaning a few of the hardier greens that made it through September. "I didn't expect you so soon," she said, her rich, lazy voice affecting me like a lingering touch.

"Jenna offered to stay and close up after the last few stragglers."

I put my arms around her from behind and snuggled my face into her neck. She was wearing one of my old dirty flannel shirts with nothing underneath, so that my scent blended with her heady aura of honey and fresh bread and earth and arousal. HomeKaitlinHome....

"Jenna is a treasure," she said, as though she didn't notice what my hands were doing under her shirt, but her nipples told me otherwise. After the first compulsive cradling of her abundant, heavy breasts, I had eased off, circling my palms so that I just brushed the tips, making them strain for my touch. Which they did. Which made my own breasts ache, along with pretty much every other part of my body that could get my attention.

She started to turn in my arms. "Wait," I muttered, thrusting my knee between her legs, rubbing my crotch against her round, round ass. "You go full frontal and you're going to get it right here in the dirt and cabbages."

"It was fine in August, in the herbs," she said, that musical cello throb beginning in her voice, "but it's a little chilly now." She turned toward me anyway, slipping a hand between my thighs, pressing it up against my ache so that I arched into her touch and forgot to hold her tight.

"Come on, Andri, get a grip. You can make it!" Then,

having made nearly sure I couldn't, she slipped out of my arms and dashed toward the house, unbuttoning the flannel shirt as she ran.

Not that the bed wasn't a good idea. But I caught her at the top of the stairs, and she let me press her against the wall, hard, as though trying to merge my whole body into hers. She reached up to stroke my cropped hair, raising her breasts high against mine, and I bent my face into their full, warm comfort, needing comfort, needing something else even more with an urgency that rocked me.

Cream, honey, silk; there's no adequate metaphor for the sweetness, softness, of Kait's skin. No way to describe the sounds she makes when I touch her, primal moans vibrating through her flesh from deep within. I worked my open, hungry mouth over her bountiful curves, growing more ravenous the more I devoured. I could do this forever, if the throbbing pressure in my groin would let me. Or if Kait would let me.

Her moans grew rougher. She forced my mouth onto a swollen nipple, and pushed my hands from where they'd been kneading her rounded belly down into the unzipped waistband of her jeans. And lower still. "Dammit, Andri, bed! And get your clothes off!" She scrabbled at my belt, but I held off a little longer, sucking and licking at one breast and then the other, working my fingers delicately over the hot, wet clit that was as engorged as her nipples.

Then she bit me, hard, on the side of my neck, and squirmed away, and threw herself on the bed. Watching her wriggle out of her jeans was so engrossing, I had a hard time fumbling with my own clothes.

As my jacket hit the floor I remembered the mysterious packet, but the heat of my blood and heart overwhelmed the chill of my grandmother's shadow. Mind and senses had a more compelling focus in Kaitlin's abundant flesh. On some deep, unthinking level, I understand the impulse that made our forbears carve full-bodied goddesses out of stone and ivory. Who's to say some of those sculptors weren't women?

She stretched sensuously, grinned, and stuck out her long, mobile tongue; and when she arched her hips upward I was on her, no frills, needing nothing between us this time but our own heat.

Sometimes, when it hasn't been too long, when we can focus, yoga-like, with contemplative intensity, we can meet mound to mound, breast to breast, in slow, exquisitely precise strokes. Not this time. I straddled her, rubbing my wetness across her tender belly, then shifted so that I rode her thigh, mine pressed hard into her crotch. She clutched at my back, then my ass; her breathing came hard and fast, in counterpoint to mine. We moved against each other, with each other, and the tension mounted until I was dizzy with it.

"Now, Love, now, dammit! "Kate gasped, as harshly as her honeyed voice could get, and tugged at my arm. I braced myself with the other and slid my fingers over her damp mound, between her slippery folds, then deep, deeper into the hot, sweet, demanding mystery of her cunt.

She arched and writhed, and I picked up her rhythm, held it, accelerated along with her wordless, pleading moans; and at last she spasmed around my hand, and a sound like a chord played on a feral cello tore from her throat.

Better, more profoundly needed, than to come myself. As if I had a choice. Kait would never leave me hanging. She didn't wait to catch her breath before she began to work her mouth and hands over my body, and all my self-control began to melt, as always, under her touch. But suddenly the ripples of anticipation transformed into a violent shivering that my lowered defenses had no power to resist. "Kait...." Unshed tears burned in my throat.

"It's all right, Love," she said, knowing unerringly that

what I needed now wasn't what I needed ten seconds ago. "I've got you safe."

And she did. Her warm, sustaining flesh moved over mine, her unbound hair flowed around me, sheltered me, formed a private space for the weakness that only Kait was ever allowed to see.

"She's gone, Kait! That vicious, domineering old woman... gone! And I never told her that I loved her."

"She knew." Kait kissed me hard and deep. "She knew," she repeated, coming up for air and leaning back. "She told me how hard it was, teaching you self-discipline, or as much as you ever did learn. She said the devil in you was nearly a match for hers."

"She told you that? But you only met her once!"

"Once was enough. We had a lot in common. But she made me promise not to tell you some things while she was still alive."

That sounded like the convoluted working of my grand-mother's mind. I was still hurt. "All she said to me was that if I didn't treat you right she'd lay a curse on me."

"Damned straight, too, and don't you forget it." Kait wriggled against me, and the impulse to treat her really, really right began to revive, but she rolled off. "It's getting chilly; where's that shirt? If you ever desert me overnight again, Andri, be sure to leave me some flannel you've sweated into. It's good company. Maybe I'll even ask Jenna for a copy of the tape she made of us."

"*What* tape?"

"Didn't you know she listens to us, sometimes, when we get too enthusiastic outdoors?"

She knew damned well I didn't know. "But...she can't...."

"Let it go. I've talked to her about it."

I noticed she didn't say she'd told Jenna to cut it out. "I can't exactly blame her for wanting to hear you," I said, "but...."

"It's not me she wants to hear. It's you. She showed me her diary: 'Andri howls like a regiment of bagpipes going into battle, pennants flying, the sound enough to tear through flesh and spirit.' "

"Why the hell are you telling me?" I wasn't prepared to deal with this at all. I'd vaguely noticed bagpipe tapes being played in the apartment Jenna rents in our renovated barn, but I'd figured she was going through a phase of getting in touch with her Hibernian roots. At the moment I didn't want to consider what else she might be getting in touch with.

"Because she's right. That's what you do to me: tear through flesh and spirit, open me up, and fill me." She leaned forward and pressed her mouth hard into the hollow of my throat, which meant that her opulent breasts pressed hard against my ribs, and the smoldering ache began to flare again. "And maybe to caution you not to be too hard on her, but not to be too nice, either." Then she pulled away, even though my arms were tightening around her, and stood up.

"So," she said in a lighter tone, veering away from a subject she might not want to deal with just now, either. "Are you going to sweat a little for me if you have to leave me again?"

The way she flaunted her luxuriant ass as she crossed the room was meant to distract me. It did an outstanding job. "Sure," I said, "if you'll let me take along some of your seasoned underpants."

"Deal." She bent provocatively to scoop up my jacket, and the packet fell out. "What's this? A present?"

"A bequest," I said, and told her about the protective curse, bracing myself for whatever lay ahead.

"I can just hear her saying that." Kait hefted the packet, flat, with a thickly cylindrical object attached. "Shall I open it now?"

I wanted to say no, touch me now, I need you now, but

somehow I had to get through this first. "What the hell. Why not?"

Kait turned on the bedside lamp and sat beside me, holding on to me without touching. She forced the knotted string off the corners of the package and peeled away the tape from the edges. "It's a picture in an old frame." We stared at a brown-tinged photograph of two girls arm in arm in front of an olive tree. My grandmother's dark eyes bored into ours from a face absurdly young to hold such challenge.

"Andri," Kait whispered, "that's just how you looked when I first saw you."

"No way," I said, but it was true, in spite of her antique clothes and long hair and the fact that I'm considerably taller. "Who is that with her?" It was a rhetorical question; I was startled when Kait knew.

"Her name was Allesandra. She was killed spying on the Germans in Sicily in 1943." Just from the way the girl stood, the look in her eyes, the way she filled out the peasant blouse and skirt, it was all too obvious how she'd been able to get close enough to spy. "Your grandmother showed me this picture and then…then she said, 'But I had my vengeance for her death!' "

"She *what*? How do you know all this? Why would she tell you and not me?"

"I think she just had to tell somebody, after all those years. Somebody who wasn't quite family."

Somebody who was Kaitlin. I couldn't resist pouring myself into her, and Jenna spilled the most intimate secrets, so why should I be surprised at my grandmother's vulnerability? But I had never been allowed to think of the arrogant old woman as vulnerable. Or even human.

"What else did she tell you? Did she say…were they…."

Kaitlin just nodded. Lovers. I looked down into the picture again. My grandmother's eyes, with a glint of fierceness even in that long-ago sunlit afternoon, told me what she had never told me in life. Dammit, she had owed me that much! I came close to hating her for what she had withheld, for what she had let me suffer alone.

And then I realized some fraction of what she had suffered.

"Vengeance? How? She must have told you more!"

"No. And I couldn't ask. It hurt her enough to go as far as she did. After that she changed the subject to gardening and gave me the seeds for that weird ridged zucchini I've planted ever since. The one you call 'the French tickler of the vegetable world.' "

The wild thought crossed my mind that the implacable matriarch of my family had, in fact, meant the seeds as just such a joke. Impossible. But.... I eyed the seven-inch brown-papered cylinder Kait was beginning to unwrap. No. Please, no. There are some things you just don't want to inherit from your grandmother, no matter what.

Kate glanced sidelong at me, and the corner of her mouth twitched. She knew perfectly well what I was thinking. "Don't worry. I think I can tell what it is." She went on unwinding coil after coil of paper, until the object's shape began to emerge, and when at last she held out the little stiletto-slim dagger I took it with something as close to reverence as I'm ever likely to feel.

"Her vengeance." I ran a finger along the blade. "It's cold," I said, somehow surprised.

Kaitlin stood and took the dagger from me, laid it flat in the deep valley between her breasts, and pulled me up so tightly against her that our bodies held the steel. "Her heart," she said. "Still fiery."

She was right. I felt its heat radiating outward, not from the blade alone but from fiery hearts back through the years. We pressed against each other, Kait clutching at my back, my hands filled with the glorious curves of her ass, rocking almost imperceptibly together.

Tension mounted as the need grew for flesh to move against beloved flesh. A fine and poignant torture, worth prolonging, except that the fear of the sharp edge shifting and slicing into Kait's delectable skin made me cut it short. And made me realize just how weak I really was.

I've always needed to feel strong—to split the firewood, shovel the snow, even carry Kait, in spite of her protests, across the occasional stream. Now, as I tightened the grip of my left hand on the compelling fullness of her ass and reached between the equally compelling swells of her breasts with my right, I faced my own deepest fear.

"I couldn't do it," I said, and tossed the dagger onto the bed. "I couldn't do what she did."

"Take vengeance?" Kate's green eyes looked deeply into my dark ones, knowing me so well that she already half-understood what I meant. "Nothing could have stopped you! I can see you now, going into battle with pipes skirling and banners flying, or slipping silently through the darkness if stealth was what it took."

I dropped my head to her shoulder and wrapped her even closer in my arms, thighs, everything that could grip her, trying to hold all of her inside me. "But you wouldn't be there to see me," I muttered into her neck. "I would avenge you, no question, preferably with tooth and claw instead of a knife. But afterward.... How did she go on living? I couldn't do that—go on without you."

Kaitlin had been stroking the nape of my neck, but at that her fingers tightened and her thumbs pressed into my windpipe just enough to get my attention. I raised my head.

"Don't!" she said fiercely. "Grieve for her, but don't judge her!"

"I'm not...."

"Yes, you are. You think she *shouldn't* have gone on, shouldn't have married, raised a family, given me you!"

"No!" There might be some truth to it. But it didn't matter. The thought of life without Kait was what tore me apart.

"And don't even think about losing me, because you never will!" Her green eyes were brilliant with anger, or unshed tears, or both. She dropped her hands to my shoulders and then, in strokes so hard and furious they hurt, ran them over all of my body she could reach while I still held her so tightly. "And if...if you ever dare to say that this flesh I love wouldn't go on, if only to carry the memory of mine, I'll take that knife, Nazi germs and all, and carve my name into you where you won't ever forget it!"

My grip on her had loosened a little, maybe to give her hands more territory to punish. She managed to get them on my breasts, and then, while I was distracted, twisted away from me and picked up the knife. She backed off a step and raised her arm—and even then, even as the blade shot past me to lodge, quivering, in the wooden headboard, the undulation of her flesh in motion sent resonating waves through mine.

Then she pushed me down onto the bed, and followed to nuzzle all along my inner thigh, making me melt and tense in ecstatic contradiction. "So," she murmured between kisses turning into bites, "just where shall I mark you? Here...or here where your fine Sicilian fur would hide it...or in this tender hollow...?" She teased me, stroking and licking until my readiness verged on pain and I arched into her touch and fought to control the raw cries clawing at my throat—a battle I needed more to lose than win.

"Kait!" My voice was knife-edged with desperation. The teasing ceased, as her wide mouth moved wet and hot and demanding against my pounding clit. Tongue, hands, divinely heavy breasts pressing my thighs; no need to sort it out, no need, impossible, to keep control. She drove me surely on and on, making my voice tear free from all restraint, forcing the agonizing tension to swell, and surge, and burst at last into dark, searing brilliance.

As peace flooded in behind the slowly ebbing glow, I pulled Kait up along my body until I could kiss her, deeply, and feel her tongue on mine. I'm never more sure of who I am than when I taste myself on Kaitlin's mouth.

We lay entwined, her thigh pressed gently now against my still-throbbing mound. I began to move my mouth over her seductive skin again, and felt her ripple of response, but I felt something else, too, something I recognized. I wasn't surprised when she swung her wide, powerful hips to the edge of the bed and stood up.

She crossed to the open window, and for an instant I wished I were watching from below, seeing Kait's curves outlined in the lamplight, and wondered whether Jenna might be out there. Then I went to stand beside her, looking out over the valley at the mountains dark against a twilight sky of Maxfield Parrish blue.

Kait gripped my hand and held it against her breast. I felt, more than heard, the tremor deep within of music being born. A fragment of melody took shape, evoking the mountains before us; then came a subtle change of tone, in that mysterious way Kait has of overlaying the mellow richness of her voice with a harsher power. The tree-furred slopes became the stony sides of Sicily's bare mountains, far away in space and time.

The tune faded, but the music was still in Kait's low voice when she spoke. "Write the words for me, Andri. Her story. Her song."

"Yes," I said. " 'The Sicilian Dagger.' " Images, phrases, already stirred in my subconscious. "It's coming." My throat was still raw from cries I had made without hearing, drowned out by the storm within. I put my arms around her and bent my face into the soft, sweet warmth of her shoulder. "But for now, just hold me."

She knew how deeply into me she was already etched, with no need of any blade. She knew, too, when it was time to set thought aside and let the flesh tell what was in the heart; and, when comfort gave way again to hunger, she let me tell her once more all that burned in mine.

Cop-Out
Rosalind Christine Lloyd

Troi was into picking up girls at straight clubs. Tonight, her destination was Butter, a hip-hop club in Tribeca.

An ex-Marine and former college hoop all-star, Troi was now a New York City police detective. Her preoccupation with combat and competition defined a quiet but powerfully aggressive demeanor. She kept her 5'10", 160-pound body buffed to masculine perfection with rigorous daily workouts that involved pumping iron with the muscle queens at a gay gym in Chelsea where she matched their workout regimen to achieve similar macho results. Every inch of her was solid, sinuous, rippling muscle.

Her skin was like dark fudge, as rich and even in tone as a sinfully delicious chocolate cake. When she laughed, a mouth full of perfectly spaced teeth framed by thin, silky lips accentuated a smile that ignited the light in her unusually light brown eyes. Her hands were massive: hands designed to palm basketballs, handle heavy artillery, and apprehend suspects, among other useful things.

Tonight she opted for a pair of soft brown leather pants and a suede camel-colored shirt. She had a knack for choosing loose-fitting clothes that enabled her to neutralize any semblance of femininity. Her breasts were almost always held hostage, bound tightly beneath her clothing. She selected one of her larger dildos, the one she'd named Shaft, along with her new leather travel harness. Shaft was handmade, designed precisely to her specifications to include, among other things, a skin tone that matched her complexion. The startling replica even came equipped with a fake foreskin that made it feel that much more authentic. It served its purpose. It set her back quite a lot of money but she quickly discovered it was worth every cent and more. She finished her outfit with her favorite designer square-toe boots (for men, of course), splashed on a men's designer cologne, and dared to accessorize with a fat ruby in her left ear and a matching pinky ring for that hint of gangsta.

To throw people off her trail, she would often flash her police badge on her way into the clubs she cruised. Besides being allowed admission at no charge, she avoided being carded. This particular evening, it was obvious that Butter was seriously implementing its ID policy because of the excess crowd of underage kids hanging out behind the ropes, trying to get in.

Hip-hop clubs were perfect venues for her obsession because the social element was fiercely dark, wild, uninhibited, and crowded enough for her to move around freely without inciting any suspicion. The carnival feeling reminded Troi of her freaknik college days. Most of the men were typical in their badass attitudes, adhering to the typical negative stereotypes of male posturing, and taking the pessimistic connotations of the music way too seriously. Talk about game—all of this worked in Troi's favor because she offered an *alternative*. Her meticulous, classy, cash-money look attracted the girls' attention every time. The only problem she ever encountered were the down-low, bisexual switch-hitter boys prowling around who correctly detected her on their gaydar, but incorrectly assumed she was a gay man or something even more ambiguous. Troi found these occasions amusing but off-putting. For this reason, using the restrooms, any restroom, was strictly out of the question.

Scanning the club, she easily found her mark: a tall, red bone with the face of an angel dipped in honey, with two long French braids that went down her back tickling a fat, juicy ass squeezed into a cheap, tight, Lycra hoochie dress. The slinky fabric stretched and strained against the milk-fed curves of her breeder hips. Her calves, sprung from svelte, golden thighs, were incredibly sculpted in a pair of chic platform ankle boots that had a sci-fi effect: the entire boot, including the heel, was encased in stretched black leather. Troi liked the way they made her calves look. Long and wispy eyelashes like the fringe on a gypsy's shawl draped huge, sensuous eyes. Wearing too much jewelry, she was definitely into "bling-bling." Her nail tips were long, decorated in startling designs and colors; but her tits, piled into a push-up bra, were voluminously for real. Ms. Thing was ghetto fabulous in all its glory.

Troi watched the girl closely, studied her standing at the bar as if waiting for a bus. At least three men asked Braids to dance, but she declined them all. Braids was waiting for Mr. Right. She was waiting for Troi.

Troi sent her a glass of champagne with a shot of Hennessey poured on top (commonly known as thug's gold) and waited for the young lady's reaction. Initially, Braids hesitated with suspicion, refusing the cocktail. But when the bartender pointed at Troi, Braids stared for a moment with those eyes, assessing her admirer before smiling seductively and mouthing the words *thank you* with lusciously burgundy-coated lips. She then proceeded to sip slowly from her glass as if digesting something very precious. Troi would not allow her much time to think, knowing she would have to crank up the charm to get Braids where she wanted her.

Their eyes locked and remained so while Troi slowly walked to the end of the bar, as if she was a pimp strolling along a catwalk. Unable to read anything from the girl's eyes, Troi relied on her feminine intuition, and she felt the adrenaline surge through her. It was the same feeling she got before taking the winning layup shot or the feeling she had during a stakeout—the feeling of victory in enemy territory. Flexing her muscles, she walked right up to Braids, suddenly feeling the aura of heat emitting from the girl's body. This startled Troi for a moment. As if reading Troi's mind, Braids took another sip of champagne. Taking a deep breath, Troi leaned in toward the girl, telling herself not to inhale her whole.

"I can see you appreciate the finer things in life," Troi whispered in her ear, letting her nose brush against the length of her neck for a trace of her scent.

"Is that your best line? Now I know you can come better than that especially when you sending over champagne and everything. What's your name, Mr. Got-all-the-Right-Moves?" The dark pools turned into magnets, drawing Troi in.

"I'm Troi—and what do they call you, Ms. Got-all-the-Right-Moves?"

"If you're nasty."

"Oh, I'm plenty nasty."

"I bet you are. I'm Staci." She sipped from her glass again, her eyes lowering, her comfort level improving.

The dance floor was a virtual free-for-all. No respect was given and every liberty was taken with the feminine gender. The brothers practically mauled the girls alive and the girls appeared to enjoy the attention, but whether this was really the case was another matter altogether. But this kind of atmosphere played in Troi's favor as she gently removed the glass from Staci's hands and led her onto the crowded dance floor.

It was so hot it seemed like everyone was simulating sex. Staci wrapped her arms around Troi's neck, rubbing herself against Troi's thigh like a puppy in heat. Something was on this girl's mind.

Troi was enamored by the overture and didn't waste any time stroking Staci's back very provocatively and grabbing her ass, positioning Staci so that she was gyrating on the head of Troi's dildo.

"You a big boy, Troi. You could hurt a girl," She purred in Troi's ear.

When Staci stuck her hot, wet tongue into that same ear, Troi wanted to sink her cock right in the ass she held, but she settled for plunging her fingers through Staci's lacy thong and in between her meaty lips.

Staci felt so good riding Troi's dong and fingers, her soft breasts crushed against Troi's bound, puckered nipples. Troi could feel Staci's muscles clench in the palm of her hands. Staci found Troi's lips with her own, forcing them into a kiss so provocative it made Troi's head spin. Sucking tongues, lips, mouths like they were sucking on the world's best-tasting treat, each of them settled into some serious dry-humping, riding the crest of their quivering horniness. Before Troi realized it, the front of Staci's dress was hiked up against her hips and Staci began stroking Shaft through Troi's leather pants: a great big no-no.

Troi reached behind her belt for her handcuffs, and placed them on Staci.

"Am I under arrest, officer?" Staci was unfazed.

"Yeah, I'm taking you into custody." Troi made only a small spectacle leading Staci out of the club in handcuffs. Security and other patrons looked on suspiciously as Troi flashed the badge attached to her belt. Staci loved every minute of the crude public display.

Troi's truck was strategically parked on a secluded side street. Listening to the sounds of their heels clicking against the slick cobblestone street, Troi continued to steer her "assailant" by the cuffs. Her eyes were locked on Staci from behind, while Staci enhanced the view by shifting her ever-ripening ass with every step she took, her calves casting a spell over Troi's mind. They stopped once they reached Troi's jet-black Lincoln Navigator.

"I like your big, black truck," Staci whispered over her shoulder.

"Oh, we'll see just how much you like it," Troi whispered back, gently pressing Staci up against the hood of the truck, the girl's hips and thighs shivering as they met the cold fiberglass.

Staci giggled nervously but obediently spread her legs apart. Troi pushed herself against her; the girl was built like a gazelle, tall and graceful, with limbs so delicate and fine they seemed breakable. If only Troi could feel those long, thin hands wrapped around her Shaft, it would be a sensual nirvana. If only Troi could watch those burgundy lips wrapped tightly around her Shaft, her strong hips pumping into that burgundy mouth like a piston, she knew she could fall in love. Instead, she would have to settle for the ass, which she exposed to the cool November air, her super-tight, lacy, tiger-print thong encasing two fleshy mounds of delight.

"Cool air couldn't cool this ass off." Troi was kneeling now, her eyes taking in the vision before her.

"But I bet *you* can." Staci's tiny voice grew up in a second, morphing into a mature growl.

Troi sank her teeth gently into the flesh of Staci's right cheek, pretending to gnaw while allowing her hand to reach in between Staci's moist bush—to find that her pussy felt like a hot piece of fruit left out in the sun too long, mushy and sticky, oozing sweet nectar along her fingertips. Staci wiggled around, her breathing getting heavier as she whispered, "Come on, baby. Come on. Tear my shit up. I'm ready for you. You better take this pussy now!"

If this girl said anything else to Troi, she knew it was

entirely possible that she could come right there, just by the sound of Staci's voice and her scent, sticky on Troi's fingers and thick in the air. Troi reluctantly refrained from any more finger and oral play. Safe sex between two women felt so unnatural to her, but she could not have sex any other way with any woman, straight, gay, or otherwise.

Standing back up, she held Staci down firmly with one hand while the other reached for a condom from her back pocket, ripping the packet open with her teeth.

"What you got for me, Big Daddy?" Staci was writhing now, the handcuffs both restricting and exciting her. As Troi readied herself for the ceremony, steadying them both by shoving a leathered thigh along the slick backside of this hot young thing, Staci began breathing and moaning, as if she had watched one too many porn videos.

Young, "straight" girls really dug Troi's handcuffs. Anything considered freaky and kinky was fashionable. But the handcuffs served a much more important purpose. Troi slid the rubber along the length of Shaft, lubricating the tip with a little of her own saliva before ramming into Staci's hot pussy with a sharp thrust of her hips. Staci went flailing against the hood of the truck while Troi skillfully guided herself deep into Staci's center. They moved together, Troi going in deeper with every forceful thrust, while Staci gyrated against every push, ensuring an easy, slippery fit, full of friction. Her hips swayed and bounced, pushed and pulled, bumped and ground to some mad truncated rhythm in her head and in Troi's pelvis. Troi could have pumped inside of her until the break of dawn, but after the third set of multiple orgasms rocked Troi's body with dizzying episodes of heart-stopping miniseizures, sweat popping from what felt like everywhere, she had to disengage herself from the girl who had resigned herself to Troi in total submission. Troi had to ignore the girl's desperate pleas for more (they *always* wanted more)—a precautionary measure, as she was always in danger of giving too much away.

The drive to Staci's home in Brooklyn was quiet. These were awkward moments for Troi because nothing would ever come from these encounters. This was just how she liked it, just how she planned things. There was always the mystery of whether any of these women knew the real deal. That was part of the allure. Sometimes in the heat of passion, Troi could testify that it didn't really matter, because she knew she had skills, mad skills. She drove the girls insane with her shit.

With Staci, she had half a mind to leave the handcuffs on until they got to Staci's place, because Staci was all over her.

"I can't believe you're still hard!" Staci kept squealing whenever Troi failed to keep the girl's hand out of her lap.

Troi had half a mind to bend her over the back seat and slip her another heavy dose of Shaft, but Staci was too much into it.

In front of her brownstone, Staci wrote her phone number down.

"Can I get yours?" she inquired.

"Nah, that's not a good idea," Troi replied deliberately, not looking at her. It was all part of the routine.

"Why not?"

"It's not important. Maybe I'll see you again at Butter."

"Damn, it's like that?"

"Girl, if you knew, you couldn't handle it."

"Don't be so sure," Staci smirked, crumpling up her phone number and tossing it into Troi's lap before climbing out of the truck. Troi followed those long sculpted legs up the brownstone stairs with her own pretty, seductive, huntress eyes, before pulling away in her beautiful black truck into the cool November night.

Elizabeth
Julie Levin Russo

I am irresistible. I go where I want and I do what I please because I taught myself early to know my own desire and to live it without apology. I dress like a man. I fuck like a woman. No one confronts me in my sin because everyone finds themselves wanting to burn with me in damnation. Lovers come to me because they know I can teach them the secrets of their own cunts and cocks. But it is rare that I meet someone who understands, like me, how to rule others by *not* fucking them.

This thought occurs to me as I stand poised to enter Elizabeth, the end of my cock slick where it rubs in the juices of her wide-open cunt.

When I first arrived at the English court, Elizabeth was deep in conversation with a lord or advisor I could not identify. Her eyes flicked up once as they registered the unfamiliar grace of my stride, but she showed no other reaction to the presence of another unremarkable foreign nobleman. When I approached her and knelt in front of the throne, she turned, when she was ready, and brooked the ritualized exchange of formal greetings and ring kissing. I don't know when Elizabeth realized I am a woman. And whatever idle, salacious, or bitter talk took place between allies in the maze of back corridors, no one dared to openly defy the Queen's tacit approval. Not for something so little as one more perversion to add to the already well-filled ranks of court intrigue.

I imagine I know what these minions see when they look at me. A young man, dark-skinned and handsome, with black hair that curls around his shoulders, delicate, boyish features, and a slender, broad-shouldered frame. Perhaps they evaluate a bit, and judge me a charming recluse who laughs easily and speaks little. Perhaps instead they listen to my voice, which can silence a room, or pool in the hearer's stomach like the heat of desire. Quiet, deep, touched with a rich accent and the hint of a threatening purr, it is unmistakably a woman's voice. Whatever they saw or heard, the ladies at court flirted with me only slightly more than they did with any appealing newcomer, and I flirted back slightly less than a man would have. I was commanding and inscrutable, and a few of them started trailing in my wake, a sort of coy, feminine flotsam. I followed Elizabeth.

Seduction is more demanding than sex, but I didn't choose this life because I appreciate things that are easy. I could spend into any cultivated lady-in-waiting who thinks she's found a clever way to give up her maidenhead and keep her purity, but that is a shallow, dishonest pleasure. As dishonest as the life I was born into. And a dangerous extravagance, since my pleasure is always a transgression. I've learned to recognize the women who want what I am and not what I am not. I know a woman who wears a cock under her skirts when I see one, who rules the men around her by the set of her hips and not by the flutter of her eyelashes, but I've never seen anyone do this as breathtakingly as the Queen. She shuts her body into a shroud and then uses the mystery of it as a snare to capture those around her. Elizabeth has learned the secret of her own power, and there are only two kinds of people she would let inside her: a man more woman than she is, or a woman more man than she is. I was smitten.

I know Elizabeth's mind, or I tell myself I do. I frighten her, and that is why she tolerates my presence. There are precious few things that inspire terror in her now—she's already excised that part of herself. She's as precise as a surgeon too in the way she keeps her house, and she watches her retinue operate. I know when to cut across the room to put my hand on the back of her chair as she rises, which garden she'll be walking in at noon, and how to defer with my words while I challenge with my eyes. All this is conventional. But I am more than a lord (or less than a lady), and from me obsequiousness is less than respectful and solicitude is more than flattery.

When I passed her in the hall one morning and bowed irreproachably low, without taking my eyes from hers, she no longer knew the anatomy of the gesture. The anxiety of the undissected knotted itself into her stomach, and she finds this anxiety a rare and cherished source of amusement. So she stopped, stifling her rising laugher at my subtle audacity, and held out her ring to be kissed. I turned her hand and pressed my lips to the exposed sliver of skin at the inside of her wrist.

It is a remote stretch of corridor where the Queen often walks at the same time of day, in the same solitude, toward her customary visit to the chapel. Suitors have surprised her here—she encourages it. But my surprises are of a different character. She rounded the corner to see the tailored lines of my back curved into the shadow of an alcove. Curved, in fact, against the milky bosom of one of her high-ranking ladies-in-waiting. The wanton was pinned to the marble at her center by my dark thigh, and my hand caught both of hers above her head. Waves of red-gold hair fell loose around her shoulders. I sank my teeth into the sweet flesh below her ear, and she stretched out her throat and moaned voluptuously. Elizabeth saw her face. It was the perfect image of her own desire. She looks like that now, her skin flushed and glowing with a sweaty sheen, her hair fanned about her head like a crown of flame. But Elizabeth stares me down with her eyes wide open.

Making love and keeping your virginity is primarily an act of will. Elizabeth's pleasure is no part of her power, and she need only divide herself to free it. She has two bodies, and one is an illusion. Soon after her coronation, she had a portrait of herself painted, and prominently hung. It is all surface: the rich brocade of her extravagant gown fills the panel, glittering with jewels and gold filigree. Her white face and hands are tiny islands in the splendor, remote and pure. In life, the Queen plays the portrait. Its sacred surface is her maidenhead, and it will be eternally unbreached. When her subjects look at her, they see what she wants them to see—even her lovers. Elizabeth knows that everyone thinks about undressing her; she arranges it that way. Every excess of embroidery, every elaborate wig and enormous farthingale, tells the story of how she withholds her body like she defends England: strategically. But the body the masquerade invites them to imagine is not the body I'm about to slide my cock into.

When the Queen came upon my seduction in the hall, she swept by as if impervious. But that afternoon, I was summoned to her presence by one of her pinch-lipped sycophants. She is always direct.

"What were you doing with our lady?"

"With all respect, your Majesty, I believe that was perfectly clear."

"On the contrary, the immodest nature of your assignation was apparent. However, what you were doing, or rather what you were going to do, is not at all clear to me." Her back was to her functionaries, and she glanced speculatively at my codpiece.

"My Queen, I meant no harm or discourtesy to the lady or to your illustrious self."

"You are too bold."

"Yes, your Majesty."

"What do you think Constance wanted from you so desperately that she would openly risk my displeasure?"

I coughed demurely. "What any woman wants, I suppose, who is not chaste. Will you punish her?"

"And what do you want, then?"

"I want what any man wants."

"But you, your Grace, are not any man."

"You do too much honor to one who vexes you."

"You vex me and you intrigue me. How do you intend to make amends for your appalling behavior?"

"I do not flatter myself to think that my humble person is worthy to attend so magnificent a Queen. But if there is any service I can perform that would be acceptable to your Highness, it would be my most ardent desire to render it."

The underlings had the grace to hide their distress.

After dusk, there was a faint knock at the outer door of my modest chambers. It was my little wanton, who threw her arms around me and peppered my cheeks with kisses as soon as I had secured the entrance.

"You have found favor with the Queen?" I asked her, amused by the display. I found her lips, and tried to snake my hand through an opening in her skirts. She danced away from me, smiled coyly, and fished a folded leaf of paper out of her bodice.

"I can't stay," she purred, and slipped out with a lewd caress.

The note was from Elizabeth.

The guards and servants were conspicuously absent from the Queen's apartments and the castle still, apart from the midnight sputtering of torches, when I showed myself in as instructed. Elizabeth was seated regally in a monstrous chair, her gown billowed around her. She watched impassively as I approached and, in a carnal parody of our first decorous meeting, knelt to kiss her ring. I held her hand against my breath for a moment, and then she turned it, and ran her fingertips along the arc of my jaw to my hairline. She pulled on the knot at the nape of my neck, and my black curls fell soft into her palm. Tracing her way along the skin of my throat to the fastenings of my tunic, she slackened the ties until I could shrug it off my shoulders. Her eyes were dark against mine as her touch discovered the slight rise of my breast through the linen shirt, as her fingertips pressed roughly into the resilient flesh, and then found the peaked punctuation of a nipple to tug at. She smiled savagely and watched me struggle not to press myself into the contact. Then she dropped her gaze as she undid the buttons to reveal the chest of a woman, studying my swarthy, pointed breast, and laying her hand over it so that it filled her palm. She traced the outline of my lips, and I opened my mouth to lick at her fingers. Sliding them in deep so I was sucking, she spoke: "Show me."

I stepped back, my shirt still hanging open, and posed for her with my hips cocked arrogantly. Then I unfastened the front of my breeches and let the firm, cylindrical leather phallus spring out. It is ingenious and lovely, nearly seamless and worn buttery smooth, and Elizabeth stood up to appreciate it with genuine curiosity. She wrapped her hand around it and stroked it, and then slid her palms down my hips so that my breeches fell, and the straps that attach my cock to me were revealed. She laughed at me a little, when she saw the harness, and I snarled and pulled her hard against my body, clawing into the exposed swell of her breast, and kissing her bruisingly. She opened her mouth to the assault, biting at my tongue as it filled her. I gentled and licked over the inside of her lips, and then shifted my attentions to her ear, so I could rasp my words into it:

"You want the secret of my body? Then let me show you the secret of yours. If I'm a woman under my clothes, then so are you."

She shoved me away with her forearms, leaving only my fingers hooked under her bodice, and we stared at each other, panting. I took another step back, giving her space to strip for me. She removed her wig first, and set it on a dressing table, and then she pulled pins from her hair until a thick coppery coil fell free. I stood behind her and hefted its weight, burying my face in it. It smelled of oil and sweat. "The laces," she directed me, and I helped her begin the laborious process of extricating herself from her gown, corsets, farthingales, petticoats, and collars. It was more ritual than seduction, but with each vestment draped heavily over a chair, I could feel more of the heat of her skin slipping under the harness to swell me. I fondled the arcane and alien under things like she'd stroked my cock, letting her watch me rub them against my lips, my nipples, my crotch. With each layer she peeled away, her jaw clenched tighter with desire. Last was a modest shift, which she pulled over her head in one graceful and lascivious gesture. Elizabeth was naked.

I know how to give it to a woman, but I can't say I've ever fucked a Queen. I spread her out on her back at the edge of the bed, and she held her own knees to open herself. Her skin is freckled, and the russet marks dust the curves of her breasts down to her nipples, which are long and slightly off-center. She is too thin, and her ribs and hipbones cast dark shadows. A line of long hairs trails up the inside of each thigh to a thick auburn bush, now split and showing its slick red center. She is all flesh, all sweaty and pale and bruiseable, and the transformation arrests me. I am standing and leaning over her, the end of my cock our only point of contact. Looking at her, in a dizzy spiral of contemplation, I realize I'm afraid that if I touch her the impossible beauty of my triumph will vanish.

Impatient with my reverence, Elizabeth stares straight at me, arches her back, and says, "Fuck me" in a tone that makes it an order and not a request.

My cock throbs, overriding my meditation, and I use the sudden weakness in my knees to thrust forward, half burying myself in her. Both of us gasp. I can feel her muscles sucking me. Then I'm talking to her.

"You want me to fuck you, open you up so wide my cock will show on your face, get in you so deep you'll always feel me there...."

She fists my hair and yanks me onto her, mauling my mouth. My cock goes in hard and I grab a handful of flesh at her hip, digging in my fingernails, and start pounding. I try to bite her everywhere, leaving brutal marks along her shoulder and around her nipple. She bites me back, levering herself to meet my thrusts with her heels on my ass. Both of us are so wet our thighs slide against each other, and I slap harder against her cunt to make up for the lack of friction. It's too soon to come, so I slow down, feeling her close and open around me by excruciating inches, and watch her grit her teeth and ball her fists on my shoulders. Pushing in as deep as I can, I make small fast movements that shine my clit, and she keens and reaches between us to rub herself. I hold myself up with my arms so I can see her fingers in her cunt, circling as she swells, my cock splitting her just below. My hips start slamming in time to her strokes, and then I hit a spot that makes her scream. I punch it over and over; her brow furrows, every muscle goes taut, she yells curses and comes exquisitely. When I feel her clamp down on me, I shove in violently, bracing my clit against her bucking hips, and spend into Elizabeth.

We end up sprawled in the middle of the bed, my breath cooling her throat. She hums quietly against my temple. Then she rolls me over and crouches between my legs.

"Can you take it off?" she asks impishly, fondling my cock.

I grin and loosen the straps so I can remove my legs from the harness. She leans close to examine my cunt, parting its folds and playing in the juices still trickling out. Then she plucks the cock from my hands, studies it for a moment, and starts putting it on. She kneels over me, her hair cascading down onto my stomach, cock resting between my breasts, and tells me imperiously, "I will fuck you, milord." I would laugh, but desire is too heavy in my gut.

She puts her face beside mine, pets my sides, and speaks low and exactingly.

"I imagine you are many things to many lovers, like a snake who sheds its skin for each new season. Tell me, have you ever been a sodomite?" She reaches for my sex, but slides her fingertips down through the wetness to my asshole. I groan, and turn under her so I'm face down. She keeps stroking the sensitive pucker delicately until I'm rubbing against the bed in a delicious torment.

"Well, what do you answer? Have you seduced young boys, fresh-faced and tender as women, and penetrated them? Have you given in to one of my noblemen who look at you so darkly?"

Now, one of her hands holds my cheeks apart as her fingers push into me, slick with cunt-juices. I'm breathless. "I've fucked boys, but this sin I have never tasted."

"You're my boy tonight, and I will have you."

My legs are spread around her knees. Her cock feels immense as it opens my ass, and I try to shift away from it. She holds me down with kisses on the back of my neck. I burn, and then, as she moves minutely, I ignite, my skin and muscles finding the pleasure. I bend my head and arch into her, and she growls and grabs a handful of curls, riding deeper along the stretched and secret flesh with each clinging thrust. Finally, the tip stabs some interior joint nucleus of my clit and my spine, and my cunt clenches on the bliss as if I were filled everywhere. The Queen's cock is inside me.

Much later, Elizabeth and I lie together under the coverlet in a tangle of limbs. "I want to have your portrait painted," she says, scratching along my collarbone with her fingernails. "I want you painted in a doublet the color of blood, looking like a handsome mystery, with the fold of a dark cloak obscuring your nether parts. I want to hang you in my gallery."

I roll onto her, letting her feel my weight, and answer her. "I want to take you in your gallery, your Majesty. I want to fuck you naked on the cold marble, while we watch ourselves from the walls, and smile."

Luck of the Irish
Kyle Walker

"Thanks for coming," Alan told Mari. "I *have* to go, but I'm *not* looking forward to it, and you're better at saying something nice than I am."

He picked up their tickets at the box office of the Off-Broadway theater, and an usher guided them to excellent seats. When Mari commented on that, Alan shook his head: "Good seats to see a bad show." His boyfriend was doing the costumes for *Star of Delight*.

Mari thumbed through her playbill and spotted a name that gave her heart an odd twist.

"Brigid Flanagan? Is that the one who was on TV...?"

"Some old show before I was born," Alan said. "Back in the '60s or something...."

"*Cowboys and Girls*," Mari finished. "I loved that show. Well, I loved Brigid Flanagan...."

"I think I saw it on *Nick at Nite,* " Alan said.

Mari had seen Brigid Flanagan in her dreams. From the time she was eight until she was twelve, her Friday nights were reserved for *Cowboys and Girls,* a drama set in post–Civil

War Wyoming, following the stories of a strong, beautiful matriarch (played by '40s movie star Molly Webster), her brood of daughters, and the cowboys on her ranch. Brigid Flanagan played Maeve, the Irish cousin.

Each week, Mari waited for Cousin Maeve's scenes, fascinated with the way her auburn ringlets spilled down her back, how she clung to the horse and rode like the wind for Doc when someone broke his leg, or got bit by a snake.

In hindsight, Mari realized it wasn't a very good show, though Molly Webster had brought a level of dignity to her part, and Mari's fascination with Brigid Flanagan had taken her on quite a journey. She began to write stories about herself and Cousin Maeve in a secret notebook, adventures in which they got lost in the mountains together, or left the ranch and went to San Francisco (even at that age, Mari knew she was destined for the big city).

She rehearsed the stories each night as she fell asleep, and woke one morning from a dream in which Brigid Flanagan had smiled at her, and they had begun to kiss. In the dream they'd kissed until Mari felt herself beginning to throb. She woke from the dream and reached down to touch herself, and found her fingers were wet.

At her all-girl school, the general opinion was that boys could masturbate, but not girls (if anyone had discovered otherwise by the sixth grade, they hadn't shared it). Mari wondered if a girl could turn into a boy. She wished she could be one, so she could kiss Brigid Flanagan. The dream disturbed her for weeks, and she watched the show with a strange feeling of guilt.

She became fascinated with all things Irish, not a bad thing at a Catholic school. Her knowledge of saints, poets, and playwrights drew her toward Irish Studies in college, and her senior thesis on Boadicea, the warrior queen, got her high honors and a fellowship from a Hibernian society to graduate school. Nearly two decades into her life as an editor, she wondered what career she might have had if she'd sublimated a crush on one of the Brady girls instead.

The lights dimmed and the play began. As soon as Brigid Flanagan walked onstage, Mari's critical faculties ceased to operate. She was twelve again, sitting too close to the TV, enthralled by the Irish beauty. Brigid's voice was lower than it had been in 1968, but still clear and lilting; she appeared to have aged gracefully. Her still-excellent figure was shown off by the beautiful costumes.

She played an Irish mother whose adult daughter was visiting from the United States. The mother wanted the daughter to move back, an old beau of the daughter's tried to start things up again, and there were other events about as predictable and interesting as a fairly good television movie.

According to Alan, the playwright wrote for a popular TV series. Mari was touched by her heartfelt but misplaced desire to write for the stage. She thought up some nice things to say if they went backstage, which she desperately hoped they would.

In the second act, Brigid had one excellent scene that almost transcended the work. Mari was glad to find out that her first love had been someone with real talent; she'd briefly worried that the flesh-and-blood actress might not measure up to the memories. Mari found herself swamped again by all the powerful feelings that had swept over her each week.

She leapt to her feet and applauded at the curtain call as Brigid bowed. "Do you want to go back?" Alan asked.

"It would be polite," Mari said.

Backstage, Mari told Alan's boyfriend his costumes were fabulous, and met the playwright; she commented favorably on the production, and how much she'd liked Brigid's performance. Zoey put her hand to her heart: "She's my guardian angel! I met her a couple years ago when she did a guest spot on our show. I'd always loved her...you remember, from *Cowboys and Girls*...." Mari gave the playwright a sharp look. "I was obsessed with that show; it turned me into a writer, I swear! When I finally met her, she was just as gracious as she could be; she encouraged me to write this play."

It hadn't occurred to Mari that Brigid might have had that effect on anyone else. Perhaps they were all picking up on a little something?

"She and her husband were so good to me," Zoey went on, derailing that train of thought. "They were devoted to each other until he died. When I got married, I told my husband I wanted us to be like them."

Finally, Brigid emerged from her dressing room, tying the ribbons of a broad-brimmed hat.

"Would anyone like to grab a bite?" Zoey asked. "Brigid?" She took the actress's hand and led her over. "This is Mari Myers, an editor at a publishing house here. She saw the play and said very nice things about you."

"An editor, is it?" Brigid replied, putting her hand on Mari's arm. "Well then, you must publish something this girl writes. She's very talented, my Zoey."

Mari had had the experience of meeting people she'd admired, and had learned how not to frighten them. Still, it took all her discipline not to leap on Brigid, sobbing *I love you I love you.*

"I was just telling Zoey how much I liked your work in that last scene, Ms. Flanagan," she said. "I was one of your many fans from *Cowboys and Girls,* and it was gratifying to see you again."

"Please, call me Brigid," the actress said with an inviting smile. "I always tried to do my best, even though the show wasn't a *critical* favorite."

"I can't imagine you doing any less," Mari replied.

"That's grand to hear at this stage of the game," Brigid said.

"Have you ever thought of writing a memoir?" Mari asked, happy she had a profession that made it appropriate to ask such questions.

"I'll take my secrets to the grave!" Brigid swore with a wink.

"Well, I've got to run," Zoey said. "Do you want to come to dinner? Or can I drop you?"

"No, dear, thanks for the offer," Brigid demurred. "And you're on the West Side and I'm on the East...."

"I'm on the East Side, too," Mari said. Alan had already disappeared with his costume designer and she'd have to find her own way home. "Perhaps we can share a cab?"

It was a glorious spring day, and when they emerged from the theater, Brigid asked Mari if she minded walking. "It's hard to find people in Los Angeles who've heard of such a thing. They'll run for miles on treadmills, but here, you can actually get from place to place on your own two feet."

"Walking is one of my favorite things about New York," Mari told her. "I would miss it if I lived anywhere else."

"Oh, California has its compensations," said Brigid. "Beautiful weather, beautiful scenery, beautiful boys and girls." She put her arm through Mari's in the European manner. Mari saw herself bending Brigid back into a passionate kiss, and focused on saying something that wasn't: *you! me! here! now!*

"I lived in New York when I first came over," Brigid continued. "So exciting: you'd do stage and television and radio all in the same week. But I went out to Hollywood for a screen test, and never came back."

"It's good to have you here now," Mari told her. "Especially in the spring, when everything is coming back to life."

"Like me," Brigid said. "I needed to get away for a bit...I haven't been myself since Max died...my husband. I can't believe it was almost three years ago. Heart attack."

"I lost my...soul mate about then," Mari told her. "We learn to live with it, but I don't know that we ever get over it." Presumably Brigid knew plenty of gay people, but Mari wasn't sure how out she could be to a woman of her age and background.

"We were lucky to have loved, and been loved, weren't we?" Brigid said.

Mari invited Brigid up for a cup of tea, and Brigid seemed happy to accept.

"I don't really know anyone here anymore," she said as they entered Mari's building. "We had a wide circle of friends, and traveled quite a bit, but my husband was my favorite companion. I still know a lot of people in the business," she added. "But they seem to speak a different language. And they don't talk about anything but work."

"Oh, I've got opinions on everything," Mari said lightly as they ascended. "Some are even based on fact. I'd be happy to discuss how I think the world should be run."

"Careful," Brigid said. "That's how people got blacklisted."

"Now *that* was before your time..." Mari began.

"Bless you, dear," Brigid replied with a brilliant smile. "I was a slip of a girl when I got to Hollywood in 1959, but they still talked about the blacklist, and the careers it ruined; Hollywood was, and is, very much a place where you keep your mouth shut, and the smart ones keep their business as private as possible."

Mari's apartment was bathed in the late afternoon light, and Brigid went to the window that faced the river.

"Oh, what a grand view!" she said.

"It's even better from the bedroom," Mari replied, delivering another mental kick to herself.

"May I?" Brigid asked.

As long as you let me join you....

"Of course," Mari replied out loud. "I'll just start the tea...."

She busied herself boiling the water and selected some teas, then felt her face to make sure she wasn't still blushing. She found Brigid in the living room inspecting her mementos.

"Is this your departed soul mate?" she asked, gently picking up Mari and her partner Darby's reception photo.

"Yes. What kind of tea would you like?"

"What do you have?" Brigid asked, replacing the photo.

Lesbian tea! Crushed out, woman-loving tea that I would like to lick from your lips.

"Umm...green tea, Earl Grey, Constant Comment.... What do you like?" Mari held out the packets.

"What do *you* like?" Brigid asked, moving closer.

Mari selected the Constant Comment and managed, "How's this?"

"I like it very much," Brigid replied, taking the bag. She inhaled deeply. "The aroma brings back memories of a love affair I once had."

"I guess that's why they call it sense memory," Mari said. "There goes the kettle. I'll get the teapot."

"Take a good deep breath!" Brigid declared, thrusting the bag under Mari's nose. Mari knew what moment the smell of Constant Comment would take her to from now on.

They shared some shortbread with the tea, licking their lips for the last sweet crumbs.

"You missed one," Brigid said. "Here...." She took the bit of cookie from Mari's lip on her fingertip. Her tongue darted out and licked it. "What an intimate ritual. Max and I made it a point to have tea at least once a week."

"Darby wasn't much for tea, but she always had a cup of coffee with me," Mari said. "I miss that, as much as the other intimacy. It's so nice when your lover is also your good friend."

"Max was my husband, and my good friend, but he wasn't my lover," Brigid said. "We *did* love each other, though, make no mistake about that."

Mari said nothing. She'd long ago learned that not asking questions was one of the best ways to keep someone talking.

"Max and I were very well matched," Brigid recalled. "Molly Webster introduced us. She taught me the rules of Hollywood."

Mari had seen some of Molly Webster's movies; she played gun molls and dames of the sort who would take a bullet for their man. She'd married at least once, though some books mentioned her as one of the "Sewing Circle" of glamorous Hollywood lesbians.

"Now *there* was a fine actress," Mari offered. "You couldn't take your eyes off her when she was on the screen."

"Or in person," Brigid said. "That one knew how to get a girl's attention. Invite you to lunch in her dressing room, offer to coach you in a difficult scene."

"Would you care for an after-tea cocktail?" Mari offered.

"How is your martini, my dear?"

"Not good," Mari confessed. "I do a better gin and tonic."

"Well then, g-and-t it shall be!" Brigid giggled. " I don't often imbibe anymore," she confided. "Bad for the skin and my tongue gets loose. I never know *what* I'll say, or where I'll put my hands!" Mari poured a hefty slug of gin into a glass, and sprinkled in a drop of tonic, floating a lime on top.

They clinked their glasses, and Brigid took a long sip.

"Here's to old fans and new friends. And what's yet to come!"

"Hear, hear," Mari agreed. Brigid grew serious. Mari allowed herself to see the age that Brigid was fighting tooth and nail. There were crow's-feet by her eyes, and her jawline was not as firm as it had been. Her lip line had shrunk, and she'd filled it in, and tried to conceal the lines around her mouth. Still, her skin was fair and unblemished, and not pulled taut. Her auburn hair, several shades darker than Mari's, was full and soft and fell around still-classic cheekbones. Mari thought she was more beautiful than ever.

"There was a time, you know, when one's career could be destroyed at the whisper of a scandal. The studio could make sure you never worked again."

"It's not like that anymore, is it?" Mari asked.

"Hollywood is still the biggest closet of them all," Brigid told her. "I suppose you find that appalling."

"Who am I to judge?" Mari said. "Am I here to hurt people? Or to let them be, and maybe try and make things better?"

"Spoken like a true Catholic schoolgirl!" Brigid said.

"Bless the dear sisters..." Mari said. "Some were *so* lovely."

"Isn't that what gets us into trouble?" Brigid said, almost to herself. "A kind eye, a soft hand...a sweet voice and a spiritual nature...the next thing you know, you're sent home from school and told not to come back."

"You went far away," Mari observed.

"What else was there for it? To be a town pariah in the bog-end of Ireland? Marry some lout to prove I could drop babies like a normal girl?" Brigid took another sip of her drink. "I went to London...that's where the fallen women were supposed to go!"

"How did you survive?" Mari asked.

"Quite easily, really!" Brigid said with a grin. "I was a pretty thing!"

"Beautiful, you mean," Mari said.

"Thank you, sweetheart. A pretty girl can go far, and if she keeps her wits about her, she needn't end up being taken advantage of. Dear, would you freshen my drink?" Mari did, noting that Brigid had a way of making her requests seem like she was bestowing a favor.

"I got work as a model for art classes," she said. "The pay was good, and the boys and girls wanted to take me out. The boys spent pots of money trying to get me into bed, the girls were more gentle and seductive. And once you meet artists, you start meeting writers and actors and all sorts of interesting types...."

"Sounds like a lovely time," Mari said appreciatively. If she'd had a clue about herself before she was in her '30s, she would have picked off a few young women writers, instead of just falling in love with their work.

"At first, I kept thinking of what the nuns had taught me, what my family would say, but somehow I was able to put it behind me. Why should I put any stock in anything they said when it made me so unhappy?"

"You're a wise woman," Mari said. "I bought into it for many more years."

"Then be thankful that you eventually found out what you needed," Brigid said, laying her hand on Mari's arm again. This time she left it there.

Mari wanted to kiss Brigid, but stopped herself. Brigid was someone to be wooed delicately. A sudden lunge would put her off. Mari rather liked sudden lunges, but she would have to adjust to Brigid's tempo. The charge building between them was exhilarating.

Brigid brushed a lock of hair off Mari's forehead. "You look like you were going to say something," she commented.

"Did you have some kind of plan for what you would do?"

"I'm by nature a careful girl," Brigid replied. "Not that I'm cowardly," she added. "But while I was gathering rosebuds, I knew I needed a future. One girl took me to her acting school, and I met the head, who was a dear, loving woman, and I began to learn how to live, onstage and off. I felt so good and free when I was acting...." She ran her hands through her hair, and slipped out of her shoes. "How glorious to speak the Bard or O'Neill, or find the good bits in even a bad play, and make people pay attention and think."

"I love artists," Mari said with a sigh.

"Lots of people do," Brigid replied. "My teacher had a circle of influential friends, and got me seen for things, but I got the parts myself, on talent. It worked well for us both. She took care of me, and my success enhanced her reputation."

"Did you love her?" Mari asked hesitantly.

"I was never with anyone I didn't love," Brigid said, not offended. "I couldn't do that. I would find something loveable about them. I was only ever with someone I cared for."

"I'll bet you're a very good friend," Mari observed.

"I am," Brigid agreed. "If anyone has been good to me, I don't forget it. That much of the nuns' teaching remained... though I'm not sure Sister Mary Joseph would have been able to see it without fainting dead away!"

They giggled a bit too much, and Mari realized they ought to eat something, or risk passing out. She offered to make dinner.

"I'm pining for a home-cooked meal," Brigid said. "Max did the cooking, and I'm not the least bit talented that way."

"My repertoire isn't vast, but I can whip up an omelet...."

"My dear, you could be a professional chef!" Brigid declared a few minutes later. "May I?" she reached to Mari's plate and speared a mushroom.

"Let me..." Mari said, holding out a forkful. Brigid steadied Mari's hand with her own, and licked the fork.

"Inspired..." she said.

"I'm inspired, all right," Mari replied.

"I was hoping you might be," Brigid said, folding her napkin.

Mari pulled out Brigid's chair. As she rose, Mari gently brushed her neck with a kiss. Brigid's fair skin colored prettily, her eyes sparkled.

"I thought you might...you're very...subtle," Mari said, blushing again.

"One has to be," Brigid said, looking away. "One might want something very much, but you have to think of the risk...."

Mari suddenly realized the effort it must have taken Brigid all those years to try to find love without losing everything else. Mari knew some of her friends would scorn anyone like that as a coward and a liar. *Maybe I wouldn't have done what she did,* Mari thought. *But she's the one who had to live with her choices, and it does neither of us any good for me to turn away, and anyway I don't want to.*

"You can do and say anything, and none of it will come back to hurt you," she told Brigid.

Brigid moved into Mari's embrace, and nestled between her breasts. Mari liked being tall, and loved the feel of her arms encircling a woman, holding her, kissing the top of her head, feeling lips so close to her nipples. She kissed Brigid's upturned face, her eyelids, the tip of her nose, then a gentle brush across her lips. She was rewarded with a ragged sigh.

"Again, please," Brigid whispered. Mari complied, as bits of the stories she'd written so long ago flashed into her head. She was the passionate, ignorant adolescent, and the character she'd made up for herself in the stories was having an adventure with cousin Maeve; no, she was a grownup of deeper, more informed lust kissing a beautiful woman, who happened to be an actress, who played the first woman she'd fallen in love with, who was kissing her in her apartment in New York City later in the same lifetime.

She bent Brigid back in the kiss she'd been coveting all day. Brigid twined her arms around Mari's neck and threw back her head after their lips parted, leaving Mari to suck and bite her neck.

"Careful...I have a show on Tuesday," she murmured.

"Of course," Mari replied between nibbles. "I'll only bite the parts of you that are covered!"

"You're a thoughtful girl," Brigid sighed. "I want to *feel* something...."

"Trust me, you will," Mari said, leading her to the bedroom.

Mari's hands caressed the silk of Brigid's blouse, unzipped her crisp linen skirt; she was delighted to discover Brigid wore a garter belt and stockings. Brigid unclasped her bra, turning her body away. Mari could see her steeling herself, caught a glimpse of uncertainty, could almost hear Brigid think: *Am I pretty enough? Am I too old?*

"My, what beautiful legs you have, said the Big Bad Wolf," Mari purred as she shed the last of her own clothes. She rubbed her cheek on the silk stocking over Brigid's inner thigh. She licked the exposed flesh between the top of the stockings and Brigid's panties. She laid her body along Brigid's, touching their nipples together. She felt the wetness of Brigid's pussy. Brigid clung to her and rubbed her crotch hard against Mari's thigh.

"Do you have a cock? A big one to ride me with?" she asked hopefully.

"How big?" Mari reached under the bed for her toy bag. She pulled out a large black one that barely fit into the harness.

"Ooh! That's lovely," Brigid said. "Then, if you like, I can use it on you!" Mari laughed with delight.

She pulled the harness on and the dildo bobbed jauntily at her crotch. She'd never been able to decide whether she was more turned on by seeing a woman wearing a cock, or being that woman. Brigid went down on it, and Mari swore she could feel Brigid's lips on her actual flesh; she thrust forward as Brigid's head moved faster and faster. Her nipples stood erect as Brigid's hands stole upward to squeeze them.

She pulled the cock from Brigid's mouth and said: "I need to go in you."

"I like it from behind," Brigid told her. Her pink ass rose in the air as she thrust it upward, and Mari bent down to kiss and bite her cheeks. She ran her tongue to where Brigid's pussy began, smooth and hairless. It was quite wet, and Mari heard her mutter: *Please, yes, I'm ready....*

She guided the head of the cock into Brigid's pussy and held it for a moment, until she felt Brigid relax, then thrust it in slow and deep, guiding herself by the hard, almost relieved moans she heard, until she was deep inside.

"Ah, yes...so good," Brigid murmured. "So long...oh ride me...."

Mari pushed harder, until she was slamming into Brigid, She draped herself over the other woman, squeezing her breasts, biting her neck.

"More...more...harder!" Brigid sobbed. She suddenly breathed in through clenched teeth and fell silent. Mari could feel her orgasm, like the ocean, first drawing back, then crashing to shore. She felt her own heart beating fast, as hard as Brigid's. She gently slipped out, and Brigid slumped to the bed, eyes closed, glistening.

Mari took Brigid in her arms, and kissed her, babbling words of love and comfort. She was surprised at how undone she was, how much it had meant.

"Oh, lovey, that was brilliant," Brigid said, nuzzling Mari's neck. She licked the sweat from Mari's breastbone. "I haven't come like that in…too long." Mari grasped the dripping dildo. She ran her finger along its length and brought it to her mouth, Brigid's tongue twining with hers as she tasted the come.

"What else do you have in your bag of tricks?" Brigid asked, reaching for the toy bag. She looked through the collection of dildos, vibrators, collars, butt plugs, and other items. She selected a strand of blue silicon beads, graduated in size. "Do you enjoy a little something up the bum?"

"I'm a backdoor girl," Mari admitted.

"And here's a wee pot of lube," Brigid said. She coated the beads, and Mari grew hot watching her. Brigid knelt before her, as Mari spread her legs. With her little finger, Brigid gently began to probe Mari's anus. Mari relaxed and let the finger slide in, and soon felt the smallest of the beads entering her. Brigid crooned as she guided them in slowly, gently. She lowered her face and Mari could feel Brigid blowing on her clit, which stood hard and erect.

"What a dear pearl you have," Brigid whispered, and Mari felt Brigid's lips brushing it as the beads continued to go deeper into her.

It was slow and melting and Mari stopped thinking, let herself be swept away by the nimble, knowing lips and fingers. Brigid teased her clit and made it stand at attention and Mari growled with delight. The wave of her climax was growing, swelling, and she willed it higher before it broke. She twined her fingers in Brigid's hair and pushed herself forward to take the next bead until she was holding the entire strand, bearing a delightful fullness enhanced by the ever more intense tingling in her pussy. Brigid suddenly pulled the beads out and Mari came in a wet rush with a long, loud howl. Brigid looked up, her face damp. Mari's body shook, and she felt tears on her own cheeks.

"Oh, so you're a screamer," Brigid teased. She snuggled in next to Mari. "It's always gratifying when someone appreciates your work." Mari could tell she was proud of herself.

"Can I have your autograph, Ms. Flanagan?" she murmured. Brigid shouted with laughter. A short time later, Mari reached for the phone. She called her office and left word that she wouldn't be in the next day. Brigid looked at her hopefully. Mari rolled back into her arms.

"Now we both have tomorrow off. I'd be delighted if you'd stay."

"As long as you'll have me," Brigid said. "And I won't wear out my welcome. The show ends in a couple more weeks."

"You could stay after it closes..." Mari suggested.

"Bless you, dear," Brigid replied. "But California is my home. I would miss my house, and my garden, and my friends." Brigid squeezed her hand. "I'd ask you to come to Los Angeles, but this is *your* home."

And, Mari thought, even if she had wanted to go to L.A., she didn't want a relationship she had to hide.

"We have a few glorious weeks," Brigid told her. "And after, there're phones, and scented paper for *billets-doux,* and planes that can fly you across the country in just a few hours."

"Then we'll make the most of it," Mari said. "And when you go home, I'll hope we can stay in each other's lives."

"I'll keep you in my heart," Brigid said. Mari felt herself tearing up. "You're someone who belongs there. Somehow, you've learned to love freely, when you're moved to, with everything that's in you."

"I dreamed of kissing you when I was twelve years old," she told Brigid. "And I didn't actually kiss a woman until I was thirty. That's too many years wasted worrying about the wrong things. Once I knew what I wanted, I stopped being afraid, and love became something worth everything else combined."

"You're a true romantic," Brigid smiled. "Like my friend

Marlene Dietrich. I never met anyone who loved love as much as she did. She'd have liked you. She'd have wanted you."

Mari thought that was one of the finest compliments she'd ever received.

"You look quite pleased," Brigid said.

"And why not? I'm lying next to a beautiful woman who makes love like an angel—I assume angels make love—and I have the day off tomorrow."

"So am I, and so do I!" Brigid said. "What a coincidence!"

They rejoiced again over their mutual good fortune.

Boys

Ana Peril

"You think that one's cute?" said Mariano, pointing across the bar. I hung out with the boys every night then, watching boys, drinking and smoking and rolling and snorting and not looking for a girlfriend. Mariano got anyone he wanted, and not just on gay.com but in these sketch-ass places downtown with everyone so fucking hot and drunk, including, I hope, us. I looked where he was pointing.

I looked at you, dancing close, your hand on the guy's waist, your mouth next to his ear. Twenty-five or thirty? Maybe a grad student. Femme, but you were leading him. I felt rather than saw you press your cock against his thigh, and felt a sharp, unexpected pain between my breasts. The music was house, or something, something I was supposed to like, and just as I turned back to the boys, the cute bartender spilled a shot of dark booze across the counter. It dripped between us to the floor. "Sorry," she said, smiling at me from under blonde curls. She looked straight, but I'm not sure. I wasn't looking, but if I had been it would have been for a dyke. I looked back at you.

"I heard he fucks women," said Adam.

"I don't care. I'm not interested."

"Yeah, you are," said Mariano. "Yeah you so fucking are." But I knew that was an occupational risk of time with the boys, the continual projection of desire so intense that it seemed to spill over onto everyone. I watched him as he walked over to you.

The three of us lost Adam to some med student and somehow left the bar. You said your place was close, that we should all walk there together and smoke a little. But I was tired, almost tired enough to skip the weed and leave the two of you to it. When we got to your doorstep, you turned under the streetlight, your dark eyes serious. "Good night, Mariano. It was lovely meeting you." You kissed on the lips the way the boys do. He turned away from the house. With your strong arm, you opened the door for me, and let me, transfixed, walk in first.

Inside the house, you didn't bother to turn the lights on. You kissed me, your lips soft, sucking on my lower lip, biting. I was drunk enough to like it. You pushed me up against the wall and your knee came up between my legs. I put my hands up your shirt, stopped short for a confused moment, and in a moment of decision frantically unbound your breasts.

"Get on your knees, bitch," you said. With your hand in my hair, you jerked me around to face the wall. With the other you traced my naked spine. You licked your finger and circled my nipple with it, jerked my head back by the hair, bit my earlobe. Breathing raggedly on my neck, you moved your left hand down and stopped right above where I wanted it. You pinned me against the wall, with your whole body, your nipples hard. I arched against them. "I said get on your fucking knees." I slid down the wall, my tits and right cheek aching from the pressure. You knelt behind me. "Tell me what I'm going to do to you."

"You're going to fuck me," I whispered.

You slapped my left cheek hard. My chin banged against the wall.

"Tell me louder."

I didn't know exactly what you had to do with the university and was afraid to ask, to uncover complications. A lot of people won't fuck undergrads, a lot more than I would have thought. A lot of people have kinks they won't show to someone they'll see again, especially someone who might know or be one of their students.

"You're going to fuck me."

"I'm going to fuck the shit out of you," you answered, letting go of my hair. You ran your arm down my shoulder to my tied hands, and in one swift motion grabbed my wrists and jerked them up behind my back. I arched and cried out from the sharp pain that ran up my arms to my shoulders. You laughed, bit my neck, and twisted my nipple, a little too hard, between thumbnail and forefinger. "Beg me."

"Please," I said softly.

You slapped me again, harder. I braced myself to avoid banging my face against the wall. You pulled my wrists higher up my back. "Again."

"Please, please," I said. "Put your dick in me."

"Shut up," you said, and hit me hard across the ass, licked two fingers and plunged them in my cunt. I squeezed them with my whole body and you thrust in and out, your hand slippery, adding a third. I cried out in surprise. "Shut up!" And then a fourth finger. For a while you rammed into and slid out of me, your fingers finding that spot and pulling out, thrusting in and pulling out, your body slamming my tits and shoulders against the wall. You hurt me again and again, and each time I almost came, till I was exhausted, leaning back against you. You banged my breasts and face into the wall one last time, your hips so hard and fingers so deep into me that I thought I would break, I thought I would come, and then you pulled out again.

"You want my dick, you little cunt? You want me to fuck you?"

"Yeah," I whispered. I had played this game before, but only at parties, with all those sex-positive riot grrls and their rulebooks. I was used to knowing what was going to happen. It was a good sign that you kept asking me if I wanted you, it meant you weren't an ax murderer. Not that I cared so much at that moment. No one had ever hit me so hard, or fucked me so mercilessly, and I knew you were going to do worse. My cunt and pulse pounded in fear and frenzy. Come on.

"Face me." You jerked my head around by the hair, and I whipped around, sat on my haunches in front of you. You knelt facing me, held my hands tight against my back, untied the rope, and in one motion pulled my wrists in front of me and tied them again.

"Show me. Touch yourself."

I couldn't get in deep enough, could just play around the opening, touch the engorged lips but not hard enough. You laughed at me with your red mouth, arching your back. Your breasts were tight against your sleeveless undershirt, and your chin jutting out in the dark between us, your dick bulging against your pants. You stood up. "Unzip my pants." I brought my wet fingers to your fly, unzipped it, unbuttoned your pants, and tugged at the waist of your boxers. A little black tattoo, a long, swirling 3-shape, shone on your right hipbone. You pushed your purple dick into my mouth and then pulled out, slapped my cheeks with it twice. "Suck it, you little slut." Your hand tightened in my hair. I licked the base, circled the head with my tongue. You pushed into my mouth and I swallowed as much as I could, sucking hard. I rubbed my thighs together, felt the pounding between my legs.

"I'm so fucking hard," you said. "I'm going to fuck you in

the throat, in the cunt, in the ass. I'm going to make you beg, you little bitch, and you won't know whether you're begging for me to stop or never stop."

All of a sudden a wave of panic swept through me, and confusion, and something worse. I slumped on my haunches, rested my head on your strong hip, and started to cry. You stroked my face. "Do you want to talk about it?"

"No. I don't want to talk about it." If I let myself go in these moments, let myself have flashbacks, feel anger toward the person there with me, it can go on and on. Stopping is no solution. Or that's how it feels—that I'll never feel desire again, that I'll be flooded with unrelenting anger like pain, that I'll kill rather than feel pleasure. I can't stop. I sniffled, straightened up, wiped my face with the back of my hand, and played with the fallen waist of your sailor pants, touching the crease between them and your soft skin.

"How long have you been a boy?"

"I'm not. I pass."

I spent a long minute studying you.

"Well? Do you want me to fuck you or what?"

"Untie me," I said.

You didn't look that pissed off, just took the razor from your pocket, snapped it open, and cut the rope. It fell onto my knees, and you snapped the razor closed and threw it on the floor. "Now what?"

I jumped to my feet and pounced on you. You put your hand on my hip and I took it in mine, twisted it behind your back, and backed you up against your desk. "Oh," you gasped. Books, papers, your cell phone, and pencils crashed onto the floor. I slid my hand into your fly, under the waist of your boxers, and touched you where your dick met your body. You shuddered a little, arched your breasts into me through the thin cotton. "I'm going to fuck you," I snarled into your cheek. "I'm going to put my whole hand in you. You fucking cunt."

"No," you whispered, smiling, and edged your ass back on the desk, opening your legs a little. I slapped you hard twice across your beautiful cheekbones. "Stop smiling." I licked your lips, your teeth. We kissed. "Open your legs wider," I said, and edged two fingers against the lips of your cunt. You sighed, pulled your arm out of my grasp, and rested your palms against my chest.

We kissed again, and in one motion you knocked me onto my back. I shuddered and gasped as my head hit the floor, dizzy from pain. "Fuck you."

"I'm going to fuck you. I'm going to fuck you." You knelt next to me, held my wrists above my head in your right fist, and with your right knee pinned my struggling left leg. "Come on, play nice," you coaxed. I kicked you away with my right leg, and you took hold of my knee and held it down bent, against the floor, my legs open. I was so hot from the force and the closeness of your body that I forgot what I had wanted to do. I wanted you to make me, force me, hurt me, show me your desire. I closed my legs again and you opened them, hard, with your knee, ran your hand up between them to my clit. "You want me to fuck you so bad," you said. "So play nice and I won't hurt you." You leaned over me, your shirt hiked up your belly, your breasts smooth and swaying, still pinning my wrists and knees to the ground. With your free hand you caressed your dick, sighed a little, played with my clit, laughed at my outrage, and spit on your hand. "What's the matter? You still a virgin? You afraid it's going to hurt?"

"Yeah," I said. I pulled my right hand free and shoved you, but you didn't fall. You smacked me hard in the face and then again, across my tits. "Don't worry. It's only going to hurt when I fuck you in the ass." My cheeks and nipples stung. You spat on your free hand, passed it across your dick, and entered me, hard. Your cock was thick, and you moved in and out fast, each time making me wait a little too long and then, as I was about to cry in desire and frustration, penetrated me deep, deep. I couldn't believe you were fucking me with a dick lubed only with spit. You licked your fingers and swiftly put two in my ass, fucking me so that as your dick went in, your fingers came out. You swung your breasts over my face teasingly. "Please, please," I moaned, "please, anything you say, please. Ohhhhnnnnhh, oh, oh."

I don't know how long you fucked me, your breath coming hard, your face flushed. "Oh, god," I said. "Please, god, please, please." Your grip on my wrists tightened as you came, and you trembled and shook, thrusting harder and harder into me. I struggled against your hands, fucked your cock and fingers. I came hard, biting your neck, feeling my cunt contract over and over, fast. You knelt, panting, your face in my neck, rocking back on your haunches, sweat glistening on your auburn breasts and my come shiny on your erect dick, still making little coming noises. I held the back of your smooth neck, stroked your spine. "Shh, shh." You kissed me, tasting mysteriously of cunt. I felt a sudden, frightening wave of softness, of compassion, like my chest was open under your hand. When you finished shivering and rocking, you said in your boy's voice, "Mo? Will you make me a soft-boiled egg?"

"Sure." The dark still came in the windows. I went into the kitchen, put the water on, and turned on the radio.

LIVE: By Request
Samiya A. Bashir

platform heels so high on these boots i bent down to see you thru the sky. the brown suede snaked to the tops of my thighs and grabbed your eyes as soon as i walked in the place. textures always aroused you.

where did my terra firma brownness end and the smooth suede begin? my skirt wasn't as short as you like me to wear on my sluttier days, but it flared and reached heights too dangerous, for tonight, when i turned. i'd forgotten to think of that.

you sitting at the bar.

i remember it darker than it was perhaps. the beer in your hand almost empty. the glass the bartender gave you abandoned. your other hand poised as if just about to check your pocket

for something. i sway over to your end of the bar, try not to notice all the other butches who try not to watch me sashay my way down to you. i know that's your job. it's part of our thing tonight i come to play baby. i bend forward slightly when i reach you so the ass you grab is just ass. you think it's to show you the deep valley of barely contained cleavage my tight top presents so you let your tongue linger a moment there after we kiss. you forget to slide your hand up the warm brown suede to the top, forget how bad you wanna know if i wore panties tonight   'cuz i want a drink. now. please, baby.

we get our drinks and the almost relieved kinda jealousy washes over the face of the b-girl bartender who was trying not to cruise you before i got here. i stand behind your stool, my polished hands hide inside your jacket, between your thighs is just you tonight. good. i let you carry my drink saying nothing 'cuz i still can't tell you how that smooth, sure it isn't practiced, voice of yours turns me on, gets me wet. of course i'm not wearing panties tonight——gotta be careful as i swish not to let my backside twirl——i'm glad your hands are full of drinks.

the big back booth i wanted sits empty. you just smile, knowing you worked it out that way before i got here. i'm always late. you wait.

you hold the drinks while i sit down so i won't knock the table. these boots make my knees so high up I gotta work to keep my skirt under my ass. you sit down, take off your jacket. you look so handsome, flash me the most irresistible damn kid-caught-hand-in-cookie-jar grin that i wanna just eat you alive.   soon come.

so we talk. i haven't seen you in a week. you missed me. i want you. damn. i wanna talk, catch up, giggle with my drink, cross my legs under this too-short table. but just your voice gets me moist and i ain't got on no panties——tonight is for you. and you don't even know it yet.

it's perfect. you're feelin' yourself tonight in black jeans so tight you give the fag boys a fright when you stroll past. hair oiled just right, new boots, even the tank under your shirt is pressed. i'm impressed. i'll let you play the flirt a little while longer. it's important that this is done right. we gotta get outta here.   finish yr beer.
please, baby. you're comin' with me tonight.

i ignore the raised eyebrow—a challenge. you ignore the twinge in your cunt—the erotic fear of being known. your eyes linger too long on the butch behind the bar on the way out—you thought neither of us noticed—but that just turns me on tonight.

i feel the cool breeze on the wetness between my legs first, then coming from the cold stares of street strangers as we walk down the avenue. you tighten your arm around my waist and i fold myself more closely into you, stare my adoration into your eyes.

we'd planned dinner, but i can't wait anymore. i've got other plans so we stop off at your place. you get that knowing, arrogant smile on your lips and try to put your hand up my skirt while you get your keys.
please, baby. look don't touch
tonight. i'll tell you when you can do what you can do.

again with the eyebrows. whatever. this time i walk behind you up the stairs it's all i can do to ask for some water.
please, baby.

i'm torn trying to get my nerve up too and restrain my blistering desire to possess you here now. but i knew who'd win that internal battle. in the kitchen i walk up behind you at the sink. you look so tough as you wash a glass for me with the tenderest hands i've ever seen. i feel a drop of sweat ride my spine to my ass when i reach around you to run my nails up your stomach, pull your back into my breasts and push my pelvis into your ass, push your pelvis into the countertop like i want you—like you want to need to be when you realize what i've been hiding.

all those nights of erotic imagination didn't prepare you for this stiff reality. you didn't think i had it in me. you open your lips almost as if to protest even as your legs spread wider to meet me, even as your deep soft moan betrays you. my fingers in your mouth become a simple formality.

i gotta move quick before we talk ourselves outta this. i whisper in your ear, say: *you can be mama's queer boy tonight if you like.* my fingers run up the crotch of your jeans, you stifle a scream as my nail grazes your ass.

all butches have a black leather belt somewhere. yours is at hand as i grab it and pull your ass a little higher while you reach between your legs to feel my cock. i'm still rubbing it between your thighs when i see the stubborn relief in your eyes as you realize it's not your dick you're drippin' on. it's mine.

you never knew how much you loved me before you got down on your knees on that dark kitchen floor, lifted up my skirt, and slid my dick down your throat. i showed you mercy, took your hand as i led the well known route to the bed, sat you on it with that dazed, amazed look on your face to watch me strip.

off with my blouse—i left the red velvet bra on for a minute. pulled down my skirt—left the brown suede boots on for a minute. let my locks down and stroked my cock.

i let you take off my bra and play titty games for a while to get you comfortable—make you drip like i dripped all down my girlish thighs. i whispered all the ways i would fuck you tonight. you fought off your fright, felt your throat get tight, wouldn't let emotion overpower desire. you cowered into my breasts. you thought that way i wouldn't make you beg. remember?

i took your shirt off—left you the tank. pulled your pants to your ankles so fast you fell facedown, boxer-clad ass in the air—i'll let you think i practiced that move—tight-ass black jeans locked your legs. i let your black belt fall free—that time.

and yes i rubbed your back and whispered my love in your ear, ran my tongue from the nape of your neck to your rear before i made you say it.

and yes i loved you with every part of my body, every part of your body, while the last of your time-toughened defenses melted beneath my touch and you knew you were safe.

and when you finally begged—just a whisper—

fuck me

i knew i could tell you to say it louder. i made you beg for it again and again until i heard you cry *if you don't fuck me goddammit, right now, one of us is gonna die!*

alright then. i entered sacred space you opened to me, let you bury your face in the pillow, helped you fight the monsters of old humiliations, new fears that i wouldn't let you keep your swagger, the staggering dread that i wouldn't be able to see the strong, sexy woman you need to be anymore. you let me bite your back and grab your cunt and tits and whisper over and over that you're mine, tell you this time how good your pussy feels from the inside because we know this is the kinda love that reaches thru these barriers.

you scream your release. i do too—after fucking you some more.

we had never known love like this. we lay in bed all night, took turns feeding each other whatever we had delivered. we talked a little and loved a lot more and freed ourselves for our own acceptance. by morning i had put my dick down for a little while, and you got yours up again and it was like never before. 'cuz i knew you, and you were known and still loved

anyway. we've had a lot of those nights since then. i always try to surprise you. and when you sit in that bar, when those other b-girls try not to look at you, you can stare straight back and know that—in the next twenty minutes or so—the kinda soft/ hard love everyone wants not to speak of gonna storm thru that door on five-inch platform boots, worn for your pleasure, and lead you by the hand back home.

Keeping Up Appearances
Kenya Devoreaux

She was pretty faced and beautifully endowed, my English Literature professor, and as she leaned over for more sugar for her lemonade her C-cups fell in her brassiere like ripe peaches from a tree. I could see her nipples—*oh, Jesus, her nipples*—protruding through her crisply starched linen blouse. It was as if they were whispering to me, *"Norma. Please...."* My own ached, they hadn't been sucked for so long. I wanted to kiss her breasts all over. But I couldn't, could I? She was my professor, after all, and I didn't wish to breach the parameters of the teacher–student relationship. Despite the rumors of Professor Carlyle's affair with Dean Mary Shannon two years prior floating around the university, she appeared to be extremely straitlaced. And appearances *are* everything....

"The clouds are making interesting shapes this afternoon." Ms. Carlyle looked skyward, blue eyes sparkling in the California sunshine. She was nice to let me into her home this way just to discuss my research paper. I wasn't sure whether or not she would rather have been spending Saturday afternoon frolicking in the surf, her body being tossed about by the huge, playful ocean, white froth lingering on those gorgeous breasts. But literature was her favorite subject, after all. She loved words, she loved ideas. And her enthusiasm for language as an art form was infectious. I enjoyed the two of us sitting on her veranda, the sea-salty odor of the ocean before us mixing with the scent of her cologne. It was intoxicating, the converged fragrances of two of nature's wonders: the Pacific Ocean and Professor Katherine Carlyle.

"So, Norma, as for your paper. Before anything, I want you to know that I am flattered by your seeking my counsel. And I enjoy knowing one of my brightest students holds me in such high regard."

"That is encouraging, Ms. Carlyle. Thank you." I found her perfect formation of the vowels and the sharp expulsion of breath on each consonant between her gleaming creamy-whites provocative. I hoped she didn't notice my pupils dilating.

"Now tell me, dear, which genre of literature will you be discussing?"

I was researching lesbian erotica, and although I was not ashamed of my interest, I did not want to cause Ms. Carlyle to blush. Well, she didn't.

"Lesbian erotica, eh?" She raised an eyebrow and chuckled softly before lifting her glass for another sip. "That is some of the best literature in existence. You have wonderful taste." She smiled and looked off into the distance behind me. Then she turned and looked me square in the eye.

"Does it taste good to you?" Ms. Carlyle kept her glass in front of her face, only partially hiding the impish grin frisking about the corners of her bow-shaped mouth.

"Yes, ma'am. It does." It may have been the sugar in my drink or the sugar in her tone, but something was exciting me and causing the type of exquisite discomfort one usually wishes to keep secret.

"What pretty thoughts come to mind as you feel the grit of the sugar slide between your teeth and over your tongue?"

"I feel it very distinctly. The grit is what conveys the sweetness to my taste buds. The lemonade wouldn't taste so sweet if I weren't force to actually partially chew it."

"Do you like that?"

"Uh...yes. Yes...I do."

"Try and develop a mouth fetish. It will make poetry much more fun to read." Ms. Carlyle continued, "And other notable experiences will be all the more intensified." She searched my eyes for a moment and, finding what she was looking for, said with a strange sort of gentleness, "So...let the games begin."

"Okay, professor. I am comparing and contrasting lesbian erotic literature from the Victorian Era with contemporary lesbo-erotic works. Now, I went to a poetry reading and I totally fell in love with the work of this one poet—I think her name was Delaney. The texture of the language was crunchy...you could almost taste it. But the words were huge, multisyllabic. Not like small granules of sugar, but like chips of ice in a cold and sobering drink."

Ms. Carlyle looked interested.

"So anyway, this magnificent lesbian poet said at the end of her set that she was influenced by a Victorian writer by the name of Emily Wittingham. I wanted to go up to her and ask her for more information about that writer, but I didn't want anyone to think *I* was a lesbian—"

"Oh. Yes. Of course," Ms. Carlyle interjected with a sweet smile.

"So I went to the library and I looked on the Internet; I even called the Library of Congress. I can't get my hands on her!"

Ms. Carlyle pushed a real swig of lemonade up over her teeth and then gulped. "Yes, dear. I am very well acquainted with the work of Emily Wittingham. She had a way of using rhyme and meter to stimulate the subconscious of the reader. One could read a piece about a woman playing the piano—a popular pastime of middle-class women in those days—and end up turned-on without knowing why. There is one poem called 'Crushing Cotton'—I could swear it is about two lesbians pushing their pussies together."

My mind slipped out of my body and I was visited by visions of naked blondes, brunettes, and redheads with throbbing, hot-red cunts slung, sprawled, and spread-eagled on clouds of cotton before me. The all wanted my hand inside them.

"Norma. I know you're hot, baby."

"I beg your pardon? How do you mean?"

She laughed good-naturedly. "You need something wet on your hands."

I was immediately embarrassed—and so damned aroused by the possibility that she knew about the dozens of lesbians I had humping in my head.

"When the extremities are cool the entire body cools." She wiped the perspiration from my top lip with her soft fingertip. Her glance down at my hefty cleavage, which was now heaving violently, elicited from her a very soft but audible, "I *ache* to fuck you." Suddenly she sat up straight, squinted her eyes playfully, and then leaned back languidly in her chair. As she spoke with me her hand busied itself with stroking away the droplets of water that had formed on the shaft of her glass. She resumed her commentary about Emily Wittingham.

"What Wittingham is able to do, and better than any lesbian writer since, is penetrate you so deeply...that you are actually forced to abandon everything you've learned about how poetry should be interpreted and *feel* what you're reading. Don't initiate a partnership with the poet in creating the meaning, just allow me—I mean, Emily—to caress your mouth, your eyes, your ears, and even your skin as you see, speak, and feel the piece." Ms. Carlyle licked her lips in enthusiasm. "A real high-caliber writer knows how to take her own ideas and disguise them within the perspective of the character, do you know what I mean? And she'll pump and pump and keep pumping into you that part of herself that makes her original."

I nodded—trying not to lick my own lips.

"Have you ever seen the movie *God, Give Me Wings?* It starred Daisy Andersen and Celia Davis. They are a couple offscreen. Daisy does the writing, I believe. And Celia directs most of the pictures. Well, a little after the second act, the climax—which women artists are noted for fabricating better than men—Daisy slips her hand into Celia's drawers and steals the cherry—"

"Oh, yes. The only clue that she had been visited by the virgin nymph."

"Okay, darling, well that came from a Wittingham poem. Emily believed in immortality. But she lived in a period in which scientific and technological knowledge was not as vast as ours. She knew the only way she could become immortal was through her poetry. The poem itself still resonates—to those who can even find it. Technological advancement doesn't necessarily inspire good taste." She sipped a little of her lemonade at that and sucked a juicy piece of pulp through her teeth. "Fascinating isn't it, dear?"

"Quite."

"Have you ever had an artist suck you so deeply into her fantasy that way? The good stuff can be difficult to get, but the resolution of the tension is exhilarating just the same."

"I think I've just broken into another sweat."

"That's Emily. She knows how to touch you."

"Glory. When I was handling my load without you I was so tense—"

"Come in the ocean.... Swim with me."

At that moment I realized that one needn't ever say yes to a proposition such as that; a slight drop of the jaw will suffice. Professor Carlyle, serious, fiercely intelligent, and—I'd just noticed it—incredibly soft skinned, had just asked me to go skinny-dipping with her...and I couldn't wait. She rose from her chair and stood before me, looking terrific in her white linen blouse and matching pants. She took me by the hand and led me barefoot down to the beach. She came close and did to me what I'd fantasized about since the first day she had entered the lecture hall and introduced herself to the class.

With her tongue pressed into my mouth she slipped her hands under my half-shirt and pulled my breasts so firmly that I fell into her. She slid her hands from under my shirt slowly, savoring every inch of my perky, tight girlishness. She cradled my temples and pressed her face into my hair. Her long, aristocratic nose was nestled in my ear as she fumbled with the belt buckle on my denim shorts. I had to help her undo the buckle. She never broke the connection of our faces, but seemed pleased as punch when she grasped my rear to remove my panties and found I wasn't wearing any. My shorts dropped once they were completely unfastened and I stepped out of them. I stood naked as I watched her undo her own blouse, and parted my legs slightly to enjoy the sea breeze as it caressed my very moist, downy mound and labia. I reached out to assist Professor Carlyle in removing her garments, but she nudged my hand away. As she let her blouse and lace brassiere fall from her body, I gasped. *Don't show me everything, I don't want to come yet.* I was pleased to see I was not the only one standing on the sand with breasts that stood up when unbound by a bra. She got out of her pants quickly, then exposed her whiter-than-white teeth at me expectantly. I looked down at her pussy. I could see the long strands of dirty-blonde down through the lace front of her Victoria's Secret underwear. She looked down at herself, and grabbing a good portion of the material, very smoothly and with much pomp, ripped her drawers down her pelvis and hips and off. She stepped toward me gracefully—like a lady, stroked my left cheek with the lace, and pressed it gently against my nose. She dropped her underwear beside us and we just stood there, each with her hands about the other's waist. Each woman's cunt pressed firmly against the other's cunt. She kissed me.

I sucked my middle finger and tickled her asshole a little.

She chuckled. "Shall we?"

"Let's."

The surf had risen a couple of inches on the waterfront, washing our feet and our clothes away at the same time. I would be naked with her forever. We'd removed all our garments and waded into the deep, wet sea. Stripped of our clothes—and all pretenses.

At Long Last
Madeleine Oh

This was it.

As the train slowed, I snapped my novel shut and pulled my suitcase from between the seats. In a few minutes we'd be face to face after thirty years. Was it curiosity or obsession that had me haring up to Scotland to see the man who'd shattered my twenty-two-year-old heart when he married my cousin, Penelope?

Why was I here? To see how the years had treated Alec? Did I hope to find him sporting a massive beer gut or sagging jowls? Perhaps recovering from a triple bypass and double hip replacements? Sitting in a wheelchair pushed around by his brand-new trophy wife?

If he looked the same as he had at twenty-five, I would rail against the injustice in the world. He didn't. But he wasn't the one who was recognized first.

"Jasmine Waters! May I call you Jasmine?"

It was Emily, wife number two. One of my faithful readers. "Of course you may. It's my name."

"But is seems so....You being so famous and...."

"You must call me Jasmine. Alec does." She all but blush-ed. How deliciously English and young she was, like a fat ripe plum, ready to drop off the branch into my hand.

"He calls you Jazzikins."

He would. He had. Couldn't call me Jazz or Jasmine the way everyone else did. He had to make up a special name that still had the power to tweak my soul. Standing beside her was my old heartache himself. "Hi, Alec."

A man who had left his wife with an autistic teenager and a senile mother-in-law had no right to thrive on it. But heaven help us all, he was still gorgeous. His dark hair was halfway gray, but it looked good on him. And as for his laugh lines, where had they come from? From smiling to himself as he walked away from his responsibilities?

"Jazzikins!" His smile was so sincere, I wanted to spit. "Fantastic to see you!"

I held out my hand before he had a chance to even think about hugging me. "Alec. It's good to see you." That wasn't a lie. I was satisfying my curiosity and, to be truthful, he was as easy on the eyes as ever. He still had a smile to invoke impure thoughts in virgins' minds. It had in mine. He'd just never delivered.

"Jazzikins." I restrained a wince. "After all these years." He grabbed my hand and pulled me into a hug before I could evade, planting a great smacking kiss on my left cheek. While I took a deep, cleansing breath, he stepped back, looking me up and down as if contemplating a purchase. "I still can't believe it! You're here, and all because of Emmsy. Who'd have thought it?"

Thought what? That I could write? That his wife could read? That he was incapable of using anyone's full name? I made a point of not snarling. "How could I not come? Invited to Scotland by a loyal and ardent reader?" He'd better not think I'd spent all day in a train for him. But he did.

"Alec," Emily put a hand on his shoulder. Marking her territory, perhaps? "Let's head for the car. I bet Jasmine wants to kick off her shoes and have a drink."

I decided I might like her, even if she had supplanted my cousin, and hoped her idea of a "drink" entailed something more than a cup of tea. I couldn't help wondering what Alec had told her about me. Was I his ex-wife's cousin, the sister of a school friend, an old, lost love? Most likely, none of the above. Maybe he never remembered breaking my heart.

His dark-green Jaguar was an improvement on the Deux Chevaux he owned the last time I'd ridden with him. His transport might have changed but his laugh hadn't; neither had his voice, or the way he drove too fast, and slid through lights as they changed. He made a very Alec crack and Emily laughed, throwing her head back a little, shaking her long, chestnut-colored hair and showing the vulnerable expanse of a long, pale neck. I'd always longed for a long neck. Still, I had bigger boobs—but she had Alec.

Did I honestly care now? Come to that, had I ever really been in the running? I'd fallen for him like a felled oak. And gotten over him, or so I always told myself. I wasn't the type to do unrequited love. But I'd hurt. Standing as bridesmaid at Penelope's wedding was an agony I hoped never to repeat. Now was payback time! Alec owed for breaking my virgin heart, leaving a gaping hole in my cousin's life, and for the handicapped son he'd abandoned. Penelope wouldn't seek revenge. She was far too kind and up to her eyes with providing care. Simon missed his father desperately, Alec's mother was too senile to realize he'd gone, and poor Penelope was aging daily.

But I was here and willing, and as we settled in the living room, overlooking the garden, I prepared to settle the score. One way or another.

Trouble was, I liked Emily. I could hardly fault her for

falling for Alec; I'd done the same when I hadn't been that much younger. And she was a fan. She had every one of my books in hardback and all but kissed my hands when I gave her an advance copy of the new one. Hard to hate a woman who admires your work and mixes a mean g-and-t.

By the time we were halfway through dinner, I was seriously thinking about smushing Alec's face into his tiramisu as he pontificated about local politics, the virtues of his new car, and the tremendous responsibilities of his job. How many more "Jazzikins" and "Emmsies" and "old things" was I prepared to endure? It was the last that got to me the worst. He had two years on me and I didn't have gray hair. Thanks to science.

Emily was far more tolerant than I. That's what love does to you. But I caught the occasional spark of irritation, and the glances of female complicity she shot my way.

I grinned back as her dark, gray eyes flashed amusement and when she hugged me for helping her load the dishwasher, I squeezed back. Her body was warm and soft and her breasts pressed nicely against mine. She was my height, her body firmer and her breasts higher, but we fit together, the old and new loves of Alec Carpenter.

"How's the coffee coming along, girls?" he called from the sitting room. Emily looked ready to give him hot coffee where it hurt.

It was an odd after-dinner conversation. Emily wanted to talk about my books. I was more than happy to oblige. Alec didn't exactly sneer at mysteries but he came darn close. Then he committed the cardinal sin. "How much do you make on a book?"

"Tell me what you earned last year, and I'll tell you what I made."

He declined the invitation with an irritating laugh. "Oh, Jazzikins! You've changed."

In more ways than he could guess.

I broke up the evening by pleading weariness. Emily kissed me good night with a promise of tea in the morning. Her lips were warm and ripe and young. Hugging her was a joy. I looked forward to my early morning cuppa.

She brought it wearing a short pink robe with satin rosebuds scattered over the yoke. It suited her, bringing out highlights in her dark hair. She blushed deliciously when I told her so. Alec had seldom told me that I looked beautiful either. She sat on the edge of my bed and I watched her firm nipples ride underneath the thin cotton. I'd found my revenge. I just had to find the means.

Alec handed it to me at breakfast.

Emily was annoyed.

I was thrilled.

"Why this weekend? Didn't you tell them you had a visitor?" Emily gave him the closest thing to a pout I'd seen yet.

"Never mind." Time to smooth some amicable oil over the marital waters. "If Alec has a crisis at work, he needs to go."

Emily muttered disagreement.

"I knew Jazzikins would understand." I got Alec's best smile, and heartfelt regrets. He did both really well. "I feel terrible mucking up your weekend when you've come so far."

"You haven't mucked it up. Emily and I will frolic together in the fleshpots of Aberdeen." Emily's face brightened. Alec glowered. No other word for it. I gave him my sweet smile. "She'll look after me, I'm certain." He looked worried. He should. "You go take care of your crisis. Don't bother about us." I sure wasn't going to bother about him. And if I had my way, neither would Emily.

He streaked off in his Jaguar. Emily and I set out in her little Fiesta. Size was of no importance.

"Take me on the tourist tour," I asked. "Show me the sights, and all the bookshops. We can stop somewhere for lunch and somewhere for tea and somewhere for a drink, and if we really feel like it, another somewhere for dinner."

She giggled like a schoolgirl let out of boarding school. We visited the bookstores, and had coffee in a dark-paneled café where we sat close in a corner and she confided in me that Alec worked terribly long hours. His new wife felt neglected. She took me to the rose garden and the maze. We got nicely lost, and held hands muddling our way out.

She drove us to the beach. "It's almost deserted," I said looking at the great crescent of golden sand. "No one's swimming."

"Too damn cold. This is the North Sea."

It wouldn't stop me. "I've got to put a toe in after coming this far."

I left my shoes in the car and ran across the beach. Emily hesitated a few seconds, before following me. The tide was out. I zigzagged over the hard sand, glancing over my shoulder. Emily followed, cutting corners to catch up. I let her, just as we neared the water.

"Chicken?" I teased as I jumped in. Emily hadn't been kidding! An icy wash hit my ankles. She stared. I took a step deeper and held up my skirt.

"Never!" She followed me, and gasped. "This is ridiculous!"

I wouldn't argue. We ran along the water's edge, keeping to the firm sand. My toes were tingling with cold as I outran Emily again. The girl was no marathoner, that was for sure, so I slowed to take her hand, as I made a beeline for the car.

By the time we got there, my feet were numb and turning red, and my calves stung from salt water and North Sea wind. Emily was shivering. "Alec will never believe we did that!" Her right eye watered from the cold, but she grinned.

"Why need he know? Do you tell him everything?"

She shook her head. Slowly. "Not everything."

256

Smart girl.

We wiped our feet on Alec's cricketing sweater. The closely knitted wool warmed our skin as it absorbed the damp and the sand. The sweater was unwearable by the time we were finished. Emily shook her head at it. "He'll throw a wobbly when he sees that."

"Let's save him the worry, then." I took the sand- and salt-encrusted heap and tossed it toward the beach, where the wind caught it momentarily, whipping it higher before it fell, wet and heavy, on the sand.

Emily watched it arc up and fall. I wasn't too sure of the look on her face. Regret? Shock? Worry? Until she smiled. "I doubt he'll miss it until next summer." She shrugged. A wry smile twisted her mouth. She took my hand and squeezed.

I pulled her to me. Slowly. Giving her time to draw back, I wrapped my arms around her and dropped a soft kiss on her forehead. "I'll never tell," I said. She kissed back, a soft whisper of skin on my chilled lips. The warmth of her breath was lost in the wind but the heat of her body wasn't. We stood, arms entwined, warming each other against the wind. It wasn't enough. Emily shivered. "We need to get out of the cold," I said. "Where's the nearest place for a drink?"

The all-but-deserted bar of a vast Victorian hotel.

Dark Lincrusta covered the walls and the rings of generations of damp glasses marred the oak tables. Emily ran her fingers up and down her glass. I raised my drink and savored the best single malt whiskey the bald-headed bartender had to offer. Watching Emily over the rim of my glass, I drank. The old codger's best was pretty good. I took another taste, holding the whiskey in my mouth and working it over my tongue before swallowing.

Emily's manicured nails tapped the side of her glass. She hadn't tasted it beyond a first sip when I'd proposed our mutual health. "Drink up."

"You want to go home?" Her eyes were dark with unspoken wants.

"I think we both need a nice, hot bath."

Her full lips parted. Slowly lifting her glass, she tilted it and drank half the whiskey down with one swallow. I expected her to choke and splutter but she just smiled. "That's good." Her glass made a dull thud on the table as I nodded.

"I never settle for less than the best you can have...or give," I said. Her hand rested on the table, palm down. I covered it with mine. Her skin was still cold. Emily moved her hand so our fingers meshed. There was no mistaking the look in her eyes. She would appreciate what Alec had refused.

She bit her lower lip with one very white tooth. "I'm glad Alec is at work."

"So am I." I swigged the last of my whiskey almost as fast as Emily did hers, ignoring the burning as I swallowed.

We were back in the house in minutes and upstairs in seconds. On the landing, with its ornate railings and decorative cornice, I paused. Her room or mine?

She settled that. Sweet, quiet Emily dragged me into the bathroom. Squeezing my hand, she leaned over the claw-foot tub. Steam rose, misting the gilt-framed mirror as Emily stood upright, and hesitated.

I didn't. I reached out and released her hair from the pale-blue scrunchee. As she shook her head and ran her fingers through her hair, I unbuttoned her blouse.

Did she and Alec share this tub? How hard did he get, seeing her firm, creamy skin swelling above her pink lace bra? Did he lust after her young body? Who was I kidding? They were married! They did this every night. Except when he hared off to save the day and left her alone. But today Emily wasn't alone and she hankered for me. Her nipples weren't hard from the cold this time.

I unsnapped her bra and cupped her breasts. They were

round and sweet, just like her. I pushed aside the lace and slipped the straps and her shirt off her shoulders and unsnapped her jeans. She wore a pretty lace thong that matched her bra. They ended up together on the floor. Her legs were long, her thighs smooth, and her tummy flat. Her breasts hung high and firm with nipples the color of the inside of a Venus shell. I'd looked like that once, back when Alec had rejected me. Now I had crepe thighs and a belly stretched by three pregnancies, but along with the cellulite, I'd gained experience and I knew what pleased women.

I eased my hands down her belly and watched her face. My mouth curled with anticipation. Emily smiled back. I didn't wait any longer. Cupping the back of her head with my hand, I pulled her face to mine. I started soft and slow, just a brush of lips on lips, but she opened her mouth and swallowed the kiss and my breath. Her lips were warm, moist, and as eager as a virgin's. Hell, she most likely *was* one, with a woman. I kissed back, trailing my other hand down between her shoulder blades and holding her steady in my arms.

As I broke off the kiss, I whispered, "Get in the tub." Like a good child, she obeyed. As she stepped in, I couldn't resist skimming my hand over the curve of her lovely, smooth haunch.

"Aren't you coming in?" When I nodded, she reached for a bottle and poured fragrant oil into the bath. The room was now filled with lavender-scented steam. I dropped my clothes on the tiled floor and joined her.

Perfumed water rose to our breasts as I sat down. Brits may not have figured out about ice in cold drinks, but they have hot baths right. As I soaped Emily's breasts with scented foam, she closed her eyes, sighing as my fingers trailed lower. I soaped her all over like a child, having her kneel up as I washed between her legs and down her thighs.

After I rinsed her with a damp washcloth, she washed

me with a touch that left me impatient and ready. Damp and heated, we patted each other dry with warm towels that wrapped us from shoulders to knees.

Emily raised her fingers to my face. "Jasmine," she said, her voice tight and her eyes bright with curiosity and need.

"Come on!" I grabbed her hand and led her down the hallway to the room I'd slept in last night.

She tugged me in the opposite direction.

It took a couple of seconds for me to register where we were headed. She pulled open the door and pulled me inside. After all these years, I was, at long last, ending up in Alec Carpenter's bed.

I grinned as I yanked back the covers, climbed in, and pulled Emily beside me. She tumbled onto her belly and the smooth expanse of her back and lovely, curvy butt inspired me. "Don't move! I'll be back in a minute."

I was down the hall to the bathroom and back with a jar of lavender lotion in less time than it takes to tell.

"What are you doing?' Emily asked, looking over her shoulder as I walked through the doorway.

She hadn't moved.

"Pleasuring you." I squeezed out a dobbit of lotion and rubbed my hands together to warm it before easing my palms across her shoulders and down her back to the curve of her waist. She sighed with pleasure, so I reached for the lotion again. I anointed her. Kissing her neck and shoulders as I stroked lotion into her back and arms. Fluttering my tongue on the soft pale skin behind her knees as I massaged her thighs and butt. She went limp and relaxed under my touch. Lovely. But I didn't want her too loose. I needed her sweating with want as her body arched under me and her eyes blazed her need.

I rested a hand on the curve of her hip and nudged. "Roll over."

Emily didn't need asking twice. She flipped onto her back, giving me an uninterrupted view of her delicious, firm breasts. I ran my tongue up from her rib cage to her nipple and felt her excitement as I worked it between my lips. She gasped as I pulled it into my mouth, and let out a slow moan of contentment as I worked my lips to her other nipple.

"Don't stop," she whispered as I pulled away.

"I won't," I promised.

I could smell her arousal over the scent of lavender but I took my time, running my fingertips over her curves and tasting her skin. As I rested my hand on her bush, she was whimpering with need. I spread her legs with my shoulders and opened her with my fingertips, reveling in the scent of her sex. Gently I breathed on her moist flesh and ran the tip of my tongue from fore to aft. Her head came off the pillow with a jolt, and the eyes that met mine were wide as her cunt.

"Jasmine!" It came out on the tail of a gasp. "There? No one ever...."

Can't say I was surprised. Alec always was a selfish bastard but... "Shhh." I didn't say anything else. My tongue was busy.

She was sweet and fresh as morning and as ready as sunrise. I'd hoped to take longer but in minutes she climaxed with a series of little cries and frenzied jerks of her hips as frantic hands grasped my hair.

She was still gasping, her breasts rising and falling with each pant as I eased up the bed and took her face in both hands. I kissed her very gently, letting my lips linger before opening her mouth so she could taste the joy I'd given her. She was halfway to fainting when I let her go. I settled for gathering her close, delighting in her warmth and scent and, I have to be truthful here, thrilled that I'd upstaged Alec.

Nasty of me. Bitchy of me. But in the circumstances....

"Jasmine?"

"Yes." I smiled at her as I ran my hand over her hair.

"You haven't come?'

I shook my head. "Not yet." It could wait. I was enjoying a different satisfaction.

Emily disagreed. Propping herself on one elbow, she bent her head to my breast and carefully worked her way down. When she reached my cunt, she delved in with the enthusiasm and ardor of a convert. I came three times before she finally paused and I insisted we take a nap. She might not need a rest at her age, but I did.

We slept the day and night around, waking as the early sun streamed in through the open curtains.

After a slow morning loving, Emily lent me Alec's toweling robe to eat breakfast in. We sat in the bay window, sipping coffee and spreading creamy butter and tart Seville marmalade on butteries. These were heavy, fatty pastries I'd have disliked in anyone else's company but now they tasted of Emily.

We were debating the wisdom of more coffee, or back to bed, when Alec walked in, clothes rumpled, hair on end, and eyes red from lack of sleep. I was scared he'd smell the sex on us but all he seemed to notice was food. Muttering a couple of sentences about idiot crews who don't maintain equipment properly, he wolfed down the remaining four butteries and the better part of the second pot of coffee his nice wife Emily fixed. Apparently Alec had not enjoyed the past twenty-four hours as much as his wife and I had, and unfortunately, he wobbled off to bed to restore himself so that put paid to an encore for us. But there would be other times. I was a patient woman.

"So glad you two get on so well together," Alec said that evening as we walked down the platform to my sleeper. "Some people have been unbelievably snooty. Peter hardly talks to me now."

Can't say I blamed Peter. He was bound to take his sister's

part. Heaven help me! Had I really loved this man? He was so self-centered, patronizing, and just plain thick! I had, once, when I was young and equally thick, but now I was well and truly cured. "Nice of you to ask Emmsy to your book signing in Edinburgh," Alec went on, as I hugged her goodbye

"It'll be nice to see someone I know." I gave a wave and hopped on the train. "I'll let you know the date." Something good had come out of the hurt of Alec Carpenter. I was going to have to call my publisher and insist they add Edinburgh to my next book tour. They wouldn't need to provide any escort. I could arrange that. I settled back in my seat, thinking. I was a trifle torn between genuine fondness for Emily and our promising affair and the certainty that Penelope would get a kick out of knowing I'd made Alec a cuckold.

Gravity Sucks
Skian McGuire

"Oh, shit! Fuck! Goddamn!" I sucked my bleeding knuckle in spite of the grease and shut my smarting eyes against the shower of rust and undercarriage gunk that sprinkled down on my face like fairy dust from hell. Between that and the sixty-watt droplight frying my ear, I never noticed the garage door closing.

There was no point wiping my eyes. Nothing on me was clean enough. I blinked against the tears and groped for my lost wrench, cursing again. How far could it have gone? I scooted the creeper a little ways out and froze. The radio had come on. Holding my breath, I listened while somebody tuned it to a country station.

For one foolish moment, I imagined I would be invisible if I stayed completely still, like a rabbit. As if half of me wasn't hanging out from under the rattletrap '67 Mustang I called Baby. I forced my voice to work.

"Who's there?" I tried to sound gruff. Big and butch. Yeah, they could see my big threatening butch legs. Right.

No answer. With a shaking hand I switched off the light

and squinted into the dark, willing my eyes to adjust. If I could see, I could recognize the intruder's ankles, maybe. If they happened to be in the quarter of the garage available to my sideways, immobile vision.

No such luck. "Fuck," I whispered, barely audible over my jackhammer heart. I dug in my heels and pulled the creeper as hard as I could, right into something solid and warm against my upraised knee.

Someone giggled.

"Natalia?" I breathed, relief flooding in.

The leg that had stopped my creeper pressed against the inside of my thigh, shifted, and then there were two, pressing my legs apart.

"Jeez, Nat," I said in a rush, "you nearly gimme a heart attack. I thought maybe an ax murderer...," I trailed off. What would an ax murderer do, hack off my feet? Still, the thought gave me a shiver. "Natalia?"

The feet stepped back. Awkwardly, I pulled the creeper out and came smack up against the legs again.

Again, the giggle.

Now I was getting pissed. "Come on, Nat. I gotta get this frigging thing off so I can put a new parking brake cable on." I was whining, and I knew it. I tried to sound calmer and more reasonable. "If I don't put a new cable on, the parking brake won't work. If the brake doesn't work, it won't pass inspec—" Cool fingers pushed aside my waffle-knit shirt and grappled with the button of my jeans.

"Whoa!" Startled, I sat up. "Yah!" My head hit the frame. I dropped back, eyes streaming. "Fuck," I whispered and spit a mouthful of rust and gunk bits, hands useless at my sides.

More giggles. The hand worked my zipper down. I lay there, forehead throbbing. I heard a rustle and a little grunt as she knelt between my feet.

Fingers pushed past my underwear and dove unerringly for

my snatch, zinging my clit with what seemed like an electric charge.

"Eeep!" I squeaked. Reflexively, I tried to close my legs. She shifted her weight and shoved them apart even harder. Her forefinger set up a hypnotic rhythm, insistent but not drubbing, teasing but effective. My clit hummed to its tune. My legs fell open, suddenly nerveless.

"Eeeeeeeeeee," I breathed. She laughed out loud. My head didn't hurt at all.

Fingers spread my lips and dipped into the flood of juice I was producing. Wet fingers slithered and danced between clit and hole. My hips bucked. "Ohhhh, jeeez!" I moaned.

The hand yanked out of my pants. "Awww!" I protested, my heels shifting for purchase. I don't know where I thought I was going.

Her hands seized the waistband of my jeans. "Upsy-daisy," a familiar voice said. Familiar, but Natalia? While my fuck-fogged brain tried to puzzle this out, my hips obliged her, all by themselves. Hands tugged my jeans and underwear down past my butt, past my thighs, past my knees, coming to rest at my ankles. I sighed, quivering with anticipation. A cool draft wafted over my thighs as I waited. And waited.

"Natalia?"

Stillness. Silence. "Uh, Nat?" I tried again nervously.

"Whoa!" Hauled by the jeans around my ankles, my legs shot into the air. The creeper trundled backward. Under the car, my arms flailed for something to hang on to. "Whoa, whoa, whoa!" Hands scrabbling on the concrete, I tried to pull my legs down. My bare knees thumped against cold metal.

"Relax," that familiar voice said, "you're bungeed to the door handle."

"Oh," I said, as if that explained it. I craned my neck for a view. All I could see was a denim bell-bottom and the hem of a long crushed-velvet coat. I ransacked my mental inventory of Nat's wardrobe and came up blank.

The air in the garage was more than cool on my naked ass, but I was sweating in my long-john and filthy Carlux hoodie. Before I knew it warm breath had enveloped my pussy, and her mouth touched down like Soyuz docking Mir. "Na'zdorovye!" I shouted, inspired.

Her tongue flicked back and forth and sluiced up and down my labia, darting into my hole like a fish. Her lips closed over my throbbing nub and sucked. Her teeth teased my clit hood and tugged at my short hairs. My legs bounced on their tether as I strained to meet her mouth, the creeper rocking and rolling ever so gently as I moved. I was weightless, trapped in a tin can, floating in space.

My arms stretched out, Christlike, for ballast as I swayed. There was my wrench: the thought drifted through my brain. I panted and licked rust-gunk off my dry lips. Orgasm was inevitable; my lower half was on autopilot. Now that less of me was under the car, maybe I could see my benefactress? No. My own pale goose-pimply thighs blocked the side view. Straight down the middle, tucking my chin hard into my chest and scraping my forehead—"Ouch!"—against the car, only the top of a dark brown head was visible. Carefully, I drew my arms in.

Her tongue moved faster. She stuffed it into my dripping hole, and I clenched and opened, rising to it, trying to draw the slithery coyness of it deeper.

"Oh, yeah," I moaned. In slow motion, my hands met on the silky bobbing top of her head. I twined my fingers in her hair. Her rather longish hair. Had it gotten that long since I'd seen her last? How long had it been? I'd seen Nat two weeks before. No, wait, it was only....

Under her relentless tongue, the heat and pressure in my groin achieved supernova. Her thumbs dug into the soft flesh of my thighs as I came, bucking, a tiny lightship tossed in the solar wind.

"Cosmic," I breathed.

Her giggles were warm, moist puffs against my engorged clit. I shivered.

"Oh, Natalia," I breathed, the last spasms twitching through my rapidly cooling flesh. "Natalia?" I unwrapped my fingers from her hair—gee, how long was it, anyway?—and groped toward her face like Helen Keller with a load on.

"Ah, ah, ah!" she said, pulling away. Without thinking, I grabbed for her.

"Aaaack!" The creeper teetered sideways. My head hit the car. My shoulders slid toward the floor. My arms, trapped between my pinioned legs, came back too slow to keep my sweaty ass from stuttering off the canted creeper onto icy concrete. My splayed thighs slapped against the car door and bounced maddeningly on the bungee.

"Shit," I muttered. A giggle tinkled out from across the dark garage, somewhere behind me. I didn't dare open my eyes. I spit oily crud and called out, "Natalia? Wait a minute, honey. Help me get out of...."

The garage door opened. And closed.

I snaked a ten-inch breaker bar out from under my left ass cheek and scooted sideways. Far and wee, a twangy male voice tunefully exhorted God to bless Texas. I thought of Houston, and Ground Control, and empathized with all those nameless astronauts who came down hard on dry land in dark little capsules and waited, waited, waited, to be set free.

In the end, I toed off my sneakers and tugged numb feet and ankles out of their denim prison, my numb legs flopping uselessly back to earth. I thought about the glory days of Mercury and Apollo while the circulation gradually returned and my cold bare behind absorbed spilled transmission fluid and waste oil from the grimy garage floor. I thought of

Natalia—it was Natalia, wasn't it?—and unearthly bliss and my own shocking touchdown on the unforgiving planet.

But what can I do? I am a fool in love, or even in lust, as I suspected it might boil down to. I called Natalia after work the next day. She'd be happy to meet me at Taco Villa for "tapas, or maybe something more?" She breathed into the phone, "I just love eating South-of-the-Border, don't you?"

It took three-quarters of an hour to get the crud out from under my nails. She was waiting at the bar when I finally got there, nursing the last inch of a Corona and bobbing her head to Hank, Jr., on the jukebox.

I stopped dead in my tracks.

"Natalia," I finally managed as she bounced up to give me a hug, "you got a haircut."

"Yes, this afternoon," she whirled and patted her hardly-longer-than-a-crewcut locks. "Do you like it?"

"Ah, sure," I began faintly, until the look on her face told me I was about to make a horrible mistake, "yes, I love it. It's terrific. Absolutely gorgeous."

She took my arm as the waitress led us to a booth in the back. In the dark. My unruly imagination slipped the surly bonds of Earth, and I wondered what I would do if she slid down the padded vinyl bench and disappeared beneath the table.

She ordered a Corona for both of us. "Upsy-daisy," I murmured, remembering.

"I beg your pardon?" She cocked her head, smiling the kind of smile no virgin had a right to.

Our drinks arrived at something approaching the speed of light.

"Na'zdorovye!" She tipped her bottle toward me. I sprayed beer across the table.

She graciously helped me mop up the mess and even signaled the waitress for more napkins. Already as mortified as I could be, I forged ahead, boldly going where I fervently hoped no man had gone before.

"Natalia," I began, "did you by any chance stop by my house yesterday? While I was, uh…" I paused, feeling my ears turning hot, "…working on the car?"

"Did I ever tell you, darling," she reached for my hand and gazed deeply, earnestly, into my eyes, only the faintest hint of amusement playing on her lips, "that my father was a member of the KGB?"

"No," I answered weakly, "I didn't know."

"He was assigned to Martina Navratilova. When she defected, so did he. What else could he do?"

"Really." Her fingers were stroking my palm.

"So, you see," she smiled, "secrets run in my family." Her toe nudged my ankle. My heart threatened to achieve escape velocity.

Appearing out of nowhere, the waitress hovered over our table, her pad at the ready.

"We'll have the number five combo, and the number three," Natalia told her, "and the number six as well, hmm?" She looked at me for confirmation. I licked my lips. She took that as a yes. "Unless you'd rather…." She squeezed my hand and cut a look at the exit.

"Could we get that order," I asked the waitress, "to go?"

"Pre-par-ing for takeout…" she enunciated as she wrote.

Time is relative; you don't need a Grand Unified Theory to know that. Several billion years later, we loaded our steaming cartons of enchiladas and chimichangas into the Baby's backseat, where they were swiftly forgotten in our warp speed race across the galaxy to my bedroom. We left a trail of clothing through the house behind us, planetary detritus forming an asteroid field in our wake. I never found out for sure if it was Natalia's mouth I rendezvoused with in the lightless depths of my garage, and I don't know if pistoning fingers and slick thighs actually convert matter into energy. Minutes and seconds can't measure the rate of propulsion of a body rocketing toward orgasm. But this one thing is immutable physical law: when the Big Bang happens, time stops.

Einstein didn't know the half of it.

Loved It and Set It Free
Lisa Archer

In 1985, my first dildo drifted out into the Baltimore Harbor on a broken bookshelf. I'd owned this dong for less than a day, but we'd been through a lot together. The night before, I'd eased it inside me, while my high school best friend lay next to me faking sleep. Most people keep their first dildos until they rot. But I was different. I loved mine and set it free.

"The Boss" was a single piece of beige rubber shaped like a billy club or toy sword—with a handle, a cross-guard, and a ten-inch dong in place of a blade. The label on the package said "anatomically correct," but even then I knew ten inches was a little on the long side.

I first laid eyes on The Boss when my friend Kim took me to a porn shop on East Baltimore Street. Kim was a born comic with gawky limbs and a wide, pouty mouth. The summer before our senior year, she carried bottles of Sun-In and hydrogen peroxide wherever she went. When we weren't swimming, she poured them over her head and lay in the sun.

By the time we went back to our all-girls school that fall, Kim's hair hung in clumps like bleached snakes. People said she dyed her hair orange to match school colors—orange and green. So she dyed it green for one of the field hockey games. This was in the mid-'80s, before Grunge Rock.

Around that time, Kim and I were playing "I Never"—one of the few games you can win through sheer inexperience and naïveté. In "I Never," players take turns confessing things they've never done. If the other player has done something you haven't, she owes you a penny. I won two cents easily, because I'd never bleached my hair or dyed it green.

It took me a bit longer to come up with my third confession. Finally I said, "I've never really gotten a good look at another person's genitals."

This was true: Although I'd made out with both boys and girls, we rarely took off our clothes. Instead, we groped each other in dark, semipublic places—fumbling with buttons, bras, belt buckles, and zippers, and glancing over our shoulders every few seconds, expecting our parents to catch us in the act. I'd even lost my virginity in the classic sense on the floor of a toolshed. In short, I'd had plenty of action, but little chance to look at naked bodies or genitalia. I had rarely ever seen boys naked, except when our neighbor little Billy ran across our backyard with his babysitter chasing him. I saw girls' bodies in locker rooms, but felt much too self-conscious to stare.

I expected Kim to question my confession, but she just nodded and tossed me another penny.

"You should come over and watch porn movies the next time my parents go away. That'll give you plenty of chances to check out other people's genitals."

Unlike my parents—the last in town to buy a microwave or any new appliance—Kim's family owned a VCR. When her mom and dad went out of town, Kim rented porn. We planned our porn adventure months in advance and waited for her folks' next vacation.

Kim rented porn videos from a seedy shop on "the Block." The Block—the 400 block of East Baltimore Street—is Baltimore's red-light district, where the locals go to see naked girls dancing and buy porn. Growing up in the sub-suburban sprawl of Baltimore County, I'd never been to the Block, so we drove me past it one night, when Kim borrowed her mom's Honda Civic.

"That's the Block." Kim pointed out the window. "Look now, or you'll miss it."

I pressed my face against the passenger window. Neon lights danced against the starless sky; then darkness swallowed the neon, as we dove back into the night.

"Was that it?"

"Yeah. It's only one block. I'll go around again."

The second time, she drove more slowly, so I could read the neon signs: Golden Nugget Lounge, the Crystal Pussycat, Gresser's Gayety Liquors, Savetta's Psychic Readings, Crazy John's, and the Plaza Saloon. Glamorous names—at least for kids growing up in Baltimore.

We didn't rent videos that night. We just drove by, and Kim pointed out Sylvester's Videos, the store where she rented porn.

"They have booths in the back where you can watch videos, but you don't want to go in there. The walls are sticky and gross. Let's just wait until my parents go away, and we'll rent videos to take home."

Finally Kim's parents scheduled an overnight camping trip. They left on a Friday; my heart and stomach fluttered all day at school. After our last class, Kim and I met in the locker room and changed out of our school uniforms and into jeans.

"Hurry up," said Kim. "I want to get down to the Block while it's still light out, so no one will break into my mom's car." Kim had her mom's car for the weekend. We slung our backpacks over our shoulders and walked out.

As we drove downtown, I pressed my face against the window and marveled at the dirt on the streets. City dirt is different from country dirt. Where I come from, dirt is brown like mud or red like sandstone. In the city, black grit cakes under your fingernails and sticks to the concrete. The wind writes messages on the sidewalk with black dust and dead leaves. I soon realized we were driving in circles, passing the same buildings.

"Are we lost?"

"No, I'm looking for parking."

"Where are we?"

"The Block, silly."

I winced. "It looks different by day."

While night had hidden everything but the neon signs, the sun exposed gray concrete buildings and trash in the street. Turned off, the neon signs were only pale plastic tubing and dusty electrical cords. We passed the same ones I'd seen at night—the Crystal Pussycat, Savetta's Psychic Readings, the Plaza Saloon. At night, they had seemed intimidating, but seeing them by day was like watching a flashy porn star sleep in her underwear and snore.

"Why didn't you take that parking space we just passed?" I asked.

"I want to park in front of the porn shop so I can keep an eye on the car."

After we'd made several more loops, a car pulled out right in front of us, across the street from Sylvester's Videos. Kim pulled up alongside the space.

"That's tiny. You can't fit in there."

"I'm going to try." She cranked her steering wheel all the way to the right and backed into the space much too fast. As her back tires rammed the curb, her elbow struck the horn with a loud honk. A siren squealed in the distance. Across the street, the door to Sylvester's Videos creaked open, and a guy with beady eyes and slicked-back gray hair stepped out of the store and glared at us.

"Shit, Kim. Let's get out of here."

"Get out and direct me," she said calmly.

Trembling, I climbed out of the passenger seat and motioned her into the space. When I glanced over my shoulder, the beady-eyed man had vanished. Kim got out of the car.

"That's the first time I've parallel parked since my Driver's Ed test," she said.

I followed her across the street. The door to Sylvester's Videos was covered with ripped, faded posters and random thumbtacks. The paint was chipped. It hadn't been painted in years.

I looked at Kim.

"Come on, let's go in." She hoisted the door open—revealing a heavy black plastic curtain. Glancing at me, she pulled aside the curtain and slipped inside. I followed her into a dimly lit square room. Videos lined the walls floor to ceiling.

The beady-eyed man—the same one who had glared at us outside—sat behind the cash register.

"Howdy, girls." He smiled with crooked yellow teeth.

At the sound of his voice, two customers in the front room turned and peered at us. Both were bent over videos, with their collars turned up and hats pulled down over their eyes. Kim and I were the only two women in the store—perhaps the only women who had been there in a long time.

Kim took me on a tour of the narrow, low-ceilinged rooms, pointing to X-rated videos with titles like: *The Penile Colony, Hannah Does Her Sisters, Astropussy Strikes Back, Public Enema Number One, Two,* and *Three.*

"The booths are in the back." Kim pointed to a man slipping behind a black plastic curtain. "You can rent your video, close the curtain, pop your video in the slot, and jerk off—Lisa...Lisa!" She poked me.

I had frozen facing a wall of rubber penises and sundry other body parts, including hands and arms. I had never looked at a penis this way before. For the first time in my life, I could look at it without worrying about what the person attached to it thought of me. At the time I was too inexperienced to know that one never quite looks at penises the way one looks at dildos, propped up on shelves, strapped onto harnesses, or packaged in plastic, hanging from hooks on walls—like toys in Toys "R" Us, or meat in a butcher shop. Through my entire childhood, I had been looking at Ken dolls without penises. Suddenly I was looking at the opposite of Ken dolls: penises without bodies attached.

Given my deprivation, this wall of "anatomically correct" models—in black, brown, and beige, complete with rippling rubber veins—was an embarrassment of riches. Some of them, labeled "stints," were hollow and attached to elastic straps. One even had leather straps. What were they for? Then I saw the flying-saucer-shaped "butt plug." Why would anyone need that? Plugs were those things you put in sinks to stop the water from draining. Was a butt plug the opposite of an enema? I was used to things having practical purposes. This was the first time I'd encountered something intended strictly for sexual pleasure, and I just didn't get it.

"Haven't you ever seen a dildo before?" asked Kim.

"N-no," I stammered.

"Check this out." She pointed to a plastic package containing a foot-long rubber forearm with the hand clenched in a fist. I'd never seen anything like it, except those dismembered arms you find in Walgreens at Halloween.

"What do you think you're supposed to do with this?" Kim asked. "Bonk somebody over the head?" I was pretty sure that wasn't what you were supposed to do, but before I could say anything, she yanked the plastic package off the hook and bonked me over the head with the rubber forearm.

"Kim! Stop!"

She clasped her hands over her mouth and burst into giggles, shoulders shaking uncontrollably. Customers in the store turned and stared.

"You're going to get us kicked out of here!" I hissed.

"Shhh! Lower your voice!"

"Look. Here's the description." We huddled over the package and read the label in excited whispers:

12.5 inches long, 3 inches wide, 9 inches around
Size: Huge
Product Category: Anal stimulation
Color: Black
Made of: Rubber
For use in this part of the body: Anus

"It's for the...the...anus?" I asked in disbelief.

"That's the butt," she whispered smugly.

"I know what an anus is, but I don't see how it could fit."

She shrugged. "Don't ask me."

"Do all these things go up your butt?" I gestured to the wall of dildos and butt plugs.

"They don't go up *my* butt," she giggled. "But you can put dildos up your vagina. Haven't you ever put vegetables up there?"

"No. Have you?"

"Of course."

"You're kidding. What kind?"

"Cucumbers, carrots, and zucchini. When I was about twelve, I used to sneak them out of the vegetable drawer in the refrigerator and put them back when I was done."

"Ew! Yuck!"

Kim hung the rubber arm back on its hook. "We're not getting this," she whispered. "Let's get some dildos. Here's a thin one. It's eight ninety-nine."

Kim handed me a package. I stared at the label: *The Boss: Anatomically Correct Dong.*

"Are you suggesting I buy this?"

"Why not? I'll buy one too."

"How do you know it'll fit?"

"You just have to try your luck. You can't try it on in a dressing room like a pair of jeans."

I laughed nervously.

"Come on," she said. "Let's move on to the videos. That's what we came here for."

I followed her back into the front room, where we rifled through hundreds of video boxes and decided on two orgy movies: *Farm Family Free for All* and *Group Grope 9.*

Growing up in the '70s and '80s, I had become familiar with the made-for-TV Roman orgy—where toga-clad patricians get it on with priestesses of Isis in the Roman baths (made to look like contemporary Jacuzzis). My parents allowed me to watch these programs due to their so-called historical significance. Hence much of my early sex education came from *I, Claudius,* and the head of a penis still reminds me of a Roman centurion's helmet. When you watch orgy scenes in historical dramas, perhaps you are supposed to think, *My god, how decadent,* and believe rampant orgies caused the fall of Rome. Modern libertines should learn from history and beware! But I watched the orgies and wondered, *Why don't people do that anymore?* I thought Roman orgies, like Egyptian mummies, were ancient history. *Farm Family Free for All* and *Group Grope 9* were my first signs that the orgy lived on, at least in contemporary porn.

After nearly an hour of X-rated shopping, Kim and I finally carried our lurid wares to the cashier and spread them out on the counter. The beady-eyed man winked at us.

"You want some K-Y Jelly for those dongs?"

"That's not a bad idea," said Kim. "We'll take some."

Outside, dusk had fallen, and the neon signs flickered on in orange, pink, and green. We crossed the street. Kim's mother's car was still intact. As we drove back to her house, I shivered when a cop car whizzed by. What if they pulled us over and found the porn videos and dildos? I pictured our mug shots on the front page with photos of The Boss underneath.

When we finally made it back to Kim's, we emptied our bags onto the living-room rug and tore open our dildo packages.

"Hey, this isn't very realistic. It doesn't have balls!"

The Boss, as I mentioned earlier, had no balls. Instead, the penis-shaped shaft ended in a handle and cross-guard, like a toy sword. I looked down at the dildo in my hands.

"Darn. I really wanted to see what balls look like."

"You'll see them in the movies," said Kim. *"En garde!"* She held the dildo by the handle and brandished it like the sword Excalibur, but the rubber weenie just flopped around.

I giggled. "That's one lame weapon."

"Oh well. Let's watch the videos." Kim switched on the TV and took the videos out of their plastic boxes.

"What do you want to watch first, *Farm Family Free for All* or *Group Grope 9*?"

"How about *Farm Family Free for All*?" We unzipped our sleeping bags and curled up side by side, propping our heads up on pillows so we could see the TV. Punching buttons on the remote control, Kim fast-forwarded to the opening scene, where a well-endowed hottie, looking much like Heidi with a blonde mullet and cleavage, skipped through a cornfield in an astonishingly low-cut blue gingham dress. The scene changed to the inside of a barn, where two men in plaid flannel shirts and overalls were milking cows. The younger man stood up and stretched.

"Gee, Paw," he drawled. "Ah wish Sissy would git here with those vittles. Ah need a break."

Outside, the blonde in blue gingham peeked through a crack in the barn door. Seeing the men, she slipped one hand up her gingham skirt and opened the door.

"Did Ah hear y'all say yuh need some refreshments?"

The men turned and gaped as she stepped into the barn, toting a straw basket in the crook of her arm and fondling her breasts.

I shook my head. "God, Kim! Can you believe these accents? Nobody talks like that."

"Watch this." Kim pointed the remote control at the TV. The video flew into fast-forward. Three more people in plaid flannel, calico, and gingham speed-walked into the barn, where they all tore off each other's clothes, sprawled on the hay, and plugged themselves into each other's orifices, fucking and sucking as fast as an assembly line.

"Dammit, Kim! I'm never going to see genitals this way!" I grabbed the remote control and pushed PLAY. My jaw dropped. Two tanned, tight-bodied girls, locked in a 69, were licking each other. With identical big boobs and blonde mullets, they looked like twins. In fact, they *were* twins. This was *Farm Family Free for All*. My heart beat faster. I'd never seen two girls having sex, even on screen. Out of the corner of my eye, I peered at Kim. Did she know this was going to be in the video? I knew orgies meant sex scenes with more than one man, more than one woman, or several of both. Somehow it hadn't dawned on me that girls would be getting it on with each other. I gaped at the screen transfixed, crotch tingling under the covers. I crossed my legs and squeezed my thighs together. Finally, I couldn't stand it anymore. I slipped my hands between my thighs. Kim's elbow brushed against mine, so the tiny hairs on our arms stood on end. She was doing the same thing I was, but I didn't dare look at her. I wondered if the people at school would be able to tell we'd watched lesbian porn. Would they see it in our eyes?

In English class earlier that year we had been talking about Virginia Woolf. The class was sitting in a semicircle around the edge of the room, facing our teacher, Mrs. Byrd. My mind was wandering, when someone mentioned the word *lesbians.* Patty raised her hand.

"Have there ever been any lesbians in our school?"

"Yes," said Mrs. Byrd. "We've had some."

"How can you tell?"

"Sometimes two girls are...closer than normal."

"Does the school do anything about it?" asked Patty.

"We try to split them up," said Mrs. Byrd. "Sometimes we tell their parents."

A hush fell over the room, as we all exchanged nervous glances. I looked at Kim, who sat across the room from me doodling. She didn't look up.

If they found out, would they separate us? Tell our parents?

Meanwhile, on *Farm Family Free for All,* the rest of the family joined the girls with mullets. The scene turned into a more traditional orgy with writhing bodies—a monster with multiple arms and legs. I circled my clit with my fingertip, less interested in the family scene, but barely admitting—even to myself—the girl-on-girl porn had turned me on.

Kim grunted next to me. She was snoring.

"Come on—I know you're not really asleep."

No answer.

"Kim?" I put my hand on her shoulder.

She was really asleep. I thought about waking her up, then changed my mind and circled my clit faster, feeling lucky and slightly out of control. My back tensed and my heart quickened, as I tried not to make any noise or move anything except my hand. I had played this game before—many times. The goal was to come without waking the other person. Sometimes, no doubt, the other person woke up and just pretended she was still sleeping. I had faked sleep myself when someone was masturbating beside me.

On screen the camera zoomed in on the girls. A man fucked one of them from behind, while she licked her sister's pussy. Next to me, Kim was breathing slack-jawed—either sound asleep or damn good at pretending. Her legs twitched under the covers. Reaching my arm outside the blankets, I groped around on the icy hardwood floor. My hand landed on the dildo—cold, hard, and ribbed with veins. I dragged it into the sleeping bag and pushed its cold head against the wet lips of my cunt. With a deep breath, I tried to ease the rubber cock inside me. It didn't fit. I pushed, took another breath, and pushed again. Still no go. Suddenly I remembered the K-Y Jelly. I ran my hand over the floor and found the K-Y. It looked like a tube of toothpaste. I squeezed a glob of clear lube into my palm. I couldn't believe how cold it was. I thought of Kim's refrigerated cucumbers. I didn't want anything that cold near my pussy, but if I wanted The Boss inside me, I knew I had to get the lube in there first.

I soaked the head of The Boss in K-Y, then—wincing—squeezed the cold lube directly into my cunt. It spilled onto the sleeping bag, spreading out in a puddle under my butt. Shivering, I glanced at Kim. Her eyelids fluttered. She was dreaming. With several deep breaths, I shoved The Boss inside me. My whole body shook—my cunt was so full, it almost burned. I looked at Kim again. What would it be like to kiss her? I brushed my lips against her cheek. Mustering all my courage, I stretched out the tip of my tongue and licked her hair.

Kim stirred and turned over on her side. I froze. Was she awake? I listened for her breath. I was sure she was awake, but I couldn't stop now. I eased the dildo in and out of my cunt. The woman on the screen came like a swimmer gasping for air. The man squeezed his cock and squirted white jizz on her tits. I came with them, melting into the scene. The cock inside me was his cock. My sounds shot out of her mouth. My wave of pleasure rocked her body on the screen. My cunt contracted and spit out the dildo—wet between my thighs. Warmth spread through my belly, heart, and limbs. I sank into the floor—and yet I was floating.

Someone nudged me.

"Stop it."

"Wake up."

"What? What time is it?"

"Five-thirty."

"What the fuck?" I glanced around the dark, unfamiliar room.

"Wake up." Kim's shadowy form bent over me.

I suddenly remembered where I was—sprawled out on Kim's living-room floor. I must have dozed off after I came.

"Lisa, listen to me. We have to get rid of these now."

"Get rid of what?"

"These." She bumped me on the cheek with something rubber. I winced, as the overhead lights blinked on. What was she talking about? Then it dawned on me. *Jesus, what did I do last night?* I remembered the wall of dildos, The Boss, and licking Kim's hair—shit! Was she awake when I did that? What did she think of me?

"Lisa!" Kim repeated, bonking me on the head. "We've got to get rid of these things before my parents get home. They'll be back early this morning."

"We can't just throw them away. They weren't cheap."

"Do you want to take them home with you?"

"Shit." I peered at the dildos as my eyes adjusted to the light. "I don't think I can."

"What should we do with them then? We can't just throw them in the trash, or bury them in the backyard. The dogs'll get at them."

"Can we burn them?"

"God, no! They'd stink."

"Well then, let's just walk a few blocks down the street and throw them in someone else's trash."

"Good idea. We can take the car and drive a little ways away. We'll take the videos back to the store too." She put the VCR on REWIND.

It was still dark outside. The crickets were chirping as we stepped out into the cold, wet air. Kim drove. I dozed in the passenger seat with the dildos in my lap wrapped in newspaper. The car screeched to a stop.

"Where are we?" The sky had turned dark blue. I rolled down my window, tasting the salt air.

"We're at Fells Point. I was thinking we could throw them in the water," said Kim. We climbed out of the car. I followed her to the edge of the pier. Water was lapping at the dock, and the seabirds called out, flapping their wings. One swooped within inches of the water, a white ghost.

Holding the dildos wrapped in newspaper, I peered down into the black water.

"It's a shame to let these sink to the bottom of the harbor."

"I know! Let's float them out to sea on one of those boards over there." Kim darted away and came back seconds later, dragging a dismantled bookcase. She pulled off the top shelf and dislodged several long rusty nails.

"We'll put the dildos on a raft. That way, someone might find them."

We lowered the board into the water. Kim tore off a sheet of newspaper and wrote:

S.O.S.
FREE TO A GOOD HOME.

I leaned over and placed the dildos side by side. Wrapped in newsprint, they looked like twins in swaddling clothes.

I thought of Romulus and Remus—the twins abandoned to the elements, who washed up on shore and founded Rome. Who knew what great fortune or conquest lay in store for our dildos? Would they be suckled by she-wolves? I watched them float away, convinced that some lonely soul, who desperately needed dildos, would find them.

Does She Look Like a Boy?
Tara-Michelle Ziniuk

When I ran through the door at work I was glad I had done my hair and makeup on the way. For the past while, my boss had been pestering me to be "as ready as possible as early as possible." She and I both knew that I didn't look quite like this when I wasn't at work, but I'm not sure she understood my untended body hair or my refusing her invitations to tanning salons. I'm a femmey girl, no doubt, but not the type to get all glammed up without occasion to. The other girls at work were the straight girl equivalent to high-femme all the time, manicured and face-masked; they also did not understand.

I kissed Darlena on both cheeks then bolted to the walk-in closet, which had been home to much slut-gear as well as my personal dressing room for nearly two years. I breathed in the scent of other people's perfumes and overcompensating chemical detergents, all stale and mixed together. Not a minute after I closed the door and stripped down to begin a frantic search for my PVC bra and corset set, Darlena walked in behind me.

"The four o'clock guy called back," she began *(oh please*

don't tell me he cancelled and I rushed here for nothing), "and he wanted to know if you looked like a boy."

I laughed. "Did he look at our ad?" I asked.

"Apparently not. I directed him to the website but his Internet service was down. I wasn't sure how to respond so I just joked back with him and said, 'Well no, sir. Did you want her to?' And he said yes."

She was reading me for a reaction. This was not an environment that had fostered any sort of gender-bending positive play in the past, save a few male clients who liked to wear pantyhose. My first instinct was that it was a crank call and I was wasting my time, *grrr.*

"So, you think he'll be a no-show?"

"I don't know, he sounded pretty sincere, and you're here now. Do you have a hat?"

I spent the next fifteen minutes scrambling to get out of my makeup and find masculine clothes among the leather and stilettos. I settled on a white dress shirt from an unclaimed bag of uniforms and schoolgirl attire, and found a white tank top to go under it. One of the other women at work had left behind a pair of dark-blue jeans with a wide black belt still in them. I pulled them on and they fit snug against my ass and thighs. I found a black cock in a box of sex toys and rinsed it in the sink before resting it against my already constricted cunt, and allowed myself to feel its stillness, rubbing my middle finger along the shaft. I positioned it so that it would be noticeable but not tacky, and zipped up the now very fitting pants.

When I came out of the washroom Darlena was waiting for me with the only hat she could find, a black cap with some anonymous Celtic symbol on it. It would do. I looked myself over in the full-length mirror. I certainly didn't look macho, I looked faggoty. I hoped that was the idea. The hall clock read five-to-four, the hour I anticipated the caller's arrival.

It was a good scene to have been called in for, more interesting than the bulk of them. I knew only that it was to be a dildo-training session and that this particular client had not seen any of the other girls before. I hoped he wouldn't have any huge unavoidable flaws, specifically that he didn't stink and wasn't eighty years old and waiting for his next heart attack. Though these possibilities occurred to me, I somehow was not as panicked as I had often found myself before. I was quite intrigued by this character who wanted curvy lipstick-lipped me in drag. Why hadn't he booked a call with a male dom? I imagined complicated answers to this question until there was a knock at the door. I poured some water for myself into a crystal wine glass and went into the room to meet my new submissive.

He was definitely more masculine-looking than I had been able to pull off, an interesting element for the scene. He looked young and wide-eyed. He appeared willing and nervous, but not fearful. "Very nice to meet you. You will call me Master," I said, in what I liked to call my best warm/ cool voice. I had impressed myself already by remembering that today I would be "Master" as opposed to "Mistress." I extended a hand and he shook it firmly before kissing it. I hadn't been sure of what to expect, but this pleased me. He was blushing as I motioned for him to have a seat. "We'll just have a little chat and then get things started." He nodded. I was unable to read his anxiety. "We use the code words *yellow* and *red* here, yellow for caution, red to stop the scene. You are familiar with these?" Another nod. "Have you done this before?" I asked genuinely.

"Similar things, but not exactly." He certainly was not talkative.

"But you do have experience with BDSM and you feel confident that you know your limitations?"

"Yes, Master." I could tell by his immediate submission to

me that he did. He kept his eyes lowered, but I could see his wanting in them. There was no reason to take up more of our time together. I settled into character easily.

"I am your Master. You will do as I say, when I say to. You will be polite and courteous, and appreciative that I have taken up my valuable time to train you." As I stood he dropped to his knees in front of me.

"Yes, Sir. Thank you in advance for spending your time on me." He offered me a thick black collar with metal rings, and I thanked him by securing it tightly around his neck. He bowed his head and touched his nose to the polished tip of one of the too-large black army boots I was wearing. I rustled his hair before pulling his face up by it.

"Very good. Now why did you come here today?" No answer. "I asked you why you came here today."

"I came here to please you, Master."

"Now go back to what you were doing." He curled by my feet, tracing his nose along the seams of the boots. Then he did the same with his entire face, resting his cheek against my ankle. He slowly licked the stitching around the soles. Before he was quite done with the second one, I interrupted. "Back up on your knees." He was taller than me, and upright on his knees reached higher than my waist. I pushed him back so that he was sitting on the backs of his heels. His eye level was just below my swollen crotch. He seemed to look straight through the tops of my thighs. "You see something you like?" My voice was softer this time.

"Yes, Master. I do."

Again he lowered his head. I felt the rush of excitement that I was intending for him electrifying my own body. We made eye contact, and though his body looked tough, the steady eyes that met mine looked like they had been hurt. They were focused now on something else. I nodded simply, testing to see if he did as well. A small well-hidden smile appeared as he faced my body. He ran his face along the zipper of my jeans, like he had done with my boots. He was slow and careful already so I didn't have to direct him. He pressed his face harder and harder into me. I could feel myself getting wet as much as I tried not to, as he started kneading my cock with his face. His lips ran over it through the denim, as he looked up for my approval. He looked brave and small. I gave him another nod and he gently started kneading with his teeth. I tried my hardest not to release the gasp in my chest that so desperately wanted to be let out.

I decided to regain control of the situation and, unzipping the jeans, took the dick out inches in front of his face.

I ran my fingers over his mouth and he sucked and lapped at them with his soft tongue. I thrust myself into his mouth. He gave me the sweetest, fiercest blow job I had known, putting everything into it. He let his mouth handle the cock expertly, paying attention to its curves and shape and not leaving out anything. He was in tune to my hips' rhythm and worked with and against it. I allowed myself to breathe heavily to let him know he was doing well, but I restrained myself from making any other sounds. I didn't want to stop him, but I wanted to make sure I took over the scene before I came. I backed out of his soft wet mouth. This time when I looked at him he looked less bashful and more confident, like he had regained some of his pride giving head like that. "Did you like that?" I barked. He did not flinch. He licked his lips and gave me a look I had come to know well through various female lovers. "Did you?" they asked silently.

"Yes, very much. Thank you." He blushed, smiling obviously this time. "Master."

I wanted to see if he was hard but was unable to tell because of the way he sat. I moved along quickly, because he had paid good money for the hour, but also because I was incredibly turned-on and didn't want to ruin the moment.

"You want more?"

"Yes. Please, Master."

"Are you going to behave yourself if I give you more? You are already very lucky to have been allowed to suck your Master's big cock like that. You know that, don't you?"

"Yes, Master. Thank you." He played along, knowing full well what he was entitled to during the session.

"Okay then, you must promise to be on your very best behavior. Bring me a condom, boy." I wanted to continue as much as he did and was pleased that he returned quickly with the basket of condoms and a bottle of lube. I pretended to eye the bottle he had handed me quizzically. "Oh, you were expecting me to go easy on you, were you?" I toyed with him, for both of us. He lowered his head in response, looking like a child about to break out in giggles. I imagined him being a strong butch lover of mine as I snapped on a glove and prepared to ready his waiting ass. I had him face the whipping post on the other side of the room and undress from the waist down. Off came the work pants and a pair of gray-specked boxer briefs. I noticed he kept his body pressed tight against the post. "Are you nervous?"

"No, Master." I didn't push it, as it was ideal positioning for my own fantasy. I instructed him to step back and make sure he kept his forehead touching the post. He complied with my demands easily, and I threw in a threat about the disciplinary actions I would be forced to take if he squirmed out of position.

I entered him at first cautiously, with one finger, then two.

I realized very soon that he had more experience than he had let on. I ran my other hand through what I assumed to be sweat on his inner thigh. He was moving his body accordingly, so I knew he wanted to be fucked. I thought about what he had said when he came in about not having done "exactly" this before, and wondered what specifically he had meant by that. Was he a fag experimenting with women? A "straight man" who frequented cruise parks, having anonymous lovers nightly? Maybe he had played out similar scenes with a woman lover before, who had since left him or become ill. I speculated for a moment too long and then snapped back to reality. Or as close to reality as I chose to make it: he was my handsome boy-dyke slave, a fine butch bottom, helplessly awaiting my hot femme dick to enter and take him over.

Caught up in my own imagination, but not so much that I wasn't paying attention, I spread the soft asscheeks before me and circled the tip of the silicone dick between them. I had, at some point in this fluster of daydream, work, and sweat, remembered to put on the condom. One last time I pushed my lubed fingers in and out firmly, and then pushed myself into him. He let out something between a squeal and a sigh, sounding like a young boy. I liked the power I felt hearing his surprisingly high-pitched sounds and continued to press myself into him and pull back. As this motion quickened and we fell into each other's rhythm, I began to grind my dripping cunt against her ass, playing with her insides. I pretended that the increasing sweat pouring down his legs was sweet girl cum and held the inside of her thigh against the palm of my hand.

I noticed that as he got more turned-on and as the fucking became rougher, he pulled away from me more, and pushed his weight against the post. I brought my arm around to the front of her neck. It was soft and tight. I ran my knuckles against his jaw, finding that his teeth were clenched. I ran my hand along his jawline, also soft and unusually free of stubble. His face was trembling with what seemed like fear.

Leaving one hand on his face, I slowly moved the other hand around to the front of his thigh. It was sticky wet and also trembled to my touch. I tried to stay strong and stern, but was both confused and excited. As I inched my hand upward he jerked away from me. I pulled her close to my body. The hand I had rested on her face came down and pressed against her collarbone. I felt the tiny recognizable ripples of a tensor-bandaged chest.

She heaved the heavy sigh of someone exposing a skeleton.

I moved my hand between her legs, revealing for certain the truth to my fantasy and this boy's well-hidden identity.

I sighed a sigh of relief, of pleasure, of the unknown future. I sat down on the floor, leaning my back against the wooden post. I pulled her down and continued to hold her against me. My hand ran through her sweaty hair. We had not yet made eye contact. When she finally looked at me her eyes were intense and concerned. "Are you mad?" they asked. I flashed her the same sexually charged and wanting smile she had given me after sucking me off.

"Are you?" my eyes asked back.

To Fuck or Get Fucked
Rakelle Valencia

I like to fuck. In a fuck or get fucked world, I'm the girl, I'm supposed to get fucked. But like I said, I like to fuck.

Maybe it started with the butt boys. Oh, but it probably started before them. I'm not saying the boys were my first. Then again, I'm not saying they weren't. It was the butt boys who gave me the hunger to fuck, who showed me the power and desire of the fuck, who taught me to crave the undulation of bodies slamming and slapping in rhythm and against the rhythm. Boys just seem to know how to have fun, they know how to fuck. So yeah, it started with the butt boys.

Having someone bent over or writhing beneath me is all the same, gender-wise, and it's all very different. I'm not saying I would still do the boys, and I'm not saying I wouldn't. But the girls...girls know how to take it. A good chick likes to get fucked.

Now I know that callin' 'em chicks can sound derogatory, but it's not. I use *chick* with the highest regard. And the ones I call chicks probably call themselves chicks too. It takes a lot to stand up and say you're a chick. It takes a lot to get fucked like I'm talkin' about, and to be a good fuck.

Like this one chick, she couldn't wait for me to strap it on with her. In fact, she needed it so fast, she was always trying to get me to pack. But I don't pack. So she did the next best thing. And I'm telling you this chick was all-the-time crazy to get fucked. She made me a special strap-on. It was a beauty.

I still have it today, wouldn't be caught dead without it, and wouldn't trade it for the world. I'm talking no manufactured deal for this girl. I'm sold on this used-to-be one of a kind. The thing was pure genius with a touch of class and individualism. I like that, class and individualism.

I started callin' it The Snap-on Strap-on. The name stuck.

I heard it the other day in that well-lit, frequented, women-owned, adult toy shop one block over from Main Street. My chick, she made up a bunch and they stocked 'em. Hot item too, 'cause it's not what she does for a livin', and she can only make so many, and I think girls are finding out that the personal touch with these beauties can be real handy.

What do I mean by that? Have you ever used 'em? Strap-ons? I mean, think on it. If you're not packin' then you're not ready. Do you warm her up first, then say, "Oh, excuse me dear while I step into this ugly, drab, black harness"? Then you know what happens. You fight with the damn thing, a tangled mess wrapped around a stiff backing that always seems to be on the wrong side until you work out all of the angles. That done, your next worry is gettin' into the contraption. Meanwhile your girl's coolin' off.

Worse than that, you jump off her bed to cram one foot at a time into the leg loops, and you end up fallin' over, eliciting whoops and hollers of laughter from above. I'm not unathletic, and I'm not saying I had been drinking or was on anything, you know? But if you're still thinking on it, you tell me how you've pulled off being suave with those manufactured strap-ons. Maybe something like, "Excuse me a moment while I freshen up," as you make the mad dash elsewhere so you don't look like a fool. Like I said, your girl's coolin' off, you know?

Now let me tell you about these beauties, these Snap-on Strap-ons. Man, you can get these things on anywhere anyhow. You can get in 'em and out of 'em fast, real fast, in case you had to either way. I'm not saying I ever had to get out of one fast, I'm just saying it's an option. But I will say I've had to get into one fast.

Like that one time she had to have it, you know. We were in a memme mobile, a small sedan, and I wasn't gonna play Gumby, but she had to have a little somethin' somethin' and I was right there with her. I'm talking I was right there, wetter than a Slip 'n Slide at a family picnic on a hot July day. Nothing to worry about though, I had a Snap-on Strap-on and was ready for action in seconds.

This thing is as crazy as her. It has snaps on every strap, at every juncture. She took those beefy, plastic snaps, like you'd find on dog collars, and put one on either side of the waistband, and one on each leg strap, all in the back, off to the sides, adjustable too. In the front, a rubber ring, held in place with those silver, flat snaps that you'd find on denim jean jackets, and the works had no backing. No backing. I remember going into the toy store with her when she first presented her invention; the girl behind the counter was aghast, opening up her sweet, tiny mouth in horror, scrunching her baby-blues and freckled brow: "No backing? How does the dong stay in place?"

"YOU are the backing," came the reply. And it works, you know. No stiff, fussy, triangular-shaped piece of vinyl or leather to chafe the crease of your thighs to your pussy if you're a skinny drink like me. And the best part, the dildos are more easily exchangeable without breaking the action too long, if you know what I mean. With no backing, I've got it down one-handed, while the other hand stays busy in the slick and slippery.

But that's not what I was trying to tell you. It's not about the dick, it's about the fuck. It's about the chicks who like to get fucked. And I love to fuck. To fuck or to get fucked. Well, like I said, I'm supposed to get fucked, but I so like to fuck.

I like to crawl up between a pair of thighs and bury myself in their adjoining crevice, open, wet, and inviting. Maybe one leg is bent upward, hung over the crook of my elbow so I can grasp a fleshy thigh as I thrust in the missionary position, our torsos sopping with sweat, gliding over each other, nipples plucking at nipples.

Chicks are fascinating to fuck, and I like to be sunk home as any man does, as any boy needs, as any girl can do. Flip them over with some slap and tickle before greasing my silicone prick and hammering it home, watching her asscheeks ripple in response to my erotic pummeling. Smacking sounds of naked skin greeting naked skin, whimpers and moans entering in chorus, white knuckles gripping hip handles, and the body beneath, flushed and tensed in its buildup to release.

And I need this. I need to fuck. Sometimes the fuck is so alluring, so powerful in its promise that I beg to get off beforehand. "Get me done so I can last," as if I were a young, pubescent male ready to pop with the opening of the latest, coveted issue of *Penthouse*.

I'm not saying it's all like that, but I like to fuck for hours, where my knees get raw, my pubic bone believes that the dong is now embedded, calcified in, and muscles ache with the burn and twitch in exhaustion, and my clit is so hard that I know it would hurt to touch or that I'd pop off with the wafting of a mere breeze.

It's not about the dick, it's about the fuck. I like the fuck and I often come while doing it, in waves of spasms as she sits aloft, humping and pumping until she squirts her juices down my rubbery rod, over my flat, thin stomach, trickling past my hips and through my groin. The wetness like a salve soothes and softens the fierceness of my fuck, and it threatens to take me into a dizzying euphoria of a post-fuck snooze. But I don't want to go there, and wish she wouldn't let me. Some do. But not a chick, a chick likes to get fucked.

You Can Write a Story about It
Jera Star

1.

I wait to meet you on the porch, your silver roller blades shining all the way down the street. I finger the chain around my neck as you approach. We are still awkward at first on these casual rendezvous we've been having. You're used to fucking friends. I'm used to fucking strangers. We are neither friends nor strangers. I'm a pink-haired hippie bi chick. You're a crew-cut wannabe-cop boy dyke. Sometimes, we fuck.

"Hey, T," I say.

You've come over after watching that movie you love with the character named Troy in it. Where you got your boy name, the one you just told me about today. I haven't yet called you by it.

"Yo, what's up?" you ask. I ignore your question. I'm distracted because you're wearing a red baseball cap backward—my weakness. You sit down beside me on the porch to take off your blades. "Oh, I saw a shooting star on the way here," you tell me, excitement in your voice. You remind me of a little kid and I find it endearing. A nice change from your usual cocky, obnoxious talk. We sit for a while and talk about the stars. Then I bring you inside. You swagger up the stairs to my apartment. Follow me down the hall to the couch in the spare room.

"How was your day?" I ask.

This time you ignore my question. Instead you say, "You have strong hands." I know you are trying to move things along to what we both really want to be doing. But still, it's one of the few compliments you have ever and will ever (I realize later) offer me. I relish it. And take your bait.

"You want a massage?"

You sit on the floor in front of the couch. I start massaging your shoulders through your clothes. After a minute, you bring out a little container of strawberry massage oil from your pocket. I laugh, getting the point. I take off your shirt. Drip the oil onto your back. You say it feels like lube: cold and hot. I massage again, starting at your neck. Mold your skin. Flex my fingers around your muscles. Shoulders, upper arms. Move my hands in front to your pecs. Careful to avoid your breasts. I stretch your arms up and lay them back down against your sides. Touch my fingers to your lower spine, one of your erogenous zones. Stay there for a while, applying pressure. Playing. You cut right to the chase.

"So, Sue, tell me about your first kiss." You want to get at my fantasies. This is what we do for each other. I like the question.

"It felt so good I thought I could go on kissing him for hours. But then later, behind the portable, after school, he said, 'What do you want to do to me?' I didn't want to do anything to him. I wanted him to do things to me. I wanted him to lick my whole body. All the way from mouth to clit."

"What else?" you ask as I work on your shoulder muscles.

"Hmm, I was too shy to tell him what I wanted. So we just kissed some more," I answer, absorbed in my hands pushing into your back. "Eventually I told him I didn't want to be monogamous and he didn't like that." You laugh, not sure about it yourself.

"Tell me, Sue, what you want me to do to you. Who, what, where you want me to be."

I smile.

You try and grab my tits and I love it. You try and tickle me and I don't like it. We laugh as you try to tickle me and I tell you to stop.

"Don't," I say.

"Don't what?" you say, grabbing my tits again, putting your hands in my pants. "Don't, Boy-T? Don't, Daddy? Don't, Troy? Don't touch my tits? Don't touch my clit? Don't make me come? Huh? Don't what?" I squirm. Hot, fucking hot.

"Daddy," I moan, wanting your hand on my clit. "Daddy, please." I squirm more as you fondle me, feel me, make my clit swell. You take your hand away.

I whine, hurt, sad. "Daddy, please. Come on, Daddy. Give me. Give me, please. Daddy, please."

You give in and give me some more. Turn me over on my stomach. I moan and cry with the sensations in my cunt. Your hand still fingers my clit. I want more, you pull your fingers away. I whine.

"Oh, poor baby," you say. "What's wrong? Is there something wrong, baby?"

"Please, Daddy." I'm close to crying. You put your fingers back.

"There you go, baby. Come on. You're a good girl." You move your finger faster on my clit. I moan and say, "Please, daddy," again and come madly, sweetly, sadly in your arms.

"Do you love me?" you ask.

"Yes, Daddy, I love you."

I shed some tears. We are both quiet.

Finally I say, "And you, T, what do you want me to do, be

for you?"

I straddle you. Take off my shirt. Kiss you. Take off my bra while you watch. Take off your jeans and boxer briefs and spread your legs. Move down your body to your belly. You feel vulnerable with it exposed, I know. I linger there, my eyes on you. My tongue licking around your belly button. I start fingering your clit slowly, gently.

"Do you do this to all the boys?" you ask.

"Just my slave-boys," I say. You make small moans. I stop playing with you. Ask, "Were you a good boy today?"

"I hope so," you answer. You always make me laugh.

"You think you deserve this?" I ask.

"Yes, Mistress," you moan as I push one finger inside your cunt.

"Why do you think you deserve this?" I play with your clit some more.

"Because it feels so good." You start humping my finger. I bend down to kiss you and just when you're ready for it, I pull away. You try to bring my lips to yours again. I don't let you.

"Ah, Boy-T wants to kiss me, does he?" I say to you, holding your arms above your head.

You close your eyes. "Uh-huh," you say, still humping.

"Now why would I want to let him do that?"

"You know you want it," you say, impatient. You shake your hands out of my grasp. Pull me down against you again. I let my tongue brush your lips. Then I grab your hands and put them above your head one more time. You like it.

"Slave-boys don't kiss without asking," I say. "I want Boy-T to learn how to be a gentleman." You smile and grab my boob real quick. Cocky, as usual.

"Ask nicely," I tell you, speeding up my hand on your clit.

"Oh, fuck."

"I said ask nicely." I push two fingers in your cunt. You clutch my arm.

"Kiss me, damn it," you say as I play with your clit and move my fingers in and out of you.

"What was that?" I ask. I start fucking your wet cunt, pushing my fingers deep. My thumb on your clit. You're groaning with each thrust. Keep trying to grab me, pull me to you. I keep pushing you down. Keep thrusting.

"Please," you moan, your hips rise, try to push my fingers deeper into you with each thrust.

"Please what?"

"Please, please, kiss me, please." You pant between words.

"Ah, that's a good boy," I say. I let go of your arms above your head. You yank me down on top of you, cover my mouth with yours, groan and swear as I fuck you. You come smooth and heavy. Your moans vibrate through me.

2.

It's been a few weeks since our last encounter. Another fight. They keep happening. Our fights remind me of my best friend at ten. How we used to touch tongues in the corner of the schoolyard, get mad, and not talk to each other for weeks at a time, then one day start touching tongues again.

You call and ask me to come over. You have something you want to show me. When I hear your obnoxious laughing voice on the phone asking for me, I forget why I was so mad at you.

You come over to show off your new boy clothes. You say you really feel like a guy in them. Shirt and vest. I tell you that you look hot because I know you want to hear it. You tell me, like it's not a big deal, that I'm the only person you've mentioned all this boy stuff to. I'm surprised. Flattered. I offer to take pictures of you exploring your guy self. You refuse. But I persist and get you. Sitting on the couch, legs spread, taking up space; the rapper look, you call it. Your arm bent, scratching your chin; intellectual. Standing, doing a muscle pose;

jock. This is all leading up to one thing, only I don't know it.

You want to go out together to the local straight slutty bar. We've talked about it before. I haven't been since I was in high school. Avoided it since I came out. But I love the idea. I put on lipstick for the first time in ages. Tight jeans and a skinny-strap tank top. For me, this is a performance. Reclaiming sixteen with more power than I ever felt I had then. I know for you, this is it.

We take the bus downtown in silence. Avoid stares. It is our first public appearance as any kind of couple. Your first public appearance as a guy.

Once in the bar we meld into the place. You quickly become my tough-ass boyfriend for the night. Stand on the sidelines, cocky and casual, and watch me dance. I play up to the bio boys until you can't resist and try to feel me up on the dance floor. I pretend to protest, giddy and turned on. You work on one of the straight girls dancing beside us and I pout and act like I'm pissed off. A jealous girlfriend. Until you turn back around to me, push me up against the speaker, and dry hump me, in front of all the bio boys and their straight girlfriends. Your packing cock in your skater pants bulging against the crotch of my pretty-sixteen-year-old-girl jeans. We stay long enough to make a scene. Both of us wet.

"I've decided," you say as we head home to your place, high on the night. "I want you to fuck me with my cock."

I'm shocked. I've brought up the idea of me fucking you before, but you've always refused. Fingers, yes. But never the cock.

"The only way it's gonna happen," you say, not looking at me, "is, you've gotta be a guy."

I am never *boy*. My cunt drips.

"Are you sure?" I ask, anxious about my boy performance abilities.

"Yeah, I'm sure." You pause. We approach your apartment.

"You can write a story about it," you say finally. " 'I fucked this guy once....' "

I smile casually, acting as if I'm not completely nervous and turned on at the thought of being a guy myself, let alone fucking you. You look at me, knowing.

Once we're inside your apartment, I close the door, kick off my shoes, and push you against the living room wall. "Sounds good. But first I want slave-boy to work for his pleasure." You lift up my shirt and start playing with my boobs. "I want you to eat me out. Some good, old-fashioned, cunt licking. And if you're real good," I say slowly, "then maybe...I'll put on your big old cock and fuck you with it." Which makes you smile and move your arms into a surrender position.

"You think you can handle that, slave-boy?" You nod keenly. I push you to the floor. Unbutton my fly. "And you know what I think about good head," I say as I take off my shirt. "It's hard to come by, don't you agree?" You nod again. I unclip my bra. Get rid of my pants and underwear.

"I want it like this," I say, and kneel over you. "With a wall to cling to when I come." I put my arms, my boobs against the cold wall. You slide down onto your back. I bend over your mouth and feel your tongue. My breath catches. "But, as you know, few people can ever really satisfy me."

I bend down lower. You grab my cunt with your whole mouth. I groan. "Do you think you can, slave-boy?"

"Oh, yes, Mistress." I shiver.

"Good. Because I want to come. So you've got to keep it up good. Do you think you can, long enough? Suck my pussy with all its fur until I come? Yeah, that's right, just like that. Oh, fuck, yeah. Do you think you can keep it up, slave-boy? 'Cause I want to come and I want to come good. Long and full and all through me like electricity or something. Can you do it, slave-boy? Come on, keep it up, keep it up. Come on do it keep me coming come on, keep me coming, I'm going to come, no, keep it slow keep it slow, I don't want to come yet. I said, do it slow now, slow now, yeah, that's right. Can you keep it up, boy? Can you? Come on, more tongue, I said more tongue, boy, yeah that's right, faster now, speed it up a bit, tongue and mouth, faster...just like that. Yeah, that's right. Do it like that.... Can you keep it up? 'Cause I want to come so you better keep it up, I said yes, more, faster, faster, fucking fast I said goddamn it. Fuck, keep it coming keep it coming keep me coming there I'm there, I'm there I'm fuck I'm coming goddamn you fucking coming fuck fuck fuck fuck. Commming. Unh unh unh unhhhhhhhhh. Fuck boy, that's it. Hold me now. Just hold me."

I press my cunt into your belly and let your arms go around me. Just long enough to get myself together. Then I sit up and look at you smiling. All proud of yourself.

"So you think you deserve a fuck for that?" I laugh into your neck for a long time.

In the bedroom, you dress me up in your shirt and vest.

"So who am I?" I ask.

"Steve."

"Who's Steve?"

"Just Steve," you say. I laugh.

"And who are you tonight?" I ask, expecting you to say Troy.

"Tammy."

"Your girl name?"

"Yeah, or you can call me slut, bitch, whore."

I'm blown away. You are never girl. Talk about gender fuck. I get even wetter. Wonder if I'll be able to comply. "Those are harsh words," I say. "You know what a good girl feminist I am."

You smirk. "Just wait, you'll like it. It'll be easier than you think." You get out your big rubber dick and strap it on me. I like it. You are right. I immediately start to feel cocky. Don't know exactly what you mean by "Be a guy," but I like the feeling of the cock between my legs, attached to *my* body for a change.

"I want you to dominate me," you say. "I want it hard. Lots of swearing and shit. I'll protest, but you make me take it. Be aggressive. Be an asshole. Call me a cunt. Yeah, cunt, that's a good one."

I'm unsure of how to begin. I push you down on the bed.

"Oh, please stop," you say. Your voice is suddenly higher pitched. I take it as a sign to start being an asshole.

"Shut up, cunt, Steve's going to do whatever the hell he pleases."

You jump up at me, ferocious. I make you stop. Tell you to lie back and shut the fuck up. And you do it. You moan.

A moan I've heard many times. A pleasure moan. I still don't feel like a guy, just an asshole wearing a guy's shirt and vest. But it's enough. I start to get into my role. I put my hand on my new dick. It's hard. So am I.

"And what I please is to fuck you, bitch."

You moan again like you like it. "Please don't," you say, pulling me toward you at the same time.

"Ah, come on. I know you're a whore. I know you want my big fucking dick pumping your nasty cunt." I shock myself with what I'm saying. You like it.

"Oh, don't make me, don't fuck me," you say. Then cry, "Oh fuck yeah," when I slap the cock against your thigh. That makes me hot.

"Take your goddamn pants off and turn over, slut," I say.

I rub my hand up and down my dick. You stay where you are and watch me. "You heard me. Turn the fuck over, slut! That's right. Now just lie there while I boot up." I put on a condom, drip some lube on your ass. You moan loudly.

"Shut up, bitch," I say and put my cock against your thigh again. You catch your breath.

"Oh no, please."

"Oh yes. Lift your ass, girl. I said lift, bitch." You lift.

"Here I come. Oh yeah, take it like the whore you arc."

I slowly move my cock into you.

"Oh no, please don't." Your voice is still high. You moan a moan I've never heard before. Then grunt, "Fuck yeah." An affirmation.

"Can you feel that?" I ask. I reach my hand around in front and finger your clit. "Can you? You fucking whore." You grunt loudly.

"I said shut up and take it, bitch." I push in further and start thrusting.

"Yeah," you say, "fuck me hard."

"Oh I will. That's right. Take it. Fucking take it, bitch. Steve's going to fuck you silly. Fuck you till you can't see. Fuck you till you come all over my cock."

"Fuck. Yeah."

"That's right, Tammy, let Steve fuck you like you deserve. Take it, girl. Fucking take it till you come. You're going to gush, aren't you? All over me. I said you're going to come, aren't you? I said come, goddamnit. Fucking do it."

"Oh yeaaah, fuck me...."

"I said shut up, cunt, and come for your Daddy." And you do. Loud and labored. You soak the sheets. Your cunt throbs long after I stop thrusting. I lie on top of you, exhausted.

"Hold me," you say. You've never asked me to hold you before. Boy. Girl. T. I hold you.

3.

We don't talk for months. Why? Because you're an asshole. Because I'm a bitch. Because you're insensitive. Because I'm too sensitive. Because we walk two completely different worlds. Today, I don't remember why. Just remember wanting you. Today, I walk through this street. *I miss T* goes over and over in my head. When I get home I call you. Ask you to come over. And of course you do. You always do. No questions asked. This is what we do for each other.

I put on lipstick and meet you on the front porch, even though it's freezing out. I don't tell you about my day, even though it was bad. I don't ask about yours. I am so glad to see you. I can tell you're glad to see me too. But we pretend we're not. We stare at each other in the cold. You and I, we sure know how to pretend.

"Well, aren't you going to ask me in?"

"Yeah, yeah, come up."

You follow me to the top of the stairs, through my apartment door. "Look, T," I say, turning around. Your arm is in the air. You drop a snowball on my head.

"Oh, you bastard," I laugh.

"Aw baby, what's wrong?" Your annoying sarcasm. You laugh too. Brush the snow off my head, my shoulders. "What's wrong?" You stop laughing. "Baby?"

I don't say anything. Bring you into my bedroom. Pull you down beside me on the bed. Lie with you. You caress me. Move your fingers over my clothes, over my body. My eyes are closed. If this is the only thing we can do for each other, so be it.

"So T, tell me about your first kiss."

You don't say anything right away. Then, "I was nine. He was a man." You say it so calmly. Like it's normal. Then I wonder, what the hell is normal?

"And how was it?"

"It was an all-right kiss," you say.

I'm quiet. You continue to caress me. Slow, sensual. Unusual for us. We stay like that for a long while. Until you move your hands gently under my shirt. My skin gets goose bumps. My cunt gets wet. My body responds with movement. You take my shirt off. Get more aggressive. Kiss my body where your caresses were. Pull at the button of my jeans.

"I want you," you say.

"I want you too. I want your fist."

"You got it."

You move down my body and undo my jeans, pull them off. Slide your hand over my underwear. Apply pressure on my clit. My hips rise and grind. You take off my underwear. Slide your hand along my wetness. Rub a finger against my clit. I open up to your fingers. You push and play with my clit. In no time my cunt gathers around your whole fist. It is always faster and easier with you than with anyone else. I love it more than anything else we do. But I always have to remind you I don't want thrusts. You like getting pumped and don't understand why I don't. But you do what I ask. Just leave your fist there in me. Still.

"It feels so...comfortable," I say.

"I haven't heard that one before," you say. I smile. We're quiet. You keep it in until I'm ready for you to take it out.

"You're still bleeding." You show me your hand covered with my blood. "Do you have a piece of paper? I'll make a handprint."

I still feel full. Flayed. Prelingual.

"Well, you've got one inside you already, anyway." You lie down beside me. Lay your hand on my breast. We stay like that for a long time.

"Will you run me a bath?" I ask.

I stay in bed while you go. You clean the tub for me. Then run the water hotter than I'd like. Use shampoo to make bubbles. I know you feel chivalrous. Like this is what a guy does for a girl. Takes care of her.

"I wonder if what we are is anything like being straight," I call from the bed.

"We're still dykes," you say, sounding offended. Sometimes it's true. That's exactly what we are. Sometimes we're not. Sometimes, I guess, it just doesn't matter.

When the bath is ready, you call me. I get in and the water is too hot, like you thought it would be. I turn on the cold and swirl it around. You close the toilet lid and sit on it. Watch me. You've got your boy vest on. I like you watching. I turn off the cold water and lie back. Warm. Smothered. A feeling I rarely enjoy. When I ask you to join me in the tub, you refuse. You don't say why, but I know you well enough to understand what makes you feel vulnerable. You leave the room.

I think about how it feels to do this typical boy–girl thing with you. Sometimes I play girl, and sometimes I am girl. I get confused about which one is which. I think about who you are to me. How, sometimes, you are what I need in the most surprising ways. I hear you in the kitchen.

"Hey T," I call from the bath. You stop moving. You're quiet.

"Yeah?" you finally respond.

"Co'mere."

You come back into the bathroom with your swagger. Your casual air. "What?"

"Kneel," I tell you.

"Kneel where?" you ask, pretending to be unsure about wanting to kneel for me.

"Beside the tub," I say, pointing beside me. You just look at me for a second, making like you don't want to. But you do.

"What?" you ask again as you kneel. There's a staccato sound in your voice.

I sit up a bit in the tub and look at you. "Kiss me, Troy."

You hesitate ever so slightly. Then get yourself wet leaning in for the kiss.

Look but Don't Touch
Sparky

You look down and see the bottle of whiskey lying in casual spills of come.

You envy the boys for those quick joyous fountains.

It will take you much longer.

The walls are shiny from others before you: a glaze of sperm, sweat, other shoulders in leather jackets, and the strangely mouthwatering smell of cleaning solution.

Your shoulders are narrow. You fit neatly into this dark box.

There is no great mystery, you think, sliding a dollar into the glowing slot. Surrounded by darkness, you think of your mom, comforting you in the locker room: "We're all girls here."

But you smell like cool water for men and pomade, and you

wear your most dapper boy clothes, black leather jacket and boots. Your hair is freshly cropped and no one can tell the tinge of lip liner. Your hair is carefully in its borrowed tranny boy flip. You are prepared for a mystery date. Who is behind the glass? That is the mystery.

A bar of light widens. The black window rises.

Five women in red-gold light are surrounded by mirrors. Dancing naked with their own lush bodies, with the mirrors reflecting silver and red flashes, girls upon girls, like the room is packed. One comes over to see you, dances before you. She has small, rounded breasts, rounded hips, catlike black-rimmed eyes, and a ready, naughty smile, stands on tall vinyl stiletto boots. A black bob, a mini-version of Uma Thurman in *Pulp Fiction*.

Your face becomes hot. Your ears burn. Your expression is awe and wonderment. She grins down at you, pleased. Seductive. She shows you her breasts; their skin looks impossibly smooth and clean, with golden-rimmed, small nipples. You see the hollow of her throat, her collarbone, her little belly.

She is the loveliest being on the planet.

She is naked before you and you can do nothing but look and look.

You keep looking at her hips, peek at her pussy, and give long lustful looks to her boots.

"I bet that smile gets them every time," she purrs.

You realize you are grinning like a fool. You shake your head no but cannot stop the grin that is shy, nervous, awed.

She calls the others over. "Look how cute! Look at those dimples!"

Now you could not stop smiling if you tried.

Four of them peep in the window at you, pressing against it. They pretend to poke your dimples. "So cute!" Real smiles from them. You want to duck and you are blushing so hard but there's nowhere to go, the window's open, and your money is in there ticking away relentlessly.

They move to other open windows and you are left with little Uma Thurman. "I like your boots," you say.

You hear the click as she rests one high heel on the window ledge and bends over so you look up the spike heel and vinyl boot to her incredible round ass. She peeks at you from above her delicate pussy lips and asshole, smiling because, you think to yourself, now she knows. She knows how to get you. You feel tormented with need to be licking those boots.

She turns to face herself in the mirror and lowers herself below your window. She writhes back and forth. You realize with delight that she is fucking your imaginary cock. She's smiling sweet and wicked, as if she knows exactly how hard this gets your clit.

The black square of window lowers. She bends down to grin underneath, waving. You see the shiny toe of her boot, and are left in darkness.

You feel wired and keyed up, you've been here a long time and are likely to stay longer, not willing to jerk off like the others. You told yourself to come here for the experience but you will get yourself turned on until you want to climb the booths, kiss and claw at the glass, so near to those girls. Wanting to please them all.

The next booth smells salty and familiar. You realize it's freshly pumped semen that glitters on the floor. You feel a sense of solidarity. You put twenty into the slot. You are in for the full ride.

The window rises. You lock eyes with a new dancer, across the carpeted, mirrored stage. This one has a cute black bob with little ponytails and bangs. She has little Cupid's-bow pouty lips and huge dark eyes with long lashes. She wears white thigh-high fishnets with bits of lace at the top and high-heeled sandals.

But most of all she has a body that is so lush and curvy, it looks familiar. It could be your own. She has a rounded tummy and her hips and thighs are buttery and luscious. With her black hair and sexy tummy, she reminds you of your first girlfriend. She is innocent and powerfully sexual. It is like the glass is gone.

She looks unimaginably soft and delicious. You want to roll around on top of her and feel her up, lick up and down her luxurious hips and belly.

She comes up and licks her lips, pouting and sexy, thrusting her heavy breasts, writhing her hips against the window. Her lips are trembling. You realize it's an effort for her to keep from cracking up. Soon she cannot stop smiling. Her eyes are half-lidded. She is everything lush and full, and you want to take her around the waist and wrap her legs around you. But she's behind the glass.

You ponder what to say. Poetry? Blank verse? "You are so cute," you say at last.

She smiles for real, her eyes lingering on you. "So are you!"

Her name is Persephone and that is not, she informs you, her real hair. She leans over to pull the wig a little. Her hair is blonde and cropped short, recently shaved.

The window closes and opens again, slowly revealing her white fishnets and finally the lace trim and her ass. She's talking to the other dancers. It's late now, and the catlike Uma Thurman dancer from earlier is stretched out against one wall, naked except for her boots, a lazy smile on her face. You are one of two people still watching. The dancers lounge around naked and hot under the lights, beautiful and untouched. It looks humid. You want to fan them with palm leaves. Suck on ice cubes and breathe mist into their lips. Wear your own outfit of gold sandals, and be their altar boy or temple acolyte....

Persephone does a silly dance, climbs up the pole, and twists her way back down, does handstands for you. She comes back to your window and her eyes focus on you, serious, thinking. She undulates and smiles, showing you her ass, her tits, her shoes, her pussy, right at eye level. You cannot look away, you are enchanted. She is pink and luscious, sparkling, red-gold from the lights. She licks and bites her own nipple and you finally feel your clit so warm and hard the feeling has spread throughout your lower body, the urgency of this is unfuckingbearable. You feel overwhelmed. You do not know what to do. How do guys deal with this? You look at the pools of semen with new understanding, but you're not about to do that here. Instead you feel wild, panicked, worshipful, at a standstill, spending more and more to keep seeing the girls deliciously naked and close enough to touch but you can't, and your breath is steaming up this little stinky booth.

The window lowers. The darkness is comforting after such staring at the light.

You walk outside into the San Francisco night. You turn and the lights of the Golden Gate Bridge stretch across the bay. They are shimmering in the fog. You think of the shimmering girls in their mirrored fishbowl dancing late into the night. The bridge and the girls: glittering, remote, and comforting all at once.

Lessons

S. Bear Bergman

She slid her cock out of me slowly, so slowly, then pumped it back in once, hard, to watch me gasp and laugh and grab for it; she knows I can't take that after I've just come but she likes to do it anyhow. It's how she tests to make sure I'm really, thoroughly fucked out, I think. I reached back, grabbed her wrist, and pulled her up and onto my back like so many covers, like I do, snuggling down under her warmth, the weight of her keeping me safe and grounded. She murmured fond and ridiculous things in my ear, calling me *sweet* and *delicious, handsome* and *beautiful,* licking away the sweat on my neck and sliding a hand under my sweaty chest to hug me a bit. We snuggled and rolled with the afterglow, being silly. I sucked gently on the tips of her fingers, lazing along by my cheeks, kissed the palm of her hand, nuzzled and burrowed into it, lapping like a pup. She giggled. I made a noise, a warm one, low in my throat, something between a growl and a groan, and curled myself against her.

Every time we do this, I like it a little better, and I liked it a whole fuck of a lot to begin with. We don't get a lot of chances, living so far apart and not being Rockefellers, either one of us, but between conferences, relatives, and the occasional frequent flyer ticket, we get just enough to never feel too horribly deprived. Still—this particular meeting had been after an especially long hiatus, and I was glad for the three days, glad for the king-sized bed in the anonymous hotel room on the eighth floor, glad for the weight of her on my back and the way that it never seemed like it had been months since we'd seen each other, even though we don't really talk on the phone much.

We email, though. It's the best part about messing around with writers. The email is so, so good.

Recovering slowly, I disengaged myself long enough to dislodge the head of her dick from a tender spot just above my knee, and tugged on it, experimentally, looking to see if she were ready to take it off, to let me touch her, but also ready to let my touch modulate into a jack-off motion at any minute if she wasn't. She has a harder time with it than I do; I was brought up as a butch by sex–positive, radical perverts who thought that any bullshit about butches not liking to get fucked was so much retrograde nonsense, but she grew up someplace outside of Philly and ten years earlier, where the local lesbo culture was strictly a butch top/femme bottom arrangement, where all the butches were presumed stone until proven guilty, and butch-on-butch pairings were as taboo a thing as could be imagined. Good thing that times change.

I cruised her hard when we first met a couple of years ago at a writers' conference: She made several very smart comments during a panel we were on together, and she had a steel-gray brush cut. Sold. I invited her to have dinner with my friends and me, my dear friends who set me up with ample conversational opportunity to both mention my wife at home and discuss being poly, so this hot thing would know the score. That, plus my outrageous flirting, did the trick, and after dessert I was in her room on my knees, being called a delicious assortment of very dirty things while I struggled to get her buttonfly jeans off and a condom on using only my mouth.

I *love* writers' conferences.

Since then, she's let me talk her out of her boxer briefs and into all kinds of hot and nasty fun, and has even developed quite a liking for getting fucked with my biggest dick, one that makes her crack jokes about getting to be a size queen in her old age. But I always have to wait until she's fucked me at least once, first, like she needs to reground herself in the idea whenever we meet again, as if her gentleman butch sense of the rightness and order of the world can't allow her to experience her own desire until everyone else has been squared away first. Not to suggest that fucking me isn't one of her desires. It seems clear to me at this stage that it is. But.... You know what I mean.

I slide my body up until my mouth is right against her ear. I say, "Oh. Oh, you fucking hot thing, so good to me, I want to make you feel so good, man, I want to do you so right...." I brush my lips against her ear, buck my crotch against her hip, start to move next to her. My hands find her nipples and start to rub, gently, just how she likes. She groans, quietly. I go on: "Mmmm. AJ, I want something. I want something from you, so bad."

She picks her head up and looks at me. She loves when I say what I want, she likes it that I trust her, and that I'm so hot for her. She says low, into my ear, "What's that, hm? Tell me. Tell me what you want, greedy."

Pressing myself against her, selling it with my entire body, lacing my fingers through her hair, I let a rush of hot breath out across her ear, and say, "Please. Please, teach me how to make you come."

She draws back, shocked, looks at my face. She travels with

a Magic Wand and uses it, buzzing herself off while I fuck her and having noisy good times about it. But I have a secret hunch about her. I think maybe she's like me, that there's some other, nonelectric way to get the job done, something that requires the exact right touch and a lot of work, something she never confesses because she doesn't want to be that much work, or be that exposed, or make someone else work that hard on her behalf, but which is incredibly satisfying in a totally different way. I've seen the signs. I want to know what it is. I want to do her like that, want to make her come for me without her having to do anything at all. I want her to trust me like that.

I slide closer, out of her gaze, heart pounding, positioning my lips next to her ear again. "Please, AJ. Tell me what to do. I promise I'll do a good job for you. I swear I will. Use me to get yourself off. You deserve it, god, you deserve it."

Her big hands close around two fistfuls of hair, and she drags my head away from hers so she can see my face, mouth slack from panting to catch my breath. I hold her gaze and try to make my eyes communicate exactly what I'm thinking, what she wants to see: Yes, I mean it. Yes, I want this.

She drags my head back, my ear against her mouth, and crushes me tight against her in a hug. I wonder whether she's crying. I didn't mean to make her cry, I wanted to make her come, which is wetness at a totally different *end,* and I'm just about to start apologizing all over myself when she says, "You won't want to do it."

The hell I won't. I'd walk barefoot across a mile of burning sand to watch this butch dry dishes on videotape. "Trust me, I will," I say.

After a long, long pause, during which I have the good sense to keep quiet, she says in my ear, so quietly I can barely hear her: "Lick my asshole."

I'm elated. I groan, "Oh, holy shit, yeah," into her ear, start fumbling the harness off, looking for the plastic wrap, so excited I can't remember not to do five things at once. I knock over the lube, right it, find the plastic, get her out of the harness and flat on her back on the bed with a pillow under her hips before she can start waffling or change her mind. I tear off a piece of wrap, put it aside, and start kissing her, laying my body back along the warm, furry, delicious length of hers, kissing her soft and slow with little nips of my teeth, running my hands down the sides of her body, stroking her strong arms and her wide hips, working my way down her body, so slowly, rolling her nipples between my lips for a long time, sucking them so, so gently and making her push her cunt up to me, licking at her tattoos. I keep my knees between her legs so she can't grind. I want her to be hungry when I finally touch her, want her to want it so much. I want this to last. I want to show her what she's worth—all my attention, all my desire.

Finally, I bend my head and start nuzzling against the crack of her ass, kissing and nipping at her asscheeks, reaching surreptitiously for the Saran Wrap while I squeeze her ass between my hands, pulling her cheeks apart, smoothing the plastic into place, and sliding nose first between her cheeks. Her legs are bent at the knee. I can't believe she's so open to me but I am *not* complaining. I dig in.

I trace my tongue up and down her crack, so gently, full of hot breath. I want her to feel the heat even through the barrier, want her to be able to imagine it isn't there. I start to work my tongue in a little deeper, wriggling it against the sensitive spots, taking long, long licks from just below the opening of her cunt over and past her asshole, licking a fraction harder with each swipe of my tongue. She sighs, shifts her hips, presses against me. Encouraged, I keep on, starting to vary the pressure and depth of each lick, sometimes using the broad flat of my tongue and sometimes just the very tip, as hard as I can make it; I trace around the opening of her asshole, crinkled tightly shut, tracing my tongue along each of the tiny sunburst furrows of skin that radiate out from it, trying to get it to trust me. On one of the licks, I miscalculate and start pressing just a bit too soon, pushing the tip of my tongue right against the hole.

She moans. My cunt starts to do a slow boil, and I redouble my efforts. I kiss, lick, and nuzzle against her asshole, pushing my nose against it playfully, working against it with my tongue, feeling it start to open, starting to smell how much she likes it—when I pick up my head to say this to her, I see the small, slow stream of milky come easing its way out of her cunt and down the crack of her ass. Holy Christ. I put my head back down, and get back to work.

How do I describe this? It becomes the Zen of asslicking, the whole world gets reduced to about three inches of warm, wet flesh and every sound she makes. Her hand comes down and locks itself in my hair, she pulls me closer into her asscrack, tongue first, finally opening up enough for me to insinuate it into her hole and wriggle, just a tiny bit, but it makes her make a noise I'd never heard before, and I suddenly don't care how much my neck hurts or how hard it is to get my tongue into her, I just want her to make that noise again. I start fucking her hole with my tongue, slow and steady, the plastic wrap a mess around my face, and she starts grinding back against me, so hard it hurts my nose, but I am on a mission, now.

Suddenly she lets loose my hair, and I'm not sure what she wants, I start to pick my head up but she growls, "Don't stop, oh, please, don't, please don't stop," and grabs my hand instead, dragging it up and pulling it hard against her clit, which is harder than I have ever felt it, literally standing straight out of the hood like a tiny cock. I work it differently than I normally would, in a two-fingered jack-off motion I learned for transmen with testosterone-enhanced parts, up and down the sides with occasional swipes across the head, and she loves it, starts panting and gasping while I fuck my face further into her now-open, gripping asshole and work her clit at the same time. I can tell she's going to come, soon. I don't change a thing, I keep doing exactly what I'm doing, same speed, same pace, if I'm doing it right I want to keep doing it right, I want to do it right for her, want to make her feel as good as she makes me feel, so I keep my hand steady and blink the sweat out of my eyes and take a deep breath for one more long sally, plunging my tongue back into her ass on the downstroke and pulling it out on the up, letting her buck between the two pleasures, until she yells, "Oh, holy motherfucking god!" and comes with a bellow that even the moderately soundproofed hotel room probably doesn't contain, nearly breaking my neck as she whips her legs together around my face and squeezes them hard, hand clamping down over my hands, writhing on the bed in pleasure and riding what I hope like hell are several strong aftershocks, each one announced with a guttural cry.

Soon, she's still. I tap her on the thigh to remind her that my head is still between her legs and when she opens them, I scramble up, hurrying to cover her naked skin with mine, wrapping her up against me, holding her and whispering, "Thank you. Oh, thank you," into her ear like a mantra, over and over. She looks at me.

"That was...oh. Wow. Em, that was...." She trails off, nuzzles further into the crook of my neck, rubbing her sweaty skin against mine. We breathe together for a minute. I drag the ugly bedspread over us to keep us warm, being careful to hold her tight the whole time, not wanting to break this moment. I can't even believe she trusted me with that. It makes me feel something I can't explain, and while I'm searching for the words, so I can tell her, she picks her head back up, and whispers, so quietly for such a big, confident butch, so shyly, "Did you like it?"

I grin. I take her hand, draw it down to my soaking wet cunt, brushing her fingertips over my hard clit. "What do you think?" I ask, laughing a little into her ear.

She growls hungrily, rolls me over underneath her, and says, "I think you're a little slut, that's what I think."

I nod happily, and spread my legs wider.

Envy

Teresa Lamai

The moment I saw Aracelli, I decided I hated her.

I was nineteen. For a year, I had been scrambling in the back rows of class and rehearsal at American Ballet. She appeared one sweltering May afternoon, a new student, serene, frail, with skin that gleamed like melted caramel and indigo hair so glossy it seemed always wet. A reverent space cleared for her at the head of the class, her very first day. Fresh from the Kirov school, she was flawless, an amber figurine come to life.

A stab of envy made my spine twist. My tongue swelled hard against my teeth as if I'd swallowed something too sweet. She smiled at me and I looked away.

When she and I were paired for the final allegro of class, grands jetés across the floor, my eyes stung. I was convinced our teacher had paired us on a cruel whim. I looked like a pudgy, red-haired gnome next to her smoky opulence; her sweat-slick skin glistened with copper and turquoise lights.

I decided to pleasantly ignore her, but that only lasted a week.

"You know, Kim, the thing I like most about this place is the friendliness."

It was the first time I'd heard her voice. It trailed up my neck like a silk scarf. I turned to where she sat in a perfect split, leaning forward on her elbows, smirking up at me. Her dark breasts swelled between her arms. Her damp, pink-covered legs writhed gently into the grimy floor.

We were the last ones in the studio after a distinctly miserable class. As soon as the pianist had begun playing for the warm-up that morning—just a quiet sarabande to nudge us out of stillness—Miss Greta, our teacher, had opened her bright red mouth and let forth a stream of outraged, piercing shrieks. Where her critiques lacked clarity, they had more than enough volume. Some students responded by spreading the hate around; gaunt girls gathered in the corners between exercises, watching as the others danced and sharing elaborate pantomimes of disgust. I resolutely ignored them but couldn't escape their whispers, she—she—, like spit landing on my back.

I gazed at Aracelli for a moment after she spoke, almost convinced that she was playing with me. She drew her coltish legs into herself, resting her cheek on her knees. She blinked slowly. Her deep voice surprised me; it sounded pained and rough.

"Everyone's so well-adjusted, and kind." Her velvety eyes were wide and grave, but her mouth twitched.

A delighted laugh burst from my chest, startling me. I looked up at the ceiling, letting it shake along my spine.

"Yeah." My raucous voice echoed down the corridor. "This is the one place I just say, 'fuck it,' and be myself."

"You know it! Just let it all fucking hang out." She was rocking with laughter now, her throat flushed. When her cheeks rose, her eyes narrowed and glittered, black as onyx. Her smile was fresh with kindness and a bite of wicked humor. Irresistibly subversive.

The empty studio seemed to hum uncertainly around us, as if unused to the sound of laughter.

She rose to her feet, slow and indolent. I tried not to let my smile fade as she stood, still smirking, shifting her weight into one hip. So perfect. My throat ached. Her tapered legs were taut and sleek, her waist slender as a sapling. The twin swells of her breasts were high and full, nuzzling each other playfully when she moved.

She moved toward me, chin lowered, a half-tame gazelle. Her lashes curled toward her temples. I reminded myself that I disliked her.

"I get the feeling that we're not supposed to be friends. That's, like, against the rules here, isn't it?" She spoke more quietly than she needed to. I had never seen such a beautiful face so close to mine. Her cheekbones glinted like burnished gold.

When she was near enough to take my hand, she started whispering, a lazy purr. "How about we become friends anyway, and bust this joint wide open?" She squeezed my wrist and grinned. Her crowded teeth gave her a sly, feral look.

I couldn't help licking my lips before I spoke. I blushed, knowing it made me look clumsy and weird.

"All right, we can shake on it." I tried to regain some composure with a tinny laugh.

My laugh turned into a gasp when she kissed my cheek, swiftly. Her cool ear brushed my temple. I closed my eyes as she kissed one cheek, then the other, again and again. Her breath was sugary, her lips light as petals.

My hands twitched at my sides. Panic filled me; it seemed wrong to be this close to something so exquisite. I felt like a careless child about to smudge and drool over a priceless jeweled statue.

She kissed my forehead, my eyelids. Her scent filled my

head. She wore some brisk expensive perfume, light as white wine, but underneath it her heated skin gave off the scent of cloying swamp flowers and moss. I rested my shaking hands on her shoulders and lifted my chin toward her glowing face.

We both moaned when our lips met. My awkwardness fell away like an old dead skin, and the flesh underneath was painfully alive, hissing with a low current. She drew my mouth into hers, gentle then gently deep, as if she were tasting a new fruit. I let my palms graze over her face. My eyes squeezed shut as I felt her delicate temples, her tiny chin, her trembling arteries. I never wanted to stop kissing her; it was like gulping spring water.

Her palms glided over my ass, cradling it, lifting it lightly. I cried out. My pulse thudded in my stomach, heat pooled between my legs until I felt my clit struggling fitfully against my tights, a tiny captured bird.

When I caught the tip of her tongue and sucked on it, she growled. She lifted one leg and wrapped it tight around my waist. Our breasts pushed together, play-fighting for room. She clutched the back of my skull, sinking her nails in deep. Bobby pins clattered to the floor.

Footsteps rang in the corridor, sharp and purposeful.

I started, covering my breasts as if I were naked. I stared at Aracelli and was shocked to find her smirking again, sinking her teeth into the plump flesh of her lower lip. Her smile was steady and unsettling. She reached between my legs, resting her hand over my swollen mound, trailing her elegant fingers one after the other in an unhurried beckoning. My legs shook. Her other hand slid under my palm to my breast. She brushed my nipple with her thumb, then turned away, just as the footsteps rounded the corner.

"What is this?" Miss Greta always wore a smart checked suit and a fox stole, no matter how hot the weather. Her eyes widened at Aracelli and me as we stood, side by side, squeaking with strangled laughter.

She was inhaling deeply, preparing to raise her voice, when I grabbed Aracelli's hand and pulled her through the door. Miss Greta's blistering stare followed us down the hallway. We burst into the dressing room, screaming and giggling, breathless as if we had fallen into icy water.

We spent the rest of the sweltering afternoon in my dank closet of a room. Some violent, insatiable spirit took hold of us completely. We struggled, slick with sweat and saliva, grunting, sliding from the bed to my narrow, stained rug. Aracelli dug her nails into my ass when she came, wailing inconsolably, her back arched and still until she finally broke into furious thrashing. Her fists slammed into the wall beside me.

When sleep finally took us, it was mercifully swift and heavy. We lay unconscious, fists still wrapped in each other's hair, bodies twisted tight and covered in tiny red scratches like kitten bites.

Three weeks passed. Aracelli spent every evening in my room, her long dark body stretched beside mine.

"You know, Kim, when I first saw you, I thought you were so fucking beautiful I couldn't stand it." She laughed.

I loved to close my eyes and let her voice glide over me like heated oil. My wind chimes rang softly out on the fire escape. Broadway's traffic roared far below, a distant surf. I felt her lift partly and rest on one elbow. I lay still.

After her first orgasm, Aracelli was always transformed, losing her slit-eyed smirk and becoming winsome as a cat. She trailed one strand of her hair over my collarbone. With my eyes closed, I felt her shape shimmering beside me.

Her voice stirred the hair on my temples. "I couldn't take my eyes off you, you were just so tiny and delicious. Your vanilla-cream skin, all downy and velvety like you were covered in powdered sugar. Your mouth, like a little candy rosebud. Mmm."

She kissed me and I opened my eyes. Her hair cascaded slowly, swaths of heavy black silk over her shoulders. She looked contented and wild. With the dusk, the corners of my room were retreating into dull blue shadows. She gave off a soft crimson glow in the darkness like a banked fire.

She kept talking, her eyes moving up and down my body, her fingertips trailing across my stomach and combing through the damp, matted curls over my sex.

"You know, Kim, I first thought that I hated you, isn't that funny? But it wasn't hate, really—more that I wanted so desperately to be you, or just be close to you, all the time."

Her fingernails were like polished opals, scratching over my pale nipples. She smiled down at me when I shuddered.

"Maybe envy," she murmured, resting her lips on my forehead, "is that fine edge between hate and love."

I bit my lip. We burst out laughing at the same time.

"Come here." I lifted myself up, straining to see her face.

I gripped her shoulders, shifting down until my mouth was at her tight, salty breasts. My tongue moved restlessly, anxious as if it could never get enough of her skin. I rolled her onto her back, trailing kisses down her flat, muscled belly. I lifted her ass in my palms so that I could keep watching her face as I closed my mouth over her slippery cunt. Her hips started to writhe but I held them tight, my fingers sinking into her flesh. My forearms shook with the effort.

I kept my eyes fixed on hers as I turned my head sideways. I let my tongue glide. Her pelvis pitched up when I found her clit. Still holding her, I lapped at it, persistent and gentle, until her spine coiled and her fists clenched in the sweat-soaked sheets.

I didn't stop until she had come two more times. Aracelli was never more beautiful than when she lost control, her eyelids fluttering, her mouth working soundlessly, tendons shifting in her long throat.

Afterward, I rested my cheek on her stomach. She filled her palms with my hair, lazily drawing out tendrils and spreading them all around my head.

"Kim, are you sleeping?"

"Mmm, no." I woke up and kissed her navel.

"Let's form an unholy alliance. Let's work together this summer and go further than anyone else."

Our strategy quickly took shape. I would teach her all of American Ballet's repertoire, the uniquely angular, neoclassical style that she found so new and awkward. She would help me with my desperately weak technique. We felt we'd cracked a code, combining our strengths, each the other's secret weapon.

Gossip spread that the summer workshop performance would feature *Jewels* this year. Recruiters from every major company would be invited, ready to give contracts to the most outstanding students. We decided that I would be cast as Emerald, and she as Diamond, and absolutely nothing else would do. We had five weeks before auditions would be held.

We sneaked into the studio on Sundays, pleading with the maintenance guys until they let us have a key. I had a bootleg videotape of *Jewels* and we learned all the choreography, every phrase, from beginning to end. No matter what they threw at us in the audition, we would be ready.

One hazy Sunday, a week before the auditions, we watched each other run through each of the variations twice. Music echoed brashly, rushing to the ceiling. Aracelli finished the Diamond coda, then fell into a cartwheel, squealing with glee. She stood panting, radiant, sweat streaming down her neck. Her eyes were dilated and inhumanly black.

"Fabulous. The best one I've seen." I slouched against the mirror, applauding weakly, drumming my heels into the floor.

She peeled her leotard down and leaned to work her tights off her legs. She was still panting when she lifted her arms into her flowered red sundress. I watched her flushed body disappear under a billow of rayon. By the time she shook her sweaty head free, I was standing and struggling with my leotard straps.

"No way, Kim. You need to do those sixteen fouettés again. Seriously."

I glared. My legs were numb. "I did that phrase, like, five times today."

"No," she almost shouted. I took a step away from her. I'd never seen her like this. Small blue veins writhed in her temples.

"Aracelli, what the fuck. I did—"

"You did twelve fouettés and then, like, four half-assed turns to get through the rest of the music. Do you think no one will notice?" Her voice was so shrill my ears hummed.

She looked down. "Kim." She swallowed, turned her head sharply. Her voice became deadly quiet. "If you want to just have fun, to just chill out and dance like a corps dancer.... Then why am I wasting my fucking time with you?"

Her last words were a strangled, half-whispered scream. Her balled fist smacked into her thigh. I flinched at the impact.

I turned away, feeling my eyes darting about. The room still rang with her shrieks.

"All right. Go sit down and turn on the music." My voice wavered.

"Don't fake it this time—"

"FOR CHRIST'S SAKE, I HEARD YOU!" I yelled it as loud as I could. Anything to drown out her voice. My nails dug crescents into my palms.

The music blared again, just as I turned and saw Aracelli's blank, stricken face. She leaned her back to the mirror and sank into a squat. Her lower lip shook, her eyes filled.

I ran to my mark.

When I finished dancing, she was sitting with tears streaming down her cheeks.

I turned off the tape. She was sucking her breath between her teeth, squeaking and trembling. Her eyes followed me.

I lay back on the gritty floor, trying to fill my lungs again. I wiped the sweat off my face with my forearms.

She gulped twice before she could speak. "I'm so sorry, Kim."

"Yeah."

"I don't know what happens to me sometimes, it's like I just become this monster. I hate myself when it happens. I try, I try to control it."

I turned away from her, resting on my side. I felt I could fall asleep. The blood throbbed back into my feet and the pain made me wince.

"You think I'm a bitch, Kim, don't you?"

"Sure."

I cringed, expecting her to freak out again. Instead she was silent. When I finally rolled to face her, she was covering her face with her dress, hunched over, utterly still.

I saw my reflection just past her, pale and sweat-drenched, purple shadows under my pained eyes. Half my hair had come loose.

When I stood, stars sparked orange and silver in front of my eyes. I reached down and squeezed her shoulders. She started, staring up at me. Her face was streaked with tears and sweat. I pulled her to her feet.

She rested her forehead on mine. I cradled her skull in my palms.

She was whispering now. "Do you ever feel, like, numb and raw, like your skin's been all scabbed over?"

She glanced at me, swallowed, then kept speaking.

"Like it's all been fried, like someone poured battery acid all over it, and then it just grew back all thick, with no nerves, no feeling."

"Okay, okay, Aracelli. Shh." I spread my hands over her burning head. I hardly knew what I was saying, I just heard deep, soothing sounds coming from my chest.

"I'm sorry, Kim. It's hard to remember that other people get hurt, feel pain, that I need to act a certain way or else you'll just...."

"Shh, baby." Before I could say more she squirmed into my arms.

When our mouths met, searing lust rose up in my stomach. The room went dim around me. I bit at her mouth, her shaking neck. I pulled out her bobby pins and twisted her hair in my fingers, grabbing thick handfuls and pulling until she jerked with the pain.

We stumbled into the stool and I turned her around, pulling the straps of her dress off her shoulders. It rippled to the floor. I ran my hands along the gleaming topaz curve of her back.

My boldness made me shake. I had no idea what I intended to do. She was panting. I gently guided her, leaning her forward until her elbows rested on the stool's seat. Her hair nearly reached the floor, a heavy gleaming curtain.

"Oh god, you're so beautiful, Aracelli."

I kissed her downy spine. I wanted to bite her. Goose bumps rose along her arms. My nails left soft pale furrows on the twin swells of her ass. Her moan was low and deep.

I dropped to my knees and lifted one of her bare feet, setting it up on a side rung. The sight of her naked cunt was like an electric shock to my breastbone. My breath stopped as I ran my palms up her thighs. Her labia pouted obscenely, engorged and vulnerable. Her black curls glistened. Her scent was stronger and sweeter than I'd ever known it, rich as spiced honey.

When I touched two fingers lightly to her anus, her fluted inner lips unfurled at me, dark as plums. She bucked.

"Don't move." I rested my thumb under her clit, letting my tongue glide down one side of her labia. Her curls tickled my cheek. She sobbed and jerked, twisting toward my mouth.

"Shh, just feel it." Her hair moved under my breath.

She kept twisting. I stood and swatted her ass once, playfully. She squealed. I rested my hands on her thighs, massaging, feeling her heat radiate up through my arms. Her ribs heaved.

"You felt that too, didn't you?" I tried not to let my voice tremble. "Don't make me smack it harder."

I knelt again. Still kneading her flesh, I watched her labia contract and spread, a thick-petaled flower. When I saw her inner thighs shining, slick and golden, I couldn't resist anymore. My eyes stung with tears.

I leaned in, my tongue tracing lightly over her mound, my fingers covering her clit in tender circles. The smell of her made me lightheaded and I moaned when she finally lifted her head, her back perfectly straight, writhing furiously and shrieking. Her cunt pulsed in my mouth. She shook for a long time afterward, slow delicious aftershocks, turning her head from side to side and cooing softly to herself.

I eased her off the stool. We stretched out on the cool, dusty floor, cradling each other. Our breath became quieter as the room darkened.

We went to Aracelli's place the next night. She shared a West Village loft with her aunt, an art teacher at Cooper Union.

Aracelli had been inviting me there all summer, but I kept finding excuses to stay away. It wasn't that I hated the Village; it was glorious. The neighborhood was vibrant, endlessly complex, like a chaotic masterpiece of performance art that was just about to reveal its central theme. Each new block had something fascinating: flame-colored murals and steel statues, tiny stores packed with books, scents of lilies and fresh bread, snatches of mournful clarinet and Creole laughter. Art here was serious; there was an unspoken imperative to create constantly, to produce something that would appall and transport and devastate. To be the absolute best in your field.

I felt it should have inspired me but instead it made me numb with anxiety, wanting to curl up and hide.

"Kim, are you okay?" Aracelli was staring at me. Her face was gritty with dust. "You're all pale."

"It's just...." I rested my palm on my forehead. The crowd surged around us, bristling with energy as the sky darkened. "It's just so hot. The air's so heavy."

"It's cooler upstairs. Come on, we're here." It was an old art-deco building, gleaming in the last rays of the sun as if it were gold-plated.

Aracelli's dress puffed and floated around her legs as she bounded up the stairwell. "She's away. We get it all to ourselves. Hurry up!"

I reached the top floor in time to see her poppy-red figure disappear down the murky corridor. Muffled shouting came from the other rooms.

I sucked in my breath when I followed her through the doorway. The loft's whitewashed walls were draped with pastel silk prints and grainy, obscure photos. Half-formed statues, made of found objects and spray-painted silver, perched along the moldings like deranged household gods. A patched satin sofa was the only furniture; the rest of the front room was covered in faded, multicolored carpets and velour cushions.

I was speechless as I walked over to the window. The old-fashioned shutters opened over Washington Park. The sky was deepening to teal, with a haze of rusty brown and scarlet still glowing at the horizon. The park was a nest of tangled green shadows and flaring lights, filled with music and screams.

"I know, I know. I love it." Aracelli grabbed me from behind, clasping her arms tight around my waist and rubbing her breasts into my back. Her thin dress was already gossamer with sweat.

She raked her fingers through my hair. I shook it from my eyes. Her tender fingers found the back of my neck and I moaned.

"Kim, you look like one of those old paintings of angels." She kissed my throat. "In your little blue dress, your hair all over the place."

I sighed, leaning my head back on her thin shoulder. She ran her index fingers along my arms, from my shoulders to my wrists and back again, light as moth wings. My sex throbbed as if she were already cuddling it in her palm.

When she spoke again, her voice was hoarse. "Oh, Kim, I want to tie you somewhere and just fuck you and fuck you and fuck you until you're screaming for me to stop."

The wide darkness outside seemed to suck at me. My head spun. I tried to back away from the window but Aracelli gripped my neck and bit my ear. Her hips pressed mine into the window's ledge. I pressed my palms into the rough frame, bracing.

"Screaming and screaming until I gag you." Her nails in my throat made me whimper. "I'd gag you and make you come the way you've always needed to, come so hard you'd forget everything."

She knelt. I was already wet, panting when she pulled my panties to my knees. She tilted my hips back and just rested her languorous tongue on my still-folded cunt, soft and maddening. The darkening streets swam before my eyes.

When she finally fed me her strong fingers, one after another, my broken cries were sucked into the heavy, humid wind.

We woke late the next morning, strewn flat across her aunt's futon. We hadn't eaten anything the day before and we were weak with hunger. We clanged down the staircase and burst out to the sparkling clear day.

We started with our usual coffee and one biscotto each, just to check out a dark, stylish café. We added more pastries, growing even more famished as we ate. The second breakfast turned into lunch. We finished with an armful of chocolate bars, giggling madly on a sun-warmed stone bench in the Chinese garden, sucking the last melted bits from the foil. I couldn't remember when I'd eaten so much. My blood was so full of sugar that the world seemed painfully bright.

With my shoulder leaning on Aracelli's I looked out over the slow-moving crowd and realized suddenly it was all laughably easy. Absolutely anything was possible. I let myself tumble down and rested my head on her lap. I didn't care who saw us. Above me, she closed her eyes and lifted her sharp chin into the sunlight. Tendrils of wisteria and honeysuckle hung low, shaking vivid petals into the breeze.

We sat that way until the sun sank behind the trees.

"Come on, we shouldn't wait too long." Aracelli's voice had a leaden ring as we descended into the deserted subway station. She tugged me into the women's bathroom. Filthy shadows pooled in the corners.

"Wait for what?" I felt like I was drunk.

She knelt in an open stall, leaning over the toilet, her left arm working frantically at her mouth until her back spasmed. The smell made me retch and I stepped back.

She coughed only once and stood up, pressing a tissue into her lips. Her skin seemed to be dusted with ashes. I gulped, sucking in air around my tongue, willing my stomach to stop clenching on itself.

"What," she barked. But I still couldn't speak. She glared, her eyes dull as charcoal.

"I'm sorry." I turned away. "I don't do that. I—I don't think it's healthy."

"You don't...."

"I just, you know, diet."

"You diet!" I didn't need to see her face. Her laughter was strangely loud. "Well, Kim, no wonder...."

I faced her now. My ears rang and the miserable room went dim.

She yelled in earnest. "Don't give me that bullshit, Kim. What, you're just going to let all that sit on your stomach?" Her voice ricocheted over the tiles. "With auditions in six days? Jesus Christ, you're going to gain, like, five pounds."

I flinched, blinking. Panic flooded my mind. I felt my skirt already growing tighter around my thighs.

I knelt where she had been and looked at my hands. "I don't know how," I murmured.

Her voice was gentle, almost sweet. "Here." She crouched close beside me, holding out her long, bronze palm. "Use two fingers, hard, on the back of your throat."

I tried. It just tickled. I hadn't thrown up since I was five. My eyes became wet.

"Press really hard, on the part where your throat becomes soft." Her voice was brittle with impatience now. "Christ, either do it or not."

I reached further back, gingerly, breathing in little gasps, until I found the spot that made me gag. Before I could pull my hand away, Aracelli grabbed my wrist and shoved it toward the back of my head.

She stood up as I finished.

I couldn't stop sobbing afterward. My temples throbbed and my insides felt as though they'd been soldered into a black, smoking mess. I felt her standing over me and thought she would leave in disgust. Instead she knelt and wound her cool, slim arms around my neck, pulling until I fell back into her, holding my damp head under her chin. Her skin smelled like baby powder and vanilla lipgloss. She trailed her slender fingers through my hair.

"Kim, what did you expect?" Her voice was very quiet.

I was usually the first one at the studios in the morning, so I was surprised to hear voices in the cool, clean hallways that Wednesday as I arrived. A group of girls already huddled near the office doors. I made my way through them, slowly. I tried to listen for gossip, but there were only quick whispers, full of hissing rage.

A sheet was hung at the top of the bulletin board. Summer Workshop Performance Cast List.

Before I could read further, my shoulders tingled. I turned around. Aracelli gave me her mildest doe-eyed smile.

"What the hell, did you see this?" I pointed toward the board. "Auditions are this coming Saturday, aren't they? This must be a mistake."

"Well, they asked a few of us to audition for the principal roles last week. Everyone else will be the corps."

"They asked—" I pressed my hands to my temples. My stomach squirmed, turning ice cold. I realized my mouth was open and I shut it quickly.

"Don't get mad at *me*, Kim." Aracelli's tone was perfect; affectionate and reasonable. "Am I supposed to insist that they audition everybody?"

I laid my palms on my burning cheeks. A few girls were staring at us.

"Kim, a good solid corps dancer is so immensely valuable to a company."

I closed my eyes and felt her arm slip around my shoulders, hugging tight before she disappeared into the murmuring crowd.

Roulette
Shannon Cummings

Women got there earlier than the crowds at the nearby South of Market bars. Straight from work, proudly displaying the sweat of a day's work on their clothes. Tidying up would have been a sign of vanity, of femininity. A glob of pomade to grease the hair back was all the eveningwear they needed.

There was an unspoken rule that you couldn't park your bike in front of the club if it was smaller than someone's who had already arrived. Think your ride is better than someone else's, you better be prepared to defend it. The only exception was of course if you had a high femme riding bitch.

If you arrived late, you had to park your bike a few blocks away and hope you could get to the club without being roughed up by the neighborhood crew. A few trucks lined the alley out front. No one messed with you if you had a truck. It was assumed it was for work and was therefore off limits. Jobs were scarce, so if you could earn a living without losing your edge you were never ridiculed.

Lou had gone there on many occasions, sometimes returning home via the emergency room after bottles had been broken or blades pulled. Fights often started over motorcycles or the call of a pool shot. Or someone talking about how some stone had cracked.

The worst fight had happened after one girl had underestimated the locker room talk and bravado of both her lovers. While trading tales over whiskey, they realized just how much they had in common and ended up in a brawl. The next day they both called her to say they had defended her honor. But it was their own they were fighting for. One got a cut just above her eye; nearly blinded her, the doctor had said. The other's hand was sliced along the life-line, or was is it the love-line?, when she grabbed the blade swinging at her. She lost the use of her thumb and earned three months' disability leave from her machinists union. Women practiced their swaggers and rubbed their imaginary beards during pauses in conversation. It was a club for women with a rule of "no girls allowed." I was dying to go.

For six months, I had been crashing at Lou's place. I had run out on my last lover and showed up on her doorstep. I had taken over closet space and control of the tape deck, had started four kitchen fires, and had run up a long distance phone bill to my sister out east. Lou regularly threatened to kick me out but I would always coo to her until she got into bed so she could get to work on forgiving me. She was a good fuck and I was determined to stay. Sometimes when she was at work I would hustle some money at the pool hall to get by, pay a phone bill, or buy something sexy to wear so she wouldn't notice I had trashed her apartment. And her life. She was the first lover I ever had who knew a compliment should be taken as a request for more. I steadily stroked her ego and she let me stay.

"Dress sexy," Lou tells me. "We are going out."

I dress hurriedly and return for her approval. She looks me over, undoes another button on my blouse, and leans in to trace her tongue over the now exposed lace of my bra. "Tonight I'm taking you to the bar." She grabs her cigarettes, sighs into her nearly empty wallet, and slides both of them into her pockets.

"Who's going to be there?" I ask her, trying not to sound overtly curious.

"It will be crowded. Nanc will be there too. Just be on your best behavior."

Nanc, Lou's best friend and sometimes enemy. We had spoken on the phone a few times.

"Lou there?"

"No."

"She leave you all alone?"

"Yeah, she's out. I'll tell her you're looking for her."

"No, I mean, if you're alone, why don't I just come on over. We can wait for her together."

"I don't think that's the best idea. She'll be home soon."

"She says you're real pretty. Why don't I come over so I can tell her what I think of you."

"Maybe...some other time. I'll tell her you called."

"Ah, come on, she's been talking about how you're a wild one, that you can't ever get enough. You're probably rubbing your clit raw right now. I'll just come over and help you out. Why don't I just come over there and introduce myself to your...."

"Ummm.... I should really go. Bye."

We hadn't met but I had replayed her words in my head enough to recognize her voice anywhere. The best sex is always in your head, and Nanc had a knack for climbing into mine.

Lou parks the truck near the bar's entrance and comes around to open my door and look me over. "Who do you love?" she asks, brushing my hair back.

This well-rehearsed mantra to sooth her fragile ego spills

forth: "I love you, Lou, you know that. Only you. You know you are the only one who can keep me happy."

"Is that right?" She smiles a bit and pushes me against the side of the truck to kiss me and then she pulls back, seems to be waiting for more. It is not the cock but the compliment that is the way to a butch's heart.

So I continue. "You know you are my love. You turn me on more than anyone else ever could. How many times have I told you so? I'm not going anywhere. Don't you worry, baby."

Lou looks me square in the eyes and says, "No matter what happens tonight, you just remember that."

With her arm around my waist, we head down the damp back street. I can see the bikes in silhouette and the shape of a crowd of burly women hanging in the doorway of the bar. There is a whistle or two as we approach, then smiles and nods to Lou as she ushers me inside. The room is dim but everywhere I can see the dark huskiness of the most handsome women. There are squeaks of leather as people turn and a hand brushes my leg now and then in an almost accidental way. Now I fully understand why femmes need a chaperone here.

I like my women tough. The rougher edged and bigger, the better. I like to watch them get restless, their tough exteriors trembling under thick denim when they talk to me. I regularly call them *sir* to make them think they are passing. I admire those who don't correct me—it is a compliment. All a good butch really needs is a femme to appreciate her.

I have taken to making myself the most appreciative femme in the city. I can appreciate the fuck out of just about any butch I come across. And it is the fucking that I am really after. The trick is to find the soft spot in the hard women and tickle it until they hike my skirt up to see if my pussy is as sweet as my words. Their little way of thanking me.

Shy butches on their barstools want to be told that I can tell they are thinking deep thoughts. One drink later we are in their cars and they are thanking me as deeply as their broad-fingered hands can in such close confines.

A cropped-haired mechanic who has been tinkering on a bike that has been parked, unusable, for months on the lawn wants me to tell her what a fine ride it's going to be. Wants to hear me ask if I can sit on it for a minute, have me hitch my skirt up and place my oops-I-forgot-to-wear-panties-cunt down on the seat, lean forward so my clit slides along the leather to reach the handle bars. "I bet you can make her purr," I say, feigning revving the engine. A minute later, the shop table has been cleared off and she paws me with grease-stained fingernails while her buddies go out for lunch.

Lou had been hard and secretive and didn't fall for any of my usual ploys. Her soft spot was hard to find. Two weeks after moving in with her, I discovered a hidden stash of books. A few worn-out trashy straight novels, an instructional manual called *The Erotic Woman,* and a thoroughly uninteresting not-very-well-illustrated version of the Kama Sutra. To stay with Lou I would need to find a spot I could tease her with that could last months. Ordaining her as the best lover I have ever had was a way to keep my side of the bed vacant and to prevent her from changing the locks. She was good, so it wasn't a matter of faking it with her, as much as playing down every other encounter I had ever had. She knew I played around, but all seemed to be forgiven when I whined about how frustrated I was and how I couldn't wait to come home to be with her. She let the indiscretions go and grew increasingly interested in the fumbling details of lovers I auditioned. Lately we'd been arguing almost every day, and my stories had gone up a notch to counter her complaints. Now, not only was no one even close to her in bed, but no one else could even make me wet. Lou, who had been jamming my things into a duffle bag, stopped what she was doing when I revealed this to her. With almost a sense of pity she seemed to feel obliged to let me stay. I always carried clean panties in my pocket, which I could slip on before I came home to convince her of the lie she so wanted to believe.

We stop to get drinks before heading to the table that Lou's friends have staked out. Nanc speaks to Lou but keeps her eyes on mine, watching me scan the crowd. "Ah, so you finally let her out of the house." They laugh, giving each other a one-shoulder butch hug/pat.

The floor is already sticky with spilled beer. Lou's friends make room for us at the table and I listen to the group discuss work. How the assholes at the plant are reducing overtime, how so-and-so at the cycle shop has some thingy and such part doodad. I can't follow the conversation and don't care. I sip my beer, bouncing my ankle, trying to catch eye contact in a crowd used to avoiding it. Conversations in the room grow louder and women set their beers down so hard in anger or humor that the tables are slick from the sloshing over.

Lou gets up to go fetch more drinks and Nanc slides into her chair. "So, what d'ya think of our little bar?" She moves my hair off my shoulder, giving it a little tug. She leans in to me, one hand on my knee. In her familiar voice, she whispers the gossip of those sitting around the table. "Jess—been single for over a year, a pity she can't find a nice femme like Lou obviously has." I lean into her slightly so her mouth grazes my ear as she speaks. "And see Ron there? She passes at work. Takes shots too, when she can get her hands on a dose. Did you know testosterone raises sex drive?" She laughs alcohol-moist breath into my neck, saying she'd bet I already knew that.

Lou interrupts us, shoves Nanc back to her own seat, and pulls me out of mine.

"C'mon, let's go."

"Lou, man, we're just talking. Geez, half the time you want her to find a new man. I was just testing the waters." Nanc punctuates this with a sizzle sound.

"We're just going outside for a smoke. We'll be back."

She leads me out of the bar, squeezing the pinkies on both my hands in her fist as she pushes our way through the crowd.

Lou ignores me when we get outside even when I kiss her throat and try to jam my hands into her pockets. She has rolled us a joint she didn't want to share with her friends and we lean against the wall in silence trying to hang in the shadows. She feeds me drags between her long puffs.

Three women leaving the bar pause as they catch the scent and come over to ask directions to some other bar in an obvious ploy to get offered a hit. Lou vaguely gives them the information they want, and when they linger, she hands them the tight-rolled cig and they chat as they pass it around.

Lou introduces herself. Then she introduces me as the insatiable curse who couldn't be left alone for a minute without trying to make a pass at her best friend. Lou laughs it off and says that even if her friend had taken me into some back corner and tried to rustle up some lust, I would just have come crawling back to her.

Lou tells them that last week I went to the bathroom between pool-shots and convinced someone to feel me up. How after the woman was unsuccessful at using her fingers to arouse anything more in me than a need to pee, I came storming out, saying I'd have to use a pool cue if I wanted to get off. She tells them how she caught me crawling back into her bed with chalky hands and a blue smudge on my nose.

She complains that I am always picking up girls and going home with them, just to end up horny and frustrated and then have to steal cab money or hop a late-night bus back to her place. Like an alley cat who keeps wandering back in the window whenever you shut him out. With this, she let out a meow-moan and they laugh as if they know what it's like. It is the first time I have heard her retell these tall tales and I can see her eyes sparkle with butch pride. I see how much of herself is tied to this reality I've been weaving for her.

"Baby, tell them how no one can turn you on like I can."

I raise my eyebrows a bit and nod.

"Shit, if you can do it, you can have her." Lou says seriously as she sends the tiny butt around for one last pull from each of them.

The three step back. They look at my boots, the sheer black stockings of my thigh, the skirt that has been inching its way up as I shift from one foot to the other. "I bet I can make the bitch wet," one mumbles to another, meaning for Lou to overhear.

Lou warns them that many women have tried, even a couple of men, with no effect. But if they are willing to give it a shot, they would be doing her a favor. She drops the roach to the ground and grinds it into the sidewalk with the heel of her boot, saying she would be glad to get rid of me so she could get some sleep for a change. She tells them that I've jacked up her phone bill and owe her money. So, for $50 they can have three minutes to get a chance to make me wet. Three minutes of kissing. Lou tells them that she doesn't give a shit, throw in some tit- and ass-grabbing too if they want. She lays out the terms: They can't touch my pussy and I have to keep my hands behind my back. But most importantly, if they make me wet, they have to promise to keep me away from her.

The thought of her handing me over to these women, these biker chicks with their huge hands and rough talk and their cocky attitudes, has me on the verge of coming already. I am not sure if Lou is setting this up to be rid of me once and for all or if she wants me to prove my devotion to her in some grand Russian roulette gamble based on a lie I've been tickling her with for months. I am still wondering this when the most boisterous one of the group steps up to the bet. She watches Lou as if she is afraid it might end up being a joke worth fighting over and pulls her wallet out of her back pocket. Fifty dollars, surely an entire day's pay if she is one of those lucky enough to have a full-time job. She holds it out, as if daring Lou to take it.

Lou tells her that we need to make sure I am dry, to judge fairly. She reaches up under my skirt and with the sleeve of her shirt wipes my pussy off with a rough stroke. She turns back to the three, takes the money, and announces, "Whenever you're ready."

I can feel Lou's presence behind me. My pussy is already pulsing. I clamp down in an attempt to keep any moisture inside.

Bulldagger number one steps toward me. She chooses the direct route, kissing me confidently, open-mouthed, with her tongue darting deep into my throat. Her hands are on my shoulders, pulling me in, bending my neck back. This eager suitor smells of leather, whiskey, and motorcycle grease—a scent so bewitching I could be Pied Piper down the street with it. I hold my breath as she strangles me with her mouth. I just let her go at it, barely kissing back, resisting the urge to correct her faulty style with a few quick nips of my teeth to her tongue. I try to force my mind to wander from the situation. I try to think dry thoughts. I will win the bet for Lou and make her proud.

The three minutes are up and I have not so much as sighed. No groan. No pelvis seeking hers. No melting into her.

Lou turns to me. "Anything, honey?" she asks.

I shake my head "no" and lick the taste of whiskey off my lips.

Lou sighs and says that it's never as easy as it looks.

Number one steps back, tries to laugh it off, saying I am an uptight, frigid bitch, a fucking ice queen. She starts to walk off but her friends stop her.

The second dyke fumbles with her wallet and hands over

the cash for her chance at the challenge. She apparently thinks that if the hard teeth-clanking kiss didn't work, perhaps I am a soft femme who needs seduction. She has three minutes. She kneels at my boots, and I avert my gaze to avoid the pull of her green eyes staring up at me. She licks the rim where the leather meets my calves, runs her tongue on the underside of my knee, and slides her hands slowly up my inner thighs. Lou stops her just as her fingers disappear under my skirt. She is stopped just before I make the decision that calloused hands and warm breath are worth bending my knees for, moving myself down to cease the agonizingly slow pace. She is stopped just before I drop my cunt down to meet her palm. Temptation number two moves her hands to softly cup each breast. I stand still, knees braced so as not to lose my balance. My hands search behind me for Lou—she takes both of my pinkies into her fist and gives them an encouraging squeeze. If I can pull this off, I know it will be the best compliment I have ever paid her.

Lou tells her that her time is up. I shrug, act unimpressed.

The two who have tried, chide the third into an attempt, telling her it was a good three minutes whether they won me or not. Razz her about how all night she's been lookin' for a femmey girl and here is one standing on the street just waiting.

The third bulldagger wants to know how we are measuring. She wants to see for herself if I am wet, wants proof. Lou reaches under my skirt and runs her fingers under the elastic of my underwear—quick, unceremonious, careful not to rub my clit. Her fingers barely skim the surface, but I gulp a breath of air at the long-awaited touch and they seem sure that she's penetrated me. She takes her hand out from under my skirt, grabs number three's hand, and rubs the definitely dry fingers along her thick wrist.

Lou holds out her hand for the money and bulldagger number three hesitates slightly before lifting her wrist to her nose. Just the faintest scent of pussy assures her that she wasn't tricked. She reaches into her pocket and pulls out some crumpled bills.

Lou resumes her position behind me, taking hold of my pinkies. I take a deep breath, trying to figure number three out so I can prepare myself. She is slow, strong, suspicious. Lou clicks her tongue, worried. We are so close to winning this cruel game that I couldn't bear to lose now. Couldn't bear to disappoint her. I imagine the ways she will thank me for this public gesture of appreciation.

Number three steps forward, trying to read my face for clues as she considers the best approach. She leans heavily into my body, wrapping her arms around me. Pushes her bulk into me. Our legs are interwoven and she pulls my hips into her thigh. She starts in on a brain-fucking whisper. "Oh you smell like sex just like I knew you would. I've been looking for a hot little woman like you. I want you so fuckin' bad right now. I can feel your cunt heat on my leg, burnin' a hole right through my jeans. I can practically feel it swelling. It's making me so fucking horny just thinking about how slick and sweet you're getting for me. I already know how I am gonna fuck you." She hugs me into her and presses me harder down onto her thigh. I struggle to tilt my hips up so as not to catch the fullness of her leg rubbing my cunt. Lou's fist closes down harder around my pinkies, tugging me back enough to relieve the pressure building on my clit.

The bulldagger pulls me hard against her chest, breathing on my neck. "That round sexy ass of yours has been drivin' me crazy since I first saw you. I am getting so worked up I don't think I could stop even if you wanted me too." She clamps a hand down on my asscheek and pulls my cunt up to meet the slow swivel of her hips.

Lou puts her fingertips lightly on my back to steady me and I rest back into her hand. Allow her to ease me back and rescue me from this impending arousal. "When I get you home," she goes on, "I'll give you the fuck you've been looking for. I'm gonna work your hard little clit—just pull it right into my mouth and lick your sweet juices. Then I'll open you up with my fingers, just slide in and out. Swirl my hand into you until you beg me to fuck you harder. Beg me to fuck you deeper until you come."

I think of throwing the bet and wrapping my legs around her, opening my mouth to hers. My cunt is tired from being clamped down for so long and I have lost track of my inhales and exhales, my breath starting to sound like whimpering.

"I know how to satisfy a cat-in-heat femme like you. You won't be stumbling home at night. You'll be flat-out exhausted from all our fucking."

I wonder what Lou would do, wonder what proof would be requested after this test, wonder what I could get away with. My pinkies are locked in Lou's fist and she twists them, bending them back into a stinging stretch, clearing my head.

The three minutes is up and Lou makes sure contestant number three has backed away before she pushes me back up to hold my own weight. I am lightheaded and keep hold of Lou's hand, looking down.

"Sorry," Lou says. "Like I told you, she isn't as easy as she looks." Lou takes my waist and turns to escort me inside, but number three grabs her arm and yanks her back so she can look straight at me. I know this look, the look of having found the soft spot and waiting for the tickle to take hold.

The bulldaggers start throwing insults and accusations at us. Number three in particular thinks she's won. She continues to talk to me, starting in the now-familiar whisper ringing in my ears, but each phrase rising in pitch of anger. "I know I made you wet. I know you're just dying to grind that sweet cunt into me. Let's finish this up and get out of here. Tell them how wet I made you. Didn't I make you wet? Huh, bitch?"

I try to ignore her voice, her words.

Lou tells her to shut up for a minute and we can prove it to her.

In a gesture too quick for me to stop, Lou pushes me back against the brick wall and yanks my skirt up. I take a deep breath and keep my pussy lips clamped together as tightly as I can. Lou pulls my panties down to mid thigh in front of these three bulldaggers whose wallets have just been emptied. Three bulldaggers with wounded machismo can see that I am not glistening.

Lou takes number three's hand and folds it into hers as she would a child's, leaving two fingers out and the rest curled into a fist. Lou guides her hand from one pale thigh, over my pussy lips, to the other. Three bulldaggers who are feeling quite underappreciated hear her announce it. Dry.

"I don't fuckin' believe it. She must be fuckin' frigid. Whatever. Keep her, man. You deserve the bitch." They saunter off, play-punching each other and grabbing their imaginary cocks.

They round the corner and Lou turns to me, looking me in the eye for the first time in almost a half-hour. She smiles and tells me she is quite proud, tells me she guesses its okay if I stick around for a while longer.

We go back into the bar and sit down at the table. I excuse myself and head toward the bathroom. "Nice hip-check," I say as I pass by Nanc at the pinball machine. She follows me, leaving an unplayed ball, and locks the door behind us. After a quick slick finger-fuck that she has been promising me for weeks, Nanc leaves to resume her game and I pull my clean panties out of my pocket, wrapping the damp ones in a paper towel and throwing them in the trash. I return to the table to sit on Lou's lap, whispering to her how I much I love her, that she is the only one who can keep me happy, how she is the only one who knows how to turn me on.

Fee Fie Foe Femme

Elaine Miller

All night long she wouldn't let me kiss her because—she said—our lipstick colors clashed.

Checking the address she'd written on a piece of paper, I'd picked her up at her house earlier. Rosalie, the paper said, then her phone number and address. No last name. Dykes don't need last names when we have attributes and ex-lovers to be known by. As a dyke I'm Jez the Goth, or Sharen's-ex Jez, never Jessie Tate. And Rosalie...could be New-in-Town Rosalie, or Rosalie the Beautiful. Maybe if I was into U-Haul rental she could be Jez's Rosalie by the second date.

My heart skipped a beat as she'd appeared in the doorway dressed like an old-time movie starlet, her loose curls bouncing around her sparkling brown eyes. She'd taken my hand, and I'd leaned in for a kiss, which she dodged, laughing impishly. And explained. I was annoyed that she was right about the lipstick clashing. I was wearing my usual vampiric matte blood-red, and hers was something a worker bee would die trying to collect for her queen. Raspberry pink, glittery under the new-car deep gloss, her lips were startling and perfect jewels against her brown skin.

I took Rosalie the Beautiful to LICK, the only full-time lezzie bar in town. Once there and seated at a table beside the dance floor, we lost no time in flirting. She pretended to lose one of her gold earrings in my cleavage, necessitating that she trail her fingers around my breasts, trolling for it, while I protested that she had to find it, quick, because I wear only silver with black clothing. And of course, I only wear black clothing.

But she still wouldn't kiss me. She would dance so close to me that the lines of her face blurred in our body heat, oh yes. She would let the slick material of her skirt smooth the way as she rode my thigh to the beat of the house music. Later in the evening, she'd let me hold her tight in the dark corners of the bar, one hand cupping her full breast, my thumb strumming across her nipple as she squirmed, my other hand tangled in the hair at the nape of her neck. But every time I tried to kiss her, throughout the evening, she just laughed and twirled away, leaving a cloud of girl-scent, a flare of her skirt, and the teasing word *Lipstick*.

By the end of the night, I was cross-eyed with frustration. When Rosalie the Beautiful whispered a lewd invitation in my ear, I simply answered, "Yeah. Let's go to my house," took her hand, and pulled her out of LICK, past the approving smirks of my friends. And on the way home she wouldn't kiss me. She teasingly said that it was all about preserving her shiny, glossy pink lipstick. Besides, she wouldn't want to distract me from my driving.

We tumbled in my door as one body with eight limbs, panting and pulling at each other's clothes all the way to the bedroom. She didn't seem to want to stop for a tour. We fell across my bed and I unzipped her dress and, with her wholehearted help, peeled off every item of clothing that could get in my way. I left her the pretty white stockings and garters, but threw her pinching high-heeled shoes on the floor. I'm a femme too; I know these things.

I hastily shucked off my own clothes, especially my own damned shoes, and they made little black heaps amidst the white piles of Rosalie's clothes.

She looked…well, you can guess how she looked, smooth-skinned and plump-limbed, all curves and soft lines. But you probably haven't imagined with your other senses yet, so close your eyes and imagine the heat of her skin warming the air around us, and her scent like clean sweat from dancing, and just a hint of her sex.

She lay back against the pillows and smiled at me. She didn't say anything, but I just knew that if I leaned forward now she'd let me kiss her and to hell with the lipstick. I didn't try. Instead I pulled a few coils of rope and some bondage cuffs out from the toybox and onto the bed, knowing that with what she already knew of me she wouldn't be at all surprised. Not in the mood for protracted negotiation, I cocked an eyebrow at her in an inquiring gesture.

"Sure," said Rosalie the Beautiful, her eyes outshining her lipstick. "My safeword is 'Untie me now.' "

I tied her flat on her back, her hips held down by a wide belt of ropes crossing back and forth from two of the many eyebolts on either side of the bed. I clipped her hands to the headboard at full extension over her head, allowing her breasts to poke temptingly at the ceiling.

I buckled cuffs around her ankles, and two bigger cuffs a few inches above each knee. I passed a long, slim white rope through the bolts near her hands, and ran it through the rings on the cuffs around her strong, plump, stocking-clad thighs, and as she squeaked in a surprised way, effortlessly pulled her knees high up toward her chest, exposing her sweet, wet cunt. With a quick knot at the ring of the thigh cuffs, I pulled the ropes down to either side of the bed and ran them through two rings there, parting her thighs further. As she began to squirm in earnest, I connected the ends of the ropes to her ankle cuffs and pulled her heels tight to the backs of her thighs, hindering her from kicking or moving her legs.

I stepped back to admire her, and paused, conscious of my own wetness and of my clit pulsing with the beat of my heart. I ached to touch her, and I let that ache build as I looked at her. Warily, she watched me watch her, and relaxed when she saw that, in the symbiosis of being desired, her potent femme's power was intact. Held open like a wanton offering, Rosalie's eyes met mine steadily, proudly. She knew her own beauty; pretty, pretty girl.

"Don't just stand there," she said. "I know you want me."

"Oh yeah, I do. I'm dying to have you," I said. "That's why this is gonna hurt me more than it hurts you."

She looked startled.

I sat for a moment on the bed between her thighs, slowly looking at every intimate detail of her body, finally meeting her eyes. She licked her perfect pink lips in an unconsciously catlike gesture of nervousness.

I leaned forward, letting my long black hair brush her thighs, and made myself comfortable on my belly, my face inches from her exposed cunt. Damn, she smelled good.

I exhaled slowly, open-mouthed, warm breath blowing ever so gently across her flesh.

She squirmed.

"Do it," she muttered.

"Do what?" I breathed

"Go on, taste me."

"Maybe."

She wiggled halfheartedly, but the ropes prevented her from changing position. I moved closer still, my hair swinging once more against her skin, my lips an inch from her clit. I breathed slowly in through my nose, out through my mouth, making the flow of air as warm as possible.

"Fuck," she said, to no one in particular.

"Maybe that's what I'd like to do. Slide my fingers inside you, fuck you," I said, letting each exhaled word play over her clit.

"Yeah, fuck me."

"Maybe," I said.

I noticed the spot I was breathing on seemed to be drying a little from my hot breath, but the very entrance to her cunt was becoming drenched. I lifted up, scooched forward, and dropped a very unladylike wad of spit right at the top of her slit, then added another as I watched the first start to trickle downward.

"Ahh, fuck, what are you...why won't you...? Jez, do something!" she sputtered.

I grinned at her. "Maybe."

I went back to breathing on her, slowly, with all the warmth I could muster. Every so often she tried to shove her cunt in my face, but as she didn't have much slack, it was easy to avoid contact.

I lost myself, as if in meditation, as I pushed each exhale hotly past her clit, thinking nonthoughts about the sweet, musky scent of her cunt and her stifled growling noises. Every so often I added another bit of saliva above her clit, never touching her, but watching her twist and groan at the sudden sensation of wetness.

"There's a puddle under your ass now, not spit but cunt juice," I breathed, whispering to her clit as if it was my secret friend, not mentioning the wetness under my own hips.

"Touch me, you fucker." She started a rhythmic rocking motion, moving as far as the ropes would allow, only an inch or two each way.

I extended my tongue and made it a hard point, letting her make the barest contact between my tongue and her clit.

Immediately I felt her reaching for me with her hips, as far as she was able. But I simply held my place, using the faintest possible pressure as her clit brushed my tongue-tip on the upstroke and the downstroke.

After about a few dozen downstrokes, she suddenly sucked in and held her breath, and I leaned back and away from her, watched her pretty face contort in a snarl and the entrance to her cunt twitch hungrily. Nice.

"Why won't you lick me, you evil bitch-bastard?"

"Because I'm worried about mussing my lipstick," I said.

She started cursing, colorfully. Her cursing would have made a pirate's parrot lose feathers. It would have made a biker blush. It made me laugh, out loud and joyful.

I climbed up her body, nestled my hips between her spread thighs, and snuggled in. She gasped as my pubic hair pressed into her cunt after so long without touch, and I smiled down at her.

"Holy, you're so wet, I think I might get a steam burn."

"Fuck you."

"Is that your safeword?"

"No!" And then she started cursing again, as I lifted my body from hers and nuzzled into her tits, getting to know them. They were soft and weighty, full and rounded; the left one was slightly larger, a touching imperfection. Her large, dark nipples pointed straight at the ceiling, and went stiff as I watched.

Not every woman considers her nipples an erogenous zone, so I suckled on one for a second, to test. She gasped and bucked toward me, not away.

"Hey—are these candy?" I exclaimed happily, and dove right in.

I happily lost myself in no time again, moving from nipple to nipple whenever I thought the other might be getting lonely, lightly and experimentally sucking, biting, and licking until I thought I had deciphered the language of her curses and wriggles. What she liked best seemed to be a firm, direct suction at the tip of her nipple, with a slight graze of my teeth every so often. She never quite stopped trying to bring her body in contact with mine, but I stayed up on my elbows, with just my soft belly occasionally picking up wet streaks from her cunt. It wasn't just to tease her; I thought I might embarrass myself by coming if I humped her thigh even for a second.

Finally, I left her wet, chewed, lipstick-stained nipples and ran my tongue in a trail down the curves of her belly, across her garter belt, continuing on in a casual fashion along the length of her cunt. She hissed when I contacted her clit on the way, growled when I dipped inside her, and began to rock against me when I dragged my tongue back, making my tongue flat and soft and dragging it so very slowly up between her labia.

"Oh please," she said when her hard clit just naturally slid into my mouth, my tongue pressing underneath. "Please. That. Do that. Oh...." She sounded sniffly, so I sat up a little to check how she was. Her expression was soft and unfocused, her eyes full of tears. I felt the little spot in my heart grow even warmer with affection for her.

"What do you want, Rosalie the Beautiful?" I asked tenderly, adding my private qualifier to her name for the first time.

She smiled fuzzily at that. "Please touch me, Jez. Lick me. Fuck me. I'm going out of my mind."

"Yeah, I think maybe it's time," I said. And, watching her face, I slid one finger inside her, found she was wet enough, pulled out, and pushed three fingers back in, a little roughly. Her eyes rolled back and her whole body welcomed me in. I slid out and back in again, and her mouth opened soundlessly, her back arched. I did it again, and again, experimenting, trying to learn everything about her in a few short strokes.

I made a guess that she'd like to be fucked hard and fast, in direct contrast to my soft teasing game. Oh yeah. Then I thought maybe adding direct pressure on her G-spot would feel right, and within a second knew I'd guessed correctly. She held nothing back, her body and face telling eloquent stories about her body's responses.

Time enough later, or tomorrow, for my harness and dick. No time, right now, even to reach for the lube. She seemed close to coming already, and I didn't want to tease her for even one moment more.

I moved and took her clit in my mouth again, soon finding the steady side-to-side rhythm that made her cunt clench around my hand. I closed my eyes and put everything I had into pushing her over the edge, lost in her taste and smell, reaching as far as I could inside her with every stroke of my fingers.

Rosalie went rigid, shaking, and her soft cries grew urgent. Her cunt clamped around my fingers, almost squeezing me out, but felt I knew what she needed. I pushed harder inside her.

When I felt her muscles flex and heard the ropes attached to the headboard creak, I concentrated on her clit, flicking it hard with my tongue, once, twice, a third time…and she sucked her breath in and then wailed like a cat. She came in intense, shaking waves, her cunt's deep throbbing squeezing my fingers, and I kept going, fucking her more and more gently until the tension slowly melted out of her muscles, and it was time to stop.

I slid up her bound body, released the buckles on her wrist cuffs, and looked fondly at her. Breathing hard, flushed, and tear-streaked, she was more beautiful to me then than any woman I'd ever seen.

Despite everything we'd done in the last hour, her lipstick was still raspberry-glossy and perfect.

So I kissed her.

The Second Hour
L. Shane Conner

I spent the first hour of the party nursing exactly two beers. I wanted to be blind drunk and away from myself, but I couldn't seem to put the stuff down fast enough. I finally made it to my third beer and sat down on one of those flip-a-fuck foldable mattress chairs in a corner. I shouldn't have been tired, especially with the volume of the music. I didn't really even know why I'd come except that I didn't have anything better to do and some girls I met at a club the month before invited me. Moving to a new city's a pain in the ass. I was thinking about looking for something harder to drink when a woman I'd never seen before came right up to me and put one foot down on the chair between my legs. I thought I was imagining it for half a second; then she leaned forward, pressing her weight down through the toe of one high black leather boot directly onto my clit. I stopped breathing for a minute or a day. The party was gone and there was just the light reflecting off this knee-high leather boot and my heart beating in my clit.

Next there was her hand pulling a silver flask from the

inside pocket of her leather jacket. She drank, handed it to me, and as I drank she reached forward and tipped the flask up with just her two fingers. It was sweet and strong. I closed my eyes and let it fill my mouth until she pulled it away. Warmth coursed through me, right down to the tip of her boot. I looked up and tried to speak but she caught me with a sharp, open-handed slap, just hard enough to get my attention. My head was light but I could feel the pressure of her boot and the beginning of an even buzz in the base of my brain.

"Get up."

She stepped back and after a short battle with equilibrium and my legs, I stood. I looked at the space between her knees, the hem of her skirt just short of midthigh, and the narrow heels of her boots. She pushed me toward the door, which I opened and held for her.

I followed a step behind her as we walked to her car. It was a small kind of SUV, black, with leather seats. Once we were inside, she kissed me, hard and deep, then she made me kneel on the floor facing the seat and it didn't occur to me to object until I was already on my knees. I heard the glove box open behind me and then there were handcuffs around my wrists. She slid the seat back up and I found I couldn't move. She leaned down and whispered in my ear.

"Either I'm going to take you home and do what I like with you, or you say no and I'll let you out of the car right now."

I wanted her. I kept quiet. She pulled my head toward the dash by the short hairs at the back.

"Give me permission, then. Say yes or it stops now."

I turned my head up toward her and her hand caught my cheek again. It was more than I'd felt in months. I couldn't raise my voice above a whisper and I couldn't move.

"Yes."

She didn't answer and I thought maybe she'd lost interest.

"Please yes."

She blindfolded me then and I felt a kind of relief. If I couldn't see her anyhow, I didn't have to try to look anymore. I let my weight fall forward onto the seat but she pulled my head back again and pressed what felt like a rubber ball into my mouth. I accepted it like the mouth of the flask earlier. It was another few seconds before I realized it was a gag. As she pulled it tight I could feel my lips spread and my tongue press into the floor of my mouth. She let go and I let my chest rest on the seat again. The car lurched forward.

When the car stopped again I had no idea how much time had passed. For months I hadn't even been able to masturbate successfully, and for however long she'd been driving I'd been closer than anybody's best effort since my last relationship started to go south. The seat slid backward and I went with it. I heard her car door slam shut and for a little while I was alone, then the door next to me swung open.

She dragged me out of the car and I fell on the pavement, somehow not hitting my knees or elbows. I heard the muted sound of what remained of my voice squeeze out around the ball gag and I felt the toe of her boot push in under my face. For the first time since she'd put the gag in place, I wished it wasn't. She helped me roughly to my feet, put some kind of collar around my neck, and took a step away. I felt a tug and realized she'd put me on a leash. I followed her, stumbling blindly on steps, doing my best to keep my feet. I heard a key in a door and heard it swing open. She led me in and, I thought, through a couple of rooms until I found myself face to face with a wall. There was a click and I knew she'd taken the leash off. The handcuffs were next. I wanted to rub my wrists but I stood still, waiting.

She pulled my jacket off and tossed it across the room. Her slow, even, breath made my heart sound loud and fast. She came closer and I could feel the heat of her body through my thin shirt right before she pulled me backward, off balance. I tried to keep my feet, I think just by reflex, but she dropped me easily and smoothly to the floor. She told me to take off my boots and I fumbled, loosening the laces just enough so my socks came half off with my boots. Her voice was low and quiet and, as she directed me to undress completely, I was so focused on listening that I barely noticed what I was doing. The evenly spaced slats of the wood floor were cool under my bare ass but the room was warm. Everything was still. I heard her boots crossing the room and I felt like I was breathing in time with the even clicking of her heels against the floor.

I tried not to move, unsure of where to put my hands, wishing she would touch me again. A dull throb had started in my clit and seemed to radiate out, turning my body into a single pulsing organ. I was sure she was watching me. I heard her boots take a few steps followed by the sound of something scraping across the floor and stopping nearby. I couldn't identify the next several sounds but when I turned my head, trying to capture something more, she put a boot down on my chest just above my breasts and pushed me down. The other boot came to rest just above my pubic bone. She must be sitting down.

I felt more naked than I'd ever felt before. I heard the unmistakable sound of a cigarette lighter sparking to life, and for a moment the light-headed onrush of adrenaline blocked out everything else. I didn't even know why. As the wave of it passed over and out of me I realized she was sitting in a chair smoking, using my body for a foot rest. I became aware of my body then, beginning with the skin her boots rested on. I could feel the exact shape of them and the distribution of her weight. There was a slight draft in the room and it made me more and more aware of the growing wetness between my legs. Once I started to feel that, it held all my attention. I was sure she must see it, must be staring at it.

Suddenly her boots were gone, the chair slid back, she

stood. I wanted to move toward her, my body ached to be touched. She made me get onto my hands and knees, walked behind me, and stopped there. I heard a rustling sound followed by a small snap. I felt her gloved hand on the inside of my thigh and I couldn't breathe. I was afraid any movement might make her take her hand away. She slapped at my thigh, forcing me to spread my legs further. The muscles in my lower back tightened and I felt my ass trying to push itself higher. She moved her hand forward across my swollen labia, teasing my clit with a fingertip, letting me feel how slick I was. I felt an involuntary moan trying to escape but I closed down on the gag.

She had me crawl across the floor a little way, then she stopped me and got me up onto a bed, laying me down on my back. My body seemed to sink into the softness of it after the cool hardness of the wood floor. She ran a hand over my breasts and my back arched toward it before I could stop myself. She laughed quietly and pulled her hand away. I tried again to hold as still as possible while she fastened a restraint around my right wrist, then my ankle, and then the other side, stretching me across the bed. All my attention was on whatever part of me she happened to be touching.

She slapped my clit just hard enough to make my whole body jump and I realized how little I could move. My arms and legs tensed. There was a steady hum inside my head. I whimpered around the gag. The muscles around my clit twitched and spasmed. She tapped lightly, teasing. She tickled, she rubbed, she pushed her fingertips between my labia, just barely inside. I tried to thrust my hips toward her and I started to feel my whole body rising off the bed. If I hadn't been gagged I would have pleaded with her. I stopped trying to control the sounds coming from deep in my throat. I stopped trying to struggle and I stopped trying not to. Everything was slick and wet. I could feel her slowly stretching me open wider, pushing my resistance away. Her mouth was on my clit, sucking, nibbling, grazing me with her teeth. I wanted to spread my legs further apart, I wanted to pull her to me. I felt the wave of orgasm begin to sweep through me and then I felt the last piece of resistance give way and she was inside me. I felt the widest part of her hand slip in as I came. My body held her inside and she held me, suspended inside the wave of my orgasm. Nothing else could feel like that. Her whole fist filled me in places I never knew were empty. The universe was reduced to the places her two hands touched. Time was gone, the sunlight was fresh and warm.

Soon my arms and legs were free, the gag and blindfold were gone, and I was curled against her naked breasts. I felt like a child, completely safe. She kissed my forehead and pulled a blanket over me and I slept. In the morning she told me her name.

The Rock Wall
Peggy Munson

Stone

We are leaning against the rock wall by the high school where I have taken him because it's deserted. He has that board-splitting butch gaze. He's worn his letter jacket, the one he earned back in high school, and today he delicately wraps it around my shoulders and says, "Do you want to be my girl? Do you want me to be your Daddy boyfriend?" And I nod shyly and say, "Yeah, okay." He holds my hand and we walk.

This is how it begins. It begins with something made from stone.

The bed he has me in is firm. Daddy's callused hands are hard. Daddy's face looks like it was chiseled off Mount Rushmore. The wind is parting the curtains the way he brushes my hair back from my eyes. He gets serious. "Do you want to play a game, little girl?" he asks me. I know Daddy's games: rock beats scissors, scissors beat paper, paper beats rock. Hands equal power. Sometimes I am a paper doll and my clothes fold on with paper tabs, and Daddy undresses me absently, like he's opening mail. Sometimes I am a stone tablet,

370

the stone on which commandments are carved. Sometimes, my legs are safety scissors, lying like dull blades, waiting to be crushed by rock. And Daddy spreads them open and they pull reflexively shut. He kisses to relax me. He curls his hand into a fist, into a stone. He slides that power into me. This simple game of hands.

But this is not just a game, Daddy-Girl. This is not just a game, Paper-Scissors-Rock. These are the scissors that cut up paper guises. This is the crane that breaks buildings. This is the fist that destroys orderly origami. This is the red paper of my cunt unfolding. This is me coming. This is how real. "Take it, bitch," says Daddy's voice into my ear. "Be a good girl. Take my fist." This is me pressed against surfaces. This is the stone that does not acquiesce. This is the statue becoming a Girl.

Quarry

Some days, I hate everything about Daddy. I hate how orphaned I feel when Daddy goes to work. I hate how Daddy can choose the simplest onomatopoeia and roll it off the tongue, so that *cock* sounds as hard as it is. How I sit all day with that word jammed in my head, cock, Daddy's cock, Daddy's hard cock, spreading out with acres of modifiers, until it becomes Daddy's hard cock that isn't fucking me. I hate it that I am so Electra. I hate it that Freud is on my shoulder and that he told me so. I hate it that I need a Daddy. I hate it that words never add up to cocks.

I lie on my back all day waiting and watching TV. I like watching teenage rock stars almost as much as anorexic figure skaters. I used to read about anorexia and about gymnasts and I would think about their discipline when the dentist was drilling pain into my smile. And I would read about how the girls didn't want to grow up and I would walk around for days with the pain in my smile and it was such good pain. And with my fading numb lip I thought of how benevolent the dentist

was when he told me I was brave, and such a good girl. I hate
Daddy for not being a dentist. I watch the Britney Spears video
where she sings "Hit me baby, one more time" and dances
around in a Catholic-schoolgirl outfit. I want to pull up my
pleated skirt and show Daddy that we can end biblical racism
right here, because the devil is made of white cotton. That's
what little girls are made of. This exquisite, pretty rage.

I go to therapy and I want to talk about Daddy but I don't
even want to get into it with my shrink. I can't explain how
my girlfriend is a boyfriend who makes me call him Daddy.
Sometimes when my shrink listens to me talk he thinks about
other things. I can see the Viewmaster clicking in front of
his eyes. Sometimes he thinks about what I would look like
naked, and how he finds the professional boundary titillat-
ing. I sit in the waiting room and think about Daddy's cock
and my pussy is all wet and I decide to go wipe myself before
going into therapy but the bathroom lock has been ripped off
the wall. My shrink might walk in on me, or smell me. He
might see what a bad girl I really am. I return to the waiting
room, still wet.

I don't talk about Daddy's cock but every word I say in
therapy sounds like cock and I know my shrink can see right
through me. I know he has linguistic X-ray vision and that he
knows I am really saying cock, cock, cock and he wants me
to sit on his lap but I am thinking about Daddy. How I want
the day to go faster so that Daddy will get home from work.
My shrink tells me to have a good week but he is really saying
cock. The double doors shut behind me, cock, cock. And far
away somewhere, in San Francisco, lesbians are pouring silicone into dildo molds and not thinking cock at all. Happily
distracted, they are chattering and squeezing cock after cock
out of molds and thinking business. I hate Daddy for thinking
business. I wish he would think about my pleasure.

I hate how without Daddy I am a book with one bookend,

so I just fall and my words get crushed. I hate it how Daddy is a petty thief. Because if he steals what's petty, then what am I when he takes me? I hate how Daddy makes me sputter inarticulate phrases, so that I choke out sounds that have nothing to do with theory. I hate how Daddy makes me write him stories, because I cannot sculpt a sentence out of cock. I hate it how that word becomes so eloquent inside of me, pushing through me and out of my mouth.

I hate how Daddy's cock knows the way to hidden quarries, the watery places that were mined. How Daddy sees the drunken dives that kill sixteen, euphoric girls kissed to epiphanies on their mossy knees. Sophomoric girls getting their nipples touched on their mossy knees. And the skin scraped against sharp things, and the rustle of cops approaching, and the second before the kids run, and the hastily abandoned trunks. How he knows what to do about each truncated fuck. Of each lifetime. Daddy takes care of things.

I hate it how Daddy makes me need his cock. Because then I am a place that once held diamonds, sitting home yearning for him, waiting for a girl's new best friend. Because then I am always too ready for him. So hungry every time his key turns in the lock. So hungry for that handcuff sound of his key in the lock. So hungry for that four o'clock, drowsy, sharp sound. I hate it how Daddy walks in and feels me to see if I'm wet, and wonders what I anticipate, and then ignores me while removing his jacket. I hate it how those fingers on my pussy make me whimper like a little dog.

I hate how seconds turn to hours before Daddy leads me into the bedroom, and his belt buckle glints like it's submerged. How sweetly Daddy takes my hand and says, "Baby girl," and then pulls me to his denim lap. And how the things to be filled must be emptied, must be stripped. Daddy grips me and undoes me and lowers me to the bed. And I shiver because I need it. I give when Daddy pushes. Daddy pulls on my hair.

I hate how good and raw he strips me. How good it feels to be this bare.

The Rock Wall

Every night I go back to the rock wall. It is covered in moss and the rain is drizzling and I search for grips. I am ripped and mud-covered and hungry. My grasp is tenuous and my fingers are slipping. I'm tired of being a wide-eyed waif always scrambling over walls where there are more walls and more slippery rocks and more places to bruise and nowhere good to land. The rain is so irritating, the noise, the noise that's always a soft fuck when you need it hard, that's always a drizzle when you need a thunderstorm to break the air and shock the animals so they run frenzied— wild—crazed—scattershot—into spaces they never dared to go. The wall is unforgiving and I begin to slide. I land on my knees in a muddy pool and my dress is ripped and I'm old and there is no Daddy. The landing is soft. Nothing impaling me. Nothing tearing me and ripping me. No fairytale wolves, though I always thought they would be there, their dripping incisors and hunger, waiting for me to fall. There is nothing to wound me, no imaginary battles to reenact. No hole in the earth to open up and swallow me there.

Maybe I am already in the hole. Maybe I am the hole. This dark and damp place that feels like the inside and not the outside and my dress is ripped and I start crying. I hold my face in my muddy hands and my tears clean my hands and my hands smear the mud into my tears. Everything undoes everything. Nothing undoes me. Nothing does me.

Then suddenly, so dark and quick and I can't even scream, something reaches from behind and grabs me with its arm under my throat and drags me backward, and drags me while whispering things. "Daddy's here now, little girl. Daddy's got you." He's not comforting and not scary, just unsettling, just the kind of thing that makes me all animal, all animal splitting from the pack the way the wolves want it to be, all animal confused and asking for it. I try to flail around and pull away. I try to break the grip, the wall is waiting. Doesn't Daddy understand the wall? How I need to climb it always, climb and climb and climb it? Daddy pulls my muddy body so that I'm sitting on his lap and I still can't see him but I feel his hard cock. "Daddy's got you," he says again.

I want not to want it. I want not to feel how my thighs are smeared with mud and my pussy feels smeared, but it's not, it's just mine. There is nothing between my pussy and his cock but a thin layer of fabric. And he is rubbing his cock against my panties and I squirm. I want to squirm away but he rubs me so hard and I start to want to push down onto him. I start to push down as if the fabric will just dissolve. He pushes the tip of his cock against the fabric and the fabric goes into me. And the elastic of my panties follows the fabric and pulls me, pulls my legs, into me. I'm going to fall into me. I have to fight. I try to struggle but Daddy holds me against his moving pushing cock. "Daddy, wait," I say, but I keep pushing to make the fabric go away, and I want him. "Daddy, stop!" Daddy grabs under my arms and pushes me slowly forward so that my face is down but he pulls my hips back. "Daddy wants you to take his cock," he says. "All of it. Can you be a good girl and do that?"

I want to taste the mud. The mud smells oddly like Daddy. Daddy slides my panties down my legs so I'm just there in the night air and my pussy and my ass are high up behind me. "Daddy, no," I say, but this time weakly. This time it's all reverse psychology. This time I'm not sure at all.

"Daddy can just leave you here in the mud if you want, little girl. Is that what you want?" He snarls this.

"Daddy...no," I say. "No, please, no."

"Beg for what you want."

"I want you, Daddy."

"Beg me."

"I want Daddy. I want Daddy to fill me up."

"Daddy's very hard for you. Is this what you want?" He slides the tip of his cock into me. "Is this what you want?"

"Yes, Daddy. *Please*."

"Beg me."

"I want you inside of me. Please."

"What?"

"I want you, Daddy, please." I say it with the urgency I use to climb the walls.

Daddy starts sliding his cock into my pussy and I push back onto him but he holds my hips and makes me wait for him. And the rain gets harder, the drops batter my cheeks, the rain turns everything to mud while Daddy fills me up and my hands slide in front of me for something to hang onto but there is nothing, nothing there, nothing but my hips pushing back and Daddy's hard cock and my need. And I need to hold something. I need to hold on because I am used to holding and I need the wall and Daddy pushes in so hard and I want to scream, it feels so good. My hands are fumbling forward for any handhold but there is nothing there....

"Daddy's got you, baby," he says soothingly. "Fall back into me."

Gravel

The gravel reminds me of old roads cutting between fields to deserted places, the way it clatters and then hums, keeps me unsteady. Once I cut my chin on the gravel in the Dairy Queen parking lot, holding onto my Dilly Bar all the way to the ground. I remember losing my footing, bleeding on the car upholstery, wondering if kids found reddened chunks of rock where I landed. I think about all of these things now, now that I'm old being young, riding next to Daddy in the truck. The big wheels slide over the gravel. The dark moves from beneath trees to the sides of buildings. We are near a warehouse with broken windows. And the gravel is not the kind you buy in bags at Home Depot, but stained. I get out and stumble like a tipsy slut. I straighten my skirt and start to walk but Daddy is there already, and he grabs my arm. "No," he says, pointing. "You little whore. Right here."

I look down distastefully, then up at Daddy. "Here?" I sneer. I can't believe he means it. The rock is soaked dark with things dying, bled oil and shoe rubber. I look at him again, his stern expression, then kneel down. The rocks are sharp against my knees. Daddy gives a little push on my back so I fall forward and my palms slide through the rocks. Then, when I'm on all fours, he pulls up my skirt from behind, just flips the material so that it lands on my back and I feel the breeze trying to go into me. I've got no panties on.

"Such a pretty little ass," he says. "Untainted lily-white ass. Not dirty like the rest of you." The breeze seems to follow the current of his voice and rubs the goose bumps on my ass. "Are you afraid to have Daddy's big cock in your pretty ass?"

"Maybe," I say. I feel defiant. I feel the way the rocks are cutting me and I don't move my hands.

Daddy's hands fondle my asscheeks, spread them open, press against them so I slide forward more. He's so much stronger than I am. I let myself fall and feel the rocks against my cheek. I think of how I fell that time, when I was young, and tried to taste my blood. And how I always tried to taste my blood when I got cut. But what I liked to taste was not just mine, but also that which made me bleed. It was the thing that made the cut, the flavor mixed into the blood. It was the combination of the two, the grit that touched the cutter and the flesh. It was the generosity of both, and how my bleeding made the two combine. I think of all of this while Daddy moves his cock against the hole, and pushes hard because it's tight.

He pushes hard because it's tight, and pulls my hips against him. My face gets scraped against the gravel. My lip begins to bleed. I taste the blood and salt and earth and pain and fear and trampling. I taste the blood and all that has been done to it and lick and give it back to me. I give me back to me. And Daddy gives me, too.

"Who gives you what you need?" he asks. The natural light has fled. A streetlight shines behind his hair. I smell the tires. I smell the dew. I feel the walls that crumble into gravel. I feel the girls who must undo.

"Daddy," I say. He looks like a monument. "You do."

About the Authors

TONI AMATO has taught, edited, and coached in writing since 1992, and has had fiction published in several anthologies, including *Best Lesbian Erotica* (1998–2001). He is coeditor of *Pinned Down by Pronouns*.

LISA ARCHER, aka Lisa Montanarelli, is coauthor of *First Year: Hepatitis C*. Her work has appeared in *Best American Erotica 2004* and *2005* as well as *Playboy* magazine. Visit www.lisamontanarelli.com.

SAMIYA A. BASHIR is the editor of *Best Black Women's Erotica 2* and coeditor of *Role Call: A Generational Anthology of Social and Political Black Literature and Art.*

S. BEAR BERGMAN is a theater artist, writer, instigator, and gender-jammer. Ze lives on the web at www.sbearbergman.com and makes a home in Northampton, Massachusetts, where ze is the lucky husbear of a magnificent femme.

BETTY BLUE, just another smutty, slutty San Francisco girl, has published fiction in *Best Lesbian Erotica, Best Women's Erotica, Best Lesbian Love Stories,* and *Best Bisexual Erotica.*

LINDA A. BOULTER has written in several genres, inspired by love lost and love found, love of her children, and love of life and words. On word.

CARA BRUCE edited *Best Fetish Erotica, Best Bisexual Women's Erotica, Viscera,* and *Horny? San Francisco.* Her stories appear in *Best American Erotica, Best Women's Erotica, The Mammoth Book of Best New Erotica,* and many more.

RACHEL KRAMER BUSSEL (www.rachelkramerbussel.com, lustylady.blogspot.com) has had erotic stories published in more than fifty anthologies, including *Best American Erotica 2004* and *Best Lesbian Erotica* (2001, 2004, and 2005).

PATRICK CALIFIA, despite a gender transition, continues to believe that woman-to-woman sex has a unique power to transform the world. His new books include *Mortal Companion,* a vampire novel, and *Hard Men,* gay male leather smut.

L. SHANE CONNER is a boy-identified, rugby-playing, tattooed, sometime geek, wannabe writer with a dream and a vision and many women to satisfy.

SHANNON CUMMINGS is too shy to comment on most things, though she would likely say that the sexiest part of the human body is the synaptic cleft.

MR DANIEL is a somewhat nomadic writer, independent film and video curator, scholar, and sound artist whose writing has appeared in various publications.

KENYA DEVOREAUX, a femme lesbian and a devoted writer, is inspired by the beauty of lesbian passion and still searches for that one special lady to give her something to write about.

MARÍA HELENA DOLAN, an Aquarian changeling, lives in the Atlanta area and enjoys a life full of agitating, writing, gardening, loving, traveling, and generally smirking.

DAWN DOUGHERTY is a belly dancer, writer, and yoga teacher who recently relocated to the Midwest after a decade in Boston. Her work has appeared in numerous queer anthologies.

AMIE M. EVANS is a well-published literary erotica and creative nonfiction writer, workshop provider, and burlesque and high-femme drag performer. She is working on her MLA at Harvard University.

SANDRA LEE GOLVIN is a lesbian-centered psychotherapist and an adjunct professor of clinical psychology at Antioch University in Los Angeles.

SACCHI GREEN's stories appear occasionally in *Best Lesbian Erotica, Best Women's Erotica,* and enough other steamy anthologies to warm the nights of a long winter.

MICHAEL M. HERNANDEZ is a queer transbear, author, and public speaker who is in search of pastry nirvana and just happens to pay the bills through the practice of law.

THEA HUTCHESON burns up the pages with lust, leather, and latex in *Best Lesbian Erotica* (2001 and 2002), *Cthulhu Sex,* and *Hot Blood 11* as well as on AmatoryInk.com.

TENNESSEE JONES is an Appalachian-born transman now living in New York City. He is the editor of the punk lit zine *Teenage Death Songs.* His first collection of short stories, *Deliver Me from Nowhere,* was published by Soft Skull Press in March 2005.

TERESA LAMAI started writing fiction when she stopped dancing. Her work can also be found in *Best Women's Erotica.*

ROSALIND CHRISTINE LLOYD's work has appeared in *Best American Erotica 2001, Hot & Bothered, Faster Pussycat, Skin Deep,* and *Set in Stone,* among other erotica series.

SKIAN MCGUIRE is a working-class Quaker leatherdyke from western Massachusetts whose stories and poetry have appeared in quite a few anthologies, periodicals, and webzines.

ELAINE MILLER writes, designs websites, and teaches BDSM workshops in Vancouver, Canada. She's a polyamorous femme/butch leatherdyke daddy—and she can't stand being labeled.

PEGGY MUNSON, once an innocent midwestern girl, was turned into a smut peddler by the *Best Lesbian Erotica* enterprise, with stories in nine editions (1998–2005 as well as *Best of...*). Visit www.peggymunson.com for information on her recent work.

MADELEINE OH (www.madeleineoh.com), a transplanted Brit, retired LD teacher, and grandmother, lives in Ohio with her husband of thirty-four years. She has published her writing in the United States, United Kingdom, and Australia.

ANA PERIL has written for *Best Lesbian Erotica* (2003 and 2005), *Glamour Girls: Femme-Femme Erotica*, the *Village Voice, Out Traveler,* and the *Rough Guides.*

JEAN ROBERTA teaches first-year English classes at a Canadian prairie university, writes in various genres, and reminisces about her disreputable past.

JULIE LEVIN RUSSO is a PhD student in modern culture and media at Brown University, where she is regularly presents on erotic writing and pornography, alternative sexualities, and open relationships.

LAUREN SANDERS is the author of two novels from Akashic Books: *With or Without You* and *Kamikaze Lust,* which won a Lambda Literary Award in 2000.

ALISON L. SMITH's first book, *Name All the Animals,* was published by Scribner in 2004. Her work has appeared in *McSweeney's, Best American Erotica 2003,* and various anthologies. She can be reached at www.namealltheanimals.com.

SPARKY is a drag king, female drag performer, and burlesque stagehand. Sparky is published on Playbutch.net and Technodyke.com and writes a regular column for Dykediva.com.

JERA STAR is a pink-haired, hippie bi chick who writes erotica and makes wooden spanking paddles in Newfoundland. She loves watermelon and hates cats.

CECILIA TAN is the author of *Black Feathers, Telepaths Don't Need Safewords,* and *The Velderet.* Her erotica has appeared almost everywhere, from *Penthouse* to *Ms.* For more juicy details, visit www.ceciliatan.com.

When not roping and riding, **RAKELLE VALENCIA** is writing. Published in *Best Lesbian Erotica 2004,* she feels there's no need to mention more.

KYLE WALKER is the alter ego of a mild-mannered editor and playwright whose work has appeared in the *Best Lesbian Erotica* series, *A Woman's Touch,* and *Friction 7.*

TARA-MICHELLE ZINIUK is a writer, performer, activist, supervillain, and princess. She is at work completing her first collection of poetry and editing an anthology called *Dirt Road: Transient Tales.*

About the Editor

TRISTAN TAORMINO is the award-winning editor of the *Best Lesbian Erotica* series and the author of three books: *True Lust: Adventures in Sex, Porn and Perversion; Down and Dirty Sex Secrets;* and *The Ultimate Guide to Anal Sex for Women*. She is the editor of *Hot Lesbian Erotica*. She is director, producer, and star of two videos based on her book, *Tristan Taormino's Ultimate Guide to Anal Sex for Women 1 & 2,* which are distributed by Evil Angel Video. She is a columnist for the *Village Voice* and *Taboo Magazine*. She has been featured in over three-hundred publications including the *New York Times, Redbook, Glamour, Cosmopolitan, Playboy, Penthouse, Entertainment Weekly, Vibe,* and *Men's Health*. She has appeared on CNN, *The Ricki Lake Show,* NBC's *The Other Half*, MTV, HBO's *Real Sex, The Howard Stern Show,* The Discovery Channel, Oxygen, and *Loveline*. She teaches sexuality workshops around the country and her official website is www.puckerup.com.